WAR GAMES

Joints reinforced with polymer mesh. Nictating occular membranes. Sphincters where there were none before. Regenerated limbs. Subcutaneous vitalium wires instead of hair. They were no longer human. They were hybrids, bioformed for the express purpose of war.

Marc Detrs hadn't wanted to become a hybrid. But it was that or jail. That or have his true past discovered. That or be forced to reveal his knowledge of the all-seeing timestone. He became a hybrid, fighting for the chance to die in a guerrilla war that is waged in the frozen methane forests of Saturn's moon.

And then Grychn reappeared—a ghost from his past, the lover who knew all his secrets. They would either kill each other or help each other to find the timestone, the most valuable object in the universe.

"A rousing and evocative future war novel in the tradition of STARSHIP TROOPERS and THE FOREVER WAR. Readers will remember it long after they put the book down."
—George R. R. Martin,
Winner of the Hugo and Nebula awards

D1015953

WE HOPE YOU ENJOY THIS BOOK

IF YOU'D LIKE A FREE LIST
OF OTHER BOOKS AVAILABLE FROM

PLAYBOY PAPERBACKS,

JUST SEND YOUR REQUEST TO:
PLAYBOY PAPERBACKS
BOOK MAILING SERVICE
P.O. BOX 690
ROCKVILLE CENTRE, NEW YORK 11571

KARL HANSEN
WAR GAMES

PLAYBOY
PAPERBACKS

WAR GAMES

Copyright © 1981 by Karl Hansen

Cover illustration copyright © 1981 by PEI Books, Inc.

All rights reserved. No part of this book may be reproduced, stored in a retrieval system or transmitted in any form by an electronic, mechanical, photocopying, recording means or otherwise without prior written permission of the author. A portion of Book II appeared in *The Berkeley Showcase* as a novelette titled "Sergeant Pepper," copyright © 1980 by Karl Hansen.

Published simultaneously in the United States and Canada by Playboy Paperbacks, New York, New York. Printed in the United States of America. Library of Congress Catalog Card Number: 80-85104. First edition.

Books are available at quantity discounts for promotional and industrial use. For further information, write to Premium Sales, Playboy Paperbacks, 1633 Broadway, New York, New York 10019.

ISBN: 0-872-16837-9

First printing June 1981.

For Sharon and Alex,
who were sometimes shrill and strident
in their neglect, but patient, always

All things will pass away. Nothing remains but death and the glory of deeds.

From the *Elder Edda*

Book I

Scissors, Stone, and Paper

1

A stranger's face peered into my cylindrical cell: turquoise eyes glittered behind the transparent washers of growing nictitating membranes; healing suture lines crisscrossed a bald skull; ears and nostrils puckered with internal sphincters; black freckles would soon be confluent. Dark thoughts were hidden in the face. Thoughts I'd guessed too well.

He watched me often, this stranger. Each day his face was a little different, its metamorphosis more nearly complete. I'd become impatient to see the final form of his disguise.

Red culture media swirled between my face and his. Tiny oxygen bubbles streamed into cosmic lines. I blinked. Film cleared from the stranger's eyes. They followed my eyes, as though synchronized with gimbals. I blew media out my nose. Twin vortices spread from the stranger's nostrils.

You've guessed my secret, of course. I was the stranger.

His face was an image of my own, reflected from the concave wall of a hybridization tank. His metamorphosis was only my own transformation. For a month I'd been watching the process.

My mouth grinned widely. My plan was working perfectly. Before long, I'd be unrecognizable. My previous face and body would exist only as a holographic memory in the Corps' master personnel files. And in my memory, as a death mask yet to be: eyes shattered into eggshells and popped from their sockets; tongue protruding from a

11

mouth filled with frozen, foamy spit; skin as blue as a peeled grape. That image had tormented me for long days and longer nights before I devised a way to exorcise it from my thoughts. I had suffered considerable inconvenience and not a little discomfort to make sure I would never look like the face inserted in my mind by a vaporizing timestone. Why the paranoia? Because if I looked like that, I'd be dead.

I had always expected my own end to be random and totally unexpected—like a star winking out of an entropic sky. Death had had no substance before I wore the timestone. And after? It had too vivid an image then: frozen vitreous humor formed a filigree of frost behind ice cataracts.

I'd been warned. I hadn't had enough sense to listen. What had the sailor called his chronotropic crystal? Deathstone. Yes, that was it. He left space to try to escape the scenario of his death, not knowing the scene was to be played on Earth. You saw an image of your own death in a timestone. You knew how your end would come. You might even guess where, unless the stone tricked you. But one crucial parameter was missing—you didn't know when. A year. A hundred years. A thousand. There was no way to be sure. Not without another timestone. Mine was gone. There was only one other. I had to find it before death saw through my disguise. I knew how I was going to die. I didn't know when it would be. It was as impossible for me to accept an incomplete knowledge of my fate as it was to resist the urge to cheat destiny.

So I'd devised a plan that would accomplish both.

Of course, there was no guarantee my scheme would work. But I'd always been willing to take a gamble. Besides, I also always hedged my bets—you know, covered them both ways. So my plot had an elegant complexity beneath its apparent simplicity. Quite ingenious, actually.

How do you go about cheating death?

First, change your appearance more thoroughly than any disguise that could be purchased from a cosmetic surgeon, so even your basic gene structure is altered. Maybe that alone is enough to confuse the time matrix. But if it isn't, there is still the other timestone. If it can be found. Only one man knows where he's hidden it. And he is hiding himself, disguised in a mindrider's body—trying to cheat his own destiny by endlessly trading bodies. If I could find him, I could find the other timestone.

Become someone else and find a timestone. Easy enough. Except I was in jail at the time, about to be sent to a prison farm where I'd have no control of my destiny at all. A real bitch, you say. You don't know the half of it. But I'd figured out a way to do everything with one simple manipulation. Even get me out of jail and heading toward Titan, where I wanted to go anyway. I was a clever toad, I was.

But I couldn't rid myself of the nagging doubt that it was futile to try to impose free will on a universe ruled by predestination. I had the terrible premonition I might have only moved myself to another curve on an equation with only one solution set, one common intersection, one locus!

I paddled with my good hand, rotating in my fluid-filled tank. My new face followed me around, staying in front of me on the mirrored interface of liquid/crystal. Subtle changes had occurred. Blue-flecked melanomae contained more pigment granules. Nictitating membrane edges grew closer together. I looked down. A strange body danced before me: tall and angular; lean, hard muscles twitched as new nerve fibers inserted endplates within them; long surgical scars faded; joints were still red and swollen from the polymer mesh used to reinforce their ligaments; bones had new tuberosities from their own reinforcement. I touched places still sore from cybersurgery. Then I clutched my genitals, finding reassurance in their familiar softness. I held my penis in my hand. It seemed unchanged. It looked the same. But I knew otherwise. I flexed a newly augmented cremaster muscle. My scrotum tightened, pulling into its pouch inside my pelvis. My penis followed, slipping out of my hand to retract between my legs in reverse coitus. Pretty slick, huh?

By now you've guessed my plan. At least the first part. You know what creature I am becoming.

You must think me mad.

Sometimes I wonder.

The stranger smiled. Red light gleamed from his eyes, darkening to purple. He knew what madness lay within.

2

Starlight sparkled from somewhere overhead, blurred into red kaleidoscopy by layers of culture media. A brighter red shone from my cell's side, growing stronger. I moved toward it, pressing my face close to the wall. Across a cratered plain a bright disk rose from the horizon. White clouds swirled across blue sea. The green of land almost seemed incidental. Earth-light cast harsh shadows from crater rims.

Some way to visit Luna. Six weeks inside a hybridization pod no bigger than a coffin. On the Darkside, yet. Knowing on the other side of the Moon any vice you wanted could be found in one pleasure dome or another. Vice was one thing that never got boring. Itching did.

I'd caught an itch worse than any I'd ever got from all the stinking jail cells I'd visited on Earth. And I'd languished in plenty at one time or another. So I knew something about itches. But this one was something else.

Have you ever itched deep inside where you couldn't scratch? I mean everywhere inside. From toes to head. They said it was a side effect of the transforming viruses that inserted xenogenes into your tissues. Sort of like having internal chicken pox. Not that I'd ever had any kind of chicken pox. But I'd heard of the old plagues. And this was as close as you could get to having a disease nowadays. And there was still healing occurring around all the plastic and metal implants. Healing tissues itched as much as infected ones. But even though I couldn't scratch, I could

15

ignore those itches. The one in my mind was another matter. How do you ignore an itch in your thoughts? That was a side effect of both the vitalium wires that had been implanted in my brain and the hypnotraining broadcasts they were now receiving.

Six months of basic training and a year of advanced could thus be crammed into six weeks of hypnobeams. Hand-to-hand, small arms, jump school, Ranger training, demolitions, toxicology, heavy pulsars, you name it. That certainly avoided a lot of grunting and sweating. Small comfort.

Breathing liquid culture media wasn't all that pleasant, either. Despite the knowledge that oxygenation was occurring extracorporally, you felt like you were drowning. For six weeks.

And boring. What could be worse than floating inside a two-by-one-half-meter glass cylinder, surrounded by similar cylinders arranged into hundred-meter-diameter disks, which were in turn stacked into tiers. Like a giant glass wasp nest. Not a bad analogy. We were like pupae undergoing metamorphosis.

I brought my left arm close to my face and opened my eyes. Red culture media blurred my vision, but I could see well enough to be sure now. A bud was sprouting from the stump of my left arm. Five smaller nodules studded the surface of the bud. I resisted an urge to scratch it.

Itching. Drowning. Boring.

Believe it or not, it could have been worse. I shouldn't complain. I wasn't in jail. I was off the Earth, partway to Titan. (The Corps had their hybridization tanks on Luna. Something about needing vacuum to maintain sterility.) In two more weeks, I'd be on Titan. There to fight a war, the Lord Generals thought. Only I had other ideas. A timestone waited for me there. Or at least the mind of a miner who knew where it could be found. I needed the timestone to regain control of my own destiny. So I had better things to do than be killed in a messy little rebellion.

My name? Let me think. I've used so many. Ah, yes. Detrs. Marc Detrs. I was twenty years old.

I had already renounced a noble legacy. I could have been a Lord of Earth, for what that was worth. I'd accumulated my own fortune. Some of it in sporting ventures, the rest by illegal means. But all of it was safely laundered and hidden away in secret accounts. When my brilliant criminal career had been cut as short as my left arm, I'd turned down a hand-slap stay on a prison farm and volunteered for the Corps. All those sacrifices just so I could become an ordinary grunt combrid and be sent about a billion kilometers away to fight a foreign war. In which the average life expectancy of a combrid was just short of sixty days.

You must think I'm crazy.

Maybe I am. But there's a method also.

What desperation drove me to such rashness? That's easy. A timestone showed me my death. Rash measures are required to cheat destiny. I had to take a gamble. Shoot the works on one roll.

But let me explain. It's a little complicated, after all. There's plenty of time. About two more weeks, actually. Take my mind off the itching, anyway.

The Hybrid Wars had been going on for as long as I could remember, but they had never seemed entirely real. The holos made war into grand adventure. Each night they brought a fragment of heroic fantasy into the living rooms of old Earth. There was lots of exotic scenery: Martian deserts, volcanoes on Io, vapor canyons on Europa, Titanian crystal forests, the hydrocarbon glaciers of Iapetus. And it was the stuff of heroes: outnumbered Terran troops bravely defending the Empire from rebel brigands. Sailors scurried among the rigging of gravships patrolling the space lanes, cyrines streaked across the vacuum of boarding wires to fight hand to hand among the struts of pirate ships, sleek trigee fighters rose from their carriers to engage rebel craft —bright pulsar beams stabbed into the darkness between stars, seeking targets as fleeting as tumbling meteors. Dogfights happened so quickly the details could only be perceived by battle computers. Fighter pilots didn't have time to think; they relied on instincts transplanted into their brains with xenogenes—instincts that enabled them to react faster than thought. Death came with a silent implosion and was equally quick.

Although I admired sailors and fliers and cyrines, they were not my heroes. I didn't become one of them in my dreams. My imagination was captured by the Combrid Corps' Ghost Cavalry. Combat hybrids manned the garrisons on the colony worlds. They ended up doing most of the fighting. Earth controlled the space lanes. Rebels only made token sorties into space. But on the ground, it was another matter altogether. There, rebels had the advantage. After all, it was their native land. They knew the terrain and had the support of the local populace. The Corps tried to control strategic areas and to keep commerce from being interrupted. The rebels could have the rest; Earth only wanted the steady flow of raw material from her colonies. Permanent combrid garrisons had been established to insure this. Of course, this permanence made Corps facilities vulnerable to hit-and-run attacks by rebels. To counter this, the Corps conducted pre-emptive strikes of their own, using Ghost Cavalry units. Needless to say, I fell in love with the cavalry.

What three-year-old wouldn't? The holos gave them lots of air time. Hoverbuses darted about like flying metal spiders, disgorging combrids from their bellies. The Ghost Cavalry then floated gently to ground, supported by pseudograv thrusters in their battle packs, firing bursts of pulsar beams downward, protecting their descent. They certainly looked impressive. Combat armor blended perfectly with any background, making combrids as hard to distinguish as wraiths. Their faces were hidden behind mirrored visors. They were stronger and faster than any human had a right to be, but then they were not quite human. They were the elite of the Foreign Legions. Or so the holos made them out.

Now I know it was all recruiting propaganda. But then I didn't. For an hour each evening I could watch them doing battle in living 3-D color, courtesy of the holovision networks. I had my own one-watt, rapid-cycling laser pistol. I could stand shoulder to shoulder with my beloved combrids, fighting for the glory of the Corps, blasting elves, scorching sphinxes, wasting Martians, and sparing no quarter with sundry other rebellious hybrid races. For that hour I was as happy as I thought I could be. The stroboscopic flashes of my toy laser soothed away the frustrations of a troubled child. Later, after my parents tired of their games, I could relive that day's firefight in my dreams, sleeping with my toy gun in my hand. Before morning came, I would awaken to bright laser flashes and find my finger clenched in spasm on the trigger of the pistol.

I would have given anything to have been old enough to

run off and join the Ghost Cavalry. They wouldn't take you until you were sixteen. That became my passion, my reason for living. All day, I played make-believe, dressed in my own combat armor, firing my own toy laser. Each evening I watched Ghost Cavalry ride into battle. Later, after there were no more tears to cry and the pain from my parents' games had faded, I crept into their room, where they lay sprawled in peptide stupor. As I played harmless laser flashes across their bodies, how I wished I had a real pulsar. How I longed for the day when I could run away.

Several years later my father told me the truth about the Combrid Corps and the other Foreign Legions. He laughed when he told me I could never join. For I was heir to a Lord of Nyssa. I was the last of my line. Someday I would be a Lord myself. They would never take a sole surviving son into the Legions. *A different kind went to the Legions,* my father said. A kind I would never be.

Then his laughter became mocking. He smiled slyly. *Besides,* he said, *Henri went to the Legions first. Your brother waits for you there. Remember what he did to make them take him away from us and give him a new psyche? Remember Hide and Seek? Henri still plays that game. Henri still wants to play it with his little brother.*

The dreams bothered me for a long time after that.

And I'd believed him. I thought I couldn't run away with the Legions.

But there was nothing to keep me from just running away.

3

I started running away from home when I was ten years old. I've forgotten how many times I've been caught and returned. Only to run away again at the first opportunity. Why was I running? The usual reasons.

I still remember the first time. After they beat me nearly to death, my parents lay in their usual stupor, minds gripped tightly in narcospasm. They were naked; dawn-light shone from mahogany skin. Their bodies sprawled at the edge of a marble swimming pool, like toppled Greek statues. They had the same build, lean and lithe, although my father was taller and heavier. They both had amber curls cut short, and wore earrings and necklaces of sonic gems. Sonic jewelry glittered from fingers and toes as well. Her breasts were faint swellings, scarcely more noticeable than his. His penis, though limp, was still red-streaked.

I'm not sure how old they actually were—over a hundred anyway—but they appeared young, with a physiologic age of twenty.

I had crawled from the house and made it halfway to the pool before passing out from pain. My back was a network of welts. Blood dripped between my legs. As I gathered strength, I knew I had two choices: drag my parents' comatose bodies into the pool and watch them drown, or get away myself. I decided I lacked the strength for the former. Or the courage.

So I ran instead.

You learn a lot on the street. When you get hungry

enough, you do things you never thought you'd ever do. Ironically, they're quite similar to the things at home you're running from. After a while, they don't seem nearly so bad.

But hustling on the street is not without risk. There are still lots of antiquated laws on the books. And plenty of unimaginative vice varks around to enforce them. You're a little green at first.

My first time away, I was pinched in a public park with my pants down, squatting over the face of a woman old enough to be my grandmother. Such a harmless perversion, really. Her dog had recently died. She paid well, so the varks let her go. I had nothing to bribe them with, so it was off to jail for me. Shortly thereafter, I was home again.

4

After that first time, I ran away from home regularly. I gradually became more street-wise. Each time it took them a little longer to catch me. But catch me they did, until I found the timestone. I'm coming to that part later. Now let me tell you more about me. A real sob story. Got your crying towel handy?

I was the youngest of three brothers; twelve years younger than Henri, eight years younger than Robrt. I was the only one of us left. I was the last of my line. Robrt was dead and burned. Henri was off with the Legions, which was as good as dead.

How did it happen? The usual way. As a result of a game.

Henri made Robrt and me play Hide and Seek with him. Sounds innocent enough, doesn't it? But not the way he played. Robrt and I always had to try to hide, then Henri came looking for us. When he found us, he played a different game—the Executioner Game. He would pretend to shoot us, or gas us, or electrocute us, or cut off our heads. Real fun.

The game evolved into something nasty. After finding us but before his mock executions, Henri would bind our limbs. When we were helpless, he would lower his trousers to show his erect penis. Then he would make use of our rear passages or make us take it in our mouths, or both.

One day he got a little carried away. He had tied us up and made us stand on a fallen log. (We played the game outside, on the grounds of our estate.) Then he placed nooses around our necks and threw the ropes over an overhanging branch, before making their ends secure around a tree. We had to stand on tiptoe to keep from choking. Henri proceeded to bugger us from behind. I was first, then Robrt. His thrusts were a little too vigorous with Robrt. They pushed him off his log. The noose tightened around his neck. His eyes bulged and his tongue protruded blue. But Henri was too caught up in his sexual frenzy to notice. He kept up his sodomy. His thrusts continued. By the time his tension was relieved, Robrt was dead.

The authorities came and took Henri away. They gave him a new psyche and conscripted him into the Legions.

That left only me to receive the tender ministrations of my parents.

My parents were Lord and Lady Detrs. Even now, I don't blame them for their cruelty. They were as much the victims of the aristocracy as I. Heir to incredible wealth, recipients of both longevity and antiagathic genes, they had all the time in the world to accomplish nothing.

My parents had long since become bored.

Maybe they should have set themselves goals: power, wisdom, even possessions. But they didn't. They escaped ennui with decadence. There was no perversion they hadn't tried at one time or another. Procreation was only another form of depravity. How well I came to understand that. And peptide addiction was the most depraved affliction known. But it only gets part of the blame.

Let's take a little jump in time now. Like an image glimpsed on the surface of the timestone when I still had it.

I was riding in a police cruiser, skimming over the treetops of my parents' estate on the outskirts of Nyssa. To the west icesea shimmered blue, pierced by the silver needle of a gravchute. A vortex of pseudograv surrounded the chute —incoming ships spiraled down in counterclockwise helices, like pinballs going down a drain. Outgoing gravships hurtled up the chute like photons streaming out a glass fiber.

I was twelve at the time. I'd been on the run for over ten weeks that time before I was caught. A silly mistake. I'd rolled a pephead for his chargering. I hadn't realized how quickly the credit computers would discover it had been stolen. I'd tried to use it to pay a hotel bill with room-service charges. Needless to say, I was perturbed when the charge console wouldn't register. But the dog-hair machine wouldn't release my finger, either. To get away I'd have to leave my pinky behind. I decided it wasn't worth it. I'd learned another lesson the hard way.

The bunco varks quickly figured out who I was. They knew my parents were good for the bills I'd run up. They figured there was likely to be a reward for my return. In a matter of hours, I was on my way home.

The house was visible now. It perched on the edge of a sandstone cliff, like an aggregate of rhomboid quartz crystals. The cruiser swooped low and landed in front. Sonic manacles were unclasped and I was pushed out. They watched to be sure I went inside.

My father waited there. His eyes were dark and hollow, but endocaine burned within their depths. He held an alphawhip in his hand. Ions dripped to the floor and bounced around like sparks from a grinding wheel. I knew it was going to be bad when he didn't scream at me. The whip did his screaming, crackling with ionic fire each time he swung it. I did the only thing I could, what I'd learned to do a long time ago: covering my face with my arms, I fell to the floor and rolled into a protective ball, letting the whip land on my back and legs. It felt as if liquid fire were being poured over me. Each time the lash cracked across my back, I yelled in agony. Between swings, I wailed pitifully. But Father was not to be satisfied easily. Fortunately, I lost consciousness before his rage had dissipated.

When I woke, I was lying on the floor of my room. My right ankle was shackled to a chain bolted to the floor. I winced at the stabs of pain as I sat up. My skin still glowed with alpha particles. Every muscle was sore as Pittsburgh. But I knew I'd be OK. That was the good thing about an alphalash—it didn't leave scars. And it did no permanent damage. The chain rattled when I moved.

"I heard you were back," someone said from behind.

Grychn sat on the edge of my bed. She tried to smile. Rather unsuccessfully. Her eyes were amber, her hair as white as ermine fur.

Grychn Willams lived on a neighboring estate. She was the same age as I. We'd played together for as long as I could remember. I'd tried to get her to run away with me once. I really needed her then. She wouldn't go. I'd never asked again. You only got one chance with me. Sometimes not even one.

"Just for a visit," I answered, shaking the chain.

"Oh, Marc. Why make it so hard on yourself?"

"That's the way I am." We'd gone over all this before. She knew how I felt.

Grychn wore a cape of spun gold and nothing else. She crossed her legs awkwardly—they were too long, as she was in the middle of her adolescent growth spurt. The skin over her breasts was blue and taut, stretched by their rapid growth. She noticed me staring and was embarrassed. I smiled and stood up. I walked over to the bed, trailing my chain, and sat beside her. She began massaging my aching back muscles, fingers soothing away the hurt. She was good; she'd done it many times before. "Are you here to stay this time?" she asked. "I guess you'll have to now, won't you?"

I said nothing.

"I miss you when you're gone." Her arms circled me, pulling my body against hers, while her fingers kneaded my chest and belly muscles. She bit my ear, then let her tongue trail down my neck. "I need you," she whispered. Her fingers found my penis; it stiffened to their tuggings. "I want to be with you. Don't leave me again."

I turned my head. Her tongue slipped into my mouth. There was brightness in her eyes. She lay back, pulling me with her, opening her legs wide to receive me. My chain rattled in synchrony to my thrusts. Grychn whispered over and over: "Don't leave me. . . ."

But I did leave her again. It was easy. As easy as running away the next time. The penultimate time. Chains couldn't hold me. I waited for my chance. It came eventually, as I knew it would, when my parents made the mistake of passing out within my reach. I then seized my father's limp hand and pressed his sonic ring against my shackle. In a second, I was free. In another minute, I was on the run again. I won't say I didn't think of Grychn. But there was no time to gather excess baggage. There never would be.

5

Three months later found me back in Nyssa. I'd been around the world in the meanwhile. I was quite proud of my ability to survive the rigors of low-living. Especially avoiding the press gangs. They were everywhere. It seems good old Mother Earth was running short of warm bodies to turn into combrids. The Hybrid Wars were going badly. The dog-eyed colonial vermin weren't giving up their silly rebellions. You couldn't divert too many criminals from the cyborg factories, or you wouldn't have enough slave minds to run them.

So groups of entrepreneurs roamed the streets, grabbing pepheads or those overcome by mnemone fumes, and hauling them down to recruitment stations. Bartenders spiked both drinks and dope, for a percentage of the take. When business was slow the gangs grabbed even alert victims and gave them a shot of something to make them sleep. That was the beauty of free enterprise. *Caveat emptor!*

I'd learned a few tricks during my travels. I met lots of people willing to pay to see those tricks. Travel was a broadening experience.

But there was something about Nyssa that drew me back. Part of the attraction was the spaceport. The constant bustle was exciting. The crowds were easy for a twelve-year-old runaway to blend into. Pockets were easy to pick —off-worlders were naive. Perversions were easy to pander to.

Port of Nyssa was a collection of permaplastic spheres

27

that lay beneath the icesea, clustered around the base of the gravchute like giant frog eggs. Huge pneumatic tubes snaked through dark water to connect the port to Nyssa proper. Nyssa was a duty-free port, so large numbers of shops catered to visiting off-worlders. There were also the usual amusements: mnemone dens, peptide parlors, orgasm emporia, casinos. Jaded tourists could purchase anything or anyone they desired. Everything had its price. Nothing was unavailable.

In short, Port of Nyssa was an ideal place for a street urchin to do a little hustling.

Which was exactly what I was doing. I'd pinched a bell-hop's uniform and was wandering around a hotel casino, carrying a silver tray with a folded sheet of gold foil imprinted with an impressive seal and reeking of pheromones. I didn't bother to page a name; that way it would appear the person to whom I was delivering the message was known to me by sight—notoriety implied importance. That way, the bell captain was less likely to bother me. Wouldn't want a V.I.P. not to get his message. Especially if it was from a sex-friend. Like I said, I'd learned a few tricks.

The casino's floor was the inside surface of a hundred-meter sphere—a field of pseudogravity created this orientation, in which gravitational vectors were centrifugal rather than centripetal. The floor was transparent—through its ten-centimeter thickness could be seen a myriad of marine creatures attached to the outer surface: kelp, anemones, shellfish, starfish, coral. Beyond, sharks cruised with mouths agape through dark, shimmering sea. Above, players stood around gaming tables, like flies hanging from the ceiling. Naked servants plied the guests, offering mnemone, peptides, and assorted alkaloids from trays. If chemical temptations failed, breasts would brush against backs, penises would be pressed against buttocks, tongues would lick what was proffered. The servants were well trained. Anything to distract a winner's concentration.

Wheels spun. Dice rolled. LED's flashed. Crystal facets glittered. Chips skittered. Tongues licked cracked lips. Sweat beaded on tense faces. Mnemone fumes rose to form a haze in the center of the sphere.

Business had been brisk. My pockets were crammed with chips and tokens I'd lifted from gamblers.

I should have taken my loot and run. I knew the key to

success in either larceny or gambling was knowing how far you could push your luck. My luck was at its limit. I'd had a good take. I should have already been in a hotel room counting it. But something made me linger in the casino. There was a frantic energy in the air. I could almost smell it—like ozone from wires leaking electricity. And there was another energy below the first, something subliminal urging me to stay. I knew better, but I stayed anyway.

I looked straight up, across the casino, through blurring fumes. A crowd of people surrounded one of the craps tables, watching a shooter throw dice. Even the servants had abandoned their trays to watch. They sat on each other's shoulders to get a better view. Most of the house dicks had also collected around the periphery—like the jackals they were. Each time the player rolled, a murmur came from the crowd. This would be the perfect time for me to leave unnoticed.

I started walking toward the door, meandering past gaming tables with their monomaniac players. I pretended to be looking for someone to give my message to—had to keep up my disguise. If I'd had more pockets, I could have cleaned up. But I restrained myself. Another minute and I'd have been out the door. Then all I'd have to do was find someone to cash in my chips for me. That would be easy. I could always have my way with certain ladies. They found me adorable.

Yet for all my good intentions, I didn't leave then. Without realizing it, I had circled toward the crowd and now found myself mingling in its edges, slowly infiltrating deeper into its mass. I let myself be guided by this strange new volition. What the Memphis, nothing ventured, nothing gained.

Soon I was squeezing between two women and pushing next to the dice table. The women glared angrily when I forced between them, but when they saw me they smiled and patted me on top of my head. I smiled back, resisting the urge to bite their fingers.

On the other side of the table, a player was throwing dice. He was a sailor—a hybrid bioformed to survive the hazards of deep-space sailing. He stood the standard two meters. His arms and legs were somewhat out of proportion in length, giving him a lean, angular appearance. Monomer sweat glistened from skin as black as obsidian with intradermal antiradiation granules. Nictitating membranes covered his eyes like silver monocles. His scalp was bald and convoluted into ridges by wires buried beneath the skin. It gleamed with conducting gel. He wore only a formal cape of spun gold—hybrids were proud of nakedness, having need for neither clothing nor modesty. An earring dangled from his left ear. The only other jewelry he wore was a platinum ring set with a stone I could not identify. A sonic knife in a sheath was strapped around his left thigh. Fingers and toes were long—each of their tips had a suction pad so the sailor could climb polished surfaces like a tree frog.

Now his fingers cradled a pair of crystal dice. He shook them in his hand and crooned to them as dice players had done for millennia. A huge stack of chips stood before him. He let them ride on his next throw. His hand went back, then forward. Diamond dice were flung into a field of pseudograv, where they were caught and held. They tumbled in midair. Tiny oscillators in the center of each die flip-flopped randomly between six choices. The dice stopped spinning. LED's lighted up each facet: two on one, five on the other. Seven. A natural. The crowd murmured. The sailor grinned.

A croupier pushed neat stacks of chips across the table. With one hand the sailor added them to his other stacks of chips. With the other he gathered up his dice and shook them again. He bet all his chips. I did a quick mental calculation. There was at least a million in front of him.

I whispered to the woman standing next to me: "How long has he been letting them ride that way?"

She laughed. "For ninety-eight straight passes. All naturals. All the easy way. Quite incredible, really." A pink tongue darted out to wet her lips. "They say he's cleaned out a different casino each night for a week. Always shooting craps. Always throwing naturals. No one can figure out how he's doing it." Her eyes narrowed. "He'll need someone to help spend it." She put her hand on my shoulder. "Come with me, just in case. You can't be sure. He might prefer boys." She began elbowing her way around the table. I followed behind her.

The sailor brought his arm back again, shaking the dice in his hand. Light glittered off his stack of chips. There was a distant look in his eyes, a look I found disturbing.

He snapped his arm forward, throwing the dice. They ricocheted in midair, skittering into the crowd. Something was wrong. They were supposed to enter the pseudograv field of the table, not bounce off it. The field strength must have been increased. The croupier retrieved the dice and handed them to the sailor. He threw again. Again the dice skipped in midair above the table.

An uneasy murmur rose from the crowd. The croupier made an unobtrusive hand signal. Almost immediately the casino manager stood at his side. She was a tall woman, almost as tall as the sailor, but well built. Her hair was short and the color of wheat stubble. Her eyes were emerald. "There seems to be a malfunction with the table," she said. Sonic earrings amplified her voice. "Technicians have already been summoned to repair it." She smiled, nodding toward the sailor. "I'm afraid our lucky guest will have to take a break while the table is being repaired. Shouldn't take too long." Mirrored fingernails flashed as she waved her hands.

"There's nothing wrong with the table," the sailor said softly. The crowd quieted.

"Of course there is. You saw for yourself."

"I saw what you wanted me to see." There was something wrong with his voice. The same wrongness lay in his eyes. "You're afraid I'm going to break this casino like I did the others. You turned up the field on the table. You want to check it out. Can't figure out how I'm winning, can you? What's the matter? Don't you believe in luck? You'll find nothing wrong with the table. Or the dice. I'm sure you've already looked me over with sensors. You can't find any force generator on my person. Why don't you save some time and turn the table back on so I can resume winning? My luck won't last forever. Maybe I'll lose on my next roll."

The crowd muttered. They knew the sailor was right. They didn't like having their fun interfered with. Most of them had been betting on the sailor.

"Nonsense," the manager said. "A circuit's shorted. Or a diode's burned out. My technicians will have it fixed in no time. Meanwhile, here's a chit for your present winnings and a room key, on the house, so you can refresh yourself while the table is being serviced."

She tossed a platinum token and a sonic key to the sailor.

He caught them both with one hand. Then he looked carefully at the manager. He suddenly seemed to recognize her. The chit he placed in his cape pocket. He threw the key back to the manager. "You'd like me to go to that room, wouldn't you, Kramr? Make your job that much easier." His lips were pulled tight across his teeth. "Are you sure you've got enough? Three is all? Not very good odds for the house. Besides, the other one is here too." He seemed to look at me when he said that. I wondered what he meant.

Servants appeared, carrying trays loaded with intoxicants. They began plying the crowd, offering their wares. Soon laughter wafted from the crowd. It wasn't long before they forgot the sailor.

The woman I was following had made her way to the sailor and now stood beside him. She put her arm around him, pressing her body close to his. He didn't notice. He was examining the back of his hand, staring into his ring. She leaned close, whispering, and then stuck her tongue into his ear. He pushed her aside, as though she was just a minor irritation. He turned suddenly and bulled his way through the crowd. Clinging hands reached for him. He shook them off, revealing surprising strength in his lean frame. All eyes watched him.

That meant they weren't watching me. It was time for me to make my move. Past time. I followed in the sailor's wake, unnoticed. I slipped out the door of the casino without difficulty, ducked into a public toilet, and got rid of the bellhop uniform. I was safe. I should have holed up with my loot. But I didn't.

Something still bothered me.

Something about the sailor.

When I came out of the restroom, I could still see him. He was just ahead, aimlessly walking down the street. He seemed to be muttering to himself. Every once in a while he would look at his ring. I could just glimpse his eyes then. A strange fire was reflected from their depths.

I followed him.

He was easy to trail. I could have tailed him for days. But it was so easy, I got sloppy. The next thing I knew, he was running and dodging down side corridors. All of a sudden, following him wasn't so easy. Those damn hybrids were fast. The only thing that allowed me to keep pace was that it was easy for me to weave through the crowds. I'd had lots of practice doing that. I tried to keep him in sight, but he changed corridors enough to make it difficult. He steadily widened the gap between us. I didn't think he was running away from me. That would be ludicrous. I was unarmed and alone. He could have broken my neck with one hand. Besides, he had a knife. I slowed down a little, thinking. I wanted to be sure I wasn't sucked into a trap.

Far ahead, the sailor darted into another connecting corridor. By the time I reached it, he was nowhere to be seen. The corridor was deserted. A dozen others opened into it; the sailor could have ducked into any of them. He had given me the slip, all right. Then I paused. Sweat beaded along my spine. I smelled a trap. He was probably waiting for me, hiding in one of the corridors, ready to jump me from behind. If I was smart, I'd turn back. No sense taking needless chances. But then I wasn't smart, was I?

I heard something that made me sweat even more—the soft hum of an open sonic knife. No, an ultrasonic harmony. More than one knife. That really made me think.

I slowly advanced, listening carefully, until I came to the opening from which the sound came. I peered in, ready to jump back. My heart beat like a trip-hammer. Blood roared in my ears. A short corridor lay before me, empty. Beyond, dim light flickered. Sound came from there also.

I crept along the corridor. It opened into a small park, complete with benches and foliage. Luminescent sea swirled against persplex overhead, flooding the chamber with flickering green light. The sailor stood in the center of the park, surrounded by three pepheads. Each held a sonic knife. Ultrasonic fire sang from crystalline blades.

Pepheads normally resorted to less violent types of crime to support their addiction. Mugging usually required too much energy. But it was known to happen. The three pepheads surrounding the sailor looked typical enough. They were thin and cachectic with bodies wasted from too many forgotten meals. Their faces were hollow and gaunt, with sunken eyes. Hair hung in scraggly patches from their heads. They appeared too frail to even protect themselves, much less attack someone else. Yet they seemed agile enough and were surprisingly quick. Must be hopped up on endocaine or endophetamine. Those peptides gave synthetic strength and courage.

The sailor was good. He seemed to anticipate his assailants' thrusts, and easily parried them. But he was outnumbered. And surrounded. There was no escape. Just as there was no doubt what the outcome of the fight would be. But I had to admire his skill. It was like watching ballet. He leaped and twisted and turned, slashing with his knife, parrying the others' blades with his wrist and ankle bands. I flashed to the holos of my childhood, of sailors fighting pirates hand to hand in the riggings of gravships. This was better. This was in person.

One of the pepheads slumped to the ground. His throat was slashed. The other pepheads and the sailor continued fighting. Their leaps and lunges slowly moved them away from me. Now was my chance to get the L.A. out.

I was about to leave, when I noticed something peculiar about the fallen pephead. I moved closer until I stood over him. My legs weakened; I sank to my knees. My stomach felt queasy.

He was changing! As I watched, the pephead was changing appearance. His face and body were fleshing out. He was dead. I was sure of that. But he was changing anyway. His skin lost its sallowness. Nose and ears became a little different. Dead eyes changed color. Soon I saw a face no one had seen for many years. I knew then he was dead. Only in death would that face be seen. You know as well as I what creatures fought the sailor. Not real pepheads. That was just a disguise to keep any witnesses from realizing who the attackers actually were. Quite simple, really. Chameleons could wear much more elaborate masks. They were quite sensitive about their anonymity.

But now I knew who they were. I knew what that meant. If I ran, they'd follow, as soon as they were finished with the sailor. The chameleons of the Intelligence Corps wouldn't stop following me until they found me. I knew what would happen then. I didn't need that kind of heat.

I had no choice. I mean, what else could I do?

The chameleon was still grasping his knife in his dead hand. I pried it from his fingers, then looked up. The sailor looked horrible, bleeding from numerous slashes. There was a stab wound in his belly—already his abdomen was becoming distended with bloated viscera. He still fought furiously, though. He was backed up against the persplex wall of the park. Phosphorescent bubbles streamed by on the other side, as bright as space dust. The two remaining pephead/chameleons closed for the kill. I would be next.

My heart beat out of control. Cold sweat ran under my arms. My vision blurred around the edges. But I knew what had to be done. And I'd seen enough holos to know how to do it.

I quickly ran across the park. Before the pepheads had a chance to turn, I slashed the closest one across his right side, below the ribs. My knife sliced deep, cutting both liver and kidney. Bright red blood splashed on the ground. He fell forward.

The other pephead glanced back to see what had happened. As he did, the sailor lunged with his blade, catching him under his chin. He fell backward, dead. It was not a peaceful death for either pephead. With death, the neural and hormonal energies maintaining their disguises relaxed. Their appearances reverted to true form—an unpleasant metamorphosis. Skin fibrillated as if worms were wiggling underneath. Muscles snapped against tendons. Bone grated and crunched as it was remodeled.

I looked away, having seen enough. The sailor had slumped against the wall. His knife lay beside him. He motioned me over. I kneeled beside him, leaning over to place my ear close to his lips.

He whispered: "Who are you?"

"I saw you in the casino."

"But *who* are you?"

"No one. Nobody important."

"Yes you are," he said. He tried to laugh, but the sound bubbled in his throat. He coughed up a clot of blood. "Your face has haunted my dreams for a long time. I thought you would be my killer, not my rescuer. When I saw you following me, I knew my time had come. Just as the deathstone foretold. I knew when I saw your face that all my plots had been in vain." He twisted his neck to look through the persplex wall. He tapped against it with his finger. "I thought this would be the wall of a dome in space. Somewhere on one of the outer moons. How was I to guess it was water swirling beyond and not liquid ammonia and methane? I came to Earth fleeing the vision of my death, not seeking it." He took a deep breath. Bubbles gurgled in his chest. "Nels was right. I, too, should have become a mindrider and lost myself in the mindcasinos of

Chronus. Should have gotten rid of this body. It'll never catch up to Nels. Nels is safe."

"I don't understand."

"You will."

"But I've never seen you before. How could you know me?"

"The stone showed me your face. No matter how hard you try you always succumb to the temptation to see your own death. I knew you'd also witness mine."

I pointed to the dead chameleons. "Why were they after you? What did the spooks want?"

"The stone, of course. Kramr wants the stone."

"The stone?"

He held out his hand. Light sparked from the gem in his ring. "Just a flawed chip of the real one," he said. "A time-stone." Then he managed to laugh. "And a deathstone for sure." He looked at me in a funny way, almost apologetically. "Here, you take it. The cycle must remain unbroken." He slipped off the ring and pushed it into my hand. Then his body shook with paroxysms of cough. Red foam ran from his nostrils. He whispered again. I leaned closer, so I could hear. He was delirious, of course. His ravings made no sense, then. He told the whole story, though. Later I would put it all together. I'm coming to that part.

After he died, I slipped the sailor's ring onto my finger. A strange warmth emanated from its gemstone. Then I took the casino chit from his cape and pocketed it. Money could do him no good now. It could do me a lot of good. I had plans. I also strapped on his knife sheath and slipped his blade into it. No cleaning was necessary. Blood didn't stick to sonic blades. I was careful to wipe my fingerprints from the other knife handle.

As I was leaving, I looked at the chameleon I'd killed. He'd reverted to his true morphology. Quite ordinary, actually. Then it hit me. This was my first killing. I admired the wound I had made in the chameleon's side. It had been easy. And the feeling wasn't at all bad.

Then I got the Frisco out. Spooks didn't like their kind being killed. I wanted to be far away when the bodies were discovered. A vendetta against me was not my idea of fun.

A week later I got pinched again. I'd made it back to Nyssa. I was picked up by a routine patrol. Fortunately, I'd cached my loot, all but the sailor's ring. I was wearing it.

But I had the foresight to swallow it when they picked me up. I didn't want to be traced back to him. No way! They didn't connect me to either him or the dead chameleons. The dimwitted varks thought I was just a runaway. All they were looking for was the bribe they'd get for returning me to my parents. If they'd guessed the truth, they could have saved themselves a whole lot of trouble later on.

But they didn't.

Guess the truth, I mean.

6

I opened my eyes. Instead of the underwater blur to which I'd grown accustomed, my vision was clear. Nictitating membranes had finally become complete. But the difference was negligible. There still wasn't much to see: cratered moonscape, bathed in Earth-light; a kaleidoscope of other hybridization pods, each containing its own human larva, metamorphosing just as I was. I brought my left hand in front of my face. Five stubby fingers grew from the stump. They wriggled at me, of their own volition. But soon both feeling and motor control would return. It would be good to have my hand back.

With my right hand, I scratched my head. The wires in my scalp no longer itched, but there was still the deeper one. That itch was as bad as ever. Yet I marveled at the grim efficiency of hypnotraining. Already I knew the twenty-three ways to kill a man using only bare hands and feet. I also knew how to dispatch a score of other creatures not quite men anymore. I was proficient with both light and heavy photonuclear weapons. I could make a bomb out of common minerals on any of the inhabited moons and planets. On those that supported carbon-based plants, I knew which plants you could eat and which ones would kill you. In a pinch, I could pilot anything from a hoverbus to a gunship to a Nova-class gravship. I could do things I'd never done, and do them well.

I laughed out loud.

I should have figured out how to get all this training

years ago. I could have saved myself some trouble. Killing wasn't nearly as hard as I'd always found it to be. If only I'd had the skills then that I had now. Oh, well. Live and learn. I smiled at my play on words.

I saw movement at the edge of my vision. My peripheral vision had been considerably enhanced. I looked up. A gravtug passed overhead in orbit, towing a long train of silver pods. I searched my new memories. Strange. I had no knowledge of what the tug was towing. It passed out of sight over the horizon. The pods followed, one by one.

Something bothered me.

Unbidden, an image formed in my mind: frost covered the face like close-cropped fur. Red filaments fanned out from the ears. Teeth were broken into shards of ivory ice.

I pushed the face away.

I had more pleasant memories. I was telling you about myself, wasn't I? You've seen the face I was fleeing. Maybe you've figured out why I was afraid of it. I probably told you sometime. But you don't know the complete plan. I left out part of what the sailor told me. You don't really know what the timestone was. Remember Nels, the mind-rider. He can tell you all about timestones. If you can find him. If you can get him to talk. But I'll tell you what I know about timestones. I paid the piper once. I'm ready to pay again.

Listen.

I was home for the last time. You figure out what that means.

I'll spare you the gruesome details of my homecoming —my father worked me over with an alphawhip; my mother got in a few licks herself. What happened after I passed out, I couldn't say. I've got educated guesses, from the various places that hurt, but you're not interested in guesses. Before I lost consciousness, for some reason I thought of the sailor. I made some sense out of what he had said.

I came to late the next morning. My vision was still a little blurred, but it cleared rapidly. A sonic shackle clasped my ankle, attached to a long chain. I was in my room.

I stumbled into the bathroom, unsteady on my feet. I examined myself in the mirror. Except for a few scrapes and bruises, I looked all right. No scars, this time. I stepped into the shower stall. Ultrasonic fingers massaged my skin. After a few minutes, the soreness left my muscles. I stepped out, walked to the toilet, and sat down. Sonification beams warmed my bottom. Reflex took over. Smooth muscle contracted; sphincter tone relaxed. Then I remembered. I jumped off the toilet and squatted over the floor. I barely made it in time. Stool plopped against smooth marble. I'd often wondered how smugglers did it. Now I knew. They shit on the floor and poked through it with a pencil. It wasn't as bad as it sounds. Kind of fun, really. Infantile fixations, and all that.

Anyway, I found what I was after. I fished out the ring and washed it in the sink. Then I cleaned up the other mess. I didn't want the maidmech to blow a fuse. Or be hanging around any longer than necessary.

I lay in bed and examined the ring. The setting was plain platinum; quite cheap-looking, in fact. The stone was nothing to rave about, either. It was deep blue, almost black, like an amalgam of tourmaline and obsidian. The exposed face was crudely cut on an oblique angle to the other facets, which were much finer. But then it was a chip from a larger gem, wasn't it? That's what the sailor had said. And he'd told me more.

I looked deep into the stone, letting my mind relax. A shiver ran up my back. I smiled.

I got up and rummaged through my closet. I found a children's game board with a set of dice. The next hour I spent rolling naturals. Or any other number I wanted. It was easy. You just thought about it real hard, until you could see an image of the dice inside the stone. Then you made them show the number you wanted. When you threw the real dice, they came up that way. Simple. Took the gamble out of gambling. No wonder the sailor had wiped out all those casinos. But his brashness had gotten him killed. I'd be more careful.

Someone coughed behind me.

I turned around, already knowing who stood there. I mean, I knew! I'd known several minutes before she had come into my room.

"Practicing for the sporting life?" Grychn asked.

"Just fooling around. Killing time." I smiled. Dogs, I was clever. "What number do you want to see? A seven?" I threw the dice. A natural rolled up in the air. "How about eight the hard way?" I rolled again. Two fours. Before the dice stopped flashing, I picked them up and flipped them again. A six and a two. Naturally. "How about snake eyes?" I rolled. Two single red spots glowed in midair.

"Trick dice?" She laughed. "You can buy them in any novelty store." She picked them out of the air and examined them closely. Her eyes widened. She'd seen the National Quasiconductor seal on each. You couldn't fake that. Not in a novelty store. "How?" she asked.

"Child's play."

I pulled Grychn close and let her stare into the ring. I told her about the sailor. I shouldn't have. I could have saved myself a lot of trouble later if I hadn't. But I was young and foolish then.

"I don't like it," she said later.

"What?"

"The ring. The timestone. It feels wrong. Get rid of it. Toss it down a dispoz."

I laughed. My hand lay on her chest, between her breasts. The timestone glittered on my finger. My timestone. She touched my lips. I took her finger between my teeth.

"I mean it," she said. "Something bad is going to happen."

"Don't be silly. I've got plans, big plans."

"You're leaving again?" She knew I was.

I said nothing. I kissed her, pressing my body against hers. We spent the rest of the day making long, slow love. Grychn was nice. I would almost miss her when I left again. Almost. But there would be others. Just as nice.

Later, in the dark, she snuggled comfortably against me.

I heard someone moving up the stairs. I didn't need a timestone to know who. "You better leave now," I whispered to Grychn.

"He's coming?"

I nodded. "Time for you to go." Ions buzzed in the air. The nocturnal ritual was about to resume.

"I want to stay."

"No you don't. Not if you value your hide. I'll be OK. I'm used to it. Get going."

"I'm staying with you."

"Suit yourself. It won't be pleasant."

The door opened. My father stood in the doorway, surrounded by blue smoke. He was naked. Thermite embers glowed in red tattoos on his skin. His eyes burned brighter with endocaine. "Your mother wants *you* now," he said. He held an alphalash in his hand. Sparks dripped from the whip and bounced from the floor. Again, I didn't need the timestone to know it was going to be bad.

He unlocked the far end of my chain and dragged me down the stairs to where Mother waited. Grychn came by herself. It must have been a treat for my parents, to have someone as nice as her. If they even noticed.

Grychn kissed me in the night. Her lips sought the places that hurt; her tongue's wetness extinguished glowing dermatographics. Lines of flame burned in her skin also, like cruel corposant, swirling over her breasts, across her belly, between her legs. Beneath each line of fire, ions beat on pain receptors. Nerve endings sang a harmony of hurt. White sparks danced in ocher eyes. Ermine hair with retained static stood out as straight as dandelion fuzz. Darker streaks marked where tears had washed away the alpha tattooing. I licked the others out, one by one, tasting the salt-sweet taste of burned epidermis. Alpha particles could burn no deeper. They didn't leave scars in skin, just temporary pain. Her tongue worked the same magic on my skin.

Finally the fires were out. We lay together, lips touching, breath mingling. A rush went from head to toe. There was no euphoria greater than agony that was past. I touched my hand to her face, resting it gently on her cheek. She opened her eyes and stared into the timestone on my finger. She stopped breathing for a moment. Her pupils narrowed.

"What's wrong?" I asked.

She covered my hand with hers. "Don't look," she said in a strange voice.

Of course I had to look then. I pulled my hand away from hers and stared into the timestone. A compressed image darted into my mind, there to expand: Grychn and I were shackled to a beam in the ceiling, hanging by our hands. We were both naked. My parents each held whips, but not harmless alphalashes. This time they wielded sonic flagella. Their eyes gleamed with peptide madness; their lips smiled wickedly. They began working the whips over our bodies. Carefully. Slowly. So that their pleasure would last a long time. Each place the whip touched, flesh exploded into red slime as tissues were sonificated. I saw Grychn and myself scream with pain as our bodies became pocked with bleeding craters. Slowly, flesh melted. Weakened belly walls burst—entrails dangled out. Eventually we were reduced to limp skeletons—bones with only tatters of muscle left. And still sonic whips sang.

I looked away from the timestone. But the images stayed in my mind. They were there yet. And I knew the vision was true. The timestone had shown me what was to be, what would happen sometime. I was convinced of that.

"You saw?" I asked Grychn.

Her face told me she had.

"Then you know what we've got to do." I looked at my parents. They lay in a peptide stupor across the room.

"Maybe it's a trick," Grychn said. "Maybe it's only a possibility, not an inevitability. Maybe it's only illusion."

"We can't take that chance." My shackle was off. They'd made that mistake once before. I crawled across the floor. Grychn followed.

"Are you sure?" she asked.

"We have no choice." I was right. We had no other choice. I shouldn't have needed the timestone to realize what would happen eventually. They'd get carried away with their game. They were hardly in control of it, anyway. It was just a matter of time before they killed me. I'd known it unconsciously. Why do you think I was running? The timestone just confirmed what I should have suspected earlier. The sailor had told me it would show me my own death. He said there was nothing you could do about it. Well, we'd see about that. I still had one choice, one chance. But no others.

Grychn helped me drag their limp bodies across the room to the pool. We floated them on top of the steaming water. My father wore a jeweled dagger strapped around his thigh. I pulled it from its sheath. Ultrasonic fire flared from the blade, sharper than any metal edge. It took only a few seconds to nick their wrists and send red blood squirting out. I dropped the knife into the pool. A double suicide. Lords and Ladies did it all the time. Very fashionable. I stood beside the pool and watched blood pump into the water. Finally it stopped. They still floated, but now were white as polystyrene statues.

What did I feel? I don't know. Feelings didn't matter. I had no other choice.

Grychn was trembling. I took her hand and led her away. In my room I let her hold me for a while. She cried on my shoulder.

Then we made love again.

As we were dressing, I asked: "Are you coming with me?" Giving her another chance.

"OK." She looked up with shimmering eyes. "I guess so." Then she saw the ring. "Marc, get rid of the ring."

I laughed. "You've got to be joking. I've got plans. Big plans."

"Please get rid of it. For me."

I shook my head.

"I can't go with you if you won't destroy that ring. It's poison. Look at the trouble it's already caused." She was trembling.

"Then stay." I was dressed and ready to leave. I looked back once. Grychn's eyes were hidden. Cheeky little tart, anyway. She'd had her chance. Two. Frog her. There'd be others just as nice.

And there were.

7

A full moon showed its face to Earth—down there it was time for lovers to take pleasant strolls, or for harvests, or for serenades. But we weren't down there. We were on the Darkside, in the cold. The only light was from faraway stars—cold and steady and uncaring—and the dim phosphorescence of transforming virus in culture media. Even that was inconstant. For an hour, the level of media had been dropping. The tank was almost drained now—only a little sloshed at my feet.

Both my transformation and training were complete. I was a full-fledged combat hybrid now. Soon I could start the second part of my plan.

You haven't quite figured it out yet, have you? There's one more part to tell. Then you'll know it all.

The lid popped off my chamber. I clambered out easily. All around, other combrids climbed from their tanks, like a cohort of wasps hatching from their hive. We leaped to the ground. Lunar dust puffed around our feet.

We stood in orderly rows on the Lunar plain, buck naked. In vacuum. In cold a hundred below. No spacesuits. No oxygen masks. We were combrids. There was enough oxygen stored in our brown adipose to last for an hour. The same layer of special fat insulated against the cold. Skin reinforced with polymer mesh and glistening with monomer sweat was impervious to vacuum. Nictitating membranes and internal sphincters protected more delicate tissues.

A gunnery sergeant stood before us, dressed in combat armor. Human eyes might not have seen him. Camofilm on the outside of his battle dress blended perfectly with the moonscape. But human eyes were not looking at him.

He laughed. We heard it in our minds, picked up by sensors embedded there. "Welcome to the Corps, *meat!*" he shouted. "You ain't civilians anymore. You is meat now. Corps meat. You ain't never going back to Earth, so don't think different. The only way you is ever going back is on the meat wagon." He pointed upward. We all looked in unison. The gravtug with its string of pods passed overhead, almost low enough to reach by jumping. On its final orbit, then. The face I was fleeing flashed into my mind: frozen eyes, icicle teeth, frost thick as blue fur. I shivered, but I wasn't cold.

The Gunny continued his welcome speech: "If you have anybody back there that cares for you—and I doubt you do—forget about them. You ain't never going to see them again. If you got an old lady or an old man, forget about them. They be all right without you. Old Jody will take care of them. You'll never see them again, anyway. You done sold your soul to the Corps. The Corps gonna be mama and papa to you. You gonna get fat eating that good Corps food. If you gonna get laid, the Corps gonna do it." He laughed again. "Anybody here want to run? Anybody homesick? Anybody want to take off, now's the time. The Corps don't want no rabbits. Want to run? That's OK. Go ahead. Nobody stop you." He waited, hands on hips. "One last time. You gonna run, you better do it now. You got enough air in your body to last an hour. You might make it someplace. You might not. But this is your last chance to run. You try it later, the spooks come after you. You won't like that." He waited. No one moved from the ranks. I was in no particular hurry to run myself. I had to make it to Titan before I ran. A miner named Nels waited for me there. He was going to tell me something. May as well let the Corps pay my passage.

Besides, I had no other choice. Not then, anyway. I was as good as dead, unless I could change the time matrix. I wasn't sure fate could be changed. But you can bet I was going to try. I mean, what did I have to lose?

Have you figured it out yet? All the clues are there to be

fitted together. You need some more help. OK. We have time for one more story before we go.

I was about to take the Plunge. The famed ski run dropped below me—a steep, narrow chute leading straight off the top of the mountain. The lights of Telluride were below, as bright as peptide dreams. Stars winked overhead. The ski slopes themselves were lit by luminescent snow. Though it was Midsummer's Eve, the air at three thousand meters held a chill. Snow machines already spewed glowing powder from their nozzles.

I pushed myself off the lip, cutting through the glowing wake that marked another skier's passage. This was my last run. I had business to attend to. I planned to make a little after-hours withdrawal from the Bank of Telluride.

After getting rid of my parents and leaving Grychn, my life took a turn for the better. The varks never did figure out I'd killed them. Grychn never betrayed our secret. They were officially victims of suicide. I became a minor success. Having the timestone helped. A little research at the library enabled me to figure out that it was a chronotropic crystal—a type of living gem that could manipulate time. The concept was logical enough. There were radianuclear crystals that could transduce every other kind of energy. Why not time? Though predicted on a theoretical basis for years, no one had yet been able to grow one. Well, somone had. Because I had a chip of one.

It really was quite useful. Not only could it provide glimpses of the future, but you could also change the future around a little, simply by willing it so. Not a lot of change, but enough for my purposes. Enough to make dice come up the way you wanted. Or cards. Or to be sure a little round ball fell in the right slot.

I was able to make quite a name for myself in sporting circles. And accumulate quite a hoard of cash. I had my own group of sycophants living on my own estate. The good life was mine.

But that's never enough, is it? I became bored. Winning games of chance wasn't fun if you took away the chance. But I found the timestone could also be used to make computer locks open a little early or to help electronic tumblers drop into place.

I wasn't content being the system's highest roller. I also had to be its most flamboyant cat burglar.

The timestone let me be both. There was only one problem with it—you could see more than you wanted to see. If you wanted to know the way you were going to die, it would show you. I'd seen a scenario of my own death once. That was enough, thank you. I wanted to live, not spend my life fleeing death. I'd take my chances not knowing the shape of destiny. But the temptation to know was almost irresistible. I had to keep firm control on my mind. I wasn't going to make the same mistake as the sailor. Not me. I intended to use the timestone, not let it manipulate me. But frogs, I was tempted more than once to see myself dead again.

Where was I? I sometimes ramble. Ah, yes. The system's most flagrant thief. I found the thrill in crime was to be able to pull off impossible capers, in front of witnesses. Then laugh when the varks tried to figure out how the job was done and who did it. I guess the timestone made me a little cocky.

So there I was, cutting tight S-turns down the Plunge, planning to rob the Bank of Telluride, in front of witnesses.

When I reached the bottom, I stacked my skis on a rack and ducked into a public dressing room. I'd rented a locker there that morning. In a private booth, I took off my ski boots and body stocking and put on formal slippers and briefs. I fastened on a jeweled chain-mail corset, then clasped an evening cape about my shoulders.

I was ready for the night's activities.

I crossed Saint Michael's River. On the other side was Shadowtown. I passed a row of cribhouses. Pathics sat naked on open balconies. Their voices called to me as I passed. Mental fingers caressed me at first, then tugged at my hands as I continued walking. I closed my mind tight. I didn't need their particular perversions. Not tonight, anyway.

The sidewalks were jammed with tourists. This was the week of the Gravglider Festival. Thousands of gliding aficionados were in Telluride to watch their heroes dash themselves to pieces in midair duels. I had counted on it being crowded. Tonight was also the grand opening of the Bank of Telluride's new Pandora Tower. I'd promised them they'd be robbed tonight. It would be more exciting if they were warned. I wouldn't want them to be disappointed.

I wandered past peptide parlors and mnemone dens, blending into the crowd. I knew undercover varks were scattered all around. They had been trying to catch me for a long time. A real shame they didn't know who I was. I turned east on Main. Laughter rose from basement stairwells, with wisps of smoke and swirling fumes. I walked on. Those perversions were not for me, either.

I could see the tower now, floating above the ruins of an ancient mine. It rose two thousand meters above the floor of the canyon. Beyond, molten sodium splashed down a three-hundred-meter cliff. A plain waterfall had been deemed too ordinary. But real snow dusted high mountaintops.

Security was tight at the bottom of Pandora Tower, though a casual observer would have thought it nonexistent. To untrained eyes, there was only a single doorman checking invitation cards. But I noticed the other varks. You could tell by their eyes; they were too interested in what was happening around them. Let them have their interest; it would do them no good in catching me.

I handed the doorman my invitation. He let me pass without comment. And why not? It was a legitimate invitation. I was a legitimate guest. I had made a substantial deposit to the bank. I hoped to make an even larger withdrawal. I stepped into a liftube and was whisked upward along the outside of the tower. I rose past sheer cliffs carved by glaciers millennia ago and soon even topped the four-thousand-meter summits of Telluride Peak and Mount Silver. Wind whipped ice crystals against the wall of the liftube. Only the stars and Club Ionosphere were above me.

The liftube opened into the club. I stepped through a doorfield and was in. Lords and Ladies milled about, sipping wine and smoking aromatic herbs. Sonic jewelry sang from ears, noses, fingers, and toes. Naked skin gleamed with synthetic sweat.

Servants circulated among the guests, carrying trays laden with comestibles and intoxicants. I waved one away. I wanted a clear head tonight. I meandered about, apparently as aimless as the other guests. I engaged in meaningless conversations, laughed empty laughter. All the time I made my way to the center of Club Ionosphere.

Several faces were known to me: Miguel Teller, body merchant and proprietor of the original hybrid shop in nearby Ophir, was with Dolores Silver, his sometime companion and gene futures entrepreneur. Carmen Mendoza had attracted her usual crowd. I only nodded or smiled or muttered a greeting. I didn't want to get tied up in a prolonged conversation. Varks were scattered about, of course. But they were easy for me to spot.

Finally, I reached my goal. A clear cylinder about a meter in diameter ran from ceiling to floor in the middle of the room. It was a fiber optic bundle. One end opened on the top of Pandora Tower, where it received data beamed by laser from orbiting satellites. The other end fed this data to the bank's computers in the old mine tunnels beneath the tower. The Bank of Telluride was a central clearinghouse for this hemisphere. Or it would be when the system became operational. Which would be in about five minutes. The bank's president was already giving his ceremonial speech. I shut him out. I didn't need to listen to speeches.

A hand touched my shoulder. I turned. She'd changed to a formal gown, but I recognized her. I'd seen her skiing earlier that day. She wasn't someone you'd easily forget. Gossamer spider-silk cascaded about her shoulders, showing lots of brown skin through it. A string of singing pearls circled her neck, glowing white hot. I remembered green eyes. And the image of her nice ass bobbing up and down over moguls as she skied.

"What's so fascinating about that glass column?" she asked. "You've been staring into it for five minutes."

"You'll see in a few minutes." I smiled. But I'd been careless. Too obvious. There were varks all over. The woman would be good cover. Nothing unusual about talking to her. Besides, there was lots of scenery revealed by her flimsy gown. I smiled my most charming smile and eyed her breasts. Not bad. The parts below were all right, too.

She pretended she didn't notice me looking at her. But she smiled back. "I saw you on top of the hill today." She laughed. "Looks like you made it down in one piece." She looked closely at me. "I thought you looked familiar. I've seen you in the holos. You're a gambler, aren't you?"

"That's me. Marc Detrs. Boy wonder of the casinos." I

handed her my card—the one with the pair of dice that always came up sevens.

"My name is Michele Kramr." She smiled again. "What's a gambler doing at the opening of a bank? There're no risks to be taken here."

"I like to be close to money. And you?"

"I came for the free refreshments. And so people wouldn't gossip about me."

There was another reason, left unsaid. I knew she'd take my offer. As soon as I completed my business, I'd tender one.

Now was the time for my withdrawal. The bank's president had finished his speech. He signaled for the lights to be turned off. Darkness surrounded us.

Stars were visible through the transparent ceiling of Club Ionosphere. Directly overhead was the brighter star of a comsat. A red beam stabbed down from the sky, striking the vertex of the tower. The fiber optic column next to me filled with laser light, sparkling like ruby sand in an hourglass. The crowd oo'd and ah'd. All except me. I had business to attend to.

Did you forget I wore a timestone on my finger? It was a useful little gadget. Each of the tiny optical fibers in the column represented around five hundred accounts. Laser light modulated the activity of those accounts. Each beam of laser light was only a photon across. Once they got in an optical fiber, they stayed there. The comsat was aligned very precisely to achieve this. But a photon wasn't very big. It was just the right size for my timestone to manipulate. I could change probability a little with it—twist the wires of coherent light a little, and make a few photons hit a few wires of my choosing.

One of the fibers was mine, representing my account. It was child's play to pad my balance out a little. There was no way to trace it or to even know it was being done. Digits flashed from the chargering on my other hand, marking my steadily increasing bank balance. The bank would know that they had been swindled—more had gone out than had come in. They would know they'd been robbed, but they wouldn't know how. They would know who had done it—I'd told them I would. Only they didn't know who I was. Pretty clever, no?

Like I said, child's play. Photons were easy to move

about. In just a few minutes, I'd siphoned off several million credits. My chargering's digits changed so fast, its register glowed a solid green.

All the time I kept up an inane conversation with the woman standing beside me, setting her up for some night games afterward. I didn't notice the way she also watched my chargering. But I did notice the hand signal she made.

Too late an image flashed in my mind: me with a set of sonicuffs around my wrists. I looked about in alarm. A couple of varks guarded each exit. The rest were unobtrusively moving toward me. The woman Michele had fingered me. She wasn't a vark. I could smell varks. I didn't have time to figure out what she was. I had to get away.

I slipped into the crowd, making my way to the far wall. There wasn't a door there, so there were no varks, either. They took their time following me, sure I couldn't escape. They thought they had me this time.

I wasn't so sure about that. I'd made a few contingency plans myself.

As I worked my way through the crowd, I got ready. I tried not to think too much about what I was going to do. I had no other choice, so there was no point worrying about it. I knelt briefly and fastened each corner of my cape to my slippers at the ankle. I slipped the shoulder clasps over each wrist. Then I pulled out a flat piece of plastique from its hiding place under my corset and worked it into a round ball.

The varks were holding back, waiting until they were all in position. Michele seemed to be directing things. They were in no hurry, figuring they had me trapped. Indeed, they did. The transparent wall of Club Ionosphere had no doors or windows. Besides, beyond the wall was two thousand meters of sheer drop. I felt like the proverbial cornered rat.

So I did what I had to do.

I threw the ball of plastique impact explosive at the wall, at the same time dropping to the floor and covering my head. A deafening explosion sounded. Flame tickled the hairs on my neck. As soon as the tickling stopped, I jumped to my feet and ran forward. A meter-wide hole gaped in the wall. Cold wind roared in through it. Without looking back, I dove headfirst through the opening. Once beyond the edges of the wall, I spread my arms and legs into a skydiver's frog. Air billowed under my cape, ballooning it into a parawing that both slowed my fall and provided forward thrust. I could steer by moving my arms and legs. Although I didn't have as good a glide coefficient as I would with a real hang glider, I could still go a long way with a two-thousand-meter start. At least as far as Ophir, where my skimmer was hidden.

I spilled air out of one side of my cape and began circling around the tower. Wind streamed past, chilling bare skin. Snow rustled against taut fabric. The lights of Telluride glowed far below, colder than the stars overhead. Brighter light blazed through the crystal pyramid of Club Ionosphere. Figures appeared in the hole I'd blasted. Faces peered out into darkness.

I stared into the timestone I still wore on my left hand, letting its warmth fill my mind. I was going to need its help. Eventually the varks would spot me.

I twisted to the right. A pulsar beam cracked the air where I'd been a moment before, just as the timestone had warned me it would. More beams flashed past, barely missing me. Even with the timestone's help, it was hard to dodge the beams of six hand pulsars taking target practice at me. But without the timestone, it would not have been possible.

I think I could have made it if the stone had not betrayed me. I was almost out of range of their handguns. In a few more seconds, I would have been. Then an image came unbidden to my mind. I tried to push it back to the depths of the timestone and found I could not. A face filled my mind's eye—my face, frozen solid, eyes bursting from ice inside them, teeth shattered from the cold, skin covered with frost as delicate as white fungus. I could not look away. The death mask pushed away the images of pulsar beams I should have been concentrating on.

Pulsar quanta came closer. The air cracked with their ionization energy. Then there was a different sound—a splattering sound, like a red-hot brand drenched in water. Only I had my left hand around that brand. I could not let go.

Suddenly the face in my mind was gone. But so were all the other images. Cold vacuum sucked at my mind.

I looked at my left hand. It wasn't there. All I could see was the fading contrail of a pulsar beam and a puff of vapor already dissipating into the wind. A sphere of white smoke was all that remained of my hand. And of the timestone. It also was vapor.

My cape had fallen off my wrist and flapped free. I couldn't grab it with a bloody stump. Damn annoying. With only three anchors, the wing had lost considerable lift and was uncontrollable. I fell to earth in a tight spiral. Below me were ski runs winding down through dark forest like lava flows. I tried to maneuver myself over one of the slopes. I was going to hit hard. Maybe the snow would soften my impact.

Then I remembered my death mask. I was destined to freeze to death. I would die in ice. That grim, unwanted knowledge was now mine. I wondered if I should head for the trees instead.

Glowing snow neared. Would it be here, now? Would I freeze on the ski slope before the varks found me, buried in synthetic snow? Maybe. But there wasn't much I could do. If I went into the trees I'd be killed for sure. I didn't need a timestone to know that. A steep, snow-covered slope was close beneath. I bent my legs and turned upright in the air. Dogs, I was going fast. This was going to hurt.

As I hit, I rolled forward. Snow exploded around me. I almost chuckled from a wry thought. I knew I would survive the impact. The timestone had told me as much. The only question was whether or not I would freeze to death in the snow afterward.

I felt a sharp crack on my head. Darkness closed over me. I might not ever know that answer.

I didn't freeze to death. You knew that. I woke in a hospital bed, sore all over. There was no serious damage. In a few days, I was transferred to jail. A few more days, and my trial began. You probably remember it. The holos had a lot of fun with me: scion son of nobility, playboy gambler, daring master thief. The networks went out of their way to show all the robberies I'd committed that had completely baffled the varks. They loved making the authorities out to be buffoons. The public loved watching it. I became a media event for the few days of my trial.

Of course I was found guilty. But only for one count of fraud against the Bank of Telluride. They couldn't prove anything else. And they didn't know how I'd siphoned off millions from the bank. The prosecution's star witness was Major Michele Kramr, on loan to the varks from the Intelligence Corps. I almost crapped when I found that out, remembering that I'd once snuffed a spook. Apparently they failed to make the connection. But so did I. I'm sure you have. Michele testified about me standing next to the fiber column and watching my chargering registering. The bank could verify that my account got fatter as others got leaner. They didn't need to prove how I did it, only that I had. They did. Which made me guilty.

Not that I put up a spirited defense. It didn't seem to matter. Nothing mattered anymore. My timestone was gone. I was going to die, and there was nothing I could do about it. I even figured out where it would be. I was destined to freeze to death. I knew that the punishment for fraud would be a year or two at a prison farm. Big deal, you say. Well, get this—the prison farms are located in Antarctica. You know, the icebox of the world.

So naturally I was found guilty. Just as certainly I would be sent to a prison farm. There I would most definitely die. Fate must be consummated. There was nothing I could do about it. Only a timestone could manipulate the time matrix. My timestone was gone.

So I was in a rather grim mood as I lay in my cell on the eve of my sentencing. I knew a hand-slap punishment would be a death sentence for me. I wasn't even cheered up by watching the coverage of my trial on the holo. I was *that* depressed.

The war news came on next. I didn't bother to turn it off. Tonight the coverage came from Titan, where the elves had launched another offensive against Chronus. They showed footage of the "bombardment." None of the elven pulsar beams even made it through the city's force-field. Life there went on as notoriously as usual. Patrons still frequented the famed mindcasinos.

Suddenly I remembered something. I could have kicked myself for not thinking of it earlier. The sailor had told me it as he died. I'd forgotten about the miner, Nels. And the other timestone. The holo scenes from Chronus reminded me. There was another timestone. Nels knew where it was hidden. He could be found among the mindriders of Chronus. Maybe I could cheat fate if I could locate the other timestone. I had done that once before. It might work

again. But how was I going to get to Titan? I was going to
be sent to Antarctica. As I watched elves eluding Terran
combrids in forests of glass, the solution came to me. Quite
simple, really. There was only one way. I had no other
choice.

The next day, before the judge could sentence me, I
asked him to let me volunteer for the Combrid Corps. The
request was a formality. He couldn't refuse me. Any citizen
had the right to go to the Combrid Corps in lieu of any
other criminal penalty. Normally, joining the Corps was the
alternative to capital punishment. But it could be substi-
tuted for lesser punishments as well.

I can still remember the surprised look on the Lord
Judge's face when he granted my request. He must have
thought me mad to trade a year or two on a prison farm
for six years in the Corps. Less than one percent of combrids survived their tour of duty. The average life span was
closer to two months. But I knew going to a prison farm in
Antarctica was the same as a death sentence for me. There
was only one way for me to cheat that destiny. I had no
other choice.

But still, I had to smirk every time I saw myself reflected
from the inside wall of my hybridization tank. My plan
was clever, no doubt about it. Even if I couldn't find the
other timestone, I might thwart the time matrix. By becoming a combat hybrid, I was changing myself into another
creature entirely. More than just superficial appearance.
Even my genes were different. I was not the same being as
I had been; I was no longer the same as the dead face the
timestone had planted in my mind.

So now you know the whole plan.

Pretty smart, eh?

Now I just had to get out of the Corps before I got my
new self killed. And I had to come up with some way to
get that dead face out of my thoughts. It was giving me the
creeps.

8

As I stood at ease with my fellow combrids, I shivered, although I wasn't cold. A thrill, then. A childhood fantasy realized. For I had never forgotten the Ghost Cavalry of my dreams. Then I wanted to join the Corps to escape my parents' cruelty. Now I'd joined for another reason entirely. No matter. The thrill was still there.

A gravtug appeared on the horizon and slowly neared, until finally it nudged into a berthing tower. The long string of pods it was towing gently settled to ground.

The Gunny pointed toward them. "Come on, meat!" He laughed. "We got to unload some other meat, to make room for you."

We formed a long line, stretching ourselves between the pods and the hybridization tanks we'd just left. Inside every pod were eight cells, each of which held a body bag with a wounded combrid who was too severely injured to be treated at a field hospital. They had been brought back to Luna for complete regeneration. In hybridization tanks, they could be stimulated to grow back an arm or a leg or a new set of intestines.

The Gunny opened the pods' hatches. I pulled each body bag out of its cylindrical cell and passed it to another combrid who passed it down the line to the tanks. There, the wounded combrid was placed in a hybridization cell whose lid was then closed.

We went down the line of pods. I tried not to look too closely at the bodies in the bags—they were depressingly similar, anyway, with mangled limbs, gaping wounds, seared flesh. A human would have died from such trauma. Combrids were a little tougher. Lucky us.

We eventually came to the last pod. The Gunny opened its hatch and stood back. I grabbed the first bag and pulled. The body inside was stiff. Right away, I knew something was wrong. I looked at the cell. Its wall was cracked right through a heating coil. A body bag was only good against cold and vacuum for a few hours. The nearest garrison was ten days out. I tugged the body out. I wished I had not.

It was frozen solid, of course. As the eyes froze, they ruptured, despite nictitating membranes. Teeth became brittle and snapped off. Water sublimated, then recondensed as frost, which covered the face like blue fur. You couldn't tell by looking that it was the face of a combrid. It could have been anybody's face. Get the picture. It could just as easily be the face in my own dreams.

All the wounded had been placed in hybridization cells. It was time to go. Each of us climbed into one of the cells in the transport pods. The Corps used the same pods to transport fresh troops out and bring wounded in. Quite efficient, that way.

The Gunny went down the line of pods, closing each hatch. I waited for him with seven other combrids. I knew the timestone had been playing with me. I'd been tricked. I couldn't fool the time matrix by becoming a combrid. Death waited for me, wanted me. In death, my face would look the same as it had before. All my plots and schemes had been in vain. Somewhere, ice waited. Not in Antarctica now. In space? On Titan? What difference did it make?

Still, I didn't know when it would be. Maybe on the trip out. A little crack. A vacuum leak. The failure of a heating coil. There was no way to know. Maybe soon. Maybe later. The only way to be sure would be to find the other timestone. Before ice found me. And maybe the other timestone would lie to me, play me for its pawn. I couldn't be sure it would not. The time matrix seemed very convoluted. Fate could be devious in achieving its ends.

The Gunny closed our hatch. Warmth began to radiate from the walls of my cell. For how long?

Singing filled my mind. The other combrids sang. I knew the words; they'd been given to me by hypnotraining. I sang along, blending my voice to a chorus of other voices. It was a marching song, the kind that had been sung by troops for millennia. The words were quaint, the meaning simple. We were off on a silly adventure. War was frivolous brutality. There was nothing noble about it. But glory could be found. We would all die eventually; that was inevitable. Only the nature of our end could be of our choosing.

But maybe that was enough. Maybe that was all there ever was to life.

Another song was sung; the words changed but the meaning stayed the same. I found comfort in the camaraderie of singing with other combrids as we sailed off to war. Childhood fantasies of glory rose in my mind. They no longer seemed silly at all. I knew I would be brave.

For the first time in a long time, I wasn't scared.

Book II

Show and Tell

1

A poker crystal lay in front of me. It was my turn to bet. I was trying to decide the best strategy. Other players watched me from across the gaming table. Just like old times, huh? You might think nothing had changed, that I was still a flamboyant playboy back on Earth. You'd be wrong if you thought that.

Lance Corporal Detrs, at your service. Pride of the First Ghost Cavalry. Veteran combat hybrid, *par excellence*. Member in good standing of the Legion of Lost Souls. Mercenary killer of elves. But I've killed for reasons other than money. But those reasons are my business.

I'd taken to soldiering like a computer takes to chess. The Cavalry was more fun than anything I'd ever done before—like a hunting trip with your buddies, half of whom were women. A real shame I was going to have to leave. Right when things were getting interesting.

I'd been in a bush garrison on Titan for over six months. You see a lot of firefights in six months—a lot of your buddies get killed. You waste a lot of elves yourself. There are good times and bad times. The initial thrill of being in the Ghost Cavalry wanes. I'd stared death in the face too many times to be afraid anymore. I'd developed a fatalistic philosophy common among combrids—when your number was up, it was up. Your time had come. There was nothing you could do about it except to make sure your death was as glorious as possible, and to be sure to get the elf that got you. I was no different from anyone else. I didn't know when my time would be; I just knew how I'd look then. An insignificant difference. I'd made a separate peace with death.

Don't think I no longer wanted to find the timestone. I did. Only my motives had changed. The Terran Empire was about to fold. There'd be a power vacuum when that happened. An enterprising young man with an advantage like a timestone could carve out quite an empire for himself. A lust for power had replaced my previous greed.

Besides, I was getting a little bored playing Cowboys and Indians.

I was just about ready to make my move. I had enough money saved to pay for the cosmetic surgery that would be needed to change my appearance. (There was nothing more obvious than a combrid deserter.) It had taken me six months to accumulate the necessary capital. I'd sat at gaming tables a lot of hours during those six months. I'd diverted a lot of goods to the black market. I had a duplicate set of keys to a ground vehicle and a forged set of travel orders that would get me to Chronus. I could leave anytime. Except for a couple of loose ends. One of those was a fem combrid named Vichsn. She knew too much about me; I'd foolishly told her too much. When I deserted, the spooks would question her. I couldn't be sure she'd keep quiet. She was becoming a real problem.

She was sitting across the table from me now. I couldn't go over the hill until I figured out what to do with her.

I glanced at my poker crystal. A black queen stared at me: the bitch of spades.

I looked beyond the green felt gaming table past shadowed faces of other players, to the noncom club's picture window. The window commanded a good view. A shame nobody cared to see its scenes. Light ebbed outside. Soon glass would turn to mirror.

Night came quickly on Titan. Darkness closed suddenly. Thick hydrocarbon fog rolled over steep mountain slopes covered with crystal forest. Before long, we would hear the banshee howls of elves as they swooped from tree to tree before eventually settling into the forest ringing the base perimeter, there to taunt us with their shrieks throughout the night. Maybe that's how they mourned their dead—the ones we'd killed that day. Maybe that's why they wailed so. It didn't matter. Lamentations couldn't wake the dead, they could only keep the living from sleeping.

I'd hoped I wouldn't be sleeping tonight. I was still wired tight from the day's shooting. But I hadn't arranged a liaison yet. The prospect of our usual sex games bored me. I was ready for something more exciting. Only I didn't know what. I was killing time playing crystal poker. Gambling was as good as any other way to wait for something interesting to happen. I prided myself on being a good gambler.

But no matter how much psionic influence I tried to exert on my poker crystal, I couldn't transmute the queen to the jack of diamonds. She continued to smirk at me from her facet in the pentagonal crystal. I hadn't been worth a dog at telekinesis since I lost the timestone. I hoped to change that inadequacy before too long.

I quickly calculated how deep I was into the pot. Pretty deep, all right. Almost a grand. I had no choice. I was going to have to bluff my way out of this mess.

I always had been a sucker for an inside straight. When I had a timestone, I knew when I'd drawn into one. I'd developed bad habits. So when diamond face cards started rolling up in my crystal, they lured me into jazzing up the pot. Besides, it wasn't that bad a draw—I also held four to a flush. The jack of diamonds would have given me a royal flush. Not a bad draw at all.

Then the bitch queen rolled up.

Busted.

A crummy pair of queens. (I was holding the diamond queen as my hole card.) But maybe I could make them think I was holding a jack instead. A royal straight wasn't a bad hand in stud poker. If you had one. I didn't. Not by a long shot.

I waited for Vichsn to bet. She was high with a pair of tens showing. She threw in a C-chip.

I bumped her a grand.

No point being timid now. Go for broke. I would be broke if she didn't bluff out. Not only were all my winnings tied up in this pot, but so was the week's pay I'd started with. There was not much to do at base anyway, but with no money it was even worse. It could be a very boring week until next payday. Unless night games broke the monotony. I had no new prospects for that. Boring!

I made sure my face was a mask of nonchalance. It

wasn't very hard. I'd risked my life too many times for less money than was in the pot. Gambling sometimes seemed silly and futile compared with the big risk. But it was better than nothing.

Besides, this was just for fun. I'd already stashed away all the money I needed.

The other crystals went blank one by one as players folded. My bluff was working.

The bet passed to Vichsn again. Light gleamed from her oiled scalp, which was convoluted into ridges by buried vitalium wires. Her ocular membrane snapped shut for a moment, then dilated. She looked into my eyes, running the tip of her tongue along the edge of fine, white teeth. She'd been trying to distract me all night by letting her tunic fall open as she threw chips into the pot, revealing glimpses of her breasts. Not that I minded. I enjoyed the show. It took more than a few flashes of taut young nipples to distract me away from gambling. Well, maybe not all that much more.

A bare foot touched my leg under the table, then stroked my shin.

Vichsn smiled. "I think you're trying to buy the pot," she said.

"It'll only cost you a grand to find out." I knew my voice carried just the right amount of flippancy. I really couldn't care less.

Vichsn toyed with the chips in front of her. Her toes continued to play footsie with my leg. She must be holding the third ten. Three of a kind wasn't a bad hand in stud. But she was thinking I had filled my straight. A straight beats three of a kind on every moon in the system. Even Titan. Her other two cards were a six of hearts and a jack of clubs. No help there. She had to be holding a ten.

"I don't think you've got the jack," she said. "I think you're trying to bluff your way out of a tight spot." She smiled. Her skin gleamed like obsidian. She wasn't going to bluff. Dogs.

Vichsn counted out her chips carefully, stacking them into a neat pile. She looked at my face. Her eyes shone blue with retinal reflections. She pushed her stack of chips into the center of the table, then delicately tipped them over so they spilled and mingled with the others. They skittered over the green felt of the table.

"Call," she said.

"Dogs," I said, and illuminated the side of my crystal facing her. The queen's image formed. "Two ladies. What's your hole card?"

"Two pair," she said. A jack of diamonds showed on her crystal. No wonder she didn't bluff out. She was holding the fourth jack. My jack. She knew all along I didn't have my straight. Sneaky little tart.

As Vichsn gathered in the chips, I got up to leave. I was broke and I didn't want to have to play with her marker. I knew how she'd want it redeemed. Be more fun to listen to the elves' taunts. Well, almost.

As I turned, I saw the Gunny standing in the doorway. He was smiling like a sandcat. "Had enough poker lessions for tonight, Detrs? Looks like you're into Vichsn pretty deep already. Ready to call it quits for the day?" He leered at Vichsn. "While you're still capable of redeeming your marker."

"I suppose. Frogging run of bad luck." I stood up from the table.

Vichsn winked at me. "Later," she said.

"What's up?" I asked the first shirt as I walked outside with him. He was stocky for a combrid, with the forearms of a miner. I'd seen him decapitate an elf with one chop of a combat glove. The Gunny didn't smile very much. I'd never asked him why. You didn't ask that kind of question. But he was smiling now.

"We're finally getting another medic," he said when we got outside. "And about damn time. It's been almost two months since Doc bought his."

"Wasn't there some hang-up Luna-side?" The Corps had their hybridization tanks on Earth's moon.

"Yeah, they're bringing out a new series of Corpsmen and ran into a few production delays. Something about needing a certain personality profile. But the tanks are on line now. They're putting out ten a week. The new medics are supposed to be the hottest hybrids since the new-model cybernetic marines came out. Completely self-contained. Entirely autosynthesizing. And we've got one waiting for our company. So I want you to grab a skimmer and move ass over to the port to pick her up."

"But it's almost dark." I put just a touch of whine in my voice. "And it's a hundred klicks to the spaceport." Then

I realized what he'd said. "Her?" I asked, suddenly interested. A new player? I mused to myself.

"That's what I said. Don't you listen to the scuttlebutt? All the new-generation medics are female genotype. Something about needing an X chromosome for the hybridization to be successful. Why do you think their mark designation is X-M-R?"

"I hadn't thought much about it." *Chi-M-Rho.* Chimera. "Chimera," I said out loud. "So that's where the name comes from."

"Sure," he said. "Now move. It's almost dark."

We both knew what dangers night would bring.

Harsh sodium light glared from each of four guard towers, brightly illuminating the supply pad. I saw the chimera standing on the pad next to a gravtug. Cargo and passenger pods were lined up behind the tug. The pods' hatches were open and stevedores were busily unloading them. Other combrids also loitered about, but I had no trouble recognizing the medic. She wore a cape with spec-five stripes on the shoulders above a medic's coiled serpent insignia. For the first time I realized how apt that symbol was for her specialty. A duffel bag lay beside her. She stood nearly two meters tall, average height for a combrid, but weighed maybe eighty kilos—definitely on the skinny side. Her arms and legs were long and lithe. Her skin was black with antiradiation pigment granules and gleamed with protective monomer sweat. Pretty standard adaptations. Just like any other combat hybrid. But if the rumors were true, her significant adaptations would be internal. Chimeras were supposed to be a new generation of combat medic.

I touched her shoulder.

She turned. Ocular membranes contracted quickly, then dilated again. Jade eyes examined me dispassionately. Men used to fight wars over a face like hers. Now they had sillier reasons. I thought I was in love. But I knew better. I could recognize the beginning of a testosterone shower.

"Lance Corporal Detrs," I said. "A Company, Second Brigade, First Ghost Cavalry. Welcome to Titan. The Gunny sent me to fetch you to the garrison." There was something wrong with my voice.

"Peppardine," she said. "Firiel Peppardine. I mean,

Specialist Five Peppardine." She laughed, then paused. Her face became lax again.

I recognized the name from somewhere. Of course, that might not mean anything. The Corps would give you a new name if you wanted. She might have taken a familiar one. She remained unmoving. Frogs! She probably expected me to salute or something. Noncoms fresh from the hypno-tanks always did. So I didn't salute. The sooner she learned the realities of a combat situation, the better for everyone. I slouched a little more than usual and gazed about laconically.

She must have gotten the message, because she shrugged and shouldered her duffel bag. I led the way to the skimmer.

Night had deepened. Fog rolled across the road like surf on a beach. During the day, logging trucks lugged cargoes of crystal trees from deep in the interior to the civilian spaceport. The trees were hauled to labs in the asteroid belt for further processing, so the elves wouldn't have the necessary technology to process radiacrystal into war matériel. That was the theory, anyway. The Lord Generals could have saved themselves some shipping charges. The elves had the technology, anyway.

A safe zone had been cleared a hundred meters on both sides of the roadway. Yellow light glared from pulverized crystals. A force-field crackled green fire at the margins of the safe zone. Beyond that was virgin forest glittering in the diffuse glow of Saturn-light. Laughing elves glided among trees of glass.

More than once, the force-field had been penetrated somewhere along the hundred kilometers of road between the base and the spaceport. It had always happened at night. Elves were more devious in darkness.

I was a little nervous as I drove the skimmer back to base. I gripped the steering handle tightly. Sometimes they managed to slip airbears through the barrier and let them wander about the road. Skimmers weren't armored. They didn't provide much protection from the explosion that resulted from a collision with an airbear. I kept glancing from one side of the road to the other. But I wasn't so nervous I didn't look at the chimera every chance I got. She was worth looking at. I hoped she'd let her cape fall open a little now that we were in the skimmer, but she didn't play the game and kept herself demurely covered. My gaze lingered on her hands. I couldn't help but look at them. I'd heard rumors. She had long, supple fingers. Their pads were formed into tree-frog suction cups, like those of sailors, the better to cling to polished surfaces. She didn't have fingernails. Instead, each finger had the retractable claw of a cat. I couldn't help but wonder if the stories told about those claws could be true.

She must have sensed my interest, for she bared her claws quickly, then retracted them again. But before they disappeared, I saw a wet, blue gleam. Nights could be dull at a combrid garrison. Those claws could make them interesting. She smiled, showing her teeth. They shone like cut sapphires. Then she laughed. Viper heat organs glowed from ridges above her eyebrows.

"Where are you from?" I asked, hoping idle conversation would distract my thoughts. From dark forest. And her hands.

She smiled. "A place called Telluride. Have you been there?"

"Once," I answered. "A long time ago." Eight months seemed a long time if you were a combrid on Titan. And I'd been most everywhere on Earth once. Especially places the beautiful and rich considered chic. How well I remembered Telluride. Telluride was very chic. I wondered what a resident of there was doing here. But you didn't ask that kind of question in the Corps. Because you wouldn't want to answer it. Everyone had his reasons. Some were more solid than others, but all were valid. "An interesting place, Telluride," I said.

"Do you think so? I suppose. I was a Lady there. Married to a Lord." She stopped speaking briefly. "Do you know what that means?"

I did, but I didn't have a chance to answer.

Ahead, shadows moved. I stomped on the accelerator and banked into a hard right turn. Ten G's pushed against me, pinning my flesh against wombskin cushions. I heard Peppardine gasp in surprise, as her breath was squeezed from her lungs.

"Toad!" I said with my own exhalation.

A pulse of red light flashed through a momentary gap in the road's force-field. Pavement bubbled into vapor where the skimmer would have been if I hadn't goosed it.

I thumbed the firing stud of the quad-50 mounted on

the roof of the skimmer. A computer sight was already aiming it. Before the breach in the field closed again, four 50mm pulsar beams of a nanosec duration fanned through it. Spent photonuclear cases streamed into the air behind the skimmer. In the forest, crystal trees exploded into millions of sharp fragments. I knew the unseen elves were dead, impaled by tiny slivers of glass. They didn't wear combat armor. They couldn't fly with the extra weight. Their mistake.

I eased off the accelerator and let the skimmer coast to a more maneuverable speed. The lights of the garrison glowed on the horizon. We were almost home.

I looked at the chimera. Ten claws gripped the arms of her seat. But she was smiling.

"You saw?" I asked.

"Of course. More than you imagine." She licked her lips with blue saliva. "Did you have to kill them that way?"

"No. We could have eluded them, anyway."

Her eyebrows arched. "Then why?"

"Because I wanted to. I like killing elves. There's no way they can claim to be civilians if they're dead."

"I see." She touched my leg. Her fingers puckered my skin. Her cape had opened along its slits. I glimpsed smooth pectus muscles, adolescent breasts, pubic hair fine as spun carbon.

Excitement swirled inside. It had been days since we'd had a new player in the outfit. That was a long time in the bush. Everyone had bedded everyone else. And there'd never been anyone like this chimera. I thought of the blue fire carried in her claws. Peptide could warm up the night. I knew peptide was dangerous. My own parents had been addicted to it. But I would be more careful than they. Scenarios flashed in my mind. I smiled to myself.

I put my hand on her leg. Her skin was soft to the touch, but with a firmness underneath due to intradermal polymer mesh reinforcement. She moved my hand along her thigh. Sharp claws scratched the back of it. I saw promise hidden in her eyes.

Then we were gliding into base. I was being tossed about by a testosterone storm—you know, hot to trot. I stopped the skimmer and dilated its doors. I carried Peppardine's duffel this time, leading the way to her hut. But at the door, she turned. Nictitating membranes had closed. She was different; something had changed.

"Let me show you to your quarters," I said, my voice intimate.

"That won't be necessary." Her voice had become flat. Something was wrong.

"OK." But I was desperate. "After you've unpacked your gear, come over to the noncom club. I'll buy you a mnemone stick."

"I think I need to be by myself."

"Maybe I can help?"

"I don't think so." She looked at me in a way I remembered.

But I was too tight with sex steroid to care about my pride. "You'll come later?" I knew she wouldn't. I knew that look. I knew that game. But why?

She turned and entered her room. She paused inside the door and looked back. "I was once a Lady of Telluride," she said, and her voice told me she'd lost more than I would ever have. Because my nobility had not been taken from me. I had run away from mine. I was an orphan by choice. They couldn't hurt me anymore.

The door hissed shut.

I waited by myself at a corner table in the club. A mnemone stick fumed from a bong sitting in front of me. I'd only taken one hit. My thoughts were disturbed enough already. I kept thinking about the sudden change that had come over Peppardine—one minute she was teasing me like a Venusian in heat and the next she was as frigid as an Antirecombinant fanatic. I was feeling sorry for myself. It wouldn't have mattered except she'd thrown me into a testosterone crisis. All that sex steroid had to be dissipated some way. I knew Peppardine wasn't going to show up. But I wanted her in the worst way. I knew I wasn't going to be able to desert from the Corps until I had her.

Someone sat down at my table. Mnemone fumes blurred my vision. For an instant, hope flared. Then my nictitating membranes blinked away the film. Vichsn sat across from me. She picked up the bong and sucked mnemone deep into her lungs.

She exhaled slowly. Blue eyes appraised me. "What's

she like?" Vichsn asked. "Though it appears you've struck out."

"Who?"

"Who? Who do you think? The new medic. The X-M-R. Didn't you pick her up at the spaceport?"

"Sure."

"Is what they say about them true?" Her smile was a leer.

"What do they say about them?" But I thought of her wonderful claws.

"You've heard the stories. They say they have the kiss of death now. Each finger can inject a different neuro-peptide hormone. They hold a hundred electric eels between their hands. They can kill in a dozen ways now. And they were killers before. What's she like?" A bare foot stroked my leg under the table. "Is she a killer?"

"She seems OK." But I thought of her fingers, each with a long, curved claw, hollow, connected to a modified venom sac in its pad. And a blue gleam. Her peptides could bring unimaginable euphoria—the ultimate natural high. Of course there was a certain risk. Peptides were the most addictive substances known. My own parents had been pepheads. I knew all about peptide psychosis—that was why I'd had to kill my own parents. But a little peptide couldn't hurt. I'd stop before I got hooked. Again I glimpsed her body, with smooth muscles rippling. I'd hoped I was going to receive her blue joy. Again testosterone fire flared. *Corpus cavernosum* engorged with blood. I hoped Vichsn wouldn't notice the bulge in front of my pants. "She says she was a Lady of Telluride," I added as an afterthought.

"You know what else they say?"

"What?"

"The ones who become chimeras all have something in common." She smiled in a sly, sinister way. "They were given a choice—the Corps or the cyborg factories."

"A lot of us were given that choice." But a scenario flashed in my mind: a glimpse of something nasty, something that would disturb even the jaded sensibilities of the wealthy Lords and Ladies of Telluride; craziness, raging passion, fury in the dark of night. And an idea began to form; I pushed it away.

"They say they killed their lovers. They each committed

a crime of passion, destroying a loved one. Something about a particular personality pattern being necessary to engram the X-M-R patterns. But then genosurgeons always double-talk. What do you think about her?"

"What about her?" I was on the defensive. Without a need to be.

"Did she do it? Did she tell you about it? Did she kill her lover?"

"I wouldn't know. I didn't ask." But I saw a mutilated body sprawled amid sonic sculpture and mutable holograms. Singing jewelry adorned his nose, ears, fingers, and toes. A spider-silk cape was tattered and bloody. His genitals had been cut off and stuffed in his mouth. Every fax in the system had carried the holo. Even on Titan. Scandal was news. A murdered Lord was scandal. *Alabaster faces smiled at me. Water steamed with red mist.*

Vichsn leaned over to kiss me. Her tongue probed my mouth. I felt taut nipples pressing against my chest.

I let her lead me out of the club, through swirling clouds of hydrocarbon fog, across the commons past parked hoverbuses, and into her barracks with its waiting bunk of pulsating wombskin. She pulled privacy curtains around us, telling her roommates they were not welcome to join us tonight. She'd been doing that a lot lately. She didn't used to be so jealous of our lovemaking. Her protectiveness disturbed me. Besides, I loved an orgy.

But I didn't feel like arguing. I had a testosterone storm brewing. I extended my genitals from their pouch. Our clothes came off quickly. My mouth took hers, accepting her tongue. Her body rubbed against mine; skin slick with sweat slid back and forth. Her lips left my face and nibbled down my body. My mouth found a breast and sucked on its nipple momentarily, before it was pulled out of my lips as she went farther down my body. Her mouth took my penis; her fingers stroked my scrotum. She straddled me on her knees. I put my arms around her and pulled her buttocks to my face. As her legs spread, her own protective sphincter opened, letting my lips nibble her clitoris while my tongue probed her vault. In less than a minute, muscle spasms gripped my tongue while warm secretions wet my face. I drank her drippings. Then she switched positions. "I want you inside me," she said. That was fine with me. She sat on my penis. We coupled. I entered her deeply, striking her cervix. She closed her genital sphincter, gripping my shaft tightly, while vaginal peristalsis milked it. With her sphincter squeezing tight, my penis stayed tumid for a long time.

Later, when our androgen rush had subsided, we lay together in the quiet. I stroked the hollow of her back. I let childhood memories surface again.

"You're thinking of that chimera," Vichsn said accusingly.

She was almost right. "Are you hurt?" I asked. I was also thinking about all I'd told her. Which was too much.

She thought for a moment. "No," she laughed. "Because I have you. You'll never leave me. I know too much about you. And you know you can't trust a lover scorned. Think about her all you want. And think about her lover." She laughed again.

There was something unpleasant about that laugh.

2

I woke to the clang of the battle gong calling general quarters.

Cursing under my breath, I leaped out of bed and ran buck naked out of Vichsn's barracks, across the commons, and into my own barracks. You'd be surprised if I told you how many other combrids were doing the same thing. Running naked back to their own baracks, I mean. But after being at the garrison for a week, you wouldn't be surprised at all. Because it happened routinely every time general quarters was called first thing in the morning. The Lord Generals had learned a long time ago it was better to allow fraternization among their troops. Horny combrids tended to be insubordinate. Chastity led to mutiny.

I quickly pulled on my combat armor and boots. I shouldered my battle pack, grabbed my assault rifle and a bandolero of ammo, and trotted out of the barracks.

Vichsn fell into step beside me. She'd been waiting outside my barracks. I should have minded, but I didn't. She looked splendid in her battle dress: body armor fit her as tight as a soft exoskeleton, boots barely made contact with the ground, ammo belts crisscrossed her chest. A layer of camofilm covered everything. You could barely see her—her image wavered like a mirage dancing in the desert. She could have been a dim holographic projection—a suit of armor brought to life by a wizard's chants. Her face was hidden behind a visor. There could just as easily be no face behind the visor. Yet I knew it was her. I knew her moves.

She flipped up her visor. Her face peered out of a glimmering hole in the air. I saw the mouth that had kissed me the night before. Her lips were smiling.

We joined a stream of other combrids running across the commons.

A hoverbus waited, hatches open.

We climbed aboard and strapped ourselves into our harness. Other combrids filed past. Except for the whine of turbines warming, it was quiet. Combat armor was as flexible as satin cloth and made no noise as it moved; a polymer coating deadened any sound produced on its surface. Elves' ears were very good. Even a little noise could be fatal. The same polymer changed color to blend into any background. Elves' eyes were also pretty good.

No one spoke. There was nothing to say. Later, when speech was necessary, it wouldn't be audible—there was a network of vitalium wires buried beneath our scalps. Their proximal ends terminated within cerebral cortex. Neuropotentials generated within our speech centers would be picked up by transducers in our helmets and transmitted on microwaves. Though we were limited to line-of-sight communication, the elves had not yet devised a way to jam the frequencies we used. Other cerebral centers controlled the servos in our armor, boots, helmets, and battle packs.

The hatch closed and the hoverbus lifted into the air. Overhead, the garrison's force-field winked as we flashed through a breach produced by phase generators in the hoverbus. Then we settled into smooth flight, skimming the treetops. Two gunships flew escort.

I stared out the window. Jagged mountains covered with dense forests of crystalline trees passed below. A century before, Titan had been lifeless, except for transplanted Terran life that lived under domes, such as at Chronus now. Yet of all the Outer Moons, Titan possessed a real atmosphere, composed of dense hydrocarbons and ammonia. Its crust was rich in silicates and other oxides. The conditions were perfect to grow living crystals. Terran eco-engineers devised an ecology of genetically engineered plants and animals, specifically adapted to the Moon's environment, and all designed to support the growth of crystalline forests. Fifty years later the first colonists had landed. Someone had to tend the forests and harvest radiacrystal. They were of human stock, but had also been adapted to the native conditions of Titan. Their changes were more than cosmetic. They still called themselves men. We called them elves. They were tall with hollow, pneumaticized long bones. A flap of skin stretched between their arms and legs. They could glide for great distances in the weak gravity and heavy hydrocarbon atmosphere of Titan by extending their limbs to make a taut airfoil out of their skin flaps. By wearing a specially fitted cape of surface-effect polymer, their so-called pseudowing, they could even fly. They had large, pointed ears to collect ultrasonic pulses emitted by bat voice boxes, allowing them to maneuver through dense forest in complete darkness. Lemur eyes easily pierced the murk of hydrocarbon mists. Dense gray fur and brown adipose under their skin insulated them from the cold. Even their metabolism had been altered. They breathed hydrocarbon air; their lungs extracted substrate for oxidative reactions from the air. Oxygen was obtained by the digestion of oxides they ate. In short, respiratory and alimentary functions had been switched. Elves were completely at home in the forests of glass we passed over. A battalion of elven guerrillas could be concealed there—or only a ragged band.

That was the trouble with counterinsurgency. Guerrilla forces fought on their terms, revealing themselves only when it was to their advantage. Intelligence estimates of their numbers usually had an uncertainty factor to a power of three.

Chances were I'd lose another buddy before the day was over. One less bed partner would be in the pool. Of course, it might be me. You could never tell. The longer I hung around the garrison, the more likely my time would come. I should take care of my business and get the Frisco away. But there was the problem of Vichsn. I couldn't take her with me. I had no room for excess baggage. And if I left her, she'd blab for sure. That left me one choice. I wasn't sure I had the stomach for that. Maybe an elf would get her on the mission. That was possible.

We were going on a search-and-destroy mission. That's what High Command called it, anyway. We grunts had another name for it—target practice. Only we were the targets.

Intelligence had located what they thought was a guerrilla camp, but they had been unable to get a spook chameleon onto the area to verify it. So our job was to confirm that intelligence and destroy the camp if it existed. Of course it was just as likely to be a dummy camp baiting a trap for us to walk into. Paid informants worked both sides of the street. Spy satellites were fallible. Someone had to investigate to know one way or the other. The someone was Ghost Cavalry. Like I said, target practice.

Even if this was an actual guerrilla camp, it would probably be abandoned by the time we arrived. The elven observers that constantly watched our base would have reported our departure and the direction of our subsequent flight would be monitored. They would have plenty of warning and lots of time to set their traps.

Titan was the elves' world. They were adapted to it, not we. They could live off the land and fight with just the equipment they could carry on their backs. They knew the hiding places. We were forced to look for them. They could snipe at us from concealment and leave behind nasty booby traps. They could poison our food and contaminate our water. They tried to taint our oxygen converters. They mutated strains of venereal disease, then tempted us to bed pelts infected with it. They fed urchins liquid plastique and abandoned them for us to find, detonating the explosive by remote control. There was no safe place to step. Not one minute of the day was secure. The life of a combrid on an off-world garrison was one of constant anxiety.

No wonder we eventually went bonkers and had to be shipped Luna-side for rehypnotraining. Unless we were killed in the attempt to subdue us. Or unless we were bonkers in the first place and liked the constant threat of death. Being a combrid was a disturbing dichotomy. Nothing was more exciting. War was the most fun of anything you could do. Sex games after a firefight were the best way possible to get your rocks off. If only it weren't for the fact you knew you'd buy your drawer eventually. I should be getting out now, while I still had all my parts in functional order.

Let's just say I was in a grim and introspective mood as the hoverbus streaked through the methane fog of Titan.

I noticed Peppardine sitting alone toward the front. That seemed strange. Combrids were a randy breed. Normally all we thought about was fighting and sex. Or sex and fighting. Or just sex. It seemed unusual that someone wasn't putting the moves on her. She looked just as good to me now as she had last night. Still gave my dingle a tingle. But Vichsn had me trapped in an inside berth. I knew she wouldn't let me change places so I could reacquaint myself with the chimera. No big deal. I'd have time to get inside her tunic. I had to stay around until I figured out what to do about Vichsn, anyway. Maybe the two problems would take care of themselves. I thought I knew a way. I remembered the chimera had been a Lady of Telluride. Maybe I would tell her of my own nobility. That should open her legs for me. Ladies were trained to accommodate Lords. My time would come. Strange that no one was trying to beat me to her, though. Maybe we should have a few sex steroid levels checked.

Then the hoverbus descended.

It was a typical landing. The fishbait pilots figured the less time they spent motionless close to the ground, the less chance they had of catching a minimissile. They had it figured right, of course. So they flew directly over the drop zone, fell a couple of thousand meters straight down, pulled ten G's decelerating, then hovered a few meters over the ground. Our pilot was no exception. And all the time she was screaming in our heads for us to jump. The jump gong beat like a drum. She'd blown the rear hatch while we were still a thousand meters up. Now she squawked like a buggered hen for us to get our tails out. Two gunships, flew circles, blasting the forest with their pulsars, clearing out a drop zone.

By this time all us meat had crowded into an aisle and were shuffling toward the rear. The bus was already moving forward. As each line of four combrids jumped, four more followed closely behind, landing a few meters away on the ground.

Vichsn and I crowded toward the rear hatch, pushed from behind. Everyone knew the pilot's nerve would soon fail. They were supposed to give you a full minute to evacuate the bus. But the pilots usually cheated by thirty seconds. You risked a sprained ankle if you were among the last to jump. So you didn't let the ones in front of you dawdle too long.

The open hatch came closer.

We were standing on the edge. Vichsn and I jumped together. I bent my knees, but the shock after drifting ten meters in the weak Titanian field was negligible. We were too low to have to use gravtubes.

Overhead, the hoverbus whined.

The pilot's nerve had broken. Already the bus accelerated upward. Even as it climbed, combrids continued to dribble from the hatch.

Catsucking pilots, anyway.

The chimera was the last to jump. When she did, the hoverbus was at least a hundred meters up. She leaped into the air, extending her arms and legs to create as much resistance as possible against the thick hydrocarbon atmosphere, thereby slowing her fall. I would have used thruster tubes, had it been me, despite our orders not to. Sometimes p-grav set off booby traps in the trees, so we weren't supposed to use thrusters on routine jumps. But a hundred meters up was hardly routine. As she neared the ground, she doubled up, rolling when she struck. After two somersaults, she came up on her feet. Smiling. A nifty maneuver. She'd had a good take on her hypnotraining. She'd be all right.

The Gunny spoke softly in my mind. I checked off, then listened as the others did the same one by one. The last to report was Peppardine. All were present. There were no drop injuries. No thanks to our sheepdip pilot.

"Detrs," the Gunny said, "you take the point. Azimuth zero-six-zero."

Dog breath! I thought. The point was the worst place to be. Well, usually the worst. You were the bait to get the enemy to reveal themselves. You were the target for target practice. Sometimes they let you pass, so they could blow away your buddies who followed. Either way, it was not a fun place to be. In a crossfire, it didn't matter whether it was friend or foe who pressed the firing stud of the pulsar that fried you. You would be just as dead from one as the other.

We fanned out from the drop zone, walking in a half-crouch on the balls of our feet, weapons held ready. I glanced to the left. Trinks was there. He was a good man to have close anytime, but particularly when the shooting started. He'd saved my skin before. I owed him a few already.

The drop zone was a natural clearing in the forest a few klicks away from the suspected elf camp. That could mean trouble. Elves had a nasty habit of booby-trapping open areas around their real camps, knowing we'd probably use those clearings as landing areas. I walked slowly and carefully, cautious of where I stepped, and watched the monitors along the top of my visor. Any metal would be detected by the variance it produced in the sensing electromagnetic field put out by the antennas of my helmet. Which was why elves seldom used metal mines anymore. Plastic explosive with sonic detonators was more difficult to detect. As were bug bombs and gas pots. But plastique, virulent bacteria, and enzyme poisons could be smelled. Olfactimeters sniffed thick hydrocarbon air for any telltale odor. Sonic triggers resonated to the sonar I put out, and hopefully would detonate to its pings before the sound of my footsteps tripped the mine.

That's why you took it real slow when you could. You wanted to give your sensors lots of time to probe the area in front of you. You didn't want to blunder into any little surprises.

We crossed the clearing in a zigzag fashion, avoiding buried mines, gas pots, and bug bombs. Yes, they were there. Fortunately, none detonated. The surrounding lethality suggested there might be a real elven camp nearby. There would be fewer booby traps among the trees. You were pretty safe from them there if you resisted the temptation to walk on a trail. But there were other dangers in the forest.

I entered the trees a few meters ahead of the rest. I knew they would be scanning the forest, hoping my entrance would stir up something. But it was quiet. I walked slowly and carefully. The trees were about a meter in diameter and stood several hundred meters high. They were composed of aggregates of oxide crystals and polymeric hydrocarbons: emerald, tourmaline, sapphire, amethyst, aquamarine, and chrysoberyl matrix complexed with polyethylene, polyvinyl chloride, polybutadiene, polyisoprene, and a dozen other natural polymers. They "grew" by continually adding complexes to their substance. The complexes naturally tended to form tubular structures, so growth occurred in a linear fashion, at the ends of the tubes. They would have collapsed in a one-G field, but could be freestanding in the lesser gravity of Titan. They were "alive" by the standard criteria: individual complexes were organized into a greater whole and kept in organization by the expenditure of energy of crystallization, thereby conserving entropy. They reproduced by direct "budding" at the distal ends of their tubules, casting "seed" complexes to the wind.

Radiacrystal was the most expensive "wood" in the system—and the most useful. Our entire technology had become dependent on it. Titan was one of the few places where it could be grown outside of the laboratory. The trouble was you had to grow lots of individual crystals to get one that was suitable. Radiacrystal was an electromagnetic transducer/multiplier. Oxide-polymer matrix acted as an amorphous semiconductor. An electric current passed through radiacrystal would produce resonation in the crystalline structure, which caused minute amounts of the oxide to be converted into energy. The type of energy radiated by the crystal depended on the arrangement of the crystalline complex and could only be determined empirically, but included gravitational, magnetic, thermal, photal, and almost all other frequencies of radiation. Crystal trees were felled, hauled to mills, cut into sections and shipped to Earth. There they were tested and calibrated. Less than one percent were efficient enough to be used. The rest were scrapped. The crystals were fine-tuned by being precisely cut into various sizes and shapes. Elves had been developed to work in the forests of Titan. It was too expensive to house, feed, and supply air to nonhybrid workers. Now the elves had become uppity. They wanted a bigger cut of the pie. Radiacrystals were worth big bucks. They wanted their fair share. You couldn't blame them. But that didn't mean you were going to let them get away with it.

If not for the elves, the crystalline forests of Titan could have been quite a tourist attraction. Swirling hydrocarbon mist condensed on the facets of leaves—liquid pentane and butane dripped from their undersides. On the rare occasions the mist lifted, Saturn-light blazed from billions of gemstones embedded in transparent plastic in a myriad of dazzling colors.

But there were elves.

No tourist in his right mind would visit Titan for pleasure.

And I should have been more concerned about what lurked in concealment within the forest than I was with admiring its unique beauty.

Too late I heard Vichsn's warning whisper in my mind. Already I felt strong legs cradling me. Long carbide claws clicked against my armor. A furry body embraced itself around my head.

I did manage to call myself a flyblown dumb son-of-an-elf before I froze, holding every muscle as still as I could. I tried not to move at all. If I did, I'd be dead in a few millisecs.

The most dangerous of elven traps were airbears. One had just fallen on me, clinging around my head. They were creatures bioformed from Terran koalas. But their modifications were more than those required to adapt them to the environment of Titan. Sure, they had respiratory and digestive functions switched like all Titanians: they breathed their food and ate their oxygen. Titanian lungs extracted hydrocarbons to be used as substrate for oxidation. Titanians derived elemental oxygen from the enzymatic degradation of crystal complexes in their alimentary tracks. They had plasmids in their cells with the coding for enzymes to convert methane and heavier hydrocarbons into carbohydrate. Otherwise their biochemistry was not much different from standard Terran; they just got the raw materials in a different fashion.

But elven genosurgeons possessed a sense of the macabre. For instead of storing free oxygen bound in brown adipose tissue, as did other Titanian creatures, airbears secreted it in distensible bladders that trailed from their backs. And they had eel bioelectricity organs in the membranes of their oxygen bladders.

They were, in effect, living bombs.

Pure oxygen exploded just as violently in the hydrogen/methane air of Titan as flammable gas would in the oxygen-rich air of Earth.

Airbears' heavy bodies were almost counterbalanced by their oxygen-filled bladders. They floated among the upper branches of the crystal forest, browsing on buds and leaves of crystalline oxides. Carbide teeth ground the gems to powder. Plastic matrix passed through their gut and became feces, binding the silicon, aluminum, beryllium, iron, chromium, calcium, magnesium, and boron residues left after oxygen was extracted. They were perfectly harmless as long as they stayed up in the trees. But if a combrid, or anything else with unaltered Terran metabolism, should pass below them, they immediately let go of the branch they were clinging to and dropped to the ground. It seems they were attracted to free oxygen. Our higher body temperatures caused us to lose minute traces of pure oxygen, which boiled through both protective monomer and armor. Airbears thought we were walking dessert. They clung to whomever happened to be below them.

As it happened, that was me.

Airbears actually were gentle creatures. They didn't normally hurt anything. But they were easily startled. The elven genosurgeons made them that way.

You were OK if you could slowly extricate yourself from their grasp. But if you scared them, they involuntarily discharged their electricity organs. This both disrupted oxygen bladders and provided a spark to ignite the contents of the bladders. The air exploded as hydrocarbon atmosphere burned with pure oxygen. The resulting concussion was relatively minor—unless you happened to be the one standing at ground zero. Then it was enough to flatten your combat armor like a crushed beer can. The flesh inside tended to take on a look of undifferentiated protoplasmic jelly.

I saw furry lips pressed against my visor, then a rough tongue scratched across the surface as the airbear tasted lingering traces of elemental oxygen. I didn't dare move. Let the creature get settled, I said to myself. To the others: "Don't come any closer, meat. And no sudden moves, please. I don't want to be smeared into pulp." Not that I had to worry about the others getting too close. They knew there probably were more airbears overhead. No one was anxious to be in my predicament. And if they were too close when my airbear detonated, they'd suffer the same fate as me.

I was desperately trying to devise a plan that would gently extricate myself from the bear's hug, when I saw movement at the edge of vision. Someone was coming toward me.

"Stay clear, frog it!" I said as emphatically as I dared. They said even voice vibrations could spook an airbear. But I took the chance and vocalized anyway; it wasn't any fun to curse silently.

"Hold still," came a voice in my mind. "I know what

I'm doing." I recognized that voice right away. I'd been re-membering snatches of conversation all day.

Peppardine approached slowly, walking with barely per-ceptible steps. Despite my situation, I almost had another testosterone storm. Combat armor fit skintight. Hers did her body credit—smooth musculature, firm belly, taut breasts, long, supple legs. She moved with lithe grace—they must have used considerable feline DNA in her xeno-gene complement. After what seemed like a long, hot summer on the bright side of Mercury, the chimera stood beside me.

I realized I was holding my breath. I let it out slowly. Water misted on the oxygen bubble surrounding my nose and mouth. I saw my face reflected from the inside of my visor; sweat beaded from my forehead.

The airbear began to suckle on my visor.

I sure as Akron hoped the chimera knew what she was doing.

She did.

Peppardine stood behind me, moving in close enough for our bodies to touch. Even through two layers of com-bat armor, I felt her nipples brush against my back and her pelvis press into my buttocks. She reached around carefully with both arms. I saw a curved claw slide out of a finger. A blue drop of liquid clung to its tip.

I knew her helmet visor was thrown back. She had little need for artificial sensors. The viper pit organs in her eye-brows scanned the bear, outlining the warmer tracks where blood flowed in vessels beneath its skin. Her claw neared the bear's arm, smoothly passed through its fur, and slipped beneath skin to pierce a vein. So sharp were her claws, the bear never felt the prick in its skin. Neuropep-tide coursed like blue fire into its bloodstream. I watched with fascination; the peptides carried by Peppardine's claws had been the subject of several hours' speculative fantasy by me. I wondered if the airbear felt the same euphoria I would have. I decided it did; its neurophysiol-ogy had not been significantly modified. The overdose of endorphine quickly went to the airbear's brain; its grip weakened, then relaxed. It floated face up in the air beside me. The chimera came around and held it gently between her hands. Her claws had retracted.

"Though unconscious from endorphine," she said, "it

could still reflexively discharge its spark." She pulled the lax body lower, gently, bringing its face close to hers. Its eyes stared wide open. The chimera pursed her lips. She nodded her head. A glob of blue spit formed on her lips, hung for a moment, then dropped like a sapphire tear. The droplet seemed to hesitate as it hit her oxygen bubble's surface-effect membrane, but only flattened a little, then passed through. It splattered into the bear's eye, spreading into a blue film to cover the conjunctiva. The bear's fur shook briefly with fasciculations, then was still. Legs hung limp from the body. Oxygen bladders hung suspended over the body.

"Endolepsin laces my saliva," Peppardine said. "A drop in the eye is enough to paralyze every nerve. Its bioelectricity cells can never fire now." She turned to me and smiled. "You owe me a favor now. When can I collect?" Again the seductive note. Would she deliver this time? I wondered. Then a shiver ran up my spine. I looked at the airbear, paralyzed with euphoria, soon to die of pleasure. Playing with her claws would be a dangerous game. She could either please or punish. Her kiss could either soothe or kill. I remembered stories of depraved frenzy hidden behind the walls of paralyzed force of one of Nyssa's floating towers—golden chains, spider-silk ropes, shining knives with jeweled blades, braided whips, rituals of torment in the night—and a sudden burst of violence ending it all. Yes, a very dangerous game. A game I should enjoy.

"Come on, Detrs," Vichsn said from behind. "Get moving. We don't have all day."

I turned to look at her, but her face was hidden behind the mirror surface of her helmet visor. I'd thought I'd heard something in her voice. Something that pleased me. Maybe she was worried about Peppardine and me. Fine. Let her worry. If I had my way, she'd soon have something to worry about.

"Let's go, Detrs," the Gunny said. "And be a little more careful this time."

I was more careful, but we didn't encounter any more airbears.

We moved slowly through the crystal forest. Broken shards of shed leaves lay scattered on the ground. Sometimes a crunching sound was heard when someone accidentally stepped on one. When that happened, we all froze, expecting to see flashes of pulsar fire from concealed snipers. But none came until we approached the elves' abandoned camp.

All that remained of it were the skeletons of criss-crossed saplings that had been their lean-to shelters, with smoldering cinders of oxide crystals in front, where their campfires had been.

The Gunny had us disperse around the periphery. Combrids scattered from tree to tree, using the trunks for cover, before finally taking positions at various vantage points. We watched the deserted camp for a long time. Sometimes elves left nasty surprises. Especially if they had sufficient warning before they left.

I cursed the spooks at Corps Intelligence as I waited. They were safe in their spook houses in orbit around Titan. When one of their sensors buzzed, we were the ones sent into the forest for target practice. Then I cursed the Lord Generals of High Command for good measure.

Everything stayed quiet. There was no detectable movement in the camp. Helmet sensors showed only an ebbing infrared glow where campfires cooled.

Finally, the Gunny had six of us advance, keeping the rest of the platoon in concealment. As before, I was on the point; Vichsn and Trinks flanked me, but were a little behind. Three other combrids followed.

As I entered the camp, I scanned the surrounding forest carefully. Everything remained quiet. Sensing fields were not disturbed. But drops of sweat had formed along my back. Something was wrong. I'd learned a long time ago to trust my intuition. I knew we were walking into a trap, but there wasn't a mousy thing I could do to avoid it. We were bait, to force any elven snipers into revealing themselves. Target practice.

I was almost at the center of the camp when the trap was sprung. My intuition saved me. All six of us were well within the clearing. The elves probably figured six were all they were going to get. Did I say elves? Make that elf, as it turned out. Anyway, the hairs on the back of my neck rose. I hit the ground, yelling a warning to the others at the same time. But my warning came too late. As I was going down, I sensed a quick flurry of movement behind crystalline foliage, followed by a burst of automatic pulsar fire fanning out across the clearing. A bright pulse passed over me, where I had been millisecs before. But Trinks wasn't quick enough. I saw him crumple as a pulsar quantum glanced off his body, partially deflected by his armor. His groans of pain sounded within my skull. But there wasn't much I could do for him. I was more worried about keeping myself alive.

The elf's fire had me pinned down; there was no cover to hide behind, nor did I dare try to move. I fired my own weapon into the forest in the general area where I'd seen the movement. Spent photonuclear cases bounced off my back. But I knew the elf had already swooped to another tree. He was more mobile than I.

I heard the Gunny calmly telling the rest of the platoon to hold their fire and wait for the elf to show himself again. As soon as his pulsar flashed, they were to sweep the section of forest with their beams. That the elf knew our tactics was the only thing saving me and the others caught in the open. The elf knew that as soon as he fired, a score of pulsar bursts would stab into his general area. So he had to shoot on the move, as he was gliding from tree to tree. That made aiming his weapon a little difficult. But not difficult enough to suit me; clouds of rock vapor puffed around me where his shots hit too close for comfort.

The standoff began to get a little tedious.

Each time the elf shot from concealment, a salvo of return fire burst into the forest, shattering oxide wood into tiny slivers that drifted through a polymer mist like floating glitter. But the elf was quick enough to avoid getting hit by either the beams or exploding fragments, and fired again from another position. One elf was tying up an entire platoon of Corps combrids, while his comrades made good their escape.

But that was their plan, of course.

Trinks continued to moan in agony, clutching his belly. A combrid left the safety of the forest and darted across the clearing toward us. Pulsar fire traced a smoking path behind the weaving and bobbing course taken by the combrid. Amazingly, he wasn't hit. Then I saw who *she* was. The combrid was the chimera. She dove beside Trinks and lay on the ground beside him. Her hands busied themselves. Fingers probed cleverly designed chinks in his combat armor. Hypodermic claws sought the veins underneath polymer-toughened skin and injected neuropeptides into sluggish blood. Endotalis flogged his failing heart, while endopamine toned blood vessels and raised blood pressure. Endosmin sealed leaking capillaries and endosteroid stabilized cell membranes. Endorphine obliterated pain.

When Trinks's physiologic functions became stable, the chimera used two other claws. Endophetamine sent synthetic courage to his basal ganglia. Endocholine speeded nervous transmission to thrice normal and strengthened muscle contractions by augmenting depolarization potentials.

All of which meant only one thing to a simple grunt combrid: Trinks stood up with blue fire in his eyes. The same fire coursed in his veins. He was now three times as strong and fast as he had been. And many times braver. He feared nothing. He felt no pain. He could do anything. He was berserk—overwhelmed with fighting rage, like a vengeful Norse warrior.

Trinks charged across the clearing, running toward the trees from which the elf sniper shot. It didn't seem possible a man could run that fast—his legs blurred with motion. A salvo of autopulsar fire streamed from the forest, but the puffs they made in the ground were behind Trinks. The elf didn't believe a man could move that fast either, and didn't lead enough. In an instant, Trinks was across the clearing and among the trees. A moment later, I saw his pulsar flash. Light flared upward, silhouetted against a sky of mist. An elven scream sounded, then the elf appeared in the air over the clearing, gliding on taut pseudowings. Singed fur marked the sites of pulsar wounds. Pulsar beams stabbed from the surrounding forest. Only charred remnants of the elf made it to the ground. Most of him became smoke that mingled with the mists of Titan.

I found Trinks propped against the side of a tree trunk. He had his visor flipped up. He looked at me through half-open eyes, blurred by nictitating membranes.

"Did I get the fairy?" he asked.

I nodded.

"Good. You want to make sure to do whatever you need to do before the rush goes away." He coughed blood and spat through his oxygen bubble on the ground beside him. There was a puddle of clot there already, like red pudding. "Horses, it's good before it goes. I think I could have taken a whole company of the devils by myself. But the fire burns out too quickly. And when it goes, there's nothing left."

"You'll be OK."

"Sure. Keep saying it. I believe you. Sure I do."

"Corpsman!" I yelled. Where was that cat-faced chimera?

"Pepper," Trinks said, "that's what she shoots into you. Hot pepper." He looked beyond me. "Here she comes now. Sergeant Pepper." He tried to laugh, but coughed more blood instead.

The chimera knelt beside him. Her fingers busied themselves again. Trinks closed his eyes.

I went back to the camp and helped the others "sanitize" the area. After a quick search and a photo session for the spooks at Corps Int, we set our own booby traps, leaving behind hundreds of needle mines that would detonate should an elf even glide over one in the air. A shaped charge of plastic explosive threw needles of isotope into a 180-degree hemisphere. Each needle was a miniature nuclear device consisting of an isotope sandwiched with a fission catalyst. When the needle struck something solid, isotope and catalyst collapsed together, reaching a microcritical mass, which fissioned and exploded. The tiny nuclear explosions produced remarkable results, particularly if they occurred within a previously living body. Needle mines were almost as devious as elf tricks. Almost. We had to post signs around the area, warning it was mined. Didn't want innocent civilians getting hurt. Frogging waste of time, all of it.

In the hoverbus, on the way back to base, the chimera held Trinks in her arms. The rest of us were quiet, each thinking our time would be coming. When turbulence buffeted the hoverbus and we were jostled, Trinks moaned with pain. His lips moved silently: Sergeant Pepper. Then the chimera would kiss his head, soothing away the moans. She murmured in his ear. Her whispers could not be heard by the rest of us. We didn't know what lies she told him. I should have noticed the strangeness that had come to hide in her eyes. But I was preoccupied.

When we docked at base, everybody got up and filed down the aisle. I paused as I passed the chimera and Trinks. His eyes were closed. I touched her shoulder.

"How is he?" I asked, remembering things I should have left forgotten.

"Dead," she answered simply, in a flat voice. Wrongness faded from her eyes.

"What happened? Why didn't you do something?"

"I did everything I could. There was nothing more to do. He didn't cry, nor hurt too much. He didn't cry," she said again.

I thought I saw a wet gleam behind her nictitating membranes, before I was crowded ahead by other combrids.

Later, I found the chimera standing alone at the base perimeter. Beyond the green-crackling force-field, bright forest gleamed in Saturn-light, hydrocarbon fog glowed like a will-o'-the-wisp. Dark flutterings marked the passage of elves among trees. Occasionally, when the elves revealed too much of themselves, pulsar beams stabbed into the murk as automatic sensors reacted to the disturbance. Sergeant Pepper. Short for Peppardine."

"Sergeant Pepper," I whispered.

"What?" she asked, turning to face me.

"Nothing. Only a name Trinks called you before he died. Sergeant Pepper. Short for Peppardine."

"Or peptide?"

"Maybe." I shrugged. It didn't matter now. "You did what you had to do," I said. "And Trinks did get the sniper. I know that was important to him. You don't like the elf that kills you to get away."

"I'm glad then." She turned away, bringing her hands to her face. She was crying. But I stared at her hands, thinking of the claws held within them. And I thought of the mind of a Lady in the body of a combrid. Ladies had their own peculiarities. So did chimeras. Trinks's death had given me an idea. It was time for night games to begin. I was ready this time. I'd learned a little since I'd run away from my own nobility. I'd been afraid of it for a long time. I found you couldn't run away. You had to use it to your advantage.

I had never told anyone but Vichsn I was the scion of old Earth nobility, son of Lady and Lord. I'd never mentioned the endless rituals of pain my parents had performed before I killed them, except to her. She knew too much about me. The spooks might trace me through her when I deserted. I knew what had to be done. But I didn't have the stomach for it. Perhaps there was another way. I wondered.

I touched Firiel's shoulder. I saw something at the edge of the forest I wanted her to see. It was time to start playing the game.

She took her hands away from her face and looked up.

I pointed to the trees beyond the force-field. A small shape was hurled into the air in our direction. Almost immediately autopulsar beams stabbed out. One of them hit the shape. It fell to the ground smoking.

"What was that?" she asked.

"An elf baby."

"What do you mean? A baby . . ." Her eyes widened in mock surprise.

"When one of their babies dies, they throw the corpse out like that, knowing the computers controlling our autopulsars can't distinguish between the living and the dead. Then they claim we shoot innocent babies, and have the charred remains as proof. Elves have no scruples. They use what they have. What else is a dead baby good for?"

Suddenly she was holding me tight. Her sobs were muffled against my chest. I stroked her back, trying to smooth away the hurt. She almost had me fooled. "What kind of a mother could do that?" she asked.

"A practical mother. They're not like us." I lied. They were the same. "But you'll get used to it."

"Will I? Is that what happens? Do you become cold with no feelings? Is that how you protect yourself? By not caring?"

"You guessed it." What else could I say? She was right. But she'd known that all along. She hadn't fooled me.

I walked her back to her quarters. Fog deepened. Mist swirled, mixed with hydrocarbon snow. In the forest, elves wailed in mock mourning of their dead baby.

At her door, she paused. This time I saw it in her eyes. She invited me inside.

Waking, the chimera stirred against me. Her eyes were dilated wide in darkness. She saw that I too was awake.

"A dream?" I asked.

She nodded. "I've been having a few lately."

"What do you dream?"

"Tonight about babies." Her voice softened. "About my baby."

"Your baby?"

She looked at me. "Didn't you know? My *dead* baby. I was once a Lady of Telluride. Lords must have heirs. It's expected of them. But babies die, don't they? They die all the time."

"Just as Lords do?" She hadn't touched me with her claws. I'd wanted her to earlier, but she wouldn't. I thought I knew a way. Vichsn had given me the idea. *They killed their lovers,* she had said. "How do Lords die?" I asked, smiling. *How do children become orphans?*

She looked at me closely. "The usual ways," she said. "Don't you read the scandal sheets? With overdoses. Or smashed in the wreckage of racers. Or trampled beneath the hooves of ponies. They drown sometimes. The usual ways."

"And sometimes they kill each other. Duels? Arguments?"

"Sometimes."

"Jealous fits of rage?"

"Sometimes."

"It's simpler out here." I took her hand. "The elves kill us. Or we kill them. That's all." I pressed the tip of her index finger. A claw slid out of its sheath. "Let me see how it feels?" I asked.

A blue drop of peptide formed on the tip of her claw.

"Not yet," she said.

"When?"

"Later. There'll be time for that. I don't want it to be like that now."

"How do you want it, then?"

"I'm not sure." She took her hand out of my grasp. Five claws gleamed. "But not that way now." She kissed me, slipping her tongue into my mouth. I tasted bitter endolepsin. But it could not affect me that way. Digestive enzymes destroyed it. She had to kiss the CNS stud on my head. In that way, the neuropeptide could gain ingress to my brain. She bit my nose, then laughed.

"What's so funny?" I asked.

"I just had a silly urge. Quite tempting, really." She laughed again.

I waited for her to continue.

"Do you ever have any *animal* thoughts?" She smiled at the profanity.

"Don't be vulgar. They don't use that much xeno-DNA in our hybridization. Do they in yours?"

"Apparently. Sometimes the urges are overwhelming. Mostly feline. Cat-thoughts are so delicious." She put her arms around me. I felt claws scratch my back. "I pounce on little mice," she said. "I bat them with my paws. Sometimes I let them think they can get away, but as they dart across the floor, I reach out and hook them with my claws."

"And when you tire of playing with them?" I asked. *The game had begun.*

"Cat-thoughts are so delicious." She smiled in the dark. "I bite off their little heads." She laughed. I'd heard that kind of laugh before. "They can't cry without their heads."

Eventually we slept again.

It was my move.

3

Battle light cast a green glow from panels in the ceiling of the hoverbus. The camofilm covering our combat armor matched both the intensity and hue of the light, as it would any illumination. The result was like a surrealistic mutaholo—blurred shapes blended into background; movement could not be distinguished from the flickerings of shadow. Fuzzy images came in and out of focus: visored helmets talked to each other; gloved fingers checked battle gear; bodies clad in skintight polymeric armor dangled from acceleration harness. Combrids in full battle dress appeared as insubstantial as wraiths—ghosts to be exorcised with incantations. No more noticeable than specters haunting dreams.

But any elf terrorist that was fooled by our camouflage was dead himself. Elves knew how dangerous apparitions could be.

The whine of the hoverbus's gravturbines sent an ache into my teeth. For some reason, their particular frequency resonated within the matrix of my tooth enamel. The resulting vibrations hurt like termites burrowing into wooden dentures. I clamped my jaws tight. Sometimes the pressure helped. This time it didn't. So I tried to think about something else. That was easy enough. I had plenty else to worry about. Like how to keep the spooks from capturing a terrorist without being burned for treason myself.

I'd had a real shock at the briefing that morning. I was still too numb to think properly. The spook briefing officer told us we were going on a mission to capture the notorious renegade, Grychn Willams. The name sound familiar? That's right, the same Grychn I knew as a child. The same Grychn who'd helped me kill my parents. The same Grychn who knew all about the timestone. That's what worried me. The spooks had been after the sailor for the timestone. That information would be in their computer files. When they started interrogating Grychn, she'd eventually tell them about me and the timestone, along with everything else in her mind. Spook interrogations went that way. The correlation would eventually be made. Once they started looking, I'd be easy enough to find, unless I'd already deserted. Then they might be able to trace me through Vichsn.

If the spooks were after me, I may as well kiss all my plans good-bye. No empire. No sycophants. No courtesans. No freedom for very long.

So I had to make sure Grychn wasn't captured alive. Dead would be OK. As long as I didn't have to kill her. I didn't want to start answering questions about why I wanted her dead.

I stared through the transparent floor. Crystalline forest passed rapidly beneath the bus. Elves lurked somewhere among glass trees.

We were skimming a zigzag course through the hydrocarbon mists of Titan, trying to stay at treetop level. In that way, we hoped to avoid detection by both elven sentries and electromagnetic sensors. Before elf gunners could plot a four-space probability fix in which to lob a minimissile, we wanted to be in a different air sector altogether.

Swirling mists shrouded crystal trees. The passage of the hoverbus disturbed the clinging fog and lifted wisps into curlicues in our wake. Sunlight sparkled from the facets of leaves uncovered by haze.

The radianuclear industry was dependent on the forests of Titan. Only here were the conditions right for the growth of living crystals to occur. Sure, they could be grown in a lab. But they cost a lot more that way. Radianuclear crystals found application in industry, medicine, transportation, communications, and weaponry. The Terran economy required a cheap, abundant supply of them. Unfortunately, that fact was not unknown to the elven guerrillas. They tried to put pressure on the Colonial Government by disrupting the harvest of crystals. It was a big-stakes game, amounting to billions of credits. More than a few lives had been lost over the dispute. *C'est la vie!* Cheap, I mean.

Before the day was over, a Terran renegade was going to have to die. I had to make sure of that. I had no choice.

The fog lifted momentarily. Linear color dazzled my eyes, as sunlight ricocheted from crystalline surfaces. An image flashed: firelight was caught and held in amber eyes. The memory hurt just a little before I pushed it away. There was no point in thinking about things that might have been. The Grychn I knew had been on Earth. We weren't on Earth now. We were on Titan. And Titan was about one billion kilometers from Earth. Someone once said you could never go back home. I believed that as surely as I knew distance was more than linear measurement. Combat hybrids never went home. Not even in body bags. They burned you on your garrison world. That was Corps tradition. Theoretically, you signed up for a specific tour of duty. If you survived your tour, theoretically you got to retire with a nice bonus and pension. There was a catch, of course. Being a combrid was the most dangerous job in the System. Almost as hazardous as being a terrorist. One rarely survived the combrid experience. That too was Corps tradition. Was I going to buck tradition? You're damn right I was.

You played the game. You cheated if you could get away with it. The Corps could kill you, but they couldn't make you not want to live. That meant my old childhood sweetheart had to die. It was me or her. I was looking out for me.

Other combrids sat beside me, cradled in acceleration harness. We were all standard combrids; we looked enough alike to be siblings: all of us were two meters tall and about ninety kilos of mass; our skin was black with anti-radiation pigment granules; nictitating membranes could close over our eyes to protect them from cold and vacuum. In a sense, we were siblings—we shared the same xenogenes that had been inserted into our cells to make us hybrids. Whatever our appearance before going into hybridization tanks, when we emerged we looked the same as every other combrid. It was more efficient that way. The military loved uniformity.

Peppardine sat in the back this time. There was a distant look in her eyes as she waited. I knew the same look was mirrored in mine. But for different reasons. My games with her would have to wait. A childhood game needed finishing.

Waiting to go into combat was always hardest on the nerves. The actual fighting was easy by comparison—you didn't have time to think too much then. But when waiting, dark memories were free to surface.

While you waited, there were a hundred things you could do to occupy your thoughts to try to keep lost images away. Helmet sensors could be calibrated; circuits could be checked for neutron leaks. You could plug your cyborg stud into the battle computer of the hoverbus, and fight mock wars with it, to condition synapses and reflex loops. Its program even let you live once in a while, so's to keep your spirits up. Weapons could be field-stripped. Photonuclear clips could be checked to insure they'd feed properly. You could do all those things and many more. But you didn't. Because you were leaving the killing behind. *Adios,* glory. *Au revoir,* valor. Just one more and you'd be through with it. Maybe two at the most. The death game had complicated rules—you were about to begin another stage of it.

Yet you couldn't rid your mind of the old images. You knew it was better to let them come now, to get their torment over with. Nights could be spent in other ways. There were other passions, other thrills.

I looked about the cabin, but I was too preoccupied even to think about arranging a liaison. And that was usually the easy part, the arranging. The hard part was making sure you came back. And making sure the one with whom you'd arranged your liaison came back also. After that, no problem. Combrids were always wired tight with blood lust after a firefight.

But I had other worries now. Like what to do about Grychn. If she were captured alive, all my plotting would be for naught.

Life sure was a bitch.

But what the hay, nobody made *me* sign on with the Corps. It wasn't a choice between the Corps and the cyborg factories. I'd made another choice. No sense having regrets over what might have been. Besides, I'd got out of worse situations than this.

So what if I was flying at treetop level in a hoverbus with thirty-nine other combrids. So what that in a few minutes more there was a reasonable certainty that I or one of my buddies would get killed. I still had a chance. That was more than I would have had on a prison farm in Antarctica. I still had my empire to build. All I had to do was to take care of a couple of loose ends. Big deal!

Blue eyes caught mine. Delight was trapped in their retinal reflections. Vichsn smiled, running the pink tip of her tongue along the edge of her teeth. The swellings and curves of her body were accentuated by skintight armor: taut breasts, rippling muscles, smooth buttocks, flat belly. She closed her eyes and touched her tongue to her nose. I knew what she wanted—a liaison tonight after the mission. Combrids were always horny after missions. Sex helped get rid of other tensions. But she'd have to look elsewhere. I was too worried about another loose end to be interested in sex. Besides, I needed a little variety. After all, I'd just taken a tumble on the wombskin with Vichsn the night before. Not that she wasn't good. There was a certain joy in her carnality. Her exuberance amazed me. I was ready for a change, though. I knew just what I needed. She was sitting in the back. Besides, I didn't want Vichsn to feel too secure about our relationship. A little jealousy would stir things up nicely. But I would have to be careful to produce just the right situation. Then the rest would take care of itself. If only Grychn could be taken care of so easily.

The door to the forward cabin opened. Red nav light mingled with green battle light, producing a brownish murk. A spook stepped through. The door closed behind him, shutting out the red. He walked slowly down the center aisle. I shivered involuntarily. Spooks gave me the creeps—my guilty conscience, I guess. This one even looked halfway human. His name was Colonel Kramr. He wore loose-fitting coveralls of camopolymer, bloused around gauntlets and boots, with a crimson beret covering his bald head. The silver skull of Corps Intelligence was pinned to the beret. I assumed he was the same spook who had briefed us earlier. Not that you could tell by looking at his face. He could wear any face he wished. Or any body. The spooks of Corps Intelligence were chameleons—they could assume the guise of almost any other hybrid. Multihued pigment granules mixed intradermally to give their skin any desired color. Feathers, hair, fur, scales, tooth and nail could be grown or shed. Subcutaneous fat could be molded to produce various physiognomies. All were under conscious control. Spooks could change their appearance at will. Spook fieldmen infiltrated the various hybrid guerrilla groups—if their disguises weren't perfect, they didn't live very long.

Kramr now looked like an ordinary combrid: his skin was black as obsidian; ocular membranes ringed his eyes like silver monocles; his scalp was bald with the skin convoluted into ripples as though wires were buried underneath. Not bad. He had only made one mistake. Who ever heard of a combrid being a commissioned officer? Officers were Lords and Ladies, not grunt combrids. A trivial point, but valid. Anyway, Kramr's face truly was a mask—only in death would neural control relax and the spook's real face appear. Until then, no one would know his actual visage. Lover or enemy, both would have to be content with masks.

I doubted if Kramr had any lovers. I'd heard stories about him. His ruthlessness was notorious. He'd torture information out of his own brother in order to advance the Terran cause. They said his zealousness was a result of his being a synthetic personality. His real persona had been stripped away and replaced with artificial memories and feelings. A real company man, all right. I briefly wondered what crime he'd paid for with his own identity. Did he even remember what he'd done? Probably not.

Spooks usually didn't go on missions with us grunts. When not under cover, they normally remained in seclusion in their orbital spook houses, plotting schemes for us grunt combrids to carry out. Kramr going with us meant the spooks wanted to catch one renegade Terran pretty badly.

And why not?

Grychn Willams was no common elf guerrilla. Elves were captured every day. There was only one Grychn. Besides being the scion daughter of Lord General Willams, she was rumored to be a lieutenant of Dr. Maizay, the leader of the elven rebellion. Grychn had been a gadfly to the Corps for over two years. Not only did she engineer particularly devious terrorist attacks, but she was the darling of the left-wing press, with her flamboyant beauty and noble heritage. And the public was still titillated by rumors of interspecial sex. Especially when the paramour was a child of royalty.

The Grychn I'd played with as a child had grown up to be much more famous than I. But that would change eventually. After I recovered my timestone.

No one knew Grychn and I had once been lovers. I can keep a secret. So can Grychn. She'd been keeping our secret for almost ten years now. How do I know she'd kept the confidence? I'm not bound by electronic chains in a cyborg factory, am I? Proof enough.

A long time ago she said she loved me. Maybe she still did; at least the memory of a preadolescent boy with whom she could share the anguish of trying to grow up amid the petty games of cruelty of the idle rich. I suppose she was hurt when I ran away. I don't know. I never looked back. You've only got one chance with me.

But I'd had to laugh every time the newsholos ran another feature on her. There was much speculation about why she had renounced her nobility to become a guerrilla terrorist. Lots of psychological theories were bandied about. But the real reason was simple: she carried the same scars as I did; she'd known the same pain as a child. The same frenzies that had made me an orphan running away from my past had made her an ideological orphan—an expatriate from her father's politics. You could seek revenge with political activism just as easily as with a sonic knife. Maybe it was sweeter that way, the hurt more deep and lingering. She had always been more devious than I.

But she'd kept our secret. She'd not betrayed me yet. But when the spooks caught her she would. They had techniques of extracting information. Foolproof techniques. Sometimes a little hard on the merchandise. Breakage was to be expected. My anonymity was safe only as long as Grychn could stay out of the hands of the spooks. Which wouldn't be much longer.

Not if Kramr had his way.

Kramr had almost caught her twice before, but both

times she'd managed to escape. It would be quite a coup for the spooks to capture her. Something that would generate lots of air time on the holos for them. Kramr didn't want anything to queer the deal. So he came along to supervise the mission himself.

Grychn had been underground in the six months since her previous near-capture. They thought she might have flown the coop. Then a spook fieldman had seen her in an elven village. She'd been covertly observed for a while, in hopes she'd lead the spooks to Maizay or that he'd surface in her vicinity. But after two weeks of waiting with no sign of the elven leader, the spooks became antsy and decided to take her alone. A bird in the hand, and all that. No telling when she'd go underground again.

A mission was launched.

That meant four hoverbuses converging on the village, with a cargo of 160 veteran combrids, and two swift gunships flying cover. All to apprehend one leftist radical. Plenty big medicine. Someone was going to die for their trouble. I wanted to make sure it wasn't me. And when they did catch her, someone was going to be in plenty of trouble. That someone was me. I had two choices: make sure she escaped, or kill her myself. Some choices.

I leaned back in acceleration harness and closed my eyes. There had to be some way out. If only Kramr hadn't come along to supervise the mission personally. If anything happened, he'd get suspicious. There was nothing more dangerous than a suspicious spook. Especially if you had something in your past you wanted to keep hidden. He'd poke around until he found some smoke. Then he'd fan the embers to flame. I had to come up with a perfect plan. In the next few minutes.

Images from the past rose in my mind. I let them. Better now than later. You can't be a fugitive from your memories. They always catch up. I'd been running for ten years. I knew there was no escape from dreams. But you could choose whether they'd be day- or night-dreams. Daydreams were easier to stand.

Two marble statues leered at me from a pool of crimson water. White flesh hardened. Eyes dulled, as scarlet water brightened. I ran over to the pool. Too late. Their faces were already stiff. As hard as I might knead with my fingers, I couldn't deform smiling lips of white acrylic. I imagined laughter echoing down empty corridors. I looked up. Another face watched mine. Its eyes studied mine seriously, with a sulfur gaze. Pale lips spoke softly. A hand took mine. We ran. Mocking voices resonated inside my own hollow skull.

4

A battle gong sounded.

Visors were lowered and the acceleration harness was unsnapped. We lined up four abreast in the aisle, facing toward the rear of the bus.

Drop hatches blew. Yellow hydrocarbon mist swirled into the cabin and frosted on its inside surfaces. Two gunships peeled off and began spraying the forest below with pulsar fire. That meant there was no clearing. We were going to have to jump through the forest. Sometimes the gunships could clear the area of booby traps. Usually they couldn't. But maybe there wouldn't be any elf snipers waiting for us.

The four combrids nearest the hatch jumped into the opening and disappeared. The rest of us shuffled down the aisle until it was our turn to jump. Nobody spoke. There was nothing to say. It was just another mission. Soon the open hatch was before me. Sulfurous fog billowed in around its edges. I stepped into the mist and dropped downward. Too fast. I nudged a flicker from the gravtubes on both sides of my pack. Concentric rings of p-grav flared down, slowing my fall. Crystalline forest waited below. Filamentous gems waved in the wind. It was cold. At least a hundred below.

I looked around. No wonder we were called Ghost Cavalry. That's just what we looked like as we dropped through the murk—ghosts. Camofilm adjusted itself to blend perfectly with the surrounding mists. We appeared as vague outlines sinking slowly into fog, like shed skins cast to the wind. Even my eyes were fooled by camofilm. But not my sensors. Infrared lenses showed heat dissipating into the surrounding cold like tongues of flame. Grav-meters displayed twin cones of pseudograv fanning down from thruster tubes. Magnetometers detected deflections in the planetary flux caused by the metal components in our battle dress. Sonar and radar pinged from solid surfaces. Olfactometers sniffed lingering traces of oxygen. I "saw" four equally spaced hoverbuses flying a circular drop pattern. Combrids streamed from their bellies and drifted silently toward the ground. A one-kilometer-diameter circle would be ringed by combrids when we all had landed. If we all landed safely. We hoped the elves didn't have electronic sensors. Camofilm could fool unaided eyes. A naive hope. Forest reached out.

Then I was drifting through the trees. It was dangerous to jump blindly into the crystalline forest. Sometimes elves left nasty little surprises waiting in the upper terraces. So I prepared myself to be blown away. No such luck. Crystal leaves crumbled to dust as I touched them. Glass branches shattered into glittering shards. Filaments broke into needles that danced in the air. Bare skin would have been sliced to shreds. But combat armor was impervious to even sharper edges. A wry thought occurred to me: I had just broken thousands of credits' worth of radiacrystals. Enough to make me a rich man on Earth. *C'est la vie.*

I passed through the upper terraces and dropped past slender trunks devoid of leaves and branches, before crashing through the underbrush. I hit the ground with my knees flexed, rolled once, and came back up on my feet with my weapon ready and helmet sensors turned to max gain. But the only movement was that of other combrids landing.

The Gunny spoke in my mind, taking roll. I checked off and listened as the others did in turn. No casualties yet. The Gunny ordered us to advance.

I walked slowly through a forest of glass. Vichsn was on one side, Peppardine was on the other. Leaves shattered underfoot. Sensors probed ahead, searching for booby traps. But the woods were clean. That meant the elf village was probably civilian. Elf guerrillas didn't bother to protect civilian villages. They knew noncombatants were safe from attack by us. Frog help us if we accidentally killed a noncom. It was good propaganda for the rebels if we did.

The nights weren't so good if there wasn't a little killing during the day. Nothing like a smoking corpse to elevate sex-hormone levels. Lethality and libido were linked. If combrids didn't get to smoke a few elves, their night games sometimes turned a little rough. Nothing nasty for me, thank you. Straight debauchery would do nicely. I'd played all the S&M games I ever wanted to before I left home. I still carried the scars to prove it, although they were all on the inside now. Everyone in the company knew it would be nasty that night if we didn't do some shooting. So I was hoping someone would get carried away and accidentally kill Grychn before she could be captured. A good firefight would provide the perfect opportunity.

The first shirt must have read my thoughts, because his voice whispered in my mind: "And remember, meat, no shooting unless we're fired on first. I don't want any accidental casualties. The sinister holofaxes are burning their tubes already about all the innocent victims you lovely folk produce. Leave us only shoot guerrillas today."

That meant one of us was going to die before we could shoot back. Elf snipers didn't miss their first shot. But only after they'd shot first could you prove they were guerrillas.

The village became visible ahead. Clusters of iridescent spheres budded from the tree trunks just below, where the crystal foliage began. Each sphere had a round hole through its bottom surface. Elves clung upside down from the sides of the crystal bubbles, gripping the smooth surface with tree-frog fingers and toes. Their wings hung limp between ankles and wrists. Gray fur glistened with hydrocarbon dew. It seemed incredible they had once been human—or that their ancestors had included humans, along with half a dozen other species. But mostly human DNA made up their genes. The miracles of modern science.

Elves watched with passive lemur eyes as we approached. Other eyes peered at us from within the openings of spheres. I imagined I also saw the blunt muzzles of auto-pulsars moving in synchrony with my cautious advance. Sweat beaded along my spine. At any moment, I expected photonuclear beams to stab out. I could almost smell the odor of burnt flesh. My flesh. I didn't much like the smell.

So I held my assault rifle at ready. I wanted to be able

to spray back a burst of fire. If the elf sniper happened to pick me out first, it wouldn't matter—I'd be dead. But I was dogged if I was going to be his second target. I wanted to make sure he didn't get a second shot. Bad enough to lose your buddy; that meant one less bedmate. No sense getting yourself shot; that meant no more bed games at all. No point dying if you could help it.

I intended to help it.

I even had an operational plan on what to do about Grychn. As soon as she flushed, I'd start a firefight, claiming I was fired on. Maybe someone would shoot her by mistake. But I had to wait until she revealed herself, or she might escape in the confusion. That would be OK, too. As soon as I saw an armed elf, I'd smoke him. That should stir things up.

We slowly closed around the elf village. It was about half a klick in diameter. Though I could not see through the trees to the opposite side of the village, my other sensors told me it was entirely ringed by combrids. Grychn would have to be lucky to escape, or get a little help. Or someone was going to have to kill her to keep her from being captured.

The Gunny must have read my thoughts again. He spoke in our minds: "Looks like we'll have to flush her. Every third in line advance and begin searching the village, bubble by bubble. The rest of you stay in position. I don't want the renegade to escape. But don't kill her under any circumstances. The spook wants her alive more than he wants you alive. There's certain things he wants her to tell him. So take her alive." He left unsaid what the spook would do to anyone impious enough to kill his plaything.

Vichsn went on into the village, leaving Peppardine and me behind. She and the other searchers began shimmying up tree trunks to peer into the openings of the spheres clustered around glass boles. Elves watched silently. But they didn't move. They knew the rest of us had our assault rifles trained on them as we covered our buddies. They thought we wouldn't need much of an excuse to open fire on them. They were right. At least about me. I kept hoping for an excuse to start a firefight. It wouldn't take much to change them from simple elven peasants to nasty guerrillas—a sudden movement, a reflection from a metal surface, a glowing pulsar tube. But I saw nothing suspicious enough to let me start firing. Not with the spook so close.

Kramr stood in the middle of the search parties, watching impassively as each tree was checked. He held his face immobile, but I knew he must be excited. I could guess how badly he wanted to capture this renegade terrorist. She'd been an annoyance to the spooks for too long. They weren't a forgiving sort.

I saw his eyes light up. I followed his gaze. There was a flurry of movement in a tree, followed by the flash of a pulsar. A combrid fell to the ground amid a shower of glass shards. Smoke rose from his body. For a fragile instant, everything was still.

Then all Cleveland broke loose.

Bursts of pulsar beams stabbed into the elven village as combrids along the periphery began firing. When a combrid fell, the area automatically became a free-fire zone. All the elves in the immediate vicinity were instantly reclassified to combatant status.

Elves dropped out of their trees like dried flies. Fur smoldered around crisp pulsar wounds. There was mad scrambling among the treetops as elves sought cover. I fired several short bursts at gliding elves and smiled as they crumpled and fell in flames. It was more fun than the grouse shoots my parents used to host on our estate on Earth. And in all the confusion, perhaps Grychn would escape or get killed by accident. Either one would be OK with me.

We couldn't keep the elves bottled up inside our circle —there were too many of them. More and more succeeded in breaching our line and losing themselves in the forest behind our backs.

Then I noticed a different shape passing overhead.

At the same time, Kramr yelled in my cortex: "That's her! That's the frogging renegade! Don't shoot her down. I want her alive. You, Detrs. After her. Don't let her get away. But don't shoot her, either."

Grychn was already in the forest behind me. I was going to have to change my plan. The solution came to me in the proverbial flash. Now was my chance.

I took off after her. You could make good time on Titan by taking long, skimming jumps. In the weak gravity, hundred-meter leaps were easy. But Grychn was airborne. I couldn't see how I was supposed to catch her without shooting her down. She was wearing pseudowings, which enabled her to fly almost as well as the elves. Polymeric wings stretched between her ankles and wrists. Gravcloth was sandwiched between two layers of surface-effect fabric, creating a wing that provided internal buoyancy combined with an augmented airfoil, as air squirted off both surfaces, providing forward thrust. By undulating her body, she could increase this thrust. When a tree got in her way, she reached out and grabbed the trunk, clambered up it as fast as she could go, then launched herself into the air again. I was forced to follow on the ground, as I couldn't use my thrusters in the forest. I'd risk breaking my neck if I used them among the trees. So I had to trail the fleeing guerrilla on foot. I could easily keep her in sight—she too was slowed by the thick timber. I didn't think she could lose me. But I couldn't catch up to her, either. That suited me fine. I'd follow her for a bit and then say I'd lost her. Gave it the old college try, but failed to catch her.

Behind, the spook followed. That complicated things a little. I wasn't going to be able to sandbag now. He'd know if I was purposely laggard. I heard Kramr's curses as he labored to keep up. His modifications were cosmetic—he only looked like a combrid; he lacked our augmented muscles that gave us four times normal strength. Not to mention our dual nervous systems. With Kramr following, I dared not let her escape, nor could I shoot her. Either one would cast suspicion on me.

I chased the girl through about ten klicks of forest, slowly narrowing the distance between us. She looked back and saw how close I was, then sprayed a clip of pulsar quanta in my direction. I quickly ducked behind a tree. Luckily, her aim was erratic. The beams only scattered foliage around me. But I made my point. I established that she was armed and dangerous. I followed at a more discreet distance. She must have guessed I was under orders not to shoot; she made no attempt to use natural cover. But she knew the lay of the land. She must have some plan of escape.

Before long, I figured out what she was trying to do. She was a clever little toad. But I was even more devious. I knew what I had to do. And it almost worked.

We had slowly gained altitude, maybe a couple of thou-

sand meters. She turned and fired at me again. I hit the
dirt. Pulsar beams cracked overhead, where I'd been standing an instant before. Her aim was improving. She could
have fried me if she'd fired again, a little lower. But she
didn't. She had another plan. She only wanted to slow my
pursuit.

Ahead, the forest ended on the edge of a cliff. Grychn
glided to the last of the trees, grabbed on to one, and
climbed to the top. She leaped into the air over the cliff
and flew away.

I made it to the edge of the forest in one jump. A deep
chasm about a klick across and a half-klick deep lay ahead
of me. The floor of the canyon was forested, but its walls
were sheer cliffs of ice and rock. Grychn was sailing
across on outstretched pseudowings. Just as I'd hoped. I
couldn't follow her on foot. No way. That left me one
choice. She'd made a mistake. I had her. I laughed out
loud, pleased as a plump lizard.

There was only one way to catch her now.

I jumped.

My first jump carried me to the lip of the precipice. As
I landed, I flexed my legs and jumped again. At the same
time, I hit the thruster button in my mind, firing the gravtubes on both sides of my pack. Ten G's tried to puddle my
flesh into my combat boots. Polymermesh-reinforced skin
resisted. But my balls starting hurting. Even though they
were retracted into their pouch. They always hurt when I
used thrusters. Maybe that's why I avoided using gravtubes
as much as possible.

Grychn was already halfway across the chasm when I
gravved on. But that didn't matter. She was flying on
pseudowings. She could go no faster than muscle power
could drive her. With a powered jump, I could overtake
her easily. I chuckled to myself. I knew what a stupid
blunder it appeared I'd committed. I looked as dumb as
a poisoned kitten.

She still had her autopulsar!

I would be an easy target in midair.

Of course, you knew that all along. But then I've been
giving you hints. So you've already guessed my ulterior
motive. You know why I wanted to appear so stupid.

Grychn had planned it the same way. Of course, she
thought I wouldn't shoot her. If I followed her across the

gorge, she could shoot me down. If I didn't, she'd get away anyway. But I *was* going to shoot her. I had no choice.

She wheeled in the air to face me, hanging on the up-drafts rising from the canyon floor. I saw her bring her weapon to her shoulder. Thin lips smiled beneath an oxygen bubble. Her eyes were hidden behind mirrored goggles. She took careful aim.

Now I was off the hook.

The way I figured it, I was safe. Because it appeared to be me or her. I would seem to fire in self-defense. My assault rifle already bore on the girl. I didn't need to aim. She hung in the air like a fat butterfly. I couldn't miss. But it would appear I shot in desperation, to save my life. The spook would see it all. Kramr would be mad as sheep. He'd have me vivisected. But he wouldn't guess the truth. He'd think I had no choice. I'd lose my stripes for being so stupid. That was OK. It would be just as easy for a buck private to desert the Corps.

My finger tightened over the firing stud. For some reason, I paused. It occurred to me that I was about to fry Grychn, my childhood sweetheart. I wasn't sure I wanted to go through with it.

I noticed movement out of the corner of my eye. I didn't have to look. Sensors already confirmed what was happening. Another combrid streaked through the air under max thrust. Rings of p-grav streamed behind her. She was lucky she didn't have any balls—they'd be screaming.

She must have paralleled my path through the forest and jumped at the same time I had. I was so concerned with Grychn, I hadn't noticed her before. I must need some R&R. I was getting awfully sloppy.

I recognized her. She was Vichsn.

Grychn glanced away from me. The muzzle of her pulsar swung away as she tried to aim at Vichsn. But she was too late. She should have tried to shoot me first, then swung on Vichsn. Of course, I would have shot her then. Now I couldn't. Not with Kramr watching.

Vichsn flashed past, knocking Grychn's weapon out of her grasp with a chopping blow. The pulsar cartwheeled toward the ground. Grychn folded her wings and tried to dive after her gun. There was only one thing I could do. I kicked my thrusters to max acceleration for a couple of millisecs and rocketed across the distance between us. I tackled her in midair, putting my shoulder into her belly and wrapping my arms around her body. Breath whistled from her nose. She gasped. Then she went limp, knocked unconscious by the impact. I hardly felt the blow on my shoulder. Combat armor was designed to absorb shock. I could have blasted into a rock cliff and sustained only a few bruises. A lady guerrilla's midsection was somewhat softer.

My momentum carried both of us to the far edge of the gorge. Kramr stood on the other side. He'd seen everything. There was nothing else I could try. I immediately jumped back, holding Grychn in my arms, not wanting her to regain consciousness before I had her back on the other side.

Kramr was waiting at the cliff's edge. "She's not . . . ?" he asked, leaving the question implied. His tone told me she had better not be.

"Of course not," I answered. "Just knocked out." There was a coldness inside me. The game was over. I was going to have to run and hide. Before I ran out of time.

The spook clasped sonic manacles on Grychn's wrists and ankles. Kramr's eyes shone with inner brightness. Then he laughed. I didn't like it.

Vichsn had jumped back. She joined us on the edge of the cliff. "Thanks, buddy," she said, and laughed as she looked at Grychn. I wasn't sure I liked her laugh any better.

I tried to smile. It was hard. I was already plotting an alternative plan. Some of it was unpleasant. And I was going to have to hurry.

Kramr had called for a bus to come and pick us up. While we waited, I looked at Grychn. I was glad I hadn't killed her. Though that would have been a kinder fate. She was still out cold. She wore loose space coveralls, so not much of her body was visible. Her hair was as short and white as ermine fur. She had good cheekbones and a fine nose. She'd grown up to be a handsome woman. When I'd last seen her, just before I'd hit the road, we were both twelve years old. She'd cried when I told her I was going. But she wanted me to get rid of my timestone. I couldn't do that for anyone. She wouldn't go with me if I took the timestone. She said she loved me. Maybe she had. But she couldn't come with me. My bridges were burned; my parents were murdered. And I had the timestone with which to manipulate events. A lot had happened to both of us since those days.

As I looked at Grychn, I had a pang of regret. I wished she'd stayed with me. She was a pretty lady. A shame she was headed for the cyborg factories. I was sorry I'd left her behind. But I'd had to choose between her and the timestone. There was no choice. I mean, pretty ladies could be found anywhere. Still Grychn was something special. A real shame the spooks had her. That meant I was going to have to run again. I'd have to hurry if I was going to find the timestone before they did. When Grychn talked, they'd find out about both me and it.

Kramr saw me looking at her. "So much for a Lord General's daughter. Her nobility will do her no good before a Colonial court. They have become a little tired of terrorism." He looked at me carefully. I got the creeps again. "Of course, she might not survive long enough to make it to trial. She has a lot to tell me. And not very much time in which to do it." He smiled. "There may be other royal brats brought to task." He laughed wickedly.

There was something in his voice I didn't like. Was he suspicious of me? Had he guessed my secret already? He couldn't have. I had covered my traces too well. Too many years had passed. No evidence was left. All that were left were my nightmares and the image of my own dead face. And Grychn's memories. No spook had glimpsed mine. But they were about to look into her head. I should be safe until that happened. She wouldn't voluntarily betray me.

But there was a disturbing familiarity to Kramr. I had heard of him even before I got to Titan. Where? Then I remembered. The woman who had fingered me in the Bank of Telluride had been named Kramr. But they couldn't be the same. No way. Besides, I had never been connected to the sailor. The spooks didn't know it was me who'd had the timestone. All they knew was that I'd figured out a way to rob banks. They wouldn't know any more without looking at Grychn's memories. It would take time to dredge them out. And more time to make the necessary correlations. I had that much time left. I could make my plans. I could take care of another loose end and then desert the Corps to look for the timestone. I tried a show of bravado: "Frogging straight. She and all her kind deserve the cyborg

factories. Even that's too good for them." *Forgive me,
Grychn.*

The spook laughed again, looking at me.

Bugs crawled up my back.

On the ground, Grychn stirred. She sat up. When she
saw Kramr, she turned away, showing her face to me. Her
eyes were like shattered amber. Something glittered from
their facets.

She didn't recognize me. Hybridization to a combrid had
changed my face beyond recognition. That didn't light up
her eyes. Something else did.

But I couldn't be sure the look of panic I glimpsed in
her eyes wasn't a reflection of my own.

The whine of a hoverbus approached.

5

Night games had begun.

Somewhere, spooks were already interrogating Grychn. But they probably weren't serious yet. They would start out just teasing her. Minds lasted a little longer if the questioning went slowly. The shock of sudden interrogation sometimes sent one into an autistic fugue. Then the questioning became a little more difficult. They wouldn't want that to happen. So they'd be patient. I should have a little time. A few weeks, maybe. Enough to get away, in any case. Enough to cover my tracks. I had made my decision. There was no other way.

Soft laughter from many throats blended into background noise. Low moans rose to orgasmic shouts throughout the barracks. Skin slipped against skin. Leather creaked. Chains rattled. Whips snapped. Mnemone fumes wafted in the air. Privacy curtains were sometimes pulled, sometimes left open. Saturn-light gleamed from naked bodies.

Everyone was enjoying himself. A good firefight always made the nights randy.

Outside, yellow fog rolled across the compound. The force-field guarding its perimeter crackled green. Elves swooped from the trees beyond, howling and shrieking. Automatic pulsar beams stabbed out if they showed too much of themselves. But the targeting computer rarely hit one of them. They weren't *that* slow. Faces from dreams formed in the mist. Wraiths melded into fog. Ghost-smiles curled into wisps.

Vichsn bit my earlobe. Breath whistled from her nostrils. "Yes, yes," she said through clenched teeth. Her eyes were open. Passion shone from retinal reflections. She spread her legs wider, the deeper to receive my thrusts. Her fingers sought places she knew pleased me. Monomer sweat shone from our bodies. Her breasts rubbed against my chest. Belly muscles undulated against mine.

My mind wandered. I couldn't concentrate on sex games. I had other worries. I couldn't be sure how long Grychn could resist the spooks. I had to think about running. But I couldn't even concentrate enough to make proper plans. I kept remembering a twelve-year-old girl who had said she loved me. I kept thinking of what she would be going through. But I was going to have to start making my own preparations. It was too late to do anything about Grychn.

Finally Vichsn's moans quieted. Peristaltic contractions waned. Her breathing slowed.

"What's wrong with you?" she asked after a few minutes.

"Nothing."

"You didn't show much enthusiasm."

"I'm preoccupied."

"You're telling me. Over her?"

"Who?"

"You know. Peppardine. I saw you looking at her." She smiled secretly.

"No, not her. Why should she interest me?" I smiled back. I didn't feel like smiling. But you had to play the game.

"Because she was once a Lady. And I'm just a commoner. But I don't mind sharing you, lover. You will always come back to me. You know you will. I know all about you. So go ahead. Play around if you have to. I mean that." She also meant something else. I had to think.

I got up from the wombskin bunk and padded on bare feet over to the window. I stood before it. A horde of elves had gathered at the edge of the base's force-field. They kept well back in the trees, to avoid triggering our autopulsars. They howled furiously. Maybe they were mourning their dead—the ones we'd killed that day. Killing was always the easiest part.

Vichsn came to stand behind me. She pressed her pelvis into my buttocks and wrapped her arms around me. "You knew the other Lady, didn't you."

"Who?"

"Grychn Willams. The guerrilla Lady. You once loved her, didn't you?"

I said nothing. You didn't ask that kind of question in the Corps. Pasts were supposed to be forgotten. Just because some fool tells you more than he should, that doesn't give you the right to know anything else. I was sorry I'd told Vichsn as much as I had. She knew too much about me already. But you had to trust someone. You had to share the hurt sometimes. Nights were too long otherwise. Then I felt a sudden chill. Vichsn shouldn't know about Grychn. I had never spoken of Grychn to anyone. I was sure of that.

"How do you know I knew Grychn Willams?" I tried to keep my voice soft, the tone casual.

Vichsn smiled sheepishly. "I have a terrible confession to make. You know when I filled in for the company clerk that time." She paused. "I feel guilty about it. But I couldn't resist. I pulled your personnel file and glanced through it." She laughed. "Awfully wicked of me. But I couldn't help it."

"What did it say?" My voice was modulated perfectly. She would never detect the anger underneath.

"Lots of interesting things. They almost gave you a synthetic personality. The Corps shrinks thought you might be too sociopathic to make a good soldier—they thought you might not follow orders and would desert eventually. But they were overruled by the big brass. And I know about how you had to kill your own parents and about your career as a gambler and robber. There was even a report from the spooks. They seemed to think you had some kind of device that let you cheat at both gaming tables and bank vaults. But they had no proof. Just suspicions. So you see, I know everything about you. Terribly nosy of me. But now you can't leave me behind, can you? You'll need to take me with you. I only did it because I love you. Am I forgiven?" She wriggled against me.

"I don't know. What else did my file have in it?"

Vichsn laughed, deep and throaty. "Don't worry," she said. "There was nothing about the other. Only I know about your plan to go to Chronus to hunt for a mindrider named Nels. Your secret is safe with me." She laughed again. "As long as you take me with you."

I said nothing. I shivered, even though I wasn't cold. It didn't make any difference. What had to be done would have had to be done, anyway. I knew that. I just had more reason now.

I watched Vichsn sleep.

Alabaster faces had bothered my dreamtime.

Her eyes were open, but they saw only inner images. A grimace contorted her face. Her mouth shaped itself into a scream that never sounded. Sweat beaded her face. She had told me of her dream. She'd had a man; he was a sculptor. He was also a pephead, and played the frenzied games of peptide. Sometimes he brought his other lovers home and made Vichsn play in a nasty *ménage à trois*. One time, a boy lover went berserk. He killed Vichsn's man with a sonic whip. Before he could turn it on her, she hit him over the head with a mallet, splattering brains all over. She still dreamed of those brains. Since hers was a crime of passion, she'd been allowed to join the Corps. That was dubious mercy. There was no honorable escape from the Corps. The only way out was to run. That was what I was going to do. After I took care of a few loose ends.

Vichsn still slept. Her dream was recycling in another stage of REM sleep. I had not wanted to hear about it. She told me, anyway. The barriers had broken down. I told her how I was going to desert and go to Chronus, that I had to find someone there. I might have even told her about the timestone. I couldn't be sure I had not. Confession was self-indulgent. Once it started there was no controlling it.

Now I had to run. I had no choice. I had to be long gone before Kramr hypnoed out of Grychn's mind the images of the dream we shared: my parents sprawled in peptide stupor; me dragging them one at a time into the spa and floating them in the hot water; opening their veins; watching their faces turn white as blood drained into steaming water, staining it crimson. She'd tell him about the timestone, how it showed us my parents would have killed the two of us. Then she'd tell him there was another timestone. He'd come after me. He'd know then I'd killed the spooks sent to get the ring from the sailor. I was going to have to move fast if I was going to find Nels before Kramr did.

Now it was time to run again. My plans were made; my bags were packed. I was ready to go except for one loose end.

Vichsn held me close in her sleep. I'd made a mistake once and left behind a witness who knew too much about me. A ghost to come back and haunt me. I wouldn't make that mistake again. Spooks were too good at extracting images from minds. I'd trusted someone else once. Never again. You only got one chance with me. Another killing wouldn't matter. They only sent you to the cyborg factories once.

I gently reached out, not disturbing Vichsn. My hand found my belt and removed a sonic knife. I snapped open the blade. Ultrasonic fire flared from its edge.

Vichsn moved in her sleep; her lips nuzzled against my chest.

Outside, elves shrieked their endless taunts. Fog swirled into the faces of wraiths.

I brought the blade near her throat, holding it a few centimeters from the soft skin there. One quick thrust and it would be over. She'd feel no pain. For some reason, that was important. There'd be no one left to talk about me when I was gone. No more ghosts to haunt me.

I realized I was making a mistake. If I deserted the same night Vichsn had her throat slit, the spooks would be damn suspicious. I had to be trickier than that. I must be getting rattled.

I closed the knife.

I remembered green fire sparking from retinal reflections. I saw claws reach out to play with mice.

There was an easier way.

But it would take a little time.

I crept out of the barracks, leaving Vichsn sleeping. I crossed the compound naked. Nothing unusual about that.

The chimera let me into her room. We lay down on a wombskin bunk.

"I've been waiting for you," she said.

"How did you know I'd come?"

She laughed, but said nothing. We lay together for a

long time—kissing, touching, feeling. Her eyes seemed to be someplace else.

Her fingers explored my body. They felt between my legs. There was nothing there. "Let it down," she whispered.

I relaxed my cremaster muscle. My penis and scrotum slid out of their pouch. The chimera fondled them as she kissed my face. My penis stayed limp. She took it in her mouth, but even her tongue could not stir life into it.

"You bastard!" she hissed. "You've been with someone else already." Her voice had changed. "How dare you come home after you've lain with one of your harlots. What's the matter with me? Am I too old? Don't I excite you anymore?" She began sobbing. "Who was she this time?"

"You've seen her," I said. "The blue-eyed one."

"You bastard!" She cried again, then stopped abruptly. "I only want my share. No more. Just what's mine. You can give the rest to your other boys and girls. What's wrong with me? Am I ugly? Do the stretch marks on my belly offend you? I can have them removed. They got there bearing your son. What's the matter with me?"

"I told you. The blue-eyed one." I smiled.

"I only want what's mine." Her fingers crept up my scalp. One poised over my CNS stud. I heard a claw slip out of its sheath. "Is that too much to ask?" Her claw touched the stud.

Blue fire flowed into my brain. Endophetamine blazed in my mind, then coursed into my body like bloody fire. Synthetic passion squeezed hormones out of endocrine glands. A testosterone storm soon raged. My penis stiffened, then hurt with tumid throbbing. My mouth and teeth worked cruelty on her breasts. She opened her legs to receive me. We coupled. With each thrust, air whistled out her nostrils.

"Oh, yes," she said. "Give me more. I must have more of you."

She had me until the peptide frenzy ebbed. Then we slept. I woke once to her talking in her sleep. Something about blue eyes.

After that, I slept uneasily.

6

A battle gong beat its persistent song.

Combrids ran across the commons to their waiting buses. Wisps of mist wafted against the force-field, dissipating when they touched it. Dawn glowed weakly on the horizon.

I shouldered my battle pack and joined the ragged lines of running combrids. I felt a hand touch mine. Vichsn ran beside me. She said something, but as we did not yet have our helmets on, it was lost to the commotion.

We boarded our hoverbus and she sat beside me. Peppardine was already sitting in the medic's seat at the front of the bus. I felt her eyes staring at Vichsn and me. Soon forests of glass passed silently below us.

Vichsn brought her mouth close to my ear. "Did she tell you about it?" she asked, speaking through barely parted lips.

"About what?"

"Did she tell you about how she killed her old man? You need to do that to qualify for X-M-R." She giggled. "And then you don't have a choice. That or the cyborg factories."

"You're jealous."

"I am not." She pretended to pout. She soon tired of that game though, and tried another. She put her hand on my leg and stroked it through combat armor. Tactile sensations were conducted quite well through the polymer fabric. She knew that. She let her hand roam higher. I looked up to see if Peppardine was watching; her eyes were hidden behind a lowered helmet visor. Vichsn whispered in my ear again. "What are they like?"

"What?"

"The chimera's peptides."

"Would you like to try them?"

"Does she swing both ways?" Her eyes opened wide in mock surprise. "Seems a little straight to me. If you know what I mean? A Lady and all. Can I join you tonight?"

"Oh, before then." I smiled slyly.

"What do you mean?"

"Get yourself wounded." I laughed at my little joke. Vichsn pretended to pout again.

We were going on another routine mission. The spooks thought they'd located an elf munitions plant. They were wrong.

We spent all morning combing a thousand hectares of forest. We didn't find any sign of a factory. And we hadn't blundered into an elf trap either, for a change.

Vichsn and I rested, sitting together beneath a tree.

"You are jealous of Peppardine," I said.

"You mean Sergeant Pepper."

"Where did you hear that name?"

"Everyone knows it. Why?"

"Nothing." I looked away.

"Does it bother you that I know her name? And how she came by it?" She nudged my foot with hers.

"Of course not. Don't be silly."

"What kind of stories did she tell you to get you into the sack?"

"The usual." I smiled. Very usual for a Lady of Telluride.

"I guess I'm not good enough for you now." She looked away. "I mean, a Lady and all. How can a simple, plain thing like me have a chance against the charms of a Lady. I was just temporary, wasn't I? Good enough until something better came along."

"If you say so."

"Just a whore to play with. Is that all I mean to you? Just someplace to get your rocks off in, then throw away like a dirty sock."

"If you say so." I wasn't really enjoying this game. But

it had to be played. I'd told her too much. Most of what I'd said had been lies. But some was true. She'd believed the lies. That was the trouble. I tried to remember what all I'd told her. It was hard to keep the stories straight. I'd been living lies for years. The hardest part was remembering to be consistent. But if she believed the lies, she'd remember the true parts also.

"Well, you can't get rid of me that easily. You're going to have to take me with you, when you go. If you don't, I'll tell the spooks everything. I'll tell them to look for you in the mindcasinos of Chronus. I'll tell them all about a miner who is a mindrider now. What was his name? Nels. Shouldn't be too hard for the spooks to find if they know who to look for." She spat through her oxygen bubble. The spittle froze solid before it hit the ground. "I've got too much time and feeling invested in you to give up now. Do you think I want to die a combrid? I want my share of the little empire you're going to establish."

"It could be like that," I lied.

"And now she has to come along and try to steal you away from me. Rather be with your own kind, wouldn't you? Forget about her. I'm the one going with you. Or I'll make big trouble." She flipped down her visor, hiding her face behind its mirrored surface.

I said nothing.

After a few minutes she said: "I'm sorry for the outburst. I'm just being silly, aren't I?"

We heard the hoverbus siren wailing. It was time to leave. The spooks had tired of Hide and Seek.

I didn't answer Vichsn. But yes, she was being silly.

I followed her through the forest toward the clearing where the bus was picking up our platoon. She must have been preoccupied. Or maybe she thought we had to hurry to keep from being left behind by a nervous pilot. For whatever reason, she was moving too fast.

I should have said something. But I didn't.

Vichsn continued to walk down the trail.

The olfactometer in my helmet began screaming in my ear. A red star glowed on my sonarscope.

I almost yelled at Vichsn. But I didn't. And it wouldn't have made any difference if I had.

An explosion shook the forest. Concussion waves bounced from tree trunks, setting them humming with resonation. A burst of light flashed, turning crystalline leaves too dazzling to watch.

I ran ahead. My own sonic field must have triggered the mine, just as it was supposed to, before I got in range. Vichsn must not have had her field on, so she was caught within the detonation field. She was pretty banged up, despite the protection of combat armor. I kneeled beside her and flipped up her visor. She opened her eyes and tried to smile. Her lips moved in silent whispers.

Shards of broken leaves drifted around us, still glowing with trapped light. For a moment, I was sorry. This had happened sooner than I had expected. But now there were other moves to be played.

"Corpsman!" I yelled.

Then waited.

The chimera's fingers had done their magic.

Vichsn rested comfortably on a stretcher in the front of the hoverbus. She was still in armor; it acted as external splints for broken bones. Apparently she had a few of those.

She had tried to speak to me once more before Peppardine had come, but I couldn't understand the words. All that came over the encephalowave was pain. But there was something in her eyes I wished I hadn't seen.

I stood beside her and held her hand. Her eyes stayed closed. If she moaned with pain, the chimera touched a finger to her arm; a claw found a vein and endorphine soothed the hurting.

We were almost back to base when it happened.

I noticed something was different. For a moment, I couldn't figure out what it was. Then it came to me. Vichsn had been making raspy breathing noises. Now she was silent.

"Peppardine!" I yelled. "She's dying."

The chimera quickly came over and felt Vichsn's neck for pulsations. She must have found none, because she then detached Vichsn's carapace, exposing her bare chest. Peppardine placed one hand between Vichsn's breasts and put the other below the left breast.

"Clear!" she said firmly.

I made sure I wasn't touching the cot.

Blue electricity arced from between the chimera's fingers. Vichsn writhed in a quick convulsion.

There was no need to feel her neck this time. The chimera's hands were sensitive enough to feel the beating of a heart. Or the worm wriggles of fibrillation. Or the quiet of cardiac standstill.

A claw extended from Peppardine's left index finger, curving at least six centimeters long. She thrust the claw like a sword beneath Vichsn's breastbone, angling toward her left shoulder. I saw bright red blood fill the hollow claw as it penetrated the chambers of Vichsn's heart. Then the red was pushed back into the heart by the blue of neuropeptide. The claw was withdrawn.

The chimera again placed her hands where palm prints had already been blistered into the skin. Again electric fire flared. Again Vichsn convulsed. Again no heartbeat was produced. It was a dramatic show. And no more than that.

Peppardine looked at me. "There's no more that can be done," she said. "Sergeant Pepper can do no more." She reached out to close Vichsn's eyes. "Her pain is gone. She didn't have to cry. No tears come from her blue eyes. I can do no more for her."

And she was right. But I knew that before. That was the next move. As Vichsn's hand cooled in mine, I had already known a chimera was incapable of reversing an overdose of her own endorphine.

I sat alone at a table at the back of the club. The room was as dark as my thoughts. Near the far wall, a bright cone of light illuminated the green felt of a gaming table. Players sat around the table: only their hands were visible, toying with stacks of chips or fingering their poker crystals; their faces were hidden in shadow. I heard snatches of friendly banter coming from the table. The game had not become serious yet.

Normally, I would have been playing, too. But not tonight. I'd not insulated myself from Vichsn as well as I thought I had. Her death bothered me more than I cared to admit. And something else was wrong. I should have been on the run already. Nothing was holding me back now. The last loose end had been snipped. I still had the keys to a skimmer. I had travel orders—I only needed to fill in the date. Nels waited for me in the mindcasinos of Chronus.

For some reason, I was staying. Some vague discomfort kept me from running. There'd be time enough tomorrow.

So I contented myself with the acrid company of mnemone fumes.

Someone stood beside my table. Her eyebrows glowed in darkness like inverted smiles. I nodded for her to join me. I knew she could see clearly through the shadows. We knew who we were.

I offered her a mnemone stick. She refused. So I sucked its vapors deep into my lungs. There was a hurting somewhere that wouldn't go away. Mnemone only pushed it deeper, where it hurt more.

Peppardine sat across from me, saying nothing. Her eyes were flawed emeralds beneath smoldering eyebrows. Teeth shone with blue saliva. She appositioned her fingertips. Sharp claws peeked out. I knew what I needed, what was wrong with me. I knew what would make the hurting go away.

I threw away my last mnemone stick.

In the dark, she moved against me. Her skin was slick with monomer sweat. She reached out and pulled me closer; her nipples pressed into my chest; her legs locked around mine. Lips nuzzled along my neck, then teeth nipped skin.

I whispered in her ear, hoping her sleeping mind would be open to suggestion: "You're the only one now. Only you can help. I hurt deep inside. Only you can make it stop hurting. Chase away my ice with your fire." I sobbed quietly in her ear.

She muttered in her sleep: "Don't cry, little man. Please don't cry."

Claws pricked, leaving tracks of blood across my back. Peptide warmth pushed away the cold, then became a fire raging inside. My head found its way between her legs; my teeth drew blood from tender flesh. She moaned, but did not awaken.

She leaped out of bed, waking me. She stood near the window, silhouetted by dawn light. Fog swirled outside. She seemed confused, disoriented. She looked about wildly. But after a few minutes the craziness left her eyes. She came back to bed and lay on the wombskin beside me and stared at the ceiling.

"Another dream?" I asked.

"I thought I heard him crying," she said. "I had to go to him, to make him be quiet. My man used to get mad if the baby cried." She looked at me. "But that was a long time ago. Why do I still hear him cry?"

"What happened?"

"To the baby?" She purposely misunderstood my question. "He died. That's all. Nothing more. He just died one day." She shivered. "Babies die all the time. But why do I still hear him cry? I tried to keep him quiet."

"And your man? What happened to him?"

"You wouldn't understand."

"I might. You see, I'm an orphan, myself."

"What do you know of the rages of nobility? We're not like common folk. We feel different passions." She paused. "But I'm not a Lady anymore. They told me to forget all that. And I tried. Why won't my dreams let me forget?"

Sunlight waxed stronger, but was still pale compared to the sunlight of Earth. And darkness was deeper there. I saw a jeweled knife hilt protruding from his chest. But he'd been cut many times before the final thrust. You could see that even in the holos. I wondered what final act of cruelty had driven her to such frenzy. Yes, I understood the rages of nobility. One game ended. Another began.

The mists of morning rose.

7

We didn't go on any routine missions that morning. No hoverbuses left the base. The only daily order was that we were to maintain ourselves on combat alert.

That made us a little nervous.

High Command always planned some kind of routine missions; they tried to keep us too busy to think too much. So maybe something big was coming down, and they were holding us back in anticipation of needing us later. There was only one thing worse than routine missions—real ones. A fella could get himself killed.

Combrids loitered about, talking together in small groups. Rumors circulated like oxide fire jumping among treetops.

I had decided to make my move that night. If I didn't get away now, I'd never be able to run. There was no addiction worse than peptide. The more I saw of the chimera, the harder it would be to leave her blue joy. Even now, I would have to suffer mild withdrawal pain. Nothing intolerable. Not yet. But if I kept taking her peptides, tolerance would develop and my habit increase, until withdrawal would be likely to kill me. Then I could never get away. So I had to go now.

Everything was ready. My money hoard had been deposited in a numbered account with the Bank of Chronus. A skimmer was gassed and oiled. Forged orders were ready to be dated. Vichsn was dead and burned—no ghost arisen from her ashes would betray me. Haunt me, maybe. But not betray me to the spooks. I only had to wait for the cover of darkness.

I just wished I could quit feeling bad about Vichsn. There was no other way. I didn't have room for excess baggage. Besides, she had it coming.

In the noncom club, a poker game formed. I watched for a bit, not really interested in playing. That's how depressed I was. But with nothing better to do, and tired of listening to idle rumors, I decided to play. I had trouble getting into the flow of play though; it didn't seem to matter. I played cautiously, not bluffing, folding if I didn't have the cards. And I didn't have the cards very often.

Peppardine came into the club. She sat alone next to the wall and watched us play. I had to force myself to not stare at her fingers. Already I began to feel a little uneasy; sweat beaded on my back. Had peptide withdrawal started already?

Morning drifted into afternoon. Mnemone fumes wafted lazily in the air. There were rumors that a big elven offensive had been launched.

I was bored. So I started jazzing up the pot, betting at least a hundred on every card. I didn't care what kind of hand I had. Money no longer mattered. And it was kind of fun watching the other combrids' faces as they tried to figure out what I had I was so proud of, what kind of game I was playing. But not as much fun as when Vichsn had been one of the players.

My first card up was a diamond queen. Eyebrows were raised when I led with a C-chip, but nobody folded on me. I knew they would play along for a while. They paused to think though, when I bet a hundred and raised another hundred on a four of hearts. There was even more thinking when I bet heavily on a ten of clubs. But everyone played along. They decided I was bluffing and trying to buy the pot. Which I was.

I was enjoying myself thoroughly. I almost forgot about Vichsn not being there. Almost.

When another queen rolled up as my last card, I nearly laughed out loud. It was all I could do to keep from grinning like a sandcat. Now I could really bluff. Two queens showing. Everyone would think my hole card was a queen. Three ladies. Not bad. So I threw a grand into the pot.

That really caused the other players to sweat.

I probably could have bought the pot.

But then the battle gong began clanging.

Everyone in the club jumped up and began putting on combat armor. Outside, combrids were already running across the commons. Hoverbuses began to warm their engines; the whine of gravturbines filled the air.

I cursed under my breath. They would sound general quarters just as I was beginning to have fun. I pulled on my armor and picked up my pack. Then I noticed Peppardine was still in the room, standing across the table from me. I turned to leave, then paused. I illuminated the dark-hole facet on my poker crystal for the first time.

I stared at it for a moment.

Then I had to laugh.

For the queen of spades stared back at me.

We were briefed while airborne in the hoverbus.

The Gunny spoke in his usual clipped speech. He was so dry and laconic you had the urge to suck on your helmet nipple. The elves had launched a major attack on our spaceport, apparently in an effort to cut our lines of supply. Other than being a predictable move, it was a good idea. But the Lords of High Command knew what a tempting target the port would be, so it was heavily defended with triple force-fields and double batteries of autopulsars. The elves had no real chance to break through its computer-directed defenses. In the past, they'd shown no inclination toward suicide attacks. So they must have some ulterior motive behind the attack. So High Command held back on sending combrid units to the port, waiting to see what would develop later in the day. They trusted the port's defense to the cold precision of battle computers firing autopulsars.

The elven attack continued without letup, but consisted of long-range bombardment with heavy pulsars. Their big guns parried with ours. They didn't mount a direct attack and risk exposing themselves to counterattack. High Command became even more suspicious. The elves looked too vulnerable. A couple of our divisions were mobilized and feigned an attack. As expected, the elves put up only token resistance as they retreated deeper into the forest. They fought only enough to try to lure us into chasing them.

Then their real attack began.

Our depot at Chronus reported being under heavy bombardment. Most of the Corps munitions and fuel were stored there. The elves hoped we would be too busy chasing their diversionary forces to defend the depot. Of course, it was just as heavily defended with force-fields and autopulsars as the port. So they would need ground forces to try to knock out our computer guns. They knew that and so did we.

That's when our unit was mobilized.

Our hoverbus hung in the air over a clearing in the forest. We were supposed to be at the rear of the elven ground forces. They were going to be trapped between us and the autopulsars defending Chronus. A pincer maneuver. A glorious victory for Mother Earth. At least that was the plan. I remembered something about mice and men and plans. I wondered if elves were included in there somewhere.

We quickly filed out of the bus and jumped to the ground. I scrambled toward the trees and made it to their cover without incident. The hoverbus was already accelerating away. The whine of gravturbines ebbed.

The Gunny had us form a V and we began advancing through the trees. Far away was the sound of heavy artillery, as faint as distant thunder. I had my sensors turned to max gain and had twelve diopters of magnification warping my visor. But the woods were quiet; nothing moved save us. My sensors detected no hidden surprises.

The forest held an eerie silence. Night approached. Fog thickened. Already hydrocarbon snow was falling, heavy and sticky with pentane and hexane rain mixed in. It was cold, at least eighty or ninety below. But combat armor kept me warm. Only my thoughts were chilled.

Ebbing light glittered from aggregates of emerald, sapphire, amethyst, and tourmaline. Serrated leaves sparkled like broken teeth. Underbrush broke into shards as we passed; fallen leaves screeched under combat boots. The trees were like giant fiber optic bundles; a translucent sheath enclosed tiny tubes that transported both hydrocarbon monomer and crystal composite upward, where the tubules fanned out at the tree's top and budded into leaves. Photopolymerization occurred in the leaves, and a matrix of complex crystals and polymer formed into geometric shapes. A forest of ripe glass dandelion heads. Silent for two or three kilometers.

Then the quiet was broken.

"Here they come!" shouted the Gunny.

I saw elves swooping from tree to tree, firing their pulsars in midair. Tree trunks picked up the flash of the weapons firing. The light was conducted distally to set their leaves glowing. Foliage quivered to the shriek of hydrocarbon gas parting for the pulsar beam, then shook with a sudden clap of thunder when the vacuum filled.

I fired my assault rifle at the swift-gliding elves in short bursts. Spent photonuclear cases arced into the air and clattered against the trunks of glass trees. I backed up slowly. The Gunny was having us form a ring, with our backs to our fellow combrids. I took cover behind a fallen tree and fanned pulsar beams at any elf who showed too much of himself.

We were just supposed to delay the elves, to make sure they couldn't escape. Reinforcements were coming to administer the coup de grace. The two divisions used earlier to fake an attack were already on their way to help. So there was no point being a hero. Just stay alive until help came. And worry the elves a little. Slow them up a little.

Which was exactly what I intended to do. I squirmed deeper into the ground beside my tree trunk, using the trunk as a rest for my weapon. I certainly didn't intend to be a hero. I planned to desert from the Corps that very night. A miner named Nels waited in the mindcasinos of Chronus. He was going to tell me where the timestone was hidden. Then I was going to find it and build myself a little empire on the ashes of the Terran Empire. Getting killed didn't figure into my plans at all.

I upped the gain on the laser scope of my assault rifle and slowly scanned the forest. I saw an elf swoop to a tree and cling to it briefly as he decided which way to launch himself. I centered the pale disk of the point of impact of the laser sight on him and touched the firing stud, squeezing off three quanta before he could move. Gray fur exploded. The elf crumpled and fell to the ground.

No problem. We could hold them here for hours, until our trap was sprung.

Me and my big mouth.

A moment later a concussion almost knocked me over. A patch of forest was missing in front of me.

"They've turned their big guns around," the Gunny whispered in my head. "They'll have the range with the next salvo. We've got to move. Everyone retreat."

I agreed wholeheartedly. No hero me. I cautiously stood up. Pulsar beams stabbed out of the forest through which we'd just come. Glass exploded over my head. Sharp fragments of crystal pinged against my armor. If I'd been an elf, I would have been skewered. Lucky me.

We were trapped between two columns of elves.

"I can't move, sarge," I bawled into my cortical mike. "They've got me pinned down with snipers." It was the same for every combrid. We were caught. That had been their plan all along. They knew they couldn't breach the walls of the depot. They'd pulled a double feint, luring us into attacking with ground forces, then trapping us in the forest with their own ground forces, where our hoverbuses couldn't evacuate us and their artillery could blow us into orbit. Devious devils. If I hadn't been the one about to be blown to bits, I would've admired their trickery.

But I was the one.

I waited nervously for the Gunny to think of something. That's what they paid him for: to think for the rest of us. I hoped he'd come up with something real quick.

Then I felt myself being lifted into the air by a giant hand. Only there wasn't any hand. Just a concussion wave. With the clarity of expanded perception, where an instant becomes stretched forever, I saw the tree trunk I'd been hiding behind turn into vapor as a blast crater formed. I seemed to float high in the air for an eternity. I knew the initial blast had broken some bones; my right thigh and left forearm felt as if hot coals had been placed under the skin and it hurt all over my chest when I tried to breathe. It felt as if a knife were sticking into my left side—a ruptured spleen or perforated viscus, I thought. And they were right: your whole life does flash before you. I saw again the endless scenes of petty cruelty as my parents slowly destroyed each other. With me in the middle, about to be destroyed myself. I saw Grychn as a child, licking out the fires of an alphalash from my skin. I saw my brother Henri, playing his Executioner Game until Robrt had choked to death. I saw again my own death mask. I knew

I was going to die here. My face would freeze on Titan. My eyes would bulge, then burst finally. All my running had been for nothing. The time matrix had caught up with me. Then I saw the face of the chimera, somehow melded with Vichsn's, until they were one.

The same hand that lifted me now flung me back to the ground as the inner core of the photon bomb imploded. Explosion/implosion shells were quite popular with elves. Particularly nasty, they said. Frogs, do the dead lose their cynicism? I hoped so. Blackness closed around me.

I woke with fire burning inside.

Fingers sought secret places; claws sought blood.

Cat-eyes peered into mine.

I recognized Peppardine's face. The chimera smiled.

I wasn't dead!

I was strong. Pain evaporated like morning mists and was forgotten. I wasn't scared. I could do anything. And I was strong. Dogs, how strong!

"You are well, soldier," she said. "You live to fight again. Be my hero." She lifted my visor. Our oxygen bubbles touched, then fused. She kissed my lips. I saw the wrongness in her eyes again. "You know what to do, Berserker." The lips smiled. Teeth shone with blue promises.

I did know what to do.

My weapon lay beside me. I picked it up and worked the action. A photonuclear case slipped easily into the chamber. It wasn't damaged. But I was, I knew that. But it didn't matter. Endosmin sealed torn blood vessels and stopped their bleeding. Endotalis flogged my heart. Endocholine speeded nervous transmission and strengthened muscles. Combat armor splinted broken bones; endosmin would keep their jagged ends from bleeding as they ground together when I ran. Pain was obliterated by endorphine.

I was strong. I was fast. I was brave . . . so brave.

I laughed.

Then ran.

I cut through the forest, weaving back and forth among the trees, bobbing up and down. Pulsar beams followed me, hitting the ground where I had been. I was too quick for them. Craters from E/I shells formed around me, but the concussion waves couldn't topple me. Then I was beyond their zone of fire and among the elves. Everything was in slow motion. Elves hung from trees. They were incredibly slow. Before they could point their pulsars toward me, I'd shot them out of their trees. I ran faster than the wind. I darted in and out as quick as a frightened coyote. Only I wasn't frightened. Just brave.

I came to an elven battery, bursting into the clearing where they had their gun set up before they even knew I was approaching. I emptied a clip into it, spraying the pulsar beams into the gunners. They all lay dead, fur smoking. I jammed another clip into place. But all was quiet.

I examined the artillery piece. The controls looked easy enough. Just like the spooks had once outlined at an orientation.

I hauled the dead elf gunner out of his chair and sat in it myself. I pushed control buttons; the detonation tube swung smoothly on gimbals. Light flashed from other batteries along the same ridge where this one was placed. I didn't need to do anything fancy. Just point the tube in the direction of the flashes and center the computer sight on the battery. Then pull the trigger. And a klick away there'd be another flash of light. Brighter. And louder. Then move the cross hairs down the ridge. The gun loaded itself. Soon the only flashes were from the shells I fired.

There was but one more duty to be discharged. (I could still smile at my pun.)

I centered the cross hairs of the gun on its own stacked crates of photonuclear cases and locked the controls in place. I dialed in a ten-second delay and pulled the trigger.

Then ran again.

I was well across the clearing before the ammo detonated. Random light flared as bright as novas. Another giant's hand knocked me down. I couldn't get back up. No matter. The game was almost over. Next move, please.

Hoverbus turbines whined.

A black queen haunted my dreams. I opened my eyes. A face watched mine. Prismatic card-eyes became green cat-eyes, following mine.

I hurt all over.

I didn't think that much pain was possible.

I lay on a stretcher in the front of the hoverbus. I could hear combrids talking. They said I was a hero, sure to get a medal, maybe the Legion of Merit. That I'd saved a whole division by taking the elven batteries. Reinforcements had arrived. We'd won.

It didn't much matter to me.

I hurt all over.

A moan pushed through my lips. I felt a claw pierce my skin. Warmth flowed up my arm. Then the pain was gone, chased away by the blue glow of endorphine.

"There, there," the chimera said. "Does my baby hurt? I'll make it better. Don't cry. You know he doesn't like to hear you cry." There was something wrong with her eyes. I'd seen it before. "Remember when I had to hold the pillow over your face," she crooned, "to keep you quiet? Don't make Mama do that again." I understood the madness behind her words. The holos hadn't found out about the dead baby. I'd guessed that part after she'd killed Trinks with endorphine. I'd used her madness to get rid of Vichsn. I thought I could play her game. Now I wondered if I knew all the rules.

The chimera stroked my head. Sharp claws left scratches in my skin. I tried not to wince. I found I couldn't move my arms and legs; they were held by straps.

Pain began to gnaw deep inside again, blending with an even deeper hurt.

The chimera kissed my cheek. "Is my baby warm enough? What can Mama do for baby? Only please don't cry. Don't make me get the pillow out." I knew what game she played in her twisted mind. I had helped to get it to surface. I thought I was going to be able to run away after I had played with her. But there was no escape. Only endless games.

Pain washed over me in waves. I bit my lip hard to keep from crying. I tasted the salty taste of blood. I had to keep from crying. Base couldn't be that much farther. I could make it. Only one more game. I could bluff my way out of this mess. After all, I had an empire to build.

Tears formed in the corners of my eyes. I blinked, squeezing them down my cheeks. I screamed inside, but no sound escaped my lips.

"There, there," the chimera crooned, her mind lost to warped fantasy. "Let Mama kiss the hurt away."

Book III

Mumblety Peg

1

I waited for morning to chase away the elf-fire that danced across the sky.

White flashes winked stroboscopically across the zenith, as though all the stars were dying in one night. Between bursts, images flashed in my mind: Ghost Cavalry jumping from hoverbuses, then drifting to ground balanced on twin cones of pseudograv; pulsar quanta ricocheting from the facets of crystal trees; elves falling with fur smoking; retinal reflections wired with lust afterward. Peppardine's face stared into mine; the chimera's cat-eyes shone with their own warped fantasy. Her claws reached for me, hooked into my skin, slipped easily into my veins. I would never forget the fire her neuropeptides sent singing into my blood. My own hormones couldn't compete with her synthetic ones. Sex, blood lust, and death wish all paled next to the rush of chimeric peptides. Life wasn't worth living without them. I might have gone back to her if I could have; but I could not.

Besides, she had served her purpose; she had made her moves in the game. Her turn was over. Now it was time for other players to take their turns at the game. I had already picked out my next partner. I hoped she would be easier to play with than Sergeant Pepper had been. Peppardine had almost killed me. And an hour of endophetamine catabolizes a lot of meat. It was six months before I could stand without leg braces. Thankfully, I didn't remember very much of that half-year. Now I was almost well. Almost. If not for the images, the remembrance of my own frozen face still to come. And a hurting deep inside. And the grim suspicion that I had not escaped from Sergeant Pepper: somewhere bared claws tipped with blue corposant reached for me; somewhere cat-eyes watched me from darkness. But I was through with her for now. I had won our game. She had only consumed my flesh; my spirit was unbroken. I was still the same Detrs, with the same quest. It would take a better player than the chimera to stop me from that.

There was still elf-fire every night.

Even with my eyes closed, I could see flashes of pulsar quanta imploding against Chronus's force-field, as elf gunners probed for weak points. Detonations beat like palpitations of night.

As a child, I remembered morning sunshine melting both my dark dreams and the glowing mists that played among the ancient redwood groves of our estate on Earth. But I was still a long way from both my childhood and Earth. On Titan the sun provided only light, not warmth. Elf-fire would vanish because elven artillery crews would stop their bombardment with the coming of dawn, retreating once more to their caves in the mountains surrounding Chronus. With daylight, hoverbuses could fly missions; combrids could search and destroy. Ghost Cavalry would ride. Pulsar batteries could be tracked during the day when their beams disturbed the solar field and our targeting computers could triangulate a fix.

It was an unusual feeling, being a soldier and knowing there was still a war but that you didn't have to go to it anymore.

And with dawn, sleep would finally come.

Endorphine burned pleasantly in my blood, pushing pain away. But too many memories tried to surface. I couldn't keep them all contained if I slept. So I stared upward through a persplex dome at a sky afire.

Jain Maure stirred beside me, rolling over to lie on her back. Hair as black as spun carbon fanned out on satin wombskin. Oiled skin shone amber with elf-fire; darker bruises had already faded. A ruby pendant hung from a gold chain around her neck. She was my doctor. And other things, too.

Her eyes opened. Copper irises appraised me. "Still

awake?" she asked. "I know something that will help you sleep." She rose and kneeled over me, brushing her breasts against my chest. Her lips kissed mine; her tongue probed my mouth. I smiled inside. But I lay passive, eyes staring straight ahead. She began to work her way down my body with her lips, circling each nipple, tonguing my navel, licking my limp member. It remained so, unstirring. Images of smoking corpses danced through my mind. Ebony dolls jerked to the pull of invisible wires. They all had the same face—mine—both corpses and dolls. You didn't have to be a genius to figure out the symbolism. I knew what they meant. And I knew what else was suppressing my libido: all the corpses had interesting wounds—or wounds in interesting places, anyway.

Jain knew what was wrong and she knew what to do about it. She picked up a crystal vial and removed its cap. Opalescent liquor swirled inside. She dipped her tongue into the vial. A drop of peptide clung to its pink tip. She lowered her protruding tongue slowly, touching it to the top of my head. Peptide was drawn into my brain through my CNS stud. Inner fire blazed with blue light, blinding me. I felt the thrill of a testosterone rush. Synthetic passion overwhelmed me. My penis pulsated with blood. We coupled. Bodies blurred with mingled sweat. Orifices touched. Secretions blended. Breasts slapped against a muscled chest. Teeth nipped earlobes, drawing blood. Fingernails scratched deep into skin. Smooth muscle spasms milked a penis from both within and without.

It was almost tender. I was glad Jain had had enough of her rougher games earlier. I was still tired from playing those.

Sometime later the frenzy of synthetic sex steroids ebbed. By then it was dawn.

Sleep finally came.

Jain Maure was gone when I awoke. I was alone in her house. She had a nice place. Cosmetic surgeons could charge fancy fees in Chronus—or at least they could before the war. Did she also exact a pound of flesh from the rest of her clients? I laughed at my little witticism.

I rolled off the wombskin and stood up, wobbling momentarily before I caught my balance. Reflex arcs were not yet completely conditioned. Proprioception always lagged a little behind. But I'd regained most of my strength, anyway. Maybe I was still a little unsteady, but six months ago I'd been too weak to do anything but lay in a Hubbard tank. My recovery hadn't been easy. Progress meant pain. I'd forgotten how many replacement grafts had been necessary. A little bit of residual nerve damage was the least of my worries. Besides, it was going to get me my discharge from the Corps. And with full disability.

I walked across the room toward a balcony. Like I said, it was plush. The floor was a living carpet of fungoid, almost as pliant as wombskin. Olfactory sculpture wafted pleasant fragrances into the air. Mutable holograms gleamed in midair. All were signed originals by the most famous artists of the System. Bonsai lounges five centuries old stood in planters on both sides of the bed. Spider-silk tapestries hung on the walls. Jewelry worth several fortunes was strewn carelessly about her dressing table—sonic gems sang in ultrasonic harmonies amid the glint of iridium and gold.

As I passed the dressing table, I had an irresistible urge. I paused before it, then took two steps closer, activating its holomirror. An image of myself sprang into the air, facing me: stainless-steel eyes, cold and unfeeling; aquiline nose; proud cheekbones; haughty lips, thin and cruel; skin brown as old copper. I touched my hands to my face and watched my image do likewise, both amazed and pleased. Because it was my face, my old face, the one I'd had before entering the hybridization tanks and becoming a combat hybrid. On leaving the tanks, combrids were almost identical in appearance and build: two meters tall, solidly muscled, well padded with brown adipose, skulls bald and convoluted by wires beneath the surface, eyes protected with nictitating membranes, skin as black as ebony with antiradiation granules and gleaming like obsidian with protective sweat. Loving uniformity, the military made quartermasters stock only one size. They also deindividualized you, and similar facial features accomplished that. But when you mustered out, the contract said they had to give you back your face. They had. Or Jain Maure had, to be precise.

Marcus Detrs, Esquire, scion son of the late Lord and Lady Detrs, the last of his line, heir to a fortune on Earth, stood before me. Lance Corporal Detrs, of the First Ghost Cavalry, was gone. At least his face was. Hybridization and cybersurgery couldn't be reversed. I'd always have the augmented muscles, reinforced tissues, laminated bones, and other survival adaptations of a combrid. All Jain Maure did was a little cosmetic surgery to restore my features and bring my skin back to standard Terran. Which suited me fine.

I admired my smooth musculature, four times normal in strength. My skin was still matrixed with polymer mesh. Brown adipose would still insulate and store oxygen. I lowered my gaze to my genitals. With a brief inspiration, I sucked both scrotum and penis into their pouch in my pelvis. If someone kicked me in the groin, all he'd get for his trouble would be a stubbed toe. When I kicked him back, I'd be splattered with ruptured guts. Although a civilian in appearance, I was still a combrid inside. I might need that advantage later.

Why? To find the timestone, of course. Have you forgotten about it? Oh, you thought the spooks would have found it by now. You thought Grychn would have told them about it. So had I, as I languished in the hospital. I waited for Kramr to come to question me. But he never did. Then I found out that Grychn had escaped before they could interrogate her. The spooks knew nothing about Nels or the timestone. They both still waited for me.

I laughed. My scheme had taken longer than I'd planned, and almost backfired, but it was back on schedule now. And now there was no hurry. I had time to be careful and do it right. Jain Maure had to think it was her idea. I knew why she'd taken me in as her lover. Not just for live-in sex—though I served that purpose, too. She had other plans for me. I knew why she was called Dr. Pepper. But I had my own plans.

I was in Chronus. I was almost a free agent again. My body was as strong and durable as a human body could be made. I could kill a man in less than three seconds, twenty-three different ways, using either my hands, feet, or head. I was almost ready to venture into Chronus's mindcasinos.

If only there weren't the dreams troubling my sleep. And the pain. And Jain Maure's night games.

Hawks shrieked outside, where they hovered in updrafts. Their voices brought me back from my reverie. They wanted breakfast.

A bowl of bloody meat sat on the table. I picked it up

and walked out on the balcony. A dozen hawks wheeled in the air outside. Raspy whistles greeted me. Jain Maure's house perched on the cliffs of Mount Erubus, the highest point in Chronus. The city sprawled across smaller hills below. The vertex of the twenty-kilometer dome of Chronus was a scant hundred meters overhead. Beyond the dome and its force-field were swirling hydrocarbon mists at seventy below. Within the dome was Earth-normal atmosphere at twenty-five above. Cypress trees grew from ledges in the cliff to rise in branching terraces past the house. Hawks made rookeries among the tangled roots on the cliff face. They rode the updrafts that rose from the city, hunting by day the rodents that had plagued Chronus since children's pets had escaped centuries before. Owls had been introduced to hunt nocturnal vermin; hawks hunted their diurnal cousins.

I tossed chunks of meat into the air, where the birds easily snatched them with their claws. Then they landed on the rail and tore at the meat with their beaks. They had become quite tame. Sometimes they would even let me stroke their feathers. When they finished eating, they leaped back in the air and began soaring in thermal updrafts once more.

I went back inside and dressed. That was easy—I was still entitled to wear a Corps uniform. I pulled on the gray body stocking we wore as fatigues. A sergeant's three stripes on a rocker were on the sleeves. The promotion came through while I was still hospitalized. Not very long after I had received the medal and commendations. I was a hero of sorts. I had made it big in the holos for about a week. I wouldn't have lasted that long except for the other —you know, the part about me being heir to the Lordship, a notorious playboy/gambler, a flamboyant criminal who chose glory with the Corps rather than go to a prison farm. The folks back home loved it. Real sensational copy. For about a week. Then I was forgotten again. Which suited me fine. I didn't want anyone recognizing me when I searched for Nels and the timestone.

I was in no particular hurry. I wanted to be completely healed from my wounds first. I'd learned my lesson in that regard. And you needed a manager if you were to become a mindrider. That's where Dr. Pepper came in. Someone had to look after your body as you played the mindgame.

I was safe. I had time to let my body heal. Nobody else was looking for Nels. Nobody but Grychn even knew who he was or where he could be found. She had escaped from Kramr. Undoubtedly she was lying low with her elf friends. I had nothing to worry about as long as she stayed free. Vichsn wasn't doing any talking. Her ghost might torment my mind, but that was all she could do. Sergeant Pepper knew nothing important. I had time to get myself well. Which I almost was. Except for peptide—I was a peptide addict now. But that couldn't be helped. That was part of my plan. Later, I could overcome my weakness for peptide. I had a plan for that, too. There was nothing more disgusting than a pephead. I'd hated my parents for their addiction. Pathetic creatures, all addicts. No better than vermin. And now I was one.

I again examined myself in the holomirror. I parted my hair to reveal a CNS stud, shining like a silver button. I had the urge to pull it out. But that wouldn't solve anything. My addiction could only be cured by suffering through withdrawal. That was the price you paid. Sometimes you died from withdrawal—if you didn't, you wished you would. I was going to have to go through it eventually or I'd never escape Dr. Pepper. I let my hair fall back over the stud. Sometime, but not tonight. Tonight I would still have to play Jain Maure's games. When she held out her tongue, gleaming with blue peptide, I would bend my head to receive her kiss. I would be tossed about on a synthetic endocrine storm. I would do things I might not otherwise do, not being able to resist the passions of peptide. Was I whining? I suppose. Why not? I've done worse. And I did still hurt inside. That worried me a little. What if the pain was still there after I underwent withdrawal? Could I stand it without the warmth of peptide?

I knew I would have to.

2

After I'd finished dressing and feeling sorry for myself,
I walked to the hospital. Although you could see the white
buildings far below from the balcony, it was a brisk walk
to get there from Jain Maure's house. Mainly because you
had to walk down the far side of the mountain, and then
detour around the large estates at its base. By air it was
less than a klick away. As a combrid, I'd made longer
jumps with thrusters. But walking made it closer to five
kilometers. I didn't mind. I needed the exercise to help re-
condition reflex arcs. Besides, it was a pleasant walk.

The road made switchbacks down steep slopes of juniper
and oak. Wild flowers grew among the trees, wafting their
perfumes over the road to mingle with other scents: musty
mushrooms, pungent spearmint, juniper oil. Tiny deer
munched acorns, unafraid. Peacocks and guinea fowl
strutted along the roadside. The air smelled always of
spring and was always the same twenty-five degrees with
fifty-percent humidity.

At the bottom were several twenty-hectare estates, with
carefully pruned trees, well-trimmed hedges, and rolled
lawns. Sometimes polo ponies galloped back and forth,
chasing a white ball. Sometimes Morgans and thorough-
breds jumped over hedges, chasing a red fox. Sometimes
I heard the sound of antique gunfire followed by the rustle
of partridge wings. Always there was the sound of laughter
floating up from the verandas, and the tinkle of ice in tall

glasses. Water splashed in swimming pools. Racquets hit balls back and forth across grass courts.

The war seemed very far away indeed. Chronus was a colonial sanctuary preserving a life-style that no longer was, that might never have been. But the peace was illusory. At night, elf-fire still flared overhead. The siege of Chronus continued, now in its sixty-first day. We had been cut off by elven gunners for sixty-one days. Gravships could neither enter nor leave the spaceport. At night the bombardment intensified. Eventually the force-field would fail. The rural garrisons were also held siege, so their combrids could not help Chronus. A fleet was on its way from Earth, with heavy cruisers and a battalion of cyrines, to lift the siege. But until they arrived, it was business as usual. The people of Chronus carried on as if nothing had changed.

The road curved around Mt. Erubus, past more estates, and finally skirted the base of red cliffs. A thousand meters up, I could see Jain Maure's house, perched on the cliff's edge. A park lay at the bottom of the cliffs. I left the road there and entered the park, walking along paths and waterways. A few combrids sat about in small groups, passing mnemone sticks. They sometimes yelled at me: "Hey, Gunny . . . What's happening? . . . How's it going at the hospital? . . . When do you get your walkin' papers?" Mnemone vapor swirled around their heads. I remembered well those acrid fumes. I sometimes longed for the rough camaraderie of a garrison post. But I didn't join them, nor would I have been welcome. I was a short-timer. Those combrids had only suffered minor wounds. They would soon be sent back to the bush, to get another chance at being killed. As soon as the siege was lifted. I was through with their war, about to begin one of my own. I no longer even looked like one of them, though I would always be a combrid inside. No, I wouldn't be welcome to join them.

The hospital was on the other side of the park.

The buildings were a collection of marble spheres of various sizes, some stacked vertically, some connected horizontally. A force-field surrounded the periphery. At the gate, a bored cyrine guard watched me pass, nodding slightly in recognition. Soon even that remnant would fade, and I would be entirely forgotten by the Corps.

In regard to that I had mixed feelings. Sometimes I even

missed the combat. Nothing was more exciting than that. I had nostalgic feelings for the forced closeness that developed among combrids, knowing your life depended on your mates' ability to fight as much as your own. And the nights had been good. Too good to believe. I wondered if sex could ever be as good as when you were wired tight with blood lust and bedding someone who had fought beside you that day, had maybe even saved your life. Probably not. It hadn't been so far. *C'est la vie!*

A little maudlin reminiscing never hurt anyone. But there was no sense getting carried away. I pushed aside my sentimental thoughts. I had more important things to worry about—like an empire to build.

I walked to the rehab dome and entered it. Inside were the various machines that had tortured my body back into shape. A sign hung just inside proclaiming: PAIN IS PROGRESS. I must have made a lot of progress.

I stripped off my fatigues and medmech zippered me into one of the rehab machines. Syntheflesh surrounded me in warmth, kneading with tiny fingers. I closed my eyes. Pins and needles started. Have you ever worn a hair shirt with nails? Probably not. The fashion passed with the old religions. But that's kind of what the rehab machine felt like. Then, later, like going over a waterfall in a barrel. And still later, like being a guest at a blanket party—you know, where thugs tie you up in a sack and start beating the doggie out of you with baseball bats. Of course, I really wasn't sustaining any damage—it just felt that way. I knew what was actually happening—muscles were contracting to electrical shocks, joints were being loosened, nerves were tingling to transcutaneous stimulation.

It was primitive and archaic, like all veterans' hospitals. The same effects could have been achieved in four weeks in a hybridization tank. But those facilities were scarce and, in any case, limited to combrids who could be salvaged for more combat duty. No sense wasting restoration services on combrids permanently damaged and due to be mustered out with a pension. There was no hurry with them. They had all the time in the world. Let them spend some of it in old-fashioned rehab machines.

Lights started flashing inside my head. It felt as if an autopulsar had shot off a clip inside a mirrored sphere. Pulses of energy bounced back and forth. Electrical pinballs caromed from the walls of my skull, ringing synaptic bells. It wasn't too bad—not if you didn't mind watching a laser light show in your head. A little intense. But I'd gotten used to it by now.

Finally the fireworks stopped. Medmech unzippered me from my machine and carried me to the shower stall. As ultrasonic spray cleansed my skin of sour sweat, I supported myself by bracing my arms against the rails on both sides of the stall. After a few minutes, my legs stopped trembling and I could stand. I opened my mouth and let the ultrasound peel away the film from my teeth. I felt better.

After dressing in clean fatigues, I walked over to the medical officer's desk. Major Bakr was his name. He wore muttonchop sideburns and a handlebar moustache. He was not a combrid. Commissioned officers belonged to another caste. He looked up from his console screens and scowled. But he motioned for me to sit. I sat.

A sheet of three-ply mylar flimsy lay on the desk in front of him.

I knew what it was. I'd been waiting a long time for this day to come.

"You know what I've got here, Detrs?" he asked.

I nodded. I knew.

"Your general discharge from the Corps," he continued. "With medical qualifications." He peered at me. "And with a service-connected disability." He lifted the mylar sheets, then let them drop. "But you know all that. You've got some powerful friends."

"What do you mean, sir?" His last statement surprised me. I had no friends, powerful or otherwise. All my real friends were dead.

Major Bakr smiled ruefully. "I was overruled by the Lord Surgeon General himself on your case. I don't know why. I triaged you myself. There was no doubt you would have been able to recover full capability if you'd been sent back to the regeneration tanks. Your nerve damage was all peripheral. The other trauma hardly mattered. Four weeks in a tank and you would have been back killing elves at one-hundred-percent efficiency. That was my recommendation. I know I was right. The machines told me that today. Your nerves will recover on their own. It will take them ten times as long to regenerate outside a tank, but they will. I knew that. Any other physician should have drawn the same conclusion. But my recommendations came back rejected. Unfit for rehybridization, they said. I was ordered to rehabilitate, civilianize, and separate you from the Corps. I've done all that. Took us six months, didn't it? But now it's done. Tell me, though, why did the Lord Surgeon General bother about you? Why are you so important?"

"I really wouldn't know, sir." I tried to keep my voice even. I was bothered by what Bakr had said. Why would the General intervene in my case? There was no reason. Bakr just had a case of paranoia. He was just afraid he'd never make colonel and was trying to explain away his own inadequacy. But what if I did get completely better? If the lingering ataxia resolved? I decided I'd caught a case of paranoia from the Major. I didn't need that. Not with an empire to build. A case of megalomania was enough for anyone.

So I decided it was just my good luck they'd made a mistake and discharged me.

Major Bakr signed the mylar flimsy and handed me the top sheet. Then he made me trade in my Corps I.D. ring for a disabled veteran's one. Big deal. The perks were the same. The bennies were better. And nobody shot at you anymore. I was officially out of the Corps. A civilian at last. Big deal.

As I stood to leave, Bakr looked up. He was almost smiling. "You should have been more careful," he said.

"What do you mean?"

"Moving in with Jain Maure was rather foolish, wasn't it?"

I stared at him, saying nothing.

"Don't think you're the first. Or the last. She squanders men faster than money." He saw the question in my face and laughed. "Don't you think I know what kind of a rehab program she had you doing after your cosmetic surgery? And peptides have been showing up in your urine for months. By the level of urinary metabolites, I'd say you've built up quite a tolerance by now." He smirked at me. "We all know the name the cyrines call her. Dr. Pepper." He laughed again.

I didn't like it at all. He'd even forgotten to shake my hand. Some send-off. Not even a marching band.

But I was out of the Corps.

I should have felt great, but for some reason I didn't. I pushed strange feelings deep, before they could surface.

I was frogged if I was going to cry in front of that sheepdip Major.

Spring still freshened the air outside the hospital. Songbirds chattered to each other from trees. Flowers bloomed in colors too vivid to be real; fragrance wafted from their blossoms. Petals littered the sidewalk, to be crushed beneath passing feet. It was always spring beneath the dome of Chronus, and the inhabitants lived their own illusion of reality. I wished I had lived there a half-century ago, when elves were content to tend their forests of glass, and true Terran Colonials worried only about who was going to be their bed partner that night. Now they had other worries. Big worries. So did we all.

What I planned next was going to be dangerous. The life of a mindrider was risky. You could die playing the mindgame, or lose your body. But the longer I waited, the less chance I'd have of finding Nels. I'd have to take my chances, or give up my quest. I wasn't the quitting kind.

I normally spent the afternoons at the VFW hall, swapping lies with other ex-combrids. (Yes, there were a few.) They had all been more seriously wounded than I; most had required considerable graftings of prosthetics and showed the signs of residual nerve damage. Yet I was accepted by them as their sibling.

This afternoon was no different. I let my feet take me toward the hall, while my mind wandered on its own. I passed quaint shops: jewelers, tailors, art merchants—displaying the finest wares that could be imported from the rest of the System. Shoppers peered into holo displays. Sidewalk cafés were found at each intersection—people sat at small round tables sipping wine from long-stemmed glasses, laughing at the things they told each other. Everywhere it was business as usual. Storerooms had been well stocked before the siege—as long as they held out there would be no shortages. War wasn't evident. At least not here, on the surface. But Chronus had many strata. Old mine shafts, tunnels, and natural caverns honeycombed the bedrock underneath. An underground life dwelt there, with peptide parlors, pathic emporia, mnemone dens, chiggies and plaguies, and the infamous mindcasinos. That is where you went to forget, to push away memories that hurt too much, or to become lost yourself. That was where I must go. And soon.

The VFW hall was a simple, unpretentious penthouse atop an office tower. An external liftube took you directly to the top. Wouldn't want a sensitive businessperson being offended by scarred and gnarled ex-combrids. The tower was in the Old Town section of Chronus—still respectable, but a little on the seamy side. Most of the veterans lived nearby in cheap apartments. A Corps pension paid enough to live on, if you weren't extravagant. But if you needed a call-body to come by once in a while, or if you craved a toot of mnemone occasionally, you didn't waste your credits on rent. And Old Town was close to the Underground. That was important. Sooner or later, you'd go Underground. And you wanted to be close to the VFW hall. You needed to talk to your buddies.

I stepped into the liftube and rose up the side of the building. How true that was—needing to talk to other veterans. I had trouble conversing with civilians. We had no common ground. I guess you could never really get away from war—it affected you too deeply, leaving too many demons in your mind. You cherished the rough camaraderie that developed between combrids—the quick anger, the quicker laughter. I looked forward to the afternoons. I was going to miss not coming to the hall. When I became a mindrider, I wouldn't have time for such diversions.

I reached the top of the liftube and stepped out into a foyer. The hall was divided into several rooms: a café, a lounge, a holo room, a gymnasium, a boudoir for casual liaisons. I chose the lounge, intending to drink my lunch. As I entered it, other veterans looked up from their tables, some nodding to me, some smiling, some inviting me to join them. The invitations I refused. I'd had several brief affairs with other veterans. I suppose I was attractive since I hadn't been mutilated by my wounds. But I lost interest in sex games. As I became more involved with Jain Maure, other liaisons were almost impossible to maintain. I had no sex partners except her now. My veteran buddies were just good friends. But I wanted to be by myself today. I knew I wouldn't be coming back. I couldn't leave cold turkey.

I took a table in a corner and ordered wine. When the barmech returned with my carafe, I sat back in my chair and sipped wine, looking around. A game room opened from the lounge—several of its machines were in use. On another day, I would have played a game or two myself. Today I was content to watch. Laughter came from other tables. Snatches of combrid talk came to me.

As I watched the others, I realized Major Bakr was right: I was not severely enough damaged to qualify for a medical discharge from the Corps. The other veterans in the lounge all had something in common—significant brain damage. They drooled, or staggered, or were deaf, or dumb, or blind, or paralyzed. Each had at least one neurologic deficit. In appearance, they were mostly normal. Cosmetic surgery could do wonders with shattered flesh. Prosthetic parts were available that were better than original equipment. But modern medicine still could not get central-nervous-system tissue to heal. An injury to brain or spinal cord was irreversible. If you were a combrid, it was your ticket out of the Corps. Any other damage could be repaired in Hubbard tanks. But not brain damage. Some ticket out.

Until talking to Major Bakr, I'd assumed my unsteadiness was permanent. He said not. I believed him. So now I had to figure out why I had my medical discharge. I didn't like the implications at all. I felt uncomfortable knowing I had anonymous friends in high places. Why should anyone want to do me any favors? I'd never taken a tumble with a Lady General.

My brooding was interrupted by someone standing next to my table. I looked up. A combrid stood there, dressed in officer fatigues. He wore a red beret. I didn't have to see the silver skull on it to know he was from Corps Intelligence. I mean, who ever heard of a combrid officer? He smiled. I didn't like it one bit. His eyes were the green of old jade. What combrid had those eyes?

"Sergeant Detrs?" he said. It was not really a question.

"Not anymore. Just plain Mr. Detrs will do nicely."

"Can I join you?" he asked, and sat down anyway.

"Why not?" I loved answering a question with a question. Especially when both were rhetorical. I hoped the spook found it annoying.

He drummed his fingers on the table. His eyes could look in two directions at once. Gave me the creeps.

"Do I know you?" I asked. Not that it mattered. Evidently he knew me.

"I think we've met once or twice. My name is Kramr." He did not hold out his hand. Just as well. I didn't want to touch it, anyway. "We have a common acquaintance—Grychn Willams."

My blood had chilled when he first said his name, but now it froze solid. I tried to relax. Kramr had nothing on me. I was safe. If I'd deserted from the Corps I would have had his kind after me. But not now. I had a ticket out. He couldn't touch me as long as Grychn was free. He couldn't know anything until he questioned her. Then why were my palms sweating?

"As I recall, you were the one who caught her for me. Back when you were Corporal Detrs." He smiled like a used-gene salesman. A barmech came and Kramr ordered. While he waited for his drink, he trimmed his nails with a clasp knife. All show, of course. He could grow them any length he wanted. "I don't suppose you know where Grychn is?" he asked finally.

I laughed. "I heard she escaped," I said, almost snickering. "By now I imagine she's back with her elf friends."

He examined the sonic blade of his knife. Blue fire swirled from its edge. "I think not. I think she's still here, in Chronus. I'm sure she hasn't made it off the planet. She has no place to go. The elves will think she talked too much before she escaped, or that we let her escape to lead us to them. They won't take a chance by taking her back."

"Did she?"

"What?"

"Talk too much?" I tried to keep my voice even, the tone casual.

"Not nearly enough. Not as much as she will when I get her back. There are several subjects on which she needs to elaborate." His voice chilled me again. I was glad Grychn was out of his grasp—both for her sake and mine.

The barmech brought his drink—mineral water. He sipped it, peering at me over the top of the glass. "I will catch her again. But my job would be a little easier if somehow I could see into the future."

My mind had been wandering, but when Kramr said that, bugs started wriggling up my back. I listened closer.

"The Lord Scientists have been working for years to develop a chronotropic crystal. No reason radiacrystal technology shouldn't be able to manipulate temporal energies. But the best they can come up with is one that will work for a few millisecs. Not enough to be of practical value. Not enough to help us put out all these colonial brushfires." He suddenly flipped his knife into the air. It tumbled slowly as it came down, then stuck into the table top next to my left hand. My skin tingled with ultrasound. I couldn't move. I felt numb all over.

Kramr reached over and picked up my hand. "Amazing how flesh can be regenerated," he said. "How did you lose your hand?" He retrieved his knife from the table.

I shrugged. "In a fight. In my youth." I didn't have to tell him. He knew.

He smiled. "That's right. You were quite a rogue. And a sportsman, as well. I don't suppose you ever met a sailor named Mikal Gy. He used to do a little gambling. He wore an unusual ring—a platinum setting with a dark blue stone. I wanted that ring. I almost had it twice. Gy's dead now. So are three of my siblings."

"No, the name doesn't sound familiar. Where did he do his gambling?" I almost stammered. I never had known the sailor's name. But I knew who Kramr meant. And I remembered where I'd heard Kramr's name before: the sailor had called a croupier that name in a casino. That meant Kramr had been after the ring himself. He knew about me. Or suspected something, anyway. That was just as bad with spooks. But Kramr must not know about Nels and the other timestone. He was on a fishing expedition. Well, he wouldn't get anything from me. I was discharged. As long as I kept clean, he'd have no excuse to hypno my brain.

Kramr watched me carefully. I tried to look nonchalant. He flipped the knife again. It arced through the air and sunk deep in the table next to my hand, shaving off a thin slice of epidermis.

"If you happen to hear from Grychn, let me know." He arched his eyebrows. "I think she might have seen the ring I'm looking for. I want to ask her a few more questions about it, anyway." He laughed, then stood up and left.

I stared at the door for a few minutes, letting my heart

slow down. I pulled Kramr's knife from the table, closed its blade, and put it in my pocket.

He knew something. Certainly more than he'd told me. I'd half expected him to haul me off for questioning. Maybe he wasn't sure what part I'd played. I was going to have to be careful from now on. I no longer had the luxury of time. I was going to have to find Nels and get away. The sooner the better.

I gulped my wine.

My furlough was over—it was time to go Underground.

3

The Underground of Chronus was a network of old mine shafts and tunnels in the bedrock beneath the city. Actually bedrock was not the proper term—the matrix was nickel/iron. A million years ago a comet had collided with Titan, fusing its substance with that of the Moon and forming a ten-kilometer lake of molten crust. Before it cooled, volcanic activity had pushed up Mt. Erubus in its center, along with a few smaller hills on the periphery. After the fireworks were over, a ten-kilometer crater with a kilometer-thick floor of nickel/iron was left. That didn't attract any miners. Nickel/iron was more easily obtained from asteroids. But the heat of the collision and subsequent volcanic eruptions allowed some interesting chemical reactions to occur. The floor of the crater was seamed with veins of radiacrystal seeds. The nickel/iron matrix was porous enough to allow hydrocarbon atmosphere to percolate through, so the seeds could grow into crude radiacrystals. For a hundred years miners had followed these gem veins with their tunnels, until living crystal biotechnology made natural radiacrystals uneconomical. Chronus started out as a mining camp, providing the miners with housing, supplies, and diversions, and continued to grow after the mines had played out. Old Town was all that remained of the original settlement. The old mines had never been capped—they were sealed and pressurized anyway—so they created no problem when Chronus's dome had been erected. Now the shallower mines housed the city's utilities and served as storage depots and warehouses. The deeper mines had been put to other uses. Varks never ventured deeper than the first level—they'd been ambushed too many times in the lower regions. Without hindrance from the authorities, business thrived in the Underground.

Jain Maure and I walked toward the portal of the Underground. We were in the middle of Old Town. Her skimmer was parked in a public lot not far away. The portal had once been the main mining shaft and provided access to all levels.

Jain wore a cape of spun gold clasped to jeweled breast cups. A chain-mail skirt was wrapped around her waist. She had on white sandals with satin gaiters wound to below her knees. Copper eyes shone with inner fire. Her tongue was dyed red. When she licked her lips they gleamed as though covered with blood. A diamond vial hung around her neck.

We walked hand in hand, as carefree as young lovers. But I was the only one of us who was young. And our relationship was a bit more complicated than one of lovers.

I wore a formal body stocking. This trip was just to reconnoiter.

Few people were out on the streets. It was still early. Later, throngs would begin the descent to the Underground. Still later, they would stagger back to the surface, filled with real and synthetic euphoria. Or they might not return.

We reached the down portal and stood before it. A hundred-meter-wide shaft dropped straight down. Warm air rose from the shaft, carrying vague scents: mnemone, narcosmin, pheromones.

A vark stood in a glass booth, looking bored. Sometimes he would take pictures of people going down, but varks no longer went themselves. Tonight he just watched.

Jain tugged at my hand. We jumped into the shaft and floated downward, supported in a field of p-grav. I briefly imagined what would happen if the p-grav generators failed —we would fall a kilometer straight down to smash into the bottom of the shaft. I shivered. I always imagined the same scenarios when in a liftube—I couldn't help it.

Vertical handrails lined the sides of the shaft—we used them to work our way to the other side. Yellow light emanated from the walls. Large chambers opened off the shaft at each separate level—they had been used to store equipment and supplies when miners were still drilling tunnels. Now they served as loitering places for the inhabitants of the Underground.

Voices called to us as we drifted past. The offers were varied: sex, pain, drugs, death. Wares were flashed for our inspection: naked bodies—male, female, hybrid, hermaphroditic; apparatus—whips, chains, shackles, needles, vials, capsules, wires and electricity; fine art—olfactory sculpture, mutable holograms, sonic tapestries, all depicting obscenity. Black-cloaked death-priests meditated with shining daggers. In the tunnels beyond could be found brothels, torture chambers, mnemone dens, peptide parlors, muticlinics, and temples of the dead. There were a few casinos for ordinary gambling. Slaves could be rented for the evening.

We passed them by, drifting ever deeper. The air became warmer and heavier. Finally we came to the chamber we sought. It was empty of loiterers. Two combrids stood guard. They were out of uniform and their pulsars weren't standard issue—deserters most likely. They nodded to Jain and let us pass. The tunnels beyond formed a maze. This deep, the gem veins had been short and convoluted, so the tunnels branched frequently and most of the branches were cul-de-sacs. They weren't marked. You had to know where you were going. Jain did. She led me down tunnel after tunnel. I soon realized we were doing considerable backtracking—she was trying to get me lost. I smiled to myself. Let her try. Let her play her little game. I still had a combrid's spatial orientation. Lost troops were dead troops. I could have been blindfolded and still found my way out.

Eventually we went down a tunnel that appeared to be another cul-de-sac. However, a combrid guard stood at the end. The tunnel opened into a chamber. The combrid allowed us passage. The chamber beyond was dimly illuminated. Tiers of seats circled a central dais. Each seat was equipped with a crystal display. A few spectators were already seated. Jain and I sat down in the front row.

Below, "handlers" were preparing their players. Handler was a better word than pimp, though not as descriptive. The players were naked, with shaven heads. They lay on couches, with their heads all pointed toward the center. There, a multifaceted crystal rested on a pedestal. Cables snaked out of the pedestal's base. At the end of each cable was a standard cerebral helmet. The handlers were fastening the helmets to the heads of their players. Probes went into each ear canal—the bony os allowed precise alignment. Each player had a CNS stud implanted at the bregma of his skull, which completed the alignment triad. That was their only permanent cybernetic hardware. When the helmets were in place, thousands of microcapillary tubes pushed through skin and bone to gently touch cerebral cortex. The tubes were only a few microns in diameter— small enough that blood cells couldn't even escape through the holes they made. These filaments carried both electricity and neurotransmitters. One by one the handlers completed their work and went to sit in the lowest tier.

Eleven players lay still on their couches. Their bodies were bathed in light flickering from the surface of the central crystal. There were six women and five men. Their bodies had once been good-looking, but now most of them had become haggard with sallow skin and sagging flesh. Their faces were hidden by shadow.

The manager of the mindcasino announced that wagers could be placed and that the game would start in five minutes.

Jain leaned over and whispered in my ear: "Which one do you like?" Her tongue touched my earlobe. "Who shall we bet on?"

"I don't know. It doesn't matter. You're the handicapper."

"So I am. That's why I have you. But this bet is just for fun. Pick the one you like."

I glanced down. It really didn't matter. Tomorrow I would be one of the players. I picked the woman with the best-looking body. That sometimes worked with horses. "Number Five," I said to Jain.

She laughed after she saw who I had picked. "The body's not important. It's all in the mind for the dreamgame. But we'll try Five." She pressed her chargering into the console. Numbers flashed across the screen, recording her wager and listing the odds on each player. She leaned back, placing her head on my shoulder.

The dreamgame started. There was not much to see on the dais. Multihued lights swirled within the central crystal. The players lay still on their couches. The only movement was an occasional involuntary twitch of a muscle. All the action was within each display monitor. Numbers flashed along the side, changing continuously. Holographic images moved within the display crystal. They were abstractions—unrecognizable shapes, strange colors, random movements. But they made me feel uncomfortable watching. My penis stiffened. Arousal must be part of it. And there was something vaguely obscene about it all. I looked away. I actually felt embarrassed. Me, the former combrid. Heck, I'd seen lots worse than that in the war.

"How do you make sense of it?" I asked Jain, nodding toward the display.

"You wear a C-helmet, if you're into *that*." She pointed around the chamber. Some of the spectators were wearing helmets. "The images you see on the display are computer symbols." She gestured to the monitor. "You need more sensory capability than your eyes alone can provide to make them identifiable. You're 'seeing' tastes, smells, sounds, and feelings displayed on the screen. Visually, the symbols only provoke vague feelings in your mind." She looked at my groin and smiled. "As you've noticed. Do you want to wear a monitor helmet? Devotees consider it vulgar."

"No." I'd be wearing the real thing too soon. "What's happening to *them?*" I nodded toward the players. "How do you play the dreamgame?"

Jain leaned back and closed her eyes. She spoke precisely, as if reciting by rote: "They lay still because they're paralyzed with endolepsin. That frees their minds from the distraction of having a body. Then endocholine is squirted into their CNS studs—enough to speed up nervous transmission about ten times. You don't want the game to take too long. Through the combination of electrical stimulation and various neuropeptides, the filaments in their brains can actually extract their minds and engram their personas into that crystal." She opened her eyes and pointed to the dais. "It's a cortical crystal—a synthetic brain of molecular semiconductors arranged within the matrix of a radiacrystal that can transduce thought. That's where the game takes place, within the crystal."

"Of what does the game consist?"

"Anything. Everything. It's different each time. The

gestalt mind of eleven players decides the exact nature of their game. The hard wiring of the cortical crystal only dictates that there will be a game, and a winner and a loser. Sometimes anarchy prevails—each man for himself. Sometimes teams form—five against six, seven and four, even ten on one. What apparently happens is perceived differently by each player—each mind translates the symbols into images it understands. The symbols are the same, but their meanings are different. A computer has been programmed to keep track of the game. That was possible because the symbols are the same each game for every player."

"How do you win?"

"You defeat your opponent or opponents in the game your minds have decided to play. The computer awards points based on the complexity of the game and the arrangement of teams. For instance, if it were ten against one, the single player could win, even though he thought he lost, if he did better than his random chance against a team of ten opponents. Scoring can get quite complicated. All kinds of coups are involved. That's why you need a computer to keep track of it."

"And what happens when you lose?"

"Your handler loses your entry fee and the money she bet on you."

"Besides that. What can happen to the player?"

She looked at me and laughed. "Don't worry. You're ready to play the game. Your rehab regimen saw to that."

"Tell me what *can* happen." I knew the answer. I just wanted her to have to tell me the risks. Since I was the one who'd be taking them.

"Sometimes the players' minds don't get back to the right bodies. Particularly if one player *wants* to switch bodies with another. Some players are into that subroutine. Occasionally a mind gets lost entirely, usually during a rather nasty game. But that won't happen to you. You're too good. I made sure of that."

"I hope you're right." I liked my own body. I'd gone to considerable inconvenience to get the modifications it had. I wanted to keep it. But I had to take the risk. That was the only way I was going to find Nels. He had something to tell me.

Suddenly, the lights flashing from the cortical crystal dimmed. Likewise, the symbols on my display crystal faded. Numbers began blinking.

Jain put her hand on my leg and squeezed. "Number Five won. With good odds, too. We're a little over a grand to the good."

Below, the handlers began disconnecting their players. Eleven new ones would play the next game. Playing more than once a day risked brain damage.

"What number do you like for the next game?" Jain asked. "Your intuition might be hot tonight."

I didn't answer. I was watching Number Five being disconnected. She'd had a fine body once. A shame it had been wasted on a mindrider. Her handler removed her C-helmet. She sat up on her couch. My heart palpitated.

She was Grychn!

I was sure of it. The same amber eyes, the same proud nose. Even though her skull was bald, I knew it was Grychn. Even though the skin sagged on her face, I knew it was her. I almost called to her.

She looked up anyway. Her eyes focused in my direction for an instant, then she turned away. I wondered if she recognized me. She could not have—I'd been twelve the last time she saw me. Since then I'd had cybersurgery, hybridization, and cosmetic surgery. I hardly resembled the lad she knew. Now I was just another spectator. Soon I would just be another player.

Her handler placed a cape over her shoulders and led her away. I stared at the doorway after they had gone. I pushed down feelings that tried to surface. I didn't need feelings. Cold thought was required now. Grychn's presence complicated my plans a little. The spooks still might find her, even though she was Underground. If they did, Kramr would find out more about me from her. He already knew or suspected too much. I tried to remember if I'd told her about Nels. I couldn't be sure I hadn't. I knew what I should do. I could make it short and simple. Get rid of the handler as well. I still knew how to do things like that. There were twenty-three ways to do it unarmed. It might come to that eventually. But now I didn't have the stomach for it. Some Emperor I'd make—too spineless to get rid of a complication. Then a disturbing thought came to me—what if Grychn's body was no longer inhabited by her mind? She might have performed a body switch to escape the spooks. I would have to find out about that. If that was the case, things would be considerably simpler.

But I was going to have to find Nels as soon as possible. Dogs, I hated complications.

"Have you made up your mind yet?" Jain asked.

I looked down. A new game was about to start. "Let's go," I said. "I've seen enough already."

She shrugged. "Whatever you say. I've certainly seen enough dreamgames.'"

We left.

On the way home, I started peptide withdrawal. I got sick to my stomach and a chill ran up my back. We were in Jain's skimmer. We should be home in a few minutes.

Elf-fire flared overhead, as the nightly bombardment resumed. Some kind of celebration was taking place in the streets. Mnemone fumes rose like wisps of fog. Crowds of people sang and danced. As detonations boomed against the force-field above, the crowd surged back and forth. I realized they were dancing to the beat of pulsar barrages overhead. Clothes were flung to the street. Naked bodies coupled on their feet. Pelvic thrusts were synchronized to artillery detonations.

Jain saw me staring. "A new cult," she said, nodding toward the crowd. "Ghost dancers, they call themselves. They dance each night, awaiting the collapse of the force-field. It's become quite fashionable. Several times I've been tempted to try it." She laughed.

"But you have me instead."

"Yes, I have you." She smiled.

I closed my eyes. My intestines were knotted with cramps. My nose ran; I blew it into my fingers. Sweat beaded on my forehead. Before long the wet-dog shakes would begin. No addiction was stronger than peptide dependence, because no withdrawal was harder. I clenched my teeth together and closed my fists tightly. My guts felt like rats were chewing their way out.

It seemed like years before we got home. I had to walk bent over double from the cramps. I staggered into the house and fell down on a floor cushion. Jain strolled in and began to get undressed leisurely. I wasn't going to beg her. I hadn't reached that stage yet. I'd die first.

She unclasped her cape and hung it from a chair. Then she took off her skirt and carefully folded it, before placing it on top of the cape. She sat on another cushion, facing me, with her legs spread wide. A labial ring glinted beneath black pubic hair. Her diamond vial swung around her breasts. She slowly unwound her sandals' gaiters from around shapely calves.

Rats were digging for cheese inside my belly. I stood neck deep in ice water while a fiend worked a blowtorch across my face. I clenched my teeth to keep them from chattering—and to keep the vomit down my throat. I had the urge to kill her, and not for the first time. I could have done so easily, as sick as I was, in any of twenty-three different ways. I had enough strength for that. But I resisted the temptation. I still needed Jain Maure—not for the peptide to make me well, I could have obtained that myself, although I let her think otherwise—I needed her to be my handler and to take care of me while I was mindriding. That was something you couldn't do alone. Once I found Nels, Jain would be expendable. I flashed into a brief fantasy about what I'd do to her then. As sick as I was, it amused me.

She finished with her gaiters and removed her sandals. She smoothed away the marks the straps had left in the skin of her calves, while wiggling her toes. I pulled my knees tight against my chest. In a few more minutes, I'd start shaking. I hoped that by then the rats would have chewed their way out.

Jain looked up and pretended to notice me for the first time. "Poor baby!" she said with mock concern. "You're sick! Why didn't you say something?"

I couldn't say anything now. If I relaxed my throat, I'd start projectile vomiting.

She came over and kneeled beside me. "Poor baby! Let Mama help." She unscrewed the lid of her diamond vial and stuck her tongue into it. Light caught in her eyes in garnet shatterings. She leaned over to touch her tongue to my head. Peptide warmth flowed into my skull. Rats ran away and hid. My throat relaxed. I lay back, letting the warmth seep into bone and muscle. Jain removed my clothes. She ran her hands over my body, kneading the cramps out of my muscles. She felt my groin. There was nothing to feel. Penis and scrotum had pulled into their protective pouch during withdrawal. They always retreated there for safekeeping.

She bit my earlobe and whispered: "Let it down."

I relaxed my cremaster muscle. Why not? I would have sooner or later. My penis slid out. Jain stroked it, but it stayed limp. The old images still danced in my brain. She placed her lips over it and stiffened it with strokes of her tongue. Images faded away.

She kneeled over me. We coupled. She undulated her ass up and down. I cupped her buttocks, digging my fingers into her flesh.

An elf barrage started overhead.

Jain's face was caught in stop-motion by pulsar detonations: her eyes held vermillion fire, broad cheekbones cast shadows to the corners of her mouth, nostrils flared wide, a flush rose from her neck. Her hair danced crazily in the air.

"Did you know Number Five?" she asked suddenly.

"Who?" But I'd heard.

"The mindrider we bet on tonight. You looked at her as though you once knew her."

"She resembled someone I used to know."

"Forget about her. You're mine now. All mine. To play with as I wish. I made you pretty just for me." She dipped her tongue in another vial, then leaned forward. Her breasts brushed my face. I took a nipple into my mouth. I felt the wetness of her tongue on my head again. This time sex steroid set my brain quivering. I almost bit her nipple off. My fingers dug deeper into her flesh.

"Yes, yes!" she said. "Be rough. Make it hurt. I want a demon tonight."

Elf-fire played across the sky, probing for weaknesses in Chronus's defenses. The force-field yielded briefly nearby; a single pulsar beam stabbed down to set trees on fire, before the breach was sealed. For an hour the elven batteries concentrated on that area, encouraged by their transient success. The detonations were deafening. The light flashes were blinding. But both palled compared to the fire that burned inside my head. Lightning crashed along my nerves, as I was overcome by a testosterone storm.

I scratched and clawed. I bit. My thrusts lifted us both into the air as my pelvis crashed into her. Flesh bruised beneath mine. Blood trickled between us.

"Oh, yes!" Jain screamed. "Make it hurt."

The fire was a long time dying.

4

The scream of hawks had awakened me that morning.

Except for them, I was alone. They wheeled in the air outside, waiting for breakfast.

I stood on the balcony naked, throwing the hawks their scraps of meat. If only they could land on my belly and pluck out the rats that skulked within. But they had no interest in imaginary rats.

After feeding the hawks, I stayed inside the rest of the day. I had nowhere to go. My bridges were burned. I thought of Grychn, living the depraved life of a mindrider. Somewhat out of character for the Grychn I'd known. She must have traded bodies. I wondered if she'd escaped after the body switch. She must have. But even one dose of neuropeptide applied directly to the brain was enough to produce an addiction almost impossible to run away from. But she must have escaped. Kramr would have come after me by now if he knew what was in her dreams. But it was possible she hadn't switched bodies. If that was the case, the spooks should have located her by now. Unless they had trouble penetrating the Underground. But they would send down a chameleon eventually. Then they'd find Grychn, if she was still in her body. Too many ifs. My thoughts were poor company, indeed.

Jain Maure came home early. She insisted on making love before we went to the mindcasino. The euphemism wasn't the proper term for what we did. She said we had to keep my tolerance for peptide high—that was the best way to make sure I'd be in control of the dreamgame. I went along with her—what other choice did I have? I don't remember all that I did to her, and I don't care to. Eventually she was satisfied.

Then we went to the Underground.

Elf-fire already blazed overhead. The entire dome glowed with absorbed energy. Rows of discrete flashes walked across the sky as barrage after barrage came from coordinated pulsar cannon. Occasionally the field would weaken and a pulsar quantum stabbed down to implode in the city itself. Fire sirens wailed. Emergency hoverbuses raced back and forth overhead. Chronus was dying that night. I knew then that the rescue fleet would arrive too late—even if the siege was lifted tomorrow, our salvation would come too late.

Ghost dancers already danced to the beat of elven artillery. Their naked bodies surged with each wave of bombardment. We had to force our way through a crowd of them to get to the portal to the Underground. Fingers plucked at my clothing. Their chanting beat into my mind with primeval intensity. Naked flesh pressed against me, hot and sweaty. Bare breasts bounced close to my face as dancers leaped. I had the urge to strip off my clothes and join their ritual.

But I had my own passion. When the end came, I wanted to be in a position to assume control. For that, I needed a timestone.

Jain and I finally reached the portal and entered it. We began our descent. We again traced a roundabout route to the casino chamber. I let her lead me. I could have found the way myself. But there was no sense letting her know that.

In a corridor outside the chamber, we paused. I peeled off my body stocking and hung it from a hook. Jain smiled. "You look splendid," she said. I did indeed. She'd done a good job on my surgery. And she was the one bruised and bleeding from our sex play.

We entered the chamber via the players' door. Ten couches were occupied. One waited for me. I glanced at the other players' faces—I did not see Grychn. Not that it mattered. Her mind was most likely elsewhere. I briefly wondered what Nels would look like. He could be any one of the players. The only way I could find out was to play the dreamgame. I lay down. Jain fitted my helmet to my head. Cold plastic probes plugged my ears, pressing tight against bone. Something snapped onto my CNS stud. Jain leaned over to kiss my lips. I closed my eyes.

A thousand needles pricked my scalp. My head started itching. I tried to scratch and found I couldn't. Nor could I move any other muscle. I couldn't even open my eyes. Then I began to get numb, starting at my toes and flowing upward. I seemed to float. The faint light that diffused through my eyelids dimmed to total darkness. Sound quieted to absolute silence. Cold and warmth became as one. I no longer smelled my own sour sweat. The bitter taste of fear was gone, replaced by nothing. All sensation disappeared—I was a detached sentience, suspended in an infinite void. Terror formed like a cancer growing. I almost went mad from the fear of sensory deprivation.

Then I was a combrid again. War had never gone away. Its grim familiarity was comforting, except for my predicament.

I lay hidden in a jumble of crystal foliage. I was alone —the rest of the patrol was blown away. Their bodies lay nearby. Elves had ambushed us with mortar fire. Before long, they'd come in person to finish the job. There wasn't much I could do to stop them—my legs were blown off. All that was left of them were two stumps. Combat armor had sealed itself and the wounds. I wasn't going to bleed to death. But my mobility was somewhat impaired. (Somewhere, I knew this was a dream, just part of a game. But even a dream was better than the isolation of total sensory deprivation.)

I had to do something. I crawled out of my concealment, pulling myself along with my arms. My stumps dragged uselessly behind. I began checking my buddies: they were all dead, from first shirt to PFC. The comman's pack looked intact. I removed his longcom transceiver and snapped it into my battle pack. Maybe I could call the cavalry to the rescue. Ha, ha. Not very funny. We were the cavalry. But I was wounded. Give me a break. I filled my ammo pouches with clips scavenged from the others. Wouldn't do them much good. Might not do me any good, either.

A pulsar beam exploded next to me. I rolled behind a log, turning my sensors to max gain at the same time.

Across the clearing I could see an elf platoon advancing. There were about ten of them. I had to get the L.A. out. I couldn't walk. I couldn't crawl fast enough to matter. That left me one other choice. I pulled myself up with my arms until I tottered on my stumps. Then I kicked on my thrusters. I shot up into the air. More pulsar fire greeted me. I put in a little lateral thrust and entered the forest. Thrusters weren't much good among trees. If you tried to go faster than the minimum, you risked hitting a tree and breaking your neck. Also, one's legs normally helped steer. I'd lost my rudder. But I had to use thrusters. I didn't have much choice.

I nudged a flicker of acceleration from them, moving ahead slowly through the trees. I didn't want to go too fast. I couldn't steer at all. When I came to a tree, I caught it and pushed myself aside with my arms. I was making some progress, but not much. The catsucking elves would catch me for sure. They could fly a lot faster than me. I needed a little help.

I put out a distress call, giving my approximate coordinates. Base acknowledged my call and said they'd dispatched a gunship. Hooray. All I had to do was to stay ahead of the elves until it got here. That was going to cut it pretty close.

It did. When I finally heard the whine of a gunship overhead, I could see the elves behind me, moving in. Pulsar beams ricocheted from crystal foliage. But a moving target was hard to hit. Especially if you were moving at the same time.

"Hey, flyboy. What kept you?"

"Thaaat yooou, little buuuddie?" The pilot's speech was distorted by resonation from his gravturbines. "Wheeere are yooou?"

I flipped on my transponder. The gunship whined past.

"I gooot a fiiix nooow. Yooou waaant sooome ooordnance ooon the groooound?"

"I sure do. Give me all you've got." The elves were getting too close for comfort. "You need a marker?"

"Yooou bet."

I launched a smoke. The grenade popped above the elves, sending red laser smoke up through the trees. "Blood marks the spot."

"Maaax is hooot. Maaax is rooolling. Cooome to saaave his little buuuddie."

The gunship rolled overhead and came in skimming the treetops. I stopped to watch. Pulsar beams fanned down, cutting a hundred-meter-wide swath. Trees exploded into crystalline shards. Leaves puffed into vapor. Elves fell to ground smoking. All but one. Nine out of ten wasn't bad. But somehow the gunship's pulsar's missed one. He glided in a clearing that hadn't been there a moment before. He seemed as slow as a fat butterfly. I couldn't miss. I squeezed off a burst of pulsar fire. I didn't miss. The elf crumpled and fell.

"Gooood shoooooting," the pilot said. "Hooold tight. I'll seeend dooown a rooope."

The gunship couldn't land in triple-canopy forest. It hovered overhead. A cable and snap was lowered. All I had to do was attach the snap to a hook on my pack and I would be hauled up to the gunship.

But something was wrong. My vision blurred. I felt dizzy. I looked down. Blood was spurting from both stumps. My wounds had opened. My armor's autotourniquet hadn't been designed to take the stress of so much movement. You were supposed to stay still when you were wounded.

The cable was beside me. The snap banged against my helmet. All I had to do was hook it to my pack. But I couldn't see it clearly. Every time I reached, it moved out of the way. My vision narrowed as though I was peering through pinholes. I lost control of my thrusters. I began to fall. I never knew if I hit the ground.

Jain Maure removed my helmet and helped me sit. I felt groggy. We left the chamber; she put her arm around me to support me. As I got dressed in the outer corridor, I said: "Sorry about that. I'll do better next time."

"What are you talking about?"

"I got myself killed in the mindgame. Kind of botched the game for you."

"You did splendidly. You won. And against ten-to-one odds."

"I'm certain that I died. If anybody won, it would have been the gunship pilot. He was the only one left."

"You didn't count right. There were ten elves, you, as a combrid, and the pilot. That makes twelve players. One too many. You were also the pilot. You split your mind into two players—one was sacrificed so the other could win. No one has tried that tactic before. You played a masterful game—I knew you had good instincts. We're going to win a lot of money, you and me."

On the way back to Jain's house, I realized that I had no idea if Nels had been in the game. I'd killed the other players without knowing their identities. If I was going to find him, I was going to have to change my tactics. After I found him, he was going to have to be made to talk. I mulled over the problem. There had to be some kind of strategy, some way to manipulate the game for my purposes.

Peptide withdrawal started before I could figure out a solution. My habit was too massive for the small doses I'd received during the game to block withdrawal. Chills, sweats, and nausea kept me from thinking about much else until we arrived home.

Jain wanted to play another kind of game that night: she administered me endophetamine laced with sex steroid.

The initial rush of testosterone had subsided; the preliminaries were over. Our sex game had been almost as much fun as when I'd been a combrid. A firefight still jazzed up the old endocrines. Blood lust made the other kind that much better.

Now the fun was over.

Endophetamine glowed in my brain, waxing ever stronger. The simple sexuality of androgen steroid began to warp—my thoughts started raveling with an emerging psychosis.

I lay naked on wombskin with Jain Maure. Red teeth marks faded from her skin; the flush in her face ebbed. In elf-light, her eyes brightened. She smiled, showing her teeth. They still gleamed blue.

"Why do you smile?" I asked.

"From thinking about my splendid new player. And games to come."

"Games to come?"

"We've just started on the cycle. You're a good player.

You'll last a long time. Father would approve of my selection."

I remembered a question I'd never asked. "Why did you choose me to be a mindrider?"

She hesitated. "Promise you won't tell?" She giggled. "No, I guess you won't. I wanted you because your brain is still a combrid's brain—its vitalium cyberwires augment the filaments of a cerebral helmet. And I had access to your medical files. Your mind has some unique qualities, not quite identified nor defined by the standard tests. They almost put you in the Pathic Division, before deciding it would be too difficult to get those latent abilities to blossom. They weren't sure what your latent abilities were, so they didn't want to take a chance by stimulating them. Psychesurgeons can be fuddy-duddies sometimes."

"But you know what they are?"

"No. But I'm willing to take a chance. I know you can apply more mental energy than an ordinary mindrider. Any combrid can do that. You can shape a dreamgame to a pattern of your choosing, one where you'll have the advantage. And you'll be able to do other things as you gain experience. Already you split into two personas— nobody has done that before. You'll become a master of the dreamgame—a champion mindrider. I was lucky to find you. Most discharged combrids have some brain damage. You'll do much better than they did." She ran a fingernail over my belly, cutting patterns in the skin.

The craziness I'd been holding back grew in my mind. Control began slipping.

"How did you happen to come to Chronus?" I asked, trying to clear my thoughts with banality. I would not be lucid much longer.

"My mother was quite religious—she pledged me as a neophyte to the Temple of the Dead."

Somehow that was supposed to explain something, but my mind couldn't grasp it.

"I'm afraid I failed her," she continued. "The discipline was too much. I wasn't strong enough to stay. I think perhaps I could now. I've been practicing. But it's too late now, of course." She smiled apologetically. "Only virgins need apply."

Endophetamine embers were fanned to flame. I pushed the madness away briefly. I had to ask her one more question. "Your other mindriders, the ones before me. What happened to them?" Angry fists beat at a door in my mind. I put a mental shoulder against it.

Her finger found an orifice and probed. I held it tight with a sphincter. Jain sighed. "They failed me. They weren't quite strong enough to play games with me." She kissed my cheek. "You'll do much better."

The door in my mind burst. A frenzied mob rushed in, waving torches and brandishing pitchforks. I let myself be swept up into their ranks. My mind caught fire.

Jain Maure looked into my eyes. "It's time," she whispered.

We were on the balcony—both naked.

The sky burned with elf-fire. My mind burned with endophetamine. A thousand flashbulbs winked overhead. Sometimes a beam stabbed down—then a real fire burned. Smoke billowed from scores of smoldering buildings, to hang over Chronus as a gray cloud. Details were obscured by murk. In the park below, ghost dancers cavorted wildly. The smoke made them appear like naked specters arising from the ground.

Jain leaned across the balcony's railing; her wrists and ankles were bound to it with silver chains. The stroboscopic flashes from above froze her writhings in stop-motion.

I worked an alphalash over her body. Static hummed in the air. As I swung the whip, sparks fanned out as though I twirled a sparkler. Each time the lash touched her skin, it left tattoos of glowing embers. Wisps of smoke rose from lines of fire that swirled over her shoulders, across her back, around her buttocks, and down her thighs. My nostrils were filled with the smell of scorched epidermis. As the lash struck, she turned her body to meet it, letting it brush across her breasts and belly.

My mind was still held by endophetamine; my body was still ruled by synthetic passion. But the initial frenzy had waned. Deep inside was a small zone of reason, like the eye of a flaming hurricane.

I flashed to remembered glimpses of my childhood, when it was I shackled to a wall and peptide madness gleamed from my father's eyes as he played a lash upon my body. The symbolism did not escape me. I remembered the harmony of hurt sung by alpha particles imbedded in cutaneous nerve endings. How I had howled and shrieked then. Jain only moaned each time the lash struck. And I was fairly certain they weren't sounds of pain.

A pulsar beam cracked past, not ten meters from the balcony. My skin tingled with ionization. Ozone stung my nostrils. I looked down. The pulsar quantum had struck into the crowd of ghost dancers below. Bodies flew into the air and fell back into a crater in the lawn, there to be burned by white-hot lava. Flames swirled high. The other dancers continued leaping around the rim of the crater, dancing in clouds of smoke and dust.

My arm kept swinging the lash.

Jain's entire body blazed with its own blue fire. She touched her tongue to her nose. Copper gleamed in her eyes. Then she called to me: "Now! It's time. Come to me now."

I dropped the lash and crossed the balcony. She leaned out over the rail, with her back toward me, spreading her legs. I stood close behind her, cupping her breasts with my hands, entering her from behind. Her buttocks settled against my pelvis, rocking to my thrusts. Her skin burned against mine, impressing a reversed pattern of fire into my flesh.

Above, the elven barrage continued. Detonations beat like rhythmic thunder. All of Chronus was illuminated in stark, flickering light. Flame licked up from burning rooftops. Smoke billowed up to hang like luminescent clouds. Ghost dancers cavorted in their death dance. Jain and I stayed coupled, undulating to destructive rhythms. Endophetamine throbbed in my brain.

It was crazy, all of it. But the rational island in my mind made sense out of the insane pattern of chaotic images. Before the fires died, it had figured out how to play the dreamgame.

There would never be another player quite like me.

5

———

The terrorist scowled at me, then spat in my face. I hit
her across the mouth with the back of my hand, splitting
her lip. I wiped the blood off my trouser leg.

I nodded to my assistants, each a schizoid persona of
myself. They fastened an interrogation helmet over her
head, despite her struggles. A little shot of endolepsin
slowed those down.

Then I began playing with her mind by tapping buttons
on a console, which caused her brain to receive various
chemical, hormonal, and electrical stimulations. The resulting mental images were picked up and translated by
a computer, which had been programmed to look for a
particular set of patterns. Her mind didn't fit into those
patterns. My helpers disconnected her from the I-helmet
and turned her over to two guards (more personas of me),
who hauled her off to her cell.

Next, please.

I was playing the old game of Search and Destroy. Only
this time I'd wised up a little. I was the spook calling the
shots. Have you grasped the simple eloquence of my
strategy? I wanted to find the mind of a mindrider named
Nels, who now inhabited another body. To do that I had
to question every other mindrider in each dreamgame.
What better way to achieve my goal than play a spook
interrogator? I'd found I could establish the pattern of the
dreamgame. I could also split my mind into multiple per-

sonas. Each time I played I was able to form more. I'd spent six months as a combrid. I was good at it or I wouldn't have survived half a year. Images of war were too vivid ever to forget. And they were too powerful for civilians to resist. I made the other players play my game, with my rules.

I made them play the Interrogation Game.

The other ten mindriders all became terrorist guerrillas. They were the bad guys. I was the good guys, having split my mind into a multitude of other personas: a company of Ghost Cavalry, gunship pilots, guards and jailers, field chameleons, and the me, me—Chief Spook Detrs, whom other mindriders began calling the Inquisitor. I took vain pleasure in the sobriquet.

The rules of the game were simple: ten terrorists tried to hide, my Ghost Cavalry captured them, they were brought to my spook house where they were interrogated by me and my computer. Sooner or later I'd play against Nels. When I did, my computer would recognize him. Then he would be made to talk.

It was an easy game to play. At least for me. Since I always used the same format and the same cast of characters, I could set it up effortlessly. Each time I played, I could maintain more personas and add more complexity to the background. Since we played my game, using my rules, I always won. The first few times a few players had escaped, but not now. I was quite methodical now. But then I wasn't playing the dreamgame for fun; I had a reason. Of course I was also winning. That meant Jain Maure was making lots of money.

The only problem was that my dreamtime began to seem as real as when I was awake. I sometimes confused which was real. The Interrogation Game was pure and simple. The rules stayed the same. Its pattern was constant. There was purpose and meaning to it. The same could not be said of my waking world, where ghost dancers cavorted to the rhythm of the elven barrage, where Chronus burned nightly, where my mind was battered by the synthetic passions of neuropeptides. My dreams were clearer and certainly more pleasant than that reality.

Even Jain Maure's madness was inconstant.

Some nights she would want to play her usual sex games. On those occasions she would overload my mind with peptides until I shared her madness and would play her way. I could only remember glimpses of those nights: sparks flying from an alphalash, bubbles rising from the nostrils of a face I held underwater, the hum of sonic shackles, the slap of flesh against flesh, the trickle of blood.

Other nights she played a different game. She would at first administer only enough peptide to keep me from withdrawing. The sex afterward was perfunctory and almost tender. She gave me endiazepam to help me sleep. Recurring dreams caused insomnia. Endiazepam chased the demons out of my dreamtime. It was also an amnesiac. I only remembered snatches of the dreams. The fragments were disturbing enough: a disembodied voice kept asking me questions, making me tell it all about the dreamgame, all about what I'd learned from my interrogations. The voice was familiar, but I couldn't identify it. And there was sex in the dreamtime. Jain had become an androgynous creature—a woman with a man's genitalia. I retracted my genitals into their pouch. When we coupled, her penis slid against mine in my pouch, caressing it, until our warm ejaculates mingled within me. I was a little bothered by the symbolism of that dream.

I knew my mind was getting close to a permanent psychosis. Eventually it would refuse to leave the structure of synthebrain, where order and purpose could be imposed on the chaos of the time matrix. It would refuse to go back to an organic brain buffeted by insane images. I would lose my body. I would never find my way back.

But until I located Nels, I had to keep playing the game. More than once, I wondered if his mind was still around to find. Perhaps he too had fled to a more rational microcosm. Maybe I should abandon the search while I could still escape with my sanity.

But I couldn't.

Besides, something happened to keep me looking.

I was conducting my usual interrogation.

Ghost Cavalry rounded up guerrillas. Guards brought them to my chamber. My computer extracted mental images from their minds. The usual routine.

Then an alarm gong sounded.

A prisoner had escaped. That hadn't happened to me for

a while. Either my control was slipping, or the escapee had an unusually strong psyche.

No matter. I would regain control of the situation. It might be Nels trying to escape.

I loosed the dogs. I sent guards searching my spook house. I surrounded it with a moat of murky water, filled with toothsome swimmers. Then I began checking intruder sensors.

I had become quite proficient at changing the reality of the game matrix. That kept the other mindriders off balance.

In a few minutes I had found my fugitive. I smiled to myself. I mean, they could run, but where could they hide? I decided to play a game of Cat and Mouse. I began re-routing corridors and locking doors. I sent guards and dogs to the chase, to keep the prisoner moving. The escapee frantically ran down hallways, trying various doors. The ones that were open were the ones I chose to leave unlocked. The only way out of the maze I'd created led into my chamber. I waited. Cat and Mouse? More like Spider and Fly. I considered changing myself into a giant spider, then thought it might be a little too theatrical.

One door remained untried. My dogs closed, teeth snapping. The escapee had no choice, and opened the door to the chamber where I waited.

She entered.

I managed to lock the door behind her, before my mind went numb.

She was Grychn.

Or at least my mind had made her appear like Grychn: amber eyes, haughty lips, eyebrows white as ermine, a body proud of its youth. No such body had been one of the ten other players. I'd looked before the game had started. There was only one reason why my mind would put a psyche in that body.

"Who are you, Inquisitor?" It was Grychn's voice. "Another spook sent to trick me? I've already told you all I know."

She didn't recognize me. She couldn't. In the role of Inquisitor, I'd made myself a combrid again. I wore the red beret and silver skull of Corps Intelligence.

I let my body change back to human form.

"Who are you now?" Her forehead wrinkled. "You look familiar. . . ."

She still didn't recognize me. The last time she'd seen my human face, I'd been twelve years old. I let myself become younger, until I was the boy she remembered.

Grychn gasped. "Marc! Is it really you? Tell me it's not another trick."

I became my current self again. "No tricks. It's me. I'm the Inquisitor."

She was still suspicious. Who could blame her?

"Prove to me you're Marc," she said.

I thought for a moment. "Do you remember a ring I once wore? Do you remember seeing the two of us being cut to pieces by a sonic whip? Do you remember what we had to do to keep that from happening?"

She was in my arms, kissing my lips. The ten years missing made no difference.

I changed the interrogation chamber into a bedchamber. An open fireplace blazed, casting both warmth and light on us. We lay on warm wombskin, soothed by its pulsations. Our bodies were naked and wet with sweat. They seemed to blend into each other, becoming one. We made love to ourselves: touching secret places, feeling again the joy of new love, discovering shared pleasure, basking in a melding of male and female orgasm.

A long time later, we separated.

Our bodies lay side by side, touching enough for comfort. We started talking, filling in ten years of gaps.

"Why did you want to become a renegade terrorist?" I asked in our fused minds. "What made you forsake your own kind?"

"You did."

"I did?"

"After you left me, I needed something to fill the emptiness you had left. I'm afraid I fell in with unsavory companions. Causes can be made to be more important than people. Besides, I was young and impressionable. It was fun to go to secret meetings with passwords and codes and safe houses. But sooner or later, it stops being a game. People get killed. I had to leave Earth. A bomb went off prematurely. The elves took me in; I was well trained in terrorist techniques."

"But why on Titan?"

"No particular reason. One place is as good as another. There's only one enemy, after all."

"The Terran Empire?"

"Certainly. We Terrans are old and decadent. The human race as a species is declining toward extinction. Hybrids will rule the future. Old Earth has to use hybrids such as yourself to fight her battles. That should tell it all. Unaltered humans are obsolete, fit only to be kept in zoos as curiosities. The species is old and tired."

"Then why are you unaltered? You are not a hybrid."

"I don't know. Maybe I have a sense of nostalgia. Maybe I haven't yet decided which kind of creature I should become. What creature would you like me to be?"

"I like you fine the way you are."

"Then you don't yet know what I am. No matter." She paused, thinking.

"Whatever happened to the timestone?" She licked my ear.

"I lost it."

"I'm glad of that." My silence caused her to guess the truth. "There's another one, isn't there?" She paused for a moment. "So that's why the Inquisitor bit? You're trying to find the other timestone." She thought for a bit longer, remembering. I'd told her too much once. Way too much. "Someone knows where the other timestone is. A mind-rider knows, who used to be a miner named Nels." She smiled. "Nels is still here, still mindriding."

"You know him?" That sparked my interest.

"I didn't say that. I met Nels once, in a dreamgame. Not long ago, I think. But it's hard to get much out of Nels, with all the mumbling and fumbled thoughts. Of course, it could all be an act. Nels is awfully scared of something."

"He told you where the stone was hidden?"

"No. Nels's ramblings aren't that coherent."

"You're not telling me something."

"No, I'm not. But it's nothing important. Just a little joke to amuse myself. Let me have my fun. There's not much left. Ask Nels about it."

"Too bad," I said. "Now I'll still have to find him." It was a shame Grychn couldn't tell me what I had to know to find the timestone. But at least I knew Nels was still mindriding. I would find him eventually.

"You want the other timestone, don't you?"

"Of course. I had big plans when you knew me in my youth. I still have big plans. Bigger. A squandered youth does have the advantage of broadening one's horizons."

Grychn smiled, then kissed my cheek tenderly. Almost regretfully. "Even if you find Nels and the timestone's location is revealed to you, you'll not be able to get it."

"Why not?"

"Mindriders are trapped by peptide. They never leave. Peptide withdrawal always brings them back. I found that out. So shall you."

I knew all about that problem. But I'd figured out how to beat it. I changed the subject. "How did you manage to escape from the spooks?" *How much did you tell them?* was what I wanted to ask.

She laughed, apologetically. "They were careless. An elf pulsar beam hit the detention area, knocking out a wall. There weren't enough guards to contain all the prisoners who tried to escape. I got away in the confusion."

Spooks were never careless. "Then what happened?" I should have guessed the truth then. But I didn't.

"I went Underground to hide. After a week or so I met a man named Jry who said he could show me an old escape tunnel to the surface that exited beyond the force-field. He wasn't giving away the information. He made me play a dreamgame before he would tell. And then another and another. What could I do? I was desperate. Before long, I was addicted to peptide. Then it was too late to run. I live here in the Underground now." She smiled ruefully. "I eventually found the tunnel on my own. I even tried to leave then. Withdrawal forced me to come back. More than once. There is no peptide to be obtained in the bush."

"Where were you going?"

"I have a trigee racer hidden in the forest a hundred kilometers west."

That interested me. I needed to know more. Mobility was always good to have. I'd been wondering how I was going to get off of Titan.

"Will you tell me where the tunnel is to be found?"

"Why not? It won't do you any good, though. There's no escape for a mindrider."

"Tell me anyway."

She did. I memorized the directions.

"I want to see you again," I said. I think I actually meant it.

"You will. In another mindgame."

"In real time."

"That doesn't happen with mindriders. Jry wouldn't allow it. My handler is quite possessive. Jain Maure wouldn't like you seeing me, either."

"You know Jain Maure?"

"Every mindrider has heard of Dr. Pepper."

"I do as I please."

"Then you're fooling yourself, if you think that. You do what Dr. Pepper tells you to do. You'll realize that eventually. Mindriders are slaves to the pimp that feeds their head with peptides. You don't want to see me as I really am. You won't like it. Besides, it's better in the dreamtime. Then we can be as we once were—a way we'll never be again. You'll discover that, too."

"Tell me where you stay, anyway."

"I dare not. I'm afraid of him."

She didn't have to tell me. I was the Inquisitor, remember. The interrogation helmet and computer and my other trappings of office were just for show. I mean, it was all a game I constructed in my head. She was in my dream. I could slip unnoticed into her head. I did. I glimpsed the location in her mind. I didn't have time to peep any deeper. If only I had glimpsed the truth then. Things would have been considerably easier later on. But she didn't know the truth.

Our minds were pulled apart. The game ended. The dream was finished. I had the momentary urge not to go back, to stay in cortical crystal and keep Grychn with me. I could have. I had the power. But I still had my ambitions. I hadn't given up yet.

I let myself be pulled into a void, then felt my body forming around my mind.

I sat up on my couch and looked around. Jain Maure stood behind me. She removed the helmet from my head.

Other mindriders were sitting up also, removing their helmets. One of them was Grychn. Which one? She hadn't said anything about a body switch, so she must be in her own body. Then I recognized her handler, the same one that had been with her before. So she was still in her own body. Almost. I scarcely recognized her, even knowing who she was. She looked haggard and worn. Her breasts hung like flaps of skin on a chest with the ribs showing through. She was skin and bone everywhere. Her eyes were sunken into her skull. How could she have changed so much since I last saw her? Peptides had taken their toll. But it couldn't have been that long ago.

She looked at me. Recognition did not show in her eyes. Yet she knew what I looked like now—I'd shown her in the dreamgame. Then she finally recognized me. She glanced at her handler, Jry. He was looking elsewhere. She let a little smile tug at her lips. Why had it taken her so long?

Her manager snapped a chain to the gold collar around her neck and led her off. She looked back once and smiled. Apologetically again.

Jain Maure leaned over and whispered in my ear: "How do you like her? Not quite what you had in mind, eh?"

"Who are you talking about?"

"Your old girl friend. That strumpet." She nodded toward Grychn being led naked on a leash.

"What do you know about her?"

"Do you think you can keep any secrets from me? I know all about your childhood sweetheart. But you can have her in your dreams. As long as you keep winning for me. You can fuck her in your mind. I have your body. You'll be mine as long as I want you." Something snapped in her hand.

Then Jain led me away by a chain attached to a collar around my neck. When had that happened? I didn't remember. I wondered what else I'd forgotten.

We left the Underground.

We climbed into Jain's skimmer. She snapped my chain to a hook inside.

Chronus was a dying city. Elf-fire blazed each night. More and more beams made it through the force-field. Once-elegant mansions had become charred ruins. Rubble littered the street. Ghost dancers roamed as mobs, breaking windows, looting, burning buildings. Drowned bodies were found in swimming pools each morning. Other bodies lay beside craters in lawns.

Yet the illusion of life went on. Parties still lasted until dawn. Polo ponies still pounded on turf. Tennis matches were still held. Fox and grouse were still hunted. A damn inconvenience to have to fish a body out of your pool before you could swim your daily laps. Maybe if you ignored the bombardment, it would go away. Each day we were told the fleet would be here soon to lift the siege.

Jain Maure and I still lived in her house atop Mt. Erubus. So far the beams had missed us. The wooded slopes were charred black, though, and pocked with craters. Dead trees stood like skinny skeletons.

When we got home, I was still bothered by Grychn's failure to recognize me at first. I'd begun to suspect a grim reality. I looked at myself in a holomirror. A stranger stood before me. A typical pephead. What had happened to the splendid creature I had once been? Now I looked like a famine victim—thin and wasted. My skin was splotched and mottled. My nose had become a sharp beak. How long had I been ravaged by peptide? I tried to remember. Days had become weeks. How many? I wasn't sure. Too long. I had to find Nels quickly now. Before I became too wasted to continue the search.

Jain was in one of her talkative moods that night. She only gave me enough endorphine to give me a gentle buzz. We lay together watching pulsar detonations play overhead.

"How is your search going? Have you found her yet?"

"What?" I had told Jain nothing about what I was doing. Or about Nels.

"Come on, I know what pattern your dreamgames are taking. The other mindriders call you the Inquisitor."

"It's just a way to play the game."

"Did your little girl friend tell you anything?"

"Like I said, it's just a way to play. Nothing else."

"You're looking for someone. Go ahead. You won't be able to do anything about it when you find her. Unless I let you. Don't forget, I own you now."

"It's just my way of playing. A way to win. You like winning, don't you?"

"A shrewd tactic. A smart way to play." Green eyes peered into mine. "Let me know when you find whom you seek. You may as well. You'll save yourself a lot of discomfort." Her eyes blinked. There was something wrong about them. She leaned over me, letting her breasts brush across my face. A wet tongue touched the top of my head.

Endiazepam flowed into my brain like warm summer rain. I went to sleep.

The dream came.

A voice asked me questions, making me repeat the answers over and over. I told the voice all about Grychn, all about Nels. It seemed to know about them, anyway. I said I hadn't found Nels, that I was still looking. Finally the voice stopped bothering me. . . . I was on my hands and knees. Someone penetrated me from behind. I felt the thrusts deep inside. A body pressed against my back; full breasts pushed on my shoulder blades. I turned my head. Jain smiled, green eyes flashed. She quickened her thrusts, slapping against my buttocks. Her hand found my penis and began stroking it, synchronizing the jerks of her hand with her pelvic undulations. As my penis squirted over her fingers, I felt her ejaculate hot in my bowels. Then her tongue touched my head. Sleep numbed my limbs. The dream faded to oblivion.

When I woke, Jain lay beside me. What I remembered of the dream bothered me. My hand stroked the inside of her legs, finding the warm place between them. Her moist vault opened for my finger. Nothing wrong there. Why the dream, then?

Something tickled between my legs. I felt wetness with my finger. I touched it to my lips, tasting the saltiness of blood.

Why the dream?

6

_____

The next day, while Jain made her rounds at the hospital, I went to the Underground by myself. But not to play a dreamgame. There was one final preparation to be made, while I still had the strength.

First I went to a storage garage I'd rented some time ago. I retrieved two heavy cases. I carried both to the portal of the Underground. The vark on duty there barely glanced up at me.

The corridors beneath Chronus were nearly deserted at this hour—its denizens had retreated to their holes. I followed the directions Grychn had given me, winding a labyrinthine path through the old mine tunnels, unused by the current inhabitants of Chronus. Eventually I came to an air lock—on the other side would be swirling hydrocarbons at a hundred below. And freedom.

I hid the cases nearby, in a blind tunnel, burying them beneath loose rubble.

Everything was ready now.

If I could only find Nels and the timestone.

My mind grew weaker.

Each dreamgame became harder to manage. I started pulling back personas, maintaining only those absolutely necessary. Subtleties were dropped for raw brutality in my interrogations. I began to deserve my sobriquet. But before long, even violence would fail.

But I saw Grychn several more times. In a dreamgame.

Each time was better than the last. When we made love, we truly made love—we became one gestalt being. We shared all the pain and joy that had happened to each of us during the last ten years apart. I held only one thing back—I never told her that I had been the combrid who had captured her for Kramr. What she held back I didn't find out until later.

And each time, it was harder to go back to bodies ravaged by peptide addiction. More and more, I had the urge to keep her with me in the casino's cortical crystal. Without minds, our bodies would die. Our minds would only survive for a few hours of real time in the crystal. But it would seem forever in dreamtime. We could be who we had not been for a long time. Didn't the perception of an event make it so? If we perceived an eternity of happiness, wouldn't it then be? The notion was very tempting. But each time I resisted, my will to do so was less.

I knew also that when the time came for me to make my escape, it would be hard to leave her behind. But I couldn't take along any excess baggage.

My strange night dreams kept coming back to haunt me. The same voice talked to me, low and persistent, making me tell everything that had happened during my interrogations. And I kept flashing to images of Jain Maure with a penis, engaging in disturbing bisexuality.

I decided I had become mad.

But my interrogations continued.

My hawks were the only constant in an equation of variables. Each day they waited for me to feed them. They would come both morning and evening, to wheel in the air outside the balcony.

That day, I forgot to feed them in the morning. I'd slept through the day, drugged with both peptides and accumulating fatigue. It was almost dark when I finally roused myself from bed. They had waited patiently. Their shrieks and whistles greeted me as I came out on the balcony with a bowl of meat.

Already, elf-fire raged overhead.

I threw bloody chunks high. The hawks grabbed them in midair with their talons. Then they came to roost on the railing and tore at the meat with their beaks. I went inside for another bowl.

As I was coming back, a flash of light blinded me. An instant later a thunderclap knocked me sprawling. My ears rang from the detonation. My nostrils stung with ozone fumes. And I smelled something else.

I crawled out to the balcony. A section of railing was missing. The balcony was littered with feathers and a few still fluttered down. I found one body. Its bright eyes were already dimming. I smoothed its feathers as best I could, then flung it into the air, watching it fall to the park below. I sat on the balcony in ebbing light and cried. I hadn't cried for a long time. But I'd lost my only friends.

A little while later, peptide withdrawal started.

I pulled my legs against my chest, resting my chin on my knees. A rigor shook me. My teeth chattered. Sweat began beading on my skin. Rats played tag with each other inside me.

Pulsar beams stabbed out of the sky like linear lightning. But no more came close. The one that had hit earlier had been a random thing, a brief weakening in the field overhead. But I wanted another to follow. I wanted to be released from the pain.

Jain Maure was late coming home. My habit was such that I needed peptide before the mindgame. She knew that. Sometimes she let me suffer a little. But I was remembering each indignity. Her time would come.

Now the rats decided to start digging.

I heard footsteps inside. It was about time she got home. I waited on the balcony. I wasn't going to crawl to her.

The footsteps came closer, pausing at the door to the balcony. I sat still, huddled next to the wall. A figure stepped out.

"Ah, there you are." I knew the voice.

Black formal boots stepped into my view. I gradually raised my eyes, seeing first gray trousers bloused around the boots, then a trim tunic without insignia, then a smiling black face. A red beret with a silver skull sat at the proper tilt on his head. Eyes as cold as Wyoming jade met mine.

"So good to see you." He stuck out his hand. I ignored it. "You remember me?" he asked. "Colonel Kramr. Corps Intelligence." He laughed apologetically. "People always say we spooks all look alike."

I said nothing. But I remembered Kramr. I'd wondered how long it would take for him to look me up again.

"I thought I might stop by and ask you a few more questions. We've been having quite a time finding that girl friend of yours." He peered brightly at me. Elf-fire glowed like emeralds in his eyes. "But we think we've located her now. In the Underground." He shrugged his shoulders. "But we're having the hardest time getting someone down there to verify the information. I understand you've been going to the mindcasinos. I don't suppose you've seen her?"

I stared ahead, showing nothing on my face. I should have guessed he knew where Grychn was. There could only be one reason he'd let her stay there. That meant he knew about Nels. But not where the timestone could be found. If he knew that, there'd be no reason to come to me. I chilled again. A rat crawled up my throat. I opened my legs and vomited between them. The rat scurried away, hiding behind Kramr.

"You're not well," he said. "Pardon me for bothering you. You should have mentioned you were ill."

Two more rats clawed their way out through my mouth.

"Maybe I can help?" Kramr pulled a vial out of his pocket. He unscrewed the lid and withdrew a dropper filled with blue liquid. He leaned over me, holding the dropper straight up and down. I felt a drop hit the top of my head. Warmth sent my muscles quivering. Another drop splashed atop my head. Embers fanned to flame. Another drop landed, as hot as molten bismuth. Heat consumed my brain. Consciousness lapsed. A dream cycled out of hippocampal gray.

I hid beneath the gnarled roots of a cypress tree. My heart pounded in my chest. I was playing Hide and Seek with my brothers in the woods of our estate. Henri was looking for me. I heard the snap of a twig, then the rustle of leaves. I held still. Silence. I held my breath. Blood roared in my ears. Suddenly, fingers grasped my neck. "I see, I see!" Henri shouted gleefully. He pulled me out from the hollow like a rabbit from its hole, and pushed me along in front of him. He had already caught Robrt, who stood beneath an overhanging tree limb with a noose tight around his neck. He had to stand on tiptoe to keep from being choked. Henri tied a rope around my legs and hoisted me up in the air to hang beside Robrt. "Now we can have some fun," said Henri. "I am the winner. The spoils are mine." He pulled down Robrt's pants and then his own. He stood behind him, pressing his penis between Robrt's buttocks. I saw it slip inside. His thrusts lifted Robrt off the ground. I knew what would happen next. I'd played the game before. Henri stood before me. My head hung at the level of his groin. His penis was still stiff. It was streaked with brown. He pressed it against my lips. "Take it," he said. I kept my mouth closed tightly. He held my nose. I vowed to pass out before I opened my mouth to breathe. I did. But when I regained consciousness, his penis was in my mouth. I began sucking. There was nothing else to do. My mouth soon filled with warmth.

I awoke. The dream started fading.

I lay naked on wombskin. The room was dark, except for flashes of elf-fire. I saw Jain Maure sitting across the room, outlined by stroboscopic bursts. I sat up. Kramr was gone.

"Is it time to go yet?" I asked.

"Past time. You were sleeping when I came home. My poor baby is tired. Let's stay home tonight. Just the two of us. We can have some fun." She crossed the room to stand in front of me. She was naked. Her pubic hair brushed my face; my tongue darted out to lick. She mounted the bed and stood over me. I put my hands behind me for support and tilted my head. She settled her crotch into my face. I nibbled at her labia, then buried my tongue deep. Elf-fire gleamed from her breasts. Her eyes shone with emotion. She lowered herself until she kneeled over me. I felt her tongue touch my head. Madness swirled like a cancer growing.

I remembered something she had once said.

"What happens at a Temple of the Dead?" I asked. "You said you were once a neophyte at one."

"Nothing important."

"But what is the ritual?"

"You have to go through it to know. There's a vow of silence as well. Why? Are you thinking of attending a service?"

"Maybe. Tell me what to expect."

Her tongue touched me again. "You lie on an altar. A priest connects you to some medical equipment—the old kind that actually pierces flesh. Then they inject some potassium directly into your heart, making it stop. They let you go for just under four minutes, then revive you. During that four minutes while you are dead, your soul is supposed to glimpse the afterlife."

"Does it?" Voices whispered in my ear, telling me to do things. Terrible things. *Do it! Do it! Do it! Do it!* "Can you glimpse anything?"

She laughed. "Who knows? I suppose a dying mind sees some image. Who knows if it's real or not?"

"What images did you see?" Her tongue was warm and wet on my skull. A tornado swirled in my mind. Madness rose, pushing aside reason. But there was one more question to ask. "Do you know what awaits us in the cold empty?" I found myself fastening sonic clasps to her ankles and wrists, then binding her to the bed of womb-skin. She strained against her bonds. Pulsar detonations froze her in stop-motion. Muscles rippled under mahogany skin. Her nipples traced circles in the air. Black hair fanned out. Vermillion fire gleamed from her eyes. "What meaning hides in the time matrix?" I opened a steel case. Instruments glittered. I removed a dermatome. "Do you know? Did you see?" I began tracing lines of blood in her skin.

"Yes," she said as she writhed in pain. "I know. How well I know."

"When will I see the truth?"

"Soon," she answered. "It's almost time."

My mind became totally psychotic. What happened afterward, it refused to remember.

That morning, no hawks roused me from sleep.

The game must go on.

I had found Nels.

An alarm light flashed from my computer console. For a moment, I was too startled to do anything. Then I got busy.

I had my guards kill the other prisoners—I didn't want to waste energy watching after them. Then I pulled in all my personas. I simplified my dreamworld, dissolving it all into one chamber.

There was just Nels and me.

I had been waiting a long time to get to talk to him. Did I say him? Force of habit. I meant *her*. Nels was a woman. I smiled. I understood now what Grychn had meant about letting her have her little joke.

She sat in a padded chair. Wrists and ankles were held by sonic straps. A spotlight glared from above.

I always did have a flair for the dramatic.

"So you found me," Nels said. "I suppose you want the same thing as the others." Her hair was short, her face burned chocolate by too much sun.

"How did you know I was looking for you?"

"You were looking for someone. All the other mind-riders knew that." She smiled. The skin wrinkled around her eyes. "Besides, the stone told me *you* would come eventually. I've been waiting a long time."

"Others have sought you?"

"I think so. They wanted the same thing you do."

"Which is?"

"The place where I hid the stone."

"Did you tell anyone else?"

"Of course not. No one else is supposed to know except you and me."

I relaxed a little. That meant Kramr couldn't force the information out of her. I would be the only one to know. "Are you going to tell me?"

"Maybe." She smiled. "Do we have to be so formal?" She glanced down at the straps.

"I suppose not." The straps and chair were gone. Nels stood before me. "Is that better?"

"A little." She came close, putting her hands on my shoulders. "Why don't you make things more comfortable for us? The story is rather long." Her fingers began loosening my cape. She kissed me. "Be nice to me first. It's lonely being a mindrider."

I shrugged. I could make her talk, or extract the information from her mind. But why be crude and brutal? Why not do it the easy way?

Suddenly we were in a bedchamber, lying naked on wombskin.

"That's better," Nels said. Her lips began moving down my body. Her hands stroked life into my penis. "You don't know how long it's been since I had a man. A woman needs a man to love her. That's all I ever wanted. And I had one, before I found the stone." She took my penis in her mouth, sliding it in and out. Her muscles were quivering. I smoothed them with my hands, quieting the fasciculations. She swung a leg over me, slipping my penis into her, and rocked up and down. I massaged her breasts with my hands. She closed her eyes. Fine teeth bit her lower lip. "Make it last a long time," she said. "Make it last almost forever. Then I'll tell you the story."

I let my penis expand to fill her vault more tightly. Breath whistled from her nostrils.

What the Frisco, an interrogator has many techniques.

Later, she lay next to me. To her, it seemed we had made love for a week. Her finger made circles in the sweat on my chest.

It was time to get down to business. The fun was over.

She sighed, knowing her delaying tactics were as exhausted as my member. "Do you want to hear it all?" she asked.

"Why not? We have all the time in the world."

"I found the stone here in Chronus. In the Underground. I was reworking some of the old mines. I found a vein in a rib that had either been overlooked or purposely sandbagged and then forgotten. I drilled it out. It contained some nice stones. Eventually the vein led to the timestone. I cut it myself. During the cutting process I chipped the stone. I made the mistake of giving the chip to my lover. No doubt you got the chip from Mikal Gy. He's dead, now?"

"Yes, to both."

"What happened to the chip?"

"It got destroyed accidentally."

"Don't be too sure of that."

"What do you mean by that?" But I knew. I'd guessed the truth myself.

"Haven't you noticed that nothing happens by chance around a timestone? Do you think it was chance that brought you and Mikal together so you could obtain that timestone? Was it chance that brought you to Titan looking for me? I doubt it. If your timestone got destroyed, it wanted to be destroyed."

"A radianuclear crystal can't want things."

"Don't bet on it. You're here because the stone wants you to be. I thought at first the timestone was just a monitor showing what events would happen in the time matrix. But now I think it manipulates them. It can change them. It can change things to suit its fancy."

"Why should it do that? It's not alive."

"I wonder. Ever hear of entropy? That's the only purpose to life—to use up entropy faster than nonlife. Well, that's what a timestone does also—its organization means more disorder has occurred elsewhere. Lots of disorder. It lives quite well."

"So what? I intend to use it to my advantage, alive or dead. I can control it."

"No, you can't. I thought I could, too. Now look where I am. The stone tried to kill me. Entropy must be conserved. Death is a great conserver of entropy. The second law of thermodynamics requires the timestone to be a killer. It did kill me once—my body, anyway. Now I have only borrowed bodies. It killed my lover. But I'm safe now. It can't find me now. I change bodies too frequently for it to know who I really am."

"Where did you hide it?"

"I'm not sure I want to tell you. Or that I should."

"I can get the information, anyway." I sharpened knives in her brain.

She shuddered. "I guess you can. Then you'll also know if I lie. I may as well tell you." She showed me the hiding place in her mind. She laughed. "No harm in letting you know. You'll never find it. Not in the Ice Mountains of Iapetus. I can't find it myself. Why do you think I chose such a place? I knew I'd be tempted to try to go back to the stone one day." She laughed again. "Besides, you won't even be able to leave Chronus." She started giggling at her own private joke.

I peeped into her mind, carefully, so she wouldn't notice. All the information I needed was there. I hope you don't think badly of me. But I couldn't let her go. Kramr might be able to get her to talk. Then he'd beat me to the stone. He could get to Iapetus a lot quicker than I could. I had to make sure Nels wasn't ever going to talk to anyone else. I could do that. But it doesn't make me a monster.

I kissed her.

Her body responded against mine.

I stroked her back and thighs, letting the suction pads pull gently on tender skin, in a way she remembered.

She opened her eyes.

I stared back at her. My image was reflected in her eyes: bald head with a scalp convoluted into ridges, mono-mer sweat gleaming from my face, eyes with silver mono-cles, an earring in my left ear.

"Mikal! Is it really you?"

"Yes," I said in a voice she remembered. "It's really me. I have a two-week furlough. Let's make the most of it."

She stared at me.

"What's wrong?" I asked.

"I just had the strangest dream. I must have dozed off just now, after we made love. We did make love?"

"Of course." I laughed. "Lots of times. Forget your dream. Let's find some good times. We have all the time in the world."

The sun set behind Ascaris Mons, visible through our hotel window. Ice storms danced in the upper air, catching sunlight in blue swirls.

"Are we on Mars?"

"Where else do lovers go on holiday?"

She smiled brightly. "Oh, Mikal. I'm so happy. Tell me you love me."

"Of course I love you."

"And that you'll never leave me."

"I'll never leave you."

We made love again, beneath the cobalt skies of a Mars I'd never seen.

A billion miles away, the real me opened my eyes. Jain Maure removed an E-helmet from my head. The other handlers did the same to their players. But one body did not sit up. One body was limp and flaccid. One mind had not made it back.

You know whose mind that was. You know who left her behind, caught up in a game of his own creation. But I had no choice. She might have told someone else what she'd told me. I couldn't take that chance.

Besides, it was better for her, too. She'd escaped a pathetic existence. I had established an elaborate pattern. I'd even left behind a persona of myself, disguised as her lover. She'd never detect the difference. They'd both be happy. And for a long time. Time was compressed within cortical crystal. The patterns of a dreamgame might only last a few minutes in real time, but it would seem forever for her. An eternity of happiness. Who could ask for anything more?

Still, I felt uncomfortable playing God. But I suppose I was going to have to get used to it, especially after I recovered the timestone. But no more dreamgames for me.

I was finished with games.

7

As we floated up the liftube out of the Underground, Jain held a chain fastened to the sonic collar around my neck. I ignored it. She'd pay for that little indignity, and soon. But not right now. I might still need her.

By hiding the timestone on Iapetus, Nels had caused a slight problem. I'd been hoping it would be hidden on Titan, preferably in Chronus. So much easier to found an empire here. But if I had to go to Iapetus, so be it. All that meant was that I had to get out of Chronus first. I'd planned for that eventuality. But how to get to Iapetus? The siege had spacecraft bottled up. There must be another way. There was. I knew what I was going to have to do.

My musings were interrupted by our arrival at the portal. We stepped out of the liftube. Outside, a crowd of ghost dancers jammed the street, chanting dirges in unison to the beat of a pulsar barrage.

Jain was ahead, leading. She glanced back. Her eyes shone copper. She pulled on the chain, leading me through the crowd.

Overhead, elf-fire burned noisily. A beam stabbed down, ripping into a nearby building. Molten steel and perma-plastic showered down. The ghost dancers loved it. They leaped and pirouetted. Their bodies surged around mine— fingers plucked at my clothing. The chain tightened around my neck, then pulled free. I retrieved it and wound it around my torso. I saw Jain being carried away from me by the crowd. She called back once. I did not answer.

My clothes had come off. Naked bodies rubbed against mine. A woman put her arms around me, pulling me tight against her. We coupled. Sweating bodies pushed from all sides. I was penetrated from behind. We rose and fell with the undulations of the crowd. The force-field above us drummed like rain on a tin roof. Sometimes beams made it through and struck close. Debris rained down on us: slag, hot globs of plastic and glass, drops of blood, fragments of shattered flesh. But still we copulated. Other orifices were offered and taken. My voice chanted a death song.

Then the sickness began: cramps knotted my bowels, rigors shook my limbs and set my teeth chattering. Cold sweat mingled with hot sweat. I withdrew my penis into its pouch and closed my other sphincters. I pushed my way through the crowd, flinging ghost dancers to both sides. Hands reached for me; I pushed them aside. Orifices were offered—I ignored them. Finally I broke out of the throng of ghost dancers.

Rats began chewing on my insides again. I had to find Jain Maure. Her house was visible atop Mt. Erubus. She'd be there, waiting.

I started walking, doubled over with cramps. My gait was a stagger. But I kept going. There was nothing else to do.

I passed buildings burning from pulsar hits. Smoke hung close to the ground. Acrid fumes made my throat raw and set my lungs coughing. I stumbled on rubble littering the street. Small animals scurried into shadows as I approached, then watched me pass with bright eyes. Soon they would be bolder. Maybe they would join their brothers in my guts.

Laughter came from intact buildings. Mnemone fumes wafted from open windows. Tendrils of optical music swirled out of doorways. My feet became tangled in musical filaments—the strands broke as I walked, enveloping me in a discordant clamor. Voices called, inviting me to join their gaiety. Pathics sat in the balconies of cribhouses. Mental whispers promised obscene delight.

I trudged on, closing my mind.

I passed elegant estates. Naked bodies splashed in swimming pools. Laughing guests stood in groups on patios.

Fluttering wings rose from concealed cages; the retort of sporting guns was lost to the louder din of artillery. Dogs bayed. A pack chased something. A woman ran before them. Sharp teeth ripped tatters from her clothing—bloody bits of skin clung to the pieces of fabric. She tried to climb a tree. The dogs tore at her legs, dragging her down. She disappeared amid snapping jaws and thrashing tails. But her screams seemed to last a long time.

I walked through the park below Jain's house. Peptide vials glittered. Heads were bowed. CSF studs shone. I was tempted to get my medicine by force, but I resisted the urge. I was already too weak for that. Peppers went armed. I was too slow now to disarm one.

Love groups lay together. Elf-fire gleamed from oiled skin. Bodies undulated to detonations. Low moans escaped their lips. I left them behind.

I climbed the switchbacks leading up the mountain. Each step was agony. I shook with rigors; ague settled into my joints. I began vomiting. But I kept climbing. I used my hands to help. Soon I was crawling on all fours.

The house was just a little farther. I kept crawling, despite the cramps that caused me to stop and retch every few meters. At first green bile came up, sour and bitter. Before long, there was blood.

I pulled myself up the porch and through the doorfield, then collapsed on the floor and lay on my back.

Jain Maure got up from a couch. She was naked except for a vial hanging from a chain around her neck. Elf-fire shone from her skin.

"Poor baby! Where have you been?" She came to me. "I've been waiting for such a long time." She kneeled over me and unscrewed the cap of a vial. She dipped her tongue in it, then bent down. Stroboscopic flashes glittered from emerald eyes. Her tongue touched my head, spreading warmth.

Somewhere far away was a tremendous explosion. A thunderclap echoed from inside the dome. Sirens wailed. A hoverbus whined overhead.

Fire flowed inside me. Quivering muscles stopped their fasciculations. Cramps relaxed. Gooseflesh smoothed out. My stomach stopped trying to turn itself inside out. I sat up.

Jain smiled. "Is my little man feeling better now that he's had his medicine? Tell me all about your busy day." She kissed my lips. Something bothered me.

Then I heard faintly a sound I could never forget—the crack of light autopulsars. I got up and went out to the balcony. A rope had been tied across the gap in the railing. The eastern edge of the dome was illuminated with flashes of yellow and red—the colors of elven and combrid light weapons. That meant troops were fighting. Which meant the walls had been breached. The Fall of Chronus was near.

Jain came to stand beside me. Far below a skimmer climbed the road to the house. I turned my head to kiss Jain on the lips. Green fire sparked from her eyes.

Something was wrong. But I couldn't remember what.

Jain held me close, pressing her breasts against my back. Her hands found their way to my penis. It remained limp to their strokings. Her tongue licked my head. More endorphine warmed me, buzzing in my mind.

"Tell me," Jain said. "What did Nels have to say?"

Why should she ask that? I'd never told her about Nels. Then I remembered the voice in my dreams. I knew whose voice it was.

A skimmer parked in front of the house.

"Where did Nels hide the timestone?" She leaned her elbows on my back. The lid to a vial screaked as it was turned. "Do you need more medicine to help you talk?"

Footsteps sounded outside.

She leaned forward to touch my head with her tongue; something pressed between my buttocks. Something warm and firm.

I pushed away from the railing, giving her a shove with my hip as I turned. She went sprawling.

I didn't need to see the erect penis between her legs to know who she was. Green eyes glared angrily. It was all in the eyes.

I ran into the house.

Another Jain walked in through the doorfield. The Jain with copper eyes. The original Jain Maure. Not a chameleon. I knew who wanted to know all about Nels and the timestone. Someone who could be either a man or a woman. Or both.

I brushed past copper-Jain and went outside. Her skimmer was parked on its pad. I hopped in and wound the turbines tight, kicking dust up as I took off.

I'd finally figured out what I had to do.

I had to get the L.A. out of Chronus, that was certain. I also had to get off-moon. There was only one way I could think of to do both.

It was a wild ride to Old Town. Combrids jetted across town on thruster tubes, to join the firefight on the eastern side. Gunships made pass after pass, trying to seal the breach in the dome. Hydrocarbon fog poured in, shrouding the buildings in clinging mists. I half expected to get shot down myself. Fortunately, both combrids and elves ignored a naked civilian in a stolen skimmer. But artillery beams blasted down all over. Several times the concussion waves almost overturned the skimmer. Globs of molten permaplastic splattered on the windscreen. Chunks of masonry ricocheted from the hull. Fires raged in every sector. Fireballs exploded when hydrocarbon and air encountered a spark. Smoke hung close to the ground.

Ghost dancers jammed the area around the portal to the Underground. Other people were trying to flee to the safety of the tunnels. Their clothes were plucked from them as they tried to force their way through the dancers. They were made to dance also. Their orifices were taken. Few made it through.

I was one who did. I could push ghost dancers aside—my arms were still combrid arms and somehow I had found a reserve of strength. I reached the portal and jumped into the down tube. I got off at a lower level and easily found my way through a maze of twisting tunnels to the old apartments that once housed miners. Grychn's directions in her mind had been good. My combrid orientation sense had been infallible.

I kicked down the door of an apartment.

Two people lay naked in a peptide embrace: Grychn and her handler, Jry. The handler reached for his gun, which lay beside the bed. Before he could swing it to bear, I had crossed the room and kicked him in the side of the neck. I both felt and heard vertebrae snap. He fell back and lay still. His neck was broken. I was rather disappointed. I would have been able to decapitate him, had I been at full strength.

I picked up his gun.

Grychn was half unconscious from peptide. If she even noticed what had happened, she'd not likely remember it. I slapped her face. Her eyes remained dazed.

I thought of a little detail that needed taking care of. I held the pulsar muzzle close to her neck and fired. Her collar fell off. I did the same to mine, burning the skin a little by accident. It was worth it, to be free of that fetter.

I waited, making plans in my mind. There was still a lot to do.

Grychn woke up.

"Marc," she said. "What are you doing here? Jry will kill you. . . ." She saw the handler's cooling body. She looked back to me. "I wanted to do that myself."

"Look closer."

She did. She saw his flesh rearranging itself to its true form. Ever see a can of worms? That was a nice way to describe the process.

"A spook!" She hid her face in her hands. "Then I never escaped. They had me all the time. Why?"

"To help them keep tabs on me."

She figured it out on her own. "The timestone. The spooks want the timestone."

"You guessed it." But the explanation was too simple, too pat. Life is always more complicated than that. I should have known better. I guess I didn't want to know the truth. I took her hand and pulled her to her feet. "It's time to go now."

"Let me get dressed."

"There's no time for that."

We ran naked along the tunnels of the Underground. No one even noticed. They had their own perversions to worry about. I held Grychn's hand in one hand, a pulsar pistol in the other.

I led. I didn't need her help to find the old air lock. I'd been there once before. First we went down a side tunnel. I pulled out the two cases I'd buried earlier. I tossed her a set of combat armor and began pulling on my own. *"Now* we get dressed," I said.

Combat armor, battle packs complete with thrusters, a survival tent, catalytic O_2 generators, and enough ration concentrates to last a month had cost me a fortune on the black market. Two autopulsars were another fortune in themselves. But I figured I'd be needing them all. Don't ask me how I knew I'd need two sets of everything but the tent. I don't like to think about that.

The armor was loose and baggy on Grychn's wasted body. It looked the same on me. I remembered how dashing I used to look in my armor. I also remembered how someone else looked. I pushed those memories away.

"Where are we going?" Grychn asked.

"You said you had a gravship. Think you can find it?"

"I think so. If we can reach it. But we'll never make it. Not before withdrawal starts. Have you forgotten about that?"

"No, I haven't forgotten. Lead the way."

She looked at me with a funny expression. Then she shrugged her shoulders. I opened the air lock and we stepped into it. An emergency gong sounded. I hoped the garrison's combrids would be too busy to investigate. Air sucked out. Cold hydrocarbon fog swirled in, frosting on the inside surfaces. The outer door opened.

We stepped out into another tunnel. A short walk took us to the tunnel's mouth, covered with underbrush. We wriggled our way through the debris until we stood on the ground. A kilometer away was the dome of Chronus. Elven pulsar beams still bombarded it.

Crystal forest lay in the other direction. We walked toward it, warm in combat armor.

Before entering the trees, I turned back once. A pulsar quantum exploded against the dome, opening a brief window in the force-field. I turned my helmet sensors to max gain.

An image flashed: I saw a house atop a high mountain. A balcony hung out over a cliff. A woman was chained to the railing. She was naked. Another figure swung an alphalash. Sparks sprayed into the air. I zoomed the image larger. Details became clearer. I could see the face of the chained woman. Elf-fire gleamed red from her eyes. Sparks glowed from her skin, tracing the pattern of the lash strokes. The other figure was also naked. She was almost the twin of the first. But her eyes were green. And she had a penis, erect with excitement. Sweat glistened from her breasts.

She swung the lash. Her penis bobbed up and down with the motion.

The image winked out. I looked away.

I was finished with that game.

Grychn took my hand.

We stepped into the forest and were gone.

Book IV

Hide and Seek

1

Grychn and I fled through the crystal forests of Titan.

Mostly we had to go on foot. But when we came to clearings, we leaped across them in powered jumps using thruster tubes. That was taking a chance. We should have skirted around the clearings, staying undercover. There could be patrols about. But we wanted to get as far away from Chronus as possible. We were too weak to run all the way.

If we had to talk, we touched helmets—I didn't want any e-wave transmissions being picked up.

It felt good to be in battle dress again, carrying an auto-pulsar. Our shapes were barely discernible, vague outlines of blurred movement. We could move as quietly as the wind.

I had my helmet sensors turned to max gain. Several times I spotted elf patrols. Then Grychn and I hid in the underbrush until they passed. Even though I felt like a combrid again, I didn't fool myself into thinking I could fight like one. Besides, I was a noncombatant now. And a fugitive. The Combrid Corps was as much my enemy as the elves. More so now.

Dawn came and went. We kept going, although we had to make more frequent rest stops. Months of peptide had taken their toll. We encountered no more elf patrols—they were holed up for the day, I suppose. There were no com-brid patrols, either—the garrisons must have had to be used for the defense of Chronus. Lucky us. I couldn't have picked a better time to escape.

But you couldn't escape the rats you carried with you. I knew that. That's why I wanted to be far away when they started chewing on my insides. So there would be no way to yield to the temptation to return to Chronus. I still had a trick or two left.

The first twinge of withdrawal came just before dark. A little early. But then I hadn't received my usual dose of peptides the night before.

We had come to a canyon about a kilometer across and a half-klick deep. It would take hours either to climb through it or go around. Our only other choice was a powered jump.

"What do you think?" I asked Grychn. "Think you can do it?"

"May as well give it a try. Can't be any worse than the last time we did something like this together." She laughed.

"When was that?"

"You remember. When you first captured me. Back when you were a combrid and I was a guerrilla."

I did remember that time. She'd tried to escape by gliding across just such a canyon. But I plucked her out of the air like a fat butterfly. I smiled to myself. But something about the memory bothered me. There was no point worrying about it now.

I let Grychn go first. She'd learned how to use gravtubes fairly quickly. Not that there was much skill required; for the Corps liked to keep things fairly simple—less chance of screw-ups that way. She took a running start, a short jump to the rim of the canyon, then gravved on. Twin cones of pseudograv pushed her in an arc across the gorge.

I followed. As usual, the acceleration made my balls ache, even though they were pulled inside their pouch. But halfway across, another ache began, deep in my joints. You guessed it. Good old peptide withdrawal. I almost doubled up with the cramps. Then they subsided. A prodromal twinge. I knew it would only get worse. That meant we'd have to hole up fairly quickly.

On the other side, we touched helmets. "It's started for me," I said. "You?"

"Not yet," Grychn answered. "But soon, I think."

I wanted to get away from the rim before we camped.

We pushed on into the forest about a klick. Then I began looking for a place to stop. Already my skin was puckered with gooseflesh.

I found the grove I sought. A giant tree had crashed into a stand of smaller trees, forming a hollow beneath its leaning trunk. Not only did it provide natural concealment from above, but anyone approaching on foot would make enough noise that we'd hear them coming before they got to us.

I took off my pack and unloaded the tent. Folded, it made a ten-by-ten-cm. package about two cm.'s thick. I set it in the center of the clearing beneath the leaning tree, pushed the button on top, and stood back. A small pseudo-grav generator sent vectors of force along conductor struts laminated to the tent fabric. The tent popped open, forming an igloo of space fabric coated with camofilm, supported by hemispherical struts of p-grav. Camofilm blended perfectly with any background. Unless you looked carefully, you wouldn't see the tent. Even then you weren't sure it was there. More than one combrid had lost his tent while on bivouac.

We crawled in and I sealed the door slit. I switched on a light. The floor was three meters in diameter; the ceiling vertex was two meters high. Real cozy. The tent functioned as a commodious set of space coveralls. An O_2 converter began making air out of hydrocarbons. Heat was provided by our bodies—space fabric was almost a perfect insulator, so excess body heat was sufficient to warm the inside to a comfortable twenty-five degrees. A small dehumidifier removed exhaled water from the air and dripped it into a flask to be recycled. Two people meant four liters per day. There was a dispoz bag near the door. I don't have to tell you what happened to waste deposited there, do I? Recycled, of course. Waste not, want not.

The tent had cost good old Mother Earth ten thousand credits to make—I purchased it from an enterprising sergeant major in the Quartermaster Corps for a tenth of that. Still a pretty piece of change. But worth every centime.

In about fifteen minutes the air was warm and breathe-able. We took off our battle dress and sat naked on the floor. We had no other clothes to wear. (You wore nothing under combat armor.) The floor had already inflated to provide an air cushion for comfort.

We didn't eat that night—there was no point in eating and then spending the rest of the night retching into a dispoz bag. Instead I broke out my medical kit. I knew eventually I'd need it. I'd packed two of everything. Does that tell you anything? I suppose it does. I guess my subconscious knew all along I'd bring Grychn with me. My subconscious must be nicer than my conscious mind—I only consciously decided to bring her along when I remembered she had a yacht stashed away. Before then, I planned to let her rot in the mindcasinos. I guess I was getting soft.

My hands shook as I prepared two infusion sets.

Sweat beaded on Grychn's body. Her skin had become mottled. She crossed her hands over her belly. I still had trouble believing how thin she'd become. And I knew I looked just as bad.

"What are you doing?" she asked. Her voice quavered. Withdrawal was starting for her.

"Fixing us some medicine."

"You mean peptide? Did you bring some along?" Her eyes gleamed. She licked her lips.

"No. Something else."

"Will it help?"

"A little, maybe. Not as much as you'd like." The only thing that would block peptide withdrawal was more neuropeptide. If you didn't want the shakes, you had to take more peptide, which produced more tolerance, which meant taking more peptide. The classic vicious circle. The only way to break the circle was to go through withdrawal. Cold turkey, that had around an eighty-percent mortality, depending on the size of one's habit. But there were ways to improve your chances.

That's just what I was doing now.

I had to concentrate to keep from fumbling. Each infusion set consisted of a flexible bag, an infusion pump, and a self-cannulating intravenous catheter. The bag already contained desiccated glucose, dextran/albumin, and electrolytes. All you did was add water and any other goodies you cared to spike it with. I carefully added a gram of noscamine to each bag.

"What's that?" Grychn asked.

"Noscamine. For sympathetic and parasympathetic blockade. Peptide withdrawal causes lots of nervous discharge to occur. That's what makes you so sick. And kills you. If you can block that nervous energy, you don't suffer as much. And you increase your chances of surviving the experience. Noscamine is supposed to do that."

"Supposed to?"

"It's not a hundred percent effective."

"How much?"

"Maybe eighty percent. Just enough to keep you from dying. The other twenty will be bad enough. But tolerable, I hope."

"Me, too."

I finished with the sets. I strapped one around Grychn's arm, then let her do the same for me. I felt a sharp prick as a needle found a vein. The infusion pump produced a comforting hum. All we had to do now was keep the bags filled with water. They would keep us alive through withdrawal.

The first was not an insignificant task—have you ever tried to fill a water bag while rats were making nests in your guts, every muscle jerked with hundred-volt shocks, and you tried to puke your rectum out your nose?

But we did manage.

We spent a lot of time holding each other, trying to synchronize our rigors, letting cold sweat become warm between our bodies.

I don't want to go into any more detail. They say you can't remember pain. I don't know about that. Peptide withdrawal you remember. I'll make book on that.

But in seventy-two hours it was over, although it seemed to last considerably longer. Like forever.

We spent the next seventy-two hours trying to eat food concentrates and sleeping. You don't do much of either during peptide withdrawal.

It seemed as if our bodies were already starting to fill out, now that we had flushed the neuropeptides out of them. Grychn started to look less ghastly. Her skin had better color. Her eyes brightened, glowing a warm amber. I found myself admiring her body. Then wanting it. She didn't seem to mind at all.

We spent another day making love. I won't say it was the same as the love we made to each other while playing dreamgames. That kind of sex was perfect, with no fumbling, no hesitation, no confusion, no awkward positions or cramped muscles. But the real kind was still pretty good.

And much more esthetic—in dreams you sometimes forgot little details, like certain textures, certain smells, or getting a hair stuck between your teeth.

Eventually there were no more excuses not to go on.

Besides, you get a little stir crazy spending a week in a tent, even if you are sick most of the time.

We put our battle dress back on.

The tent folded as easily as it went up. I stowed it away and shouldered my pack. Though still tired and weak, we made good time. We'd get stronger each day, now that peptides no longer catabolized tissue.

Sunlight burned away hydrocarbon fogs. Crystal trunks glittered with reflections. The sky was as gray as stainless steel—a clear day for Titan. We slipped through the forest like nymphs blown from fine glass.

At midday we stopped by a stream of liquid butane/pentane for a rest. We had a picnic, if you could call sitting together holding gauntlets while we each swallowed food concentrates a picnic. Sure you could. Why not?

Then we saw something that sent us scurrying for cover. Convoys of hoverbuses escorted by gunships flew past, high overhead, heading in the direction of Chronus.

"Where did they come from?" Grychn asked.

"The rescue fleet must have arrived. Apparently the Lord Generals want to keep control of Titan."

"Will anyone come after us?"

"Maybe. When Chronus is secured. Probably then. How much farther to your ship?"

"About eighty kilometers. I don't think we've come more than twenty or thirty. We'll reach an elf city first. I've got to stop there on the way. OK?"

"If you have to. Come on, we've got a long way to go." And not much time. I knew the spooks would be looking for us. I'd killed one back in Chronus. They'd come for no other reason than that. A vendetta would have been sworn against me. And now I was the only person who knew where the timestone was located. They'd come for that, too.

We pushed on until dark, then camped again. We had covered about twenty kilometers that day.

The next day we made thirty—strength was returning to our muscles. We camped at the edge of a mountain range. On the other side lay both the elven city and Grychn's gravship.

At first light, we started out, climbing up a ravine to a pass in the mountains. We had to leave the cover of the forest—trees couldn't grow on such rocky slopes. Loose rock crumbled as we climbed, sending us sliding downhill. It was going to take a long time to reach the pass. Unless we took a chance. Why not? The longer we were out in the open, the more likely we'd be spotted.

I touched my helmet to Grychn's. "Let's use thrusters," I said. She nodded in agreement.

At my hand signal we gravved on. Concentric cones of pseudograv spewed from thrusters. We rocketed uphill, skimming close to the contour of the slope. Wisps of fog streamed by. We passed over talus slides and drifts of hydrocarbon snow. Sure beats walking, as the man said. In a few minutes we'd covered ten kilometers of distance.

We landed in new hydrocarbon powder, raising a cloud of blue with the impact.

"Don't move," Grychn said. "They've spotted us."

I didn't move. I knew "they" were elves. I didn't want to be shot as an intruder.

Grychn raised her hands and went forward. I half expected to see a pulsar beam fry her on the spot. My old prejudice. I wasn't even a combatant anymore, and yet I still didn't trust elves.

Two of them stepped out from behind a rock. They held their weapons at the ready, but didn't point them at us. I looked closer and saw a cleverly concealed sentry box. I knew it would be invisible from the air to both eyes and sensors. We must be close to their city. Why else would they guard this pass? Then I looked even closer. Gooseflesh crawled up my back. The mountains bristled with the muzzles of heavy pulsars. There were also heavily fortified field-generating stations. We must be close indeed.

The two elves recognized Grychn. She had raised her helmet visor. They howled like banshees and then started hugging her and slapping her on the back, all the while jumping up and down in the air. I guess they were pleased to see her. I stayed put. I wanted to be sure she had a chance to explain about me.

She waved for me to come forward. I advanced slowly, eying the cannon mouths all around. But they weren't going to shoot me with those. A waste of energy.

"Marc, I'd like you to meet a couple of old friends of

mine, Lanaan and Aleel." I raised my visor and nodded to
the two elves. They were a male and a female, both quite
young. "Any friend of Grychn's . . ."

"You're not elf-friend yet," Lanaan said, cutting me off.
"That takes both time and proof. Until then, be careful."

"Rather gruff, isn't he?" I whispered to Grychn.

"That's the nature of elves," she answered.

Lanaan went back to the sentry post. Aleel led us down
a faint trail. She stopped at the edge of a cliff. I peered
over the rim. An elf city lay below, the largest I'd seen.

A grove of crystal trees grew next to cliffs of ice. The
trees were giants, standing over a hundred meters high,
with trunks twenty meters in diameter. Elf-houses blistered
the sides of the trees like clusters of iridescent grapes.
Elves swooped in the air. Hundreds of them. All carrying
weapons. Mouths of tunnels pocked the ice face of the cliff.

Aleel jumped over the edge, catching herself with her
wings, and began gliding down in tight spirals. Grychn followed, slowing her descent with thrusters.

What the Frisco!

I jumped.

2

We floated down among trees of glass, past glistening elf-houses. Aleel glided in spirals around Grychn and me. Elf children swooped out to greet us, chattering like winged monkeys, darting in to touch me with their hands. Counting coup, I thought. They learn early.

We headed toward a globe suspended between the two largest trees in the grove. This sphere was fifty meters in diameter. As usual, a round entrance was located at the bottom. Aleel alighted gently, and gracefully swung through the hole. Grychn was almost as adept, dropping below the opening, then firing her thrusters to pop her through. I wasn't as good and almost hit my shoulder on the edge. That probably would have cracked the elf-house rather than me.

The inside of the globe was filled with elves. Literally. Glass saplings grew toward the center from the inside surface, forming a crystal reticulum. Elves hung from the saplings by an arm or a leg or a tail—one limb seemed to serve as well as another. Several elves came to greet Grychn. She had removed her helmet. They kissed her lips through her O_2 bubble. I'm glad nobody got carried away and tried to kiss me. There was something about furry faces with lemur eyes and bat ears that made me not want to kiss their monkey lips. Bigotry? If you say so. But I always thought I was just being particular. I didn't know where those lips had been.

The globe was either well insulated or acted like a solar

collector. Probably both, since it was quite warm inside—
nearly zero degrees. Grychn and I handed our battle packs
to Aleel, then shucked off our armor. That's right, in front
of hundreds of elves. They had never developed a body
taboo—with fur, they had no need for clothing anyway. I'd
lost whatever modesty I'd had as a combrid. And Grychn
had lived among the elves.

Someone brought us jumpsuits made of space fabric.
Grychn put hers on. She was already shivering from the
cold. I handed mine back, deciding to go native. All I wore
was an O_2 converter around my neck like a neon necklace,
with its oxygen bubble around my mouth and nose. You're
not forgetting I was still a combrid inside? Brown adipose
would keep me warm in much colder climes than this.

Grychn took off across the inside of the elf-house, swinging from glass saplings. I followed her. Once you got the
hang of it, brachiation wasn't all that difficult. (Get it? The
hang of it? I guess you had to be there.) We climbed to the
ceiling, where we hung from cross branches.

Another elf greeted us there, kissing Grychn and offering his hand to me. I shook it. Suction cups pulled at my
skin. They were dry, anyway. Lemur eyes regarded my
nakedness. They blinked. A monkey face grimaced.

"Ah, now I understand," the elf said. "You were a
combrid once." He looked me over, noting my genitals
were retracted into their pouch. "A good job of cybersurgery. You could pass for standard Terran anywhere."

"A professional opinion?" I asked.

"Why not?" The elf laughed. I guess that was the bark-
ing sound he made as he grimaced. "You know my name,
then?"

"Everyone on Titan, elf or not, has heard of the notorious Dr. Maizay."

"I suppose that's so. But few remember I am also a
genosurgeon. Thank you for that."

"Maizay," Grychn said, "this is Marc Detrs."

His eyes widened and he peered at me like an owl. He
must have heard of my Legion of Merit. Not many were
handed out.

"Yes," I said, confirming his suspicions. "Former Gunnery Sergeant Detrs, once of the First Ghost Cavalry. Now
a noncombatant. Strictly neutral."

Maizay laughed again. "Don't worry. Elves hold no

grudges. We admire valor in our enemies as much as in our own warriors." He smiled, pulling back his black lips to show carbide teeth. "But your neutrality, I question. After all, you helped our little butterfly to escape. The spooks won't love you for that. They consider you a traitor already. You may as well join our side now. We always need good warriors."

"Do you think you can trust me?"

"Why not? You can't go back either to Chronus or the Corps." He grinned now. "We're all that's left."

At least on Titan, they were. I couldn't dispute that.

"But I'm neglecting my duties as your host," he continued. "You must be getting tired." He had noticed me switching from one hand to the other as I hung from a branch. He made a hand signal. An elf came with a trapeze, which he hung from the branch. Grychn and I sat in the swing. Other elves came with food, both elven and Terran, and placed it in baskets hung before us.

"Please forgive the poor fare," Maizay said. "We have few Terran visitors these days. Grychn has been gone for a long time—we've let our stocks dwindle."

He selected a crystalline fruit from a basket, took a bite, and began grinding oxide matrix to dust. His saliva contained organic catalysts that began the reduction to elemental oxygen.

Our food was standard Corps garrison rations—protein bars, carbohydrate sticks, vegetable loaves. No doubt captured from a combrid base. But I couldn't complain. Anything was better than the food concentrates we'd been eating for the past week. And there was a bottle of claret. That made up for a lot.

I listened as Grychn and Maizay reminisced. They told stories about various raids, fleeing from spooks and combrids both, hiding out in mountain sanctuaries. My mind constructed vivid images out of their words.

I already knew some of it, from what Grychn had told me earlier. But listening to an elf tell it made it different. I began to feel the old thrill again, like when I first came to Titan. The old excitement of combat came back to me—wicked and brutal. I knew Maizay felt the same way—he had the gleam in his eye. He genuinely enjoyed playing Cowboys and Indians. The elves would never give up their rebellion—they liked playing the game too much. Why not? There were worse games. I had played some myself. I was almost sorry I was out of the Corps.

For a time—maybe because of the gentle buzz produced by the wine—I was tempted to throw my lot in with the elves. I'd make a good guerrilla—and it would be fun. What difference did it make what side you played on? The game was the same. But I pushed the urge aside. I was tired of being small potatoes. When I found the timestone, I could build an empire for myself. Why waste my time in a nickel-and-dime rebellion, when there would be whole planets to conquer.

Dogs, megalomania felt good!

Another bottle of wine was brought to us. Maizay was smoking what passed on Titan for a mnemone stick—rolled leaves of living crystal. Oxides released oxygen which burned in hydrocarbon air, producing fumes from the polymer matrix of the leaf. The vapors were mildly intoxicating. They were also as pungent as L.A. But then elf lungs were used to breathing poisonous atmosphere.

I started getting mellowed out. I felt secure. The irony of it all didn't escape me. Here I was, in the middle of an armed camp of bloodthirsty elven guerrillas, and I felt safe for the first time in months. And why not? The spooks were my enemies now. Kramr was my foe. An elven city was the safest place for me.

Maizay finished his smoke. "Come on," he said. "Let me show you around. Few Terrans have ever seen my little city."

He let go of his branch and dropped to the floor in a swan dive. He shot through the opening there. Grychn and I slid out of our swing and followed more cautiously, jumping from branch to branch.

Outside, Maizay waited. He handed each of us a set of pseudowings. We clasped them to ankles and wrists. Polymer fabric billowed.

Maizay and half a dozen other elves watched as I tried out my new wings. They knew Grychn was already skilled in their use. I'm sure they expected me to flounder about, so they were waiting to be amused. I was sorry to disappoint them.

You remember my adventures in Telluride, when I leaped from Club Ionosphere atop Pandora Tower, with nothing but a cape of wingcloth. I wouldn't have done that if I had not been adept in the use of pseudowings.

The principle was simple, actually. A thin layer of grav-polymer was sandwiched between two layers of surface-effect fabric. Gravcloth neutralized the gravity field, so you were balanced between rising and falling. Surface-effect polymer caused air to flow across the wing—producing a slight forward thrust. By flapping your arms and legs, you could produce an undulation in the airfoil, magnifying this surface effect. With a little practice, you could fly like a bird—or like a bat, to be more precise.

I leaped into the air, caught some beneath my wings, then squirted it out behind, causing me to shoot upward. Then I dove toward the ground, opened my wings, and performed a couple of full loops with a half-gainer, timing my finish so I hovered in midair in front of the others.

They were suitably impressed. Maizay laughed. "Bravo, bravo! I see you've used wings before. That's good. Follow me." He took off, using his real wings. Grychn and I followed. I noticed a couple of armed elves were careful to flank both sides.

The city was about fifty hectares in area. There were about a thousand inhabitants. I wondered how it had escaped satellite detection. Maizay pointed upward. I figured out what he meant. Methane clouds hung from the cliffs above. Optical sensors would see only them. Also, the crystal foliage was quite dense overhead. He said radioactive and magnetic ores in the surrounding mountains interfered with other sensors.

Pretty clever, I had to admit.

Small garden plots were placed in clearings in the surrounding forest, where food oxides were grown. Most of the people working the plots were children or elderly—able-bodied men and women were working elsewhere. But everybody was armed. Toddlers barely able to stand brandished autopulsars as long as they were tall. Maizay told me they were proficient in the use of their weapons—I didn't doubt it.

I didn't see any evidence of technology—only elf-houses and gardens. There had to be factories somewhere, though.

I soon found out where.

After we had toured the city and its surrounding forest, we flew to the ice cliffs to the west, where we alighted on a landing area that had been carved into the sheer face of a palisade. We entered a tunnel in the cliff. The mouth of the tunnel was heavily guarded—there were four bunkers carved into the rock face on either side, each bunker housing a quad-50. About a kilometer into the mountain, the tunnel opened into a series of chambers.

"An old isotope mine," Maizay said. "Titan is riddled with old mines. But we have put them to more productive use than the Underground of Chronus."

He was right about that. The chambers were now a munitions plant.

"We have a certain advantage." Maizay laughed. "After all, we grow photonuclear crystals here on Titan."

We went from chamber to chamber. Elves made their weapons entirely from scratch. Permaplastic was made from hydrocarbon atmosphere, then poured into injection molds. The parts were trimmed and assembled into weapon frames. Photonuclear crystals were cut and calibrated and then loaded into plastic cases. Electronics labs assembled sensors, targeting computers, and autosights. Other labs made chemical and biological agents. Quite impressive. But I wondered why Maizay was showing me all this.

"We have a hundred facilities like this, in a hundred different mines. The loss of one is unimportant. All the raw materials we need are here for the taking. All that's left is the determination to continue our struggle. And we are determined. . . ."

We left the munitions plant by the same tunnel we'd used to enter. Maizay paused on the landing. Below us, two elves dueled in midair with ion sticks. A crowd watched them. Spectators were clinging to the ice cliff as well as perching on every available branch in the surrounding trees.

Ion sticks were the benign counterpart to sonic sabers. Both were the same length and weight. Ion sticks had charged particles on their surface instead of ultrasonic fire. They caused a brief paralysis when they touched, rather than slicing right on through. I was proficient with both, of course. Combrid training was anything if not complete.

The elves were good, I had to admit. Thrusts and parries and remises were difficult enough when standing on firm ground, much less in midair while hovering on wings. Their combat took the form of ethereal ballet—wings billowed, bodies undulated, swinging swords left trails of sparks marking their path. When a sword touched, the muscles beneath the blow went limp, and red light glowed from the spot. The duel continued until one of the contestants was too disabled to proceed. Then a challenger from the crowd of onlookers rose to test the champion. You could keep fighting until you lost.

The champion who was fighting now didn't look like she would ever lose. She had not been touched in half a dozen matches. She dispatched her current opponent with a slashing blow along his side, paralyzing both arm and leg. Then she hovered on her wings, awaiting her next victim. She was good-looking, for an elf. There was something familiar about her. She stood close to two and a half meters, but weighed less than thirty kilós, with her barrel chest and hollow, pneumaticized long bones. Fingers and toes were long and supple. Her dense fur shone with vitality. Yellow eyes gleamed with confidence. Again, something seemed familiar about her.

No one rose to challenge her.

Maizay touched my shoulder. He was smiling. "Why don't you give it a try? You surely remember how to fence? Let's see if a Terran can beat an elf in a fair contest."

"Why not?" I answered. "A little exercise would do me good." Someone handed me an ion stick. It fit my hand well and was properly balanced. I swung a few practice strokes; sparks cracked in the air and smoke rose in curlicues from the blade.

I glided down to where the elven maiden waited, and pulled up in the air to face her. We touched swords. Fire leaped between our blades, causing my hair to tingle with static. We withdrew.

The duel began.

She attacked, I parried to remise, thrust and parry, re-remise, break to counter. Sparks showered around us. Standard fencing. Except we were in midair. Movement of your arm was translated to movement of your wing, which changed your position in the air. If you thrust too vigorously, you might cause yourself to spin, exposing your back to a disabling blow. Follow-through was likewise exaggerated. Footwork had to occur in three dimensions—you circled your opponent from side to side or from above or below. We performed aerial ballet with swords.

Physically, I should have been superior in both speed

and strength. But I was out of shape and a little out of practice. I could hardly overwhelm her. And she was more adept at maneuvering in the air with wings, having been born with them. I had a tendency to overcompensate, making me a little off balance most of the time. The result was that we were fairly evenly matched.

Attack, parry, remise . . . break to counter. The air between us glowed with stray sparks. Smoke formed a cloud around us. Each strategy of one was thwarted by the other. I enjoyed the fight immensely. I admired her skill—she was good. I was also having more fun than I'd had in a long time. Combat was a hard habit to kick. Maybe even harder than peptide.

Under other circumstances, I might have defeated her. I was learning how to control my wings more proficiently. But I was out of shape. Months of peptide addiction had weakened me. I started getting tired. It became harder to parry her attacks. She realized I was fatiguing, and intensified the pressure.

She feigned an overhand attack, then came in from the weak side. My parry came a little too late. Her blade bounced off mine, but also glanced across my upper arm, paralyzing it. My sword hand had lost both feeling and strength, but before my saber could drop I grabbed it with my other hand. I attacked left-handed, to keep her from pressing her advantage. I was equally skilled with either hand—combrid cybersurgery mixed synapses enough to produce ambidexterity—so fighting left-handed was not a particular disadvantage. But I was still dog tired. And I couldn't maneuver very well with one wing limp.

I decided to take a chance. I didn't have much choice—it was either that or surrender.

So I double-feinted, low then high—a neat trick in midair. She parried, exposing her legs. I slashed down and across them, feeling my blade strike muscle. Then I tried to get my sword blade back up. I was too late. Her tail swung, blocking my arm. Her sword touched my shoulder. My other arm was paralyzed. There was no way I could stay in the air—neither wing functioned. I began to drop. Using only my legs, I slowed my descent. I settled to the ground, standing on my feet.

The elf was in no better shape. She could still hold a sword, but could hardly fly. She glided erratically toward

me, with sword raised. I stood my ground, wondering briefly if she intended to strike me when I was disarmed. She
didn't. As she reached me, she dropped her blade and
wrapped her arms around me. Limp legs brushed against
mine.

"You fight well, Earther." Black lips parted to show a
pink tongue. Her eyes looked into mine. "I think there was
no winner."

I recognized her. "Aleel?" I asked.

"Of course." She smiled. "But I think there was no loser,
either." She pressed her face through my oxygen bottle,
kissing my lips. Her tongue touched mine.

The elven crowd cheered.

I didn't mind either the kiss or the applause.

That evening, Aleel joined Grychn, Maizay, and me for
dinner in Maizay's house. Again there were only standard
rations for Grychn and me. The elves ate crystal fruits and
vegetables, being obligate vegans as there was no crystalline
fauna. There was more wine with the food, and later mnemone sticks for Grychn and me.

We sat around a thermonuclear crystal that glowed in
the center of the house.

Outside, the temperature dropped to around a hundred
below. Inside it stayed around zero. Any warmer and the
elves would have been uncomfortable. Grychn wore a body
stocking of space polymer. I was as naked as the elves.
More naked. I had no fur.

I'm afraid I inhaled too much of the mnemone fumes.
They and the wine went to my head. While the others talked
and laughed, I drifted into a pleasant reverie. I fell asleep.

Someone carried me to another elf-house. This one had
a Terran bed of wombskin and an oxygen atmosphere. My
oxygen bubble was removed. I lay on the bed in darkness.
Fingers stroked my skin, massaging my muscles. Lips
kissed my ears, my neck, my eyes. I let my penis slip out
of its niche. A tongue stroked stiffness into it. A tail
brushed my cheek.

I sat up.

"Grychn?" I asked, knowing she was not.

A furred body pressed against mine. "No. Aleel. Grychn's
busy. Do you mind?" Whiskers brushed my cheek.

I was too mellow with mnemone to mind anything. I

kissed her face, finding her mouth with my lips. My tongue touched hers. I stroked her fur. It felt wonderful. Static sparked blue beneath my hands. Breasts pressed against my chest. I smoothed the fur around them with my tongue, then moved down her belly to apply my tongue to the softness between her legs. She took my penis in her mouth, working her tongue over it. Her tail wrapped around my neck. Muscles fasciculated. Skin quivered. Bodies undulated in passion.

Later she rested her head on my shoulder as we lay together.

"I liked that," she said.

"So did I." I smiled. "Now we can stop being polite. Tell me why Maizay sent you here." I paused. "To keep me busy? So he can have Grychn?"

She laughed. "Certainly for that. But he didn't send me. I asked to be the one. I like you. I like your swordplay." At the double entendre, I felt her face smile next to mine. I smiled also. "I like being with other warriors," she said simply, as if that was enough.

It was. But something still bothered me. "Why all the hospitality? Why you? Maizay doesn't owe me anything."

"You brought Grychn back. He's quite fond of her."

"What else?"

She paused. The tip of her tail traced circles on my belly. "You know where to find something he wants. Something Grychn told him about. He thinks he needs it to win the war. He wants to convince you to help us."

So that was it. Maizay knew about the timestone and wanted it. Grychn had told him about it. "What about you?" I asked. "Do you want me to help you?"

Aleel laughed so low it was a growl in her throat. "Oh, yes. I want your help." She rubbed her pelvis against my leg, then wrapped her legs around me. She lifted me into the air, climbing to the ceiling on glass rods. There she hung with both hands, swinging in the air. I wrapped my arms around her and held on tight. She spread her legs wide, letting me enter, then squeezed them together. I slipped back and forth inside her. Our swings increased.

"Is this the way elves do it?"

"One of the ways."

"No hands?"

"We have something else."

"Yes?"

"Tails."

"How are they used?"

She showed me. I won't say it wasn't interesting.

3

I woke when something warm and naked crawled into bed with me, pulling a satin sheet of space polymer over us. She cupped her body next to mine, pressing her breasts against my back and pushing her pelvis into my buttocks. Bare skin felt good next to mine. Her hand went over my body and found my genitals. She fondled them.

I glanced up. Aleel slept elf fashion, hanging from a glass bar with one hand and her tail. Her legs dangled free, while her other arm was folded across her body.

"So the rumors were true," I whispered.

"What rumors?" Grychn asked.

"About you and Maizay."

"I suppose. But not like the tawdry speculation on the holos. He's sweet."

"I thought I was your lover."

"You are. You always will be one of them."

"How many more?"

"A few. Do you mind terribly?"

"Don't be silly."

"Good." She smiled. "Do you like Aleel?"

"Very much."

"I thought you would."

We both rolled over, so I cupped her as she nestled against me. My penis had stiffened to her caresses. I entered her from behind. She wiggled her bottom, settling into my lap. My hands caressed her breasts.

"That feels good. Oh my, yes." She moaned.

"Try to be quiet."

"Why?"

"We don't want to wake Aleel."

"Marc! You, a prude. I don't believe it."

"No, it's not that at all." I thought of the elf's tail. "I just don't think I could handle both of you. I'm not back to full strength yet." My thrusts continued their rhythm against her bottom.

She laughed, low and delicious. But not loud enough to wake Aleel.

The sound of a battle gong was loud enough to wake all of us.

Instinct took over. I leaped out of the bed and was halfway into battle dress before I remembered I wasn't a combrid anymore.

"What is it?" I asked Aleel as she swung down.

"The city's under attack," she said dispassionately. She picked up her weapon. "Hurry. We'll need everyone to help fight them." She dropped through the door opening.

Grychn's battle dress hung near the door, along with the pseudowings we'd worn earlier. She quickly climbed into her combat armor and I finished getting into mine. We shouldered battle packs. Before Grychn closed her helmet visor, I turned her to face me.

"I'm not going to fight anymore," I said.

"What, then?"

"I'm going to run." I looked at her. "I'd like you to come with me, but you don't have to. I can fly a trigee racer myself."

"Where are you going?"

"Away from Titan. To Iapetus."

"To look for the timestone."

"Yes."

Her eyes shimmered wet. "OK," she said. "I let you leave once. I'm not going to make that mistake again. I'll go. I'll even help you find that damned stone."

"Now you're talking sense. You'll like being my consort —we'll have our own little empire." Then I had an idea. In armor, we might be mistaken for combrids. Which would be OK if it was a combrid who made the mistake. But if it was an elf, we might get shot. I handed Grychn her pseudowings and strapped mine on. Now the elves should recognize us as friends.

We lowered our visors and picked up our weapons, then stepped through the door and dropped ten meters to the ground.

Elves swooped all around. Each was carrying a weapon. Grychn and I took off, flying toward the east. We dodged around the trees of the city. As I had hoped, the elves didn't bother us. They had more to worry about.

From the mountains above the city, optical pandemonium raged. Pulsar beams stabbed out from fortified elven batteries. Gunships screamed past overhead, making strafing runs at the placements. Troop buses hovered farther out, waiting for the gunships to secure a landing zone for them. One hoverbus circled high above.

I turned my sensors to max gain. Just as I'd suspected, I "saw" the infrared smudges of combrids dropping from the bus. A cyrine HALO company. They would free-fall as long as possible, then hit their thrusters at the last possible moment, just before impact. Their job would be to create a diversion, so Ghost Cavalry units could make conventional landings.

Pulsar lightning ricocheted from trees of glass. Detonations cracked like continuous thunder. Chunks of rock and ice were blasted from the cliffs and showered down on the city, shattering both elf-houses and trees. Fragments struck my back. Luckily none tore the fabric of our wings.

A gunship was hit as it made a strafing run. The pilot was unable to pull out of his dive and the ship rammed the cliff and exploded. Rock really flew then. But we were far enough away to avoid being struck by any of the larger pieces.

For a moment, I thought we'd get away cleanly. I started to congratulate myself on our luck. But there're two kinds of luck.

All of a sudden, a crashing came from the trees overhead. We were buried under shards of crystal, enough weight to carry us to the ground. I knew without looking what had happened—we'd blundered into the landing zone of a HALO squad. In a second, a bunch of burly cyrines would be landing on top of Grychn and me.

I stood up, flinging off crystalline debris. I dug Grychn

out of a pile of jagged fragments. Our wings were torn to shreds. But there was no time to worry about that.

"Quick, we've got to move." I grabbed her hand and pulled her along with me. We hadn't gone fifty meters before the first of the cyrines landed. I knew they had seen us. I was hoping they would ignore us. No such luck.

A burst of pulsar fire fanned out through the trees. Crystal matrix sizzled. Oxide vapor puffed, then ignited in balls of flame, as a second salvo of quanta zipped past. The resulting smoke shielded us briefly. We kept running. Again came the forlorn hope that the cyrines would lose interest. That was not to be. My magnetometer detected six disturbances in the field. They were following us. A grim suspicion came to me—maybe the cyrines had been sent after Grychn and me. Maybe a spook vendetta had begun.

There wasn't much we could do except run for it.

I sprayed a ten-second burst back through the smoke, hoping to slow the pursuit a little. I flipped open my visor and signaled Grychn to do the same. That way we could talk as we ran.

"Are they coming after us?" she asked.

"Looks that way to me."

Grychn laughed. Inappropriately, I thought. "What's so funny?"

"Just like old times. We've got to stop meeting like this."

I smiled in spite of myself. "Got any ideas?"

"Several. I haven't been playing guerrilla for two years for nothing. Combrids have chased me all over Titan. Maizay planted some nasty little surprises up ahead, just in case something like this should happen."

"Can we get through?"

"I think I remember the way. We've got to try anyway, don't we?"

"Yeah, we've got to try."

"Marc?"

"Yes."

"Don't let them take me this time. I don't want to go back to Kramr. OK?"

I knew what she meant. I didn't answer.

"OK?" she asked again.

"OK."

"You promise?"

"I said OK." I shot another clip behind me. May as well give them something to think about.

We flipped down our visors. I let Grychn lead the way. I hoped she knew where she was going.

She took a zigzag course through the forest, making long, skimming jumps. I made sure my feet landed exactly the same place hers had. Even that wasn't entirely safe. Sometimes elves put a time-delay fuse into their booby traps—she'd trip the trigger, but it wouldn't blow for a few more seconds. Like until I was standing right on top. I scanned the surrounding forest, smiling at what my sensors detected. The area bristled with lethality: trip wires stretched like cobwebs between the trees, forming a gossamer labyrinth. Some of the wires were attached to needle mines stuck to the sides of trees. The slightest tug would detonate the mine, sending hundreds of microfission needles shooting into the area. Others were attached to photonuclear bombs—the resulting flash would cause temporary blindness, even through the visual filters of a combat visor. Some of the strands were not trip wires at all—they were cutting wires. A tensile field was generated along a monomolecular strand. The combination of tiny diameter and tremendous tensile strength meant the wires would cut through anything that touched them, including combat armor. More than one combrid had been decapitated, lost his legs, or been cut in half from walking into such a wire. Clear drops beaded on other filaments, like dew on a spider thread. My olfactometers confirmed the drops were surface-effect nerve agent—one drop on combat armor would spread out into a monomolecular film which could enter the tiniest chink in the armor to kill its occupant in seconds.

For the first time, I admired the ingenuity of elves. Clever toaders, they were.

Grychn seemed to know where she was going. I followed close behind. There were various ways to get through the maze. If you knew the right one, you hardly had to slow down. If you didn't, you had to carefully work your way through, backtracking whenever you ran into a cul-de-sac. Your helmet sensors and computer helped, but to a limited degree, primarily showing you where you had been, to prevent repeating past mistakes. You constructed a grid on your datascreen. But you needed more data to fill in the blank places. That data could only be obtained by careful probing, walking meticulous patterns, and by trial and error. All that took time. The cyrines following us should be slowed down considerably. I could imagine the curses they were muttering. I could also imagine the tricks they would try. I would have tried them myself. I loaded a clip of ground-to-air minimissiles into my weapon.

The web-field was about a kilometer wide. Grychn either had a good memory or was lucky. I didn't care which. She wound her way through the maze at a brisk run, never hesitating. I stayed right on her heels. We got through to the other side uneventfully. Our cyrine pursuers would have to take considerably longer. Unless they tried something tricky.

When I heard the whine of gravturbines, I knew they had thought of the same thing I had. A hoverbus was coming from the west. Dense forest prevented me from seeing it, as well as getting a clear shot from below. The plan would be for it to drop another squad of combrids on the other side of Grychn and me, thereby trapping us between them. They would fly a circular drop pattern to try to keep us from slipping around their flank. I would have thought of the same tactics. Maybe I could keep it from happening.

I plotted several vectors on my battle computer. I knew about where the cyrines were. They knew about where Grychn and I were. The hoverbus would fly a circular drop pattern roughly a half-kilometer in diameter, with our position as its center.

I plugged my weapon's sight into my computer and fired a carefully spaced pattern of minimissiles, using radians and azimuths provided by the computer. I held it almost straight up and rotated in a semicircle, pressing the firing stud as LED's flashed. The missiles arced high in the air. They would rise about three kilometers and hover on their own p-grav thrusters, while sensors scanned the area below for a target. They were programmed to seek p-gravity— hardly standard issue for Titan. They had cost a fortune on the black market. With luck, the hoverbus would be their target.

As soon as I fired the last minimissile, Grychn and I were on the run again. We paralleled the web-field, effectively putting more of it between ourselves and the cyrines. We really moved now. Grychn was quite adept at picking a path through the forest. I had trouble keeping up with her. I remembered chasing her through the same forest a long time ago. I hadn't been able to catch her then. I suspected she could have left me behind now, had she wanted to.

A faint whine waxed louder in my auditory sensors.

Minimissiles had limited targeting capability. The bus would have to pass almost directly beneath one.

Other sensors told me the cyrines were working their way through the far edge of the web. Without help, they wouldn't be able to catch us.

Still we ran full speed. Crystal branches shattered with our passage. Silence was not necessary now. Hydrocarbon fog sent wisps snaking between the trees. Fleeting images reflected from glass tree trunks, blurred and indistinct. Like ghosts rising from the mists.

I thought of combrids riding in a hoverbus. Maybe they were Ghost Cavalry. Faces flashed in my mind unbidden: Trinks, Vichsn, Sergeant Pepper. Obsidian skin gleamed with green battle light. Retinal reflections flashed. Ocular membranes shone like silver monocles. I pushed those images away. I was playing another game now. The rules had changed.

Gravturbines could now be heard plainly. Any moment, I expected to hear the thud of drop hatches opening. Then combrids would start floating to ground. The chase would begin anew.

Instead, I heard a mach-ten crack of thunder.

I grabbed Grychn, pushed her to the ground, then fell beside her.

A minimissile had found a target—the concentric cones of force spewing from a hoverbus's gravturbines. Now it sought that target at 10,000 km/h. Positive p-grav was attracted to negative p-grav. The missile swam up a cone of force and rammed into a thruster tube, where + p-grav and − p-grav annihilated each other by becoming heat.

The blast flattened trees in a hundred-meter circle at ground zero. A concussion wave lifted Grychn and me, then tossed us tumbling to ground. Luckily, we were half a klick away from ground zero.

We picked ourselves up.

"You OK?" I asked.

She nodded.

Combat armor had kept us from being hurt by the blast.

"How far to your ship?"

"Ten or twenty kilometers."

"Can you find it in the dark?"

"Of course."

"Then let's get going before they send another APC. I'm out of minimissiles. It's almost dawn."

We ran again through the forest of glass.

4

At dawn, we reached the spaceship.

I probably wouldn't have been able to find it by myself —it was suspended in an old mine shaft in an isolated mountain range. The mouth of the shaft had been covered with camofilm. You almost had to step on it before you knew it was there. Grychn found it with no difficulty. I was glad I had her with me.

We crawled under one side of the cover and down into the shaft, where we climbed down the side of the ship on rungs recessed into the hull. The craft was painted with camopolymer, so it was difficult to see clearly, but the lines appeared sleek. Three one-meter thruster tubes were attached to a central hull with struts. Bow and stern both tapered to needle points. The ship would do well in atmosphere as well as deep space.

We came to the air lock. Grychn punched in an unlock sequence—the hatch opened. We swung ourselves into the air lock, closed the hatch, and waited for the air lock to cycle. By the time the inner door opened, the ship's synthebrain had warmed things up for us.

There were three compartments. The forward one was the control room—two acceleration chambers lay side by side, surrounded by holographic displays. The nose of the ship was transparent one-way, providing good visibility to about 120 degrees. The middle cabin was a stateroom with galley and bath. Hammocks pulled out of recessed niches and snapped to rings. The rear cabin was a cargo hold. I rummaged through it. It was still well stocked.

In a few minutes I was making breakfast—I was famished for real food.

We had crêpes and reconstituted fruit, sausages, and a bottle of white wine. I'm afraid I stuffed myself. I became bloated and a little drowsy.

We pulled out hammocks to take a nap, having decided to wait until dark to leave. I fell asleep quickly. From the wine, I suppose. But I must have been tired as well. I didn't wake until after sundown.

Grychn was not in her hammock. I rolled out of mine and went to the forward cabin. Grychn stood there, going through preflight checks. Green nav light shone from her naked body. Her muscles had filled out a little. She was looking better every day. In fact, she was looking damn good right now.

She had already gone outside and removed the cover from our "silo." Stars glittered between wisps of fog through the transparent nose of the ship. Display lights began changing from red to green as systems checked themselves. I came up behind her. She stood up. I hugged her from behind. She turned and kissed my mouth, slipping her tongue past mine. I put my hands on her buttocks, lifting her off the deck.

I carried her back to the stateroom and lay her on a hammock. "Do we have time?" I whispered.

"All the time in the world."

So I laid her. And she laid me. With some interesting variations in between. It only took until midnight—we had time to spare.

We lay in acceleration chambers, immersed in shock gel. Oxygen bubbles covered our noses. We each wore a nav helmet, connecting our brains to the electronic physiology of the ship. By doing so, we became an integral part of the ship, forming a macrocyborg. The ship's sensors became our senses. The ship's servo mechanisms were under our motor control. Afferent neurons collected data. Efferent neurons innervated effectors. Grychn's mind shared my body and mine shared hers, causing the distinction between the two of us to become blurred—our flesh melded into one and felt comfortable that way. That sharing of flesh was more intimate than any sexual act had ever been. And just as satisfying.

Yet my self remained distinct from hers, as her self did from mine.

I had never flown in a ship before, but I knew how to do it. Good old hypnotraining. The Corps called it "other duties as assigned."

Grychn whispered in my mind: "Ready?"

"Anytime."

We nudged a flicker of p-grav out of the three thrusters. We, the macrocyborg spaceship, rose out of our silo. As our stern cleared the ground, we increased our thrust. We accelerated upward at a comfortable ten G's. Hydrocarbon clouds streamed past our skin—friction warmed us like a summer breeze. Forests of glass receded; mountains dwindled to anthills.

We broke free of the clinging fingers of atmosphere. Clouds rolled beneath like orange sea swells. Ahead, stars shone steady and cold. Sunlight flared in a corona around the edge of Titan. But we stayed in the safety of shadow. As we traveled farther from Titan, Saturn appeared, expanding out from the disk margins of the Moon. The rings faced edgewise to us, appearing as black bands against the planet's ocher surface. Enceladus, Tethys, Dione, and Rhea gleamed like cyclops' eyes in black space. Mimas was on the other side of Saturn. Janus was hidden somewhere against the face of the planet. Hyperion and Phoebe hung directly overhead, separated on a north-south line; Iapetus was fifteen degrees to the west.

Iapetus was our destination.

The cone of shadow narrowed. More of Saturn came out of eclipse. We stayed in darkness, like a ghost prowling the night. And we were a ghost ship—camofilm had darkened to match ambient light, making our albedo almost zero. We were nearly invisible to photosensors. Nor did we reflect any other of the electromagnetic spectrum. Naturally we were silent—sound was not propagated in vacuum. The only trace of our passage was a slight disturbance in the gravitational flux—a cone-shaped wake of p-grav trailing behind us, soon broken up and lost among the myriad gravitational vectors produced by Saturn and his nine children. Normally we would not have been detected. Space was too big and patrols too few.

But these were not normal times.

We'd forgotten about the fleet from Earth, which now hung in orbit around Titan. But now we saw them coming around the edge of shadow, drifting like a shark pack: four heavy cruisers, ten troop tugs with their trains of personnel pods, and a half-dozen destroyers. One of the destroyers led the pack.

Sensing spectra pinged from our hull. They couldn't "see" us—camofilm didn't reflect back any radiation. But they "heard" us—gravmeters detected the variance our passage made in the gravitational flux. They knew a ship plied the void.

P-grav flared behind the lead destroyer as it accelerated toward us. The rest of the fleet stayed in their orbits. We were no menace to them. One destroyer could easily take care of a gunrunner or smuggler.

The hailing frequency hissed: "Heave to, bogey ship, and prepare to be boarded."

"What do we do?" I asked Grychn. "It won't take much of a check to figure out who we are."

We turned away from the pack, curving around Titan. Saturn lay below us. "We run for it, then," she answered.

"Heave to, and be inspected." A pulsar beam stabbed out, crossing our bows.

Grychn laughed. "I had this ship built to run blockades. Edbryn installed three of his finest thruster tubes on her. Let's see what she'll do."

P-grav roared from our stern, forming a swirling vortex in the space behind us. A hundred G's smothered our bodies. Even through shock gel, the force was oppressive. Air squeezed out of our lungs, which couldn't be reexpanded. Oxygenation had to occur extracorporally. No problem for me—I had an hour's worth stored in brown adipose. But even if I hadn't, like Grychn, oxygen was pumped into the shock gel at high concentrations, there to diffuse into our naked skins. Carbon dioxide was likewise removed by the gel. The problem was that blood circulated sluggishly, if at all, limiting the effectiveness of cutaneous exchange. Nutrient media was pumped directly into our brains, so we could think, but the rest of our internal organs were put on hold. They could only go about two hours before permanent damage resulted.

I found I couldn't move a single muscle—I couldn't even

hold my eyes open. Not that I had to—we could "see" with other sensors.

We lunged forward, streaking around Titan. A salvo of pulsar fire came, but the destroyer's targeting computer underestimated our acceleration, so the beams only sliced through our p-grav wake. The rest of the fleet disappeared behind Titan. The destroyer pursued, but it could never hope to catch us, so it did what it had to do. P-grav flared from two launching bays—two sleek fighters darted out ahead of the destroyer.

"Can we outrun them?" I asked.

"We can try."

We rolled downward, toward Saturn. Titan receded to our stern. We made random zigzags in our course. Pulsar beams occasionally zipped past, too close for comfort. The two fighters kept pace, but couldn't gain on us. That meant we couldn't gain on them either, because we were already going flat out. But maybe we could elude them.

Saturn came ever closer. We passed by his other moons —there was no safety for us on them. The rings cast black shadows on the planet. Storms raged in the upper reaches of his atmosphere.

Still the fighters chased us. Still pulsar salvos stabbed around us. Sooner or later they'd get lucky and score a hit. Gravity's hand still smothered us. I noticed that my heart had stopped beating. It would start up again when the acceleration lessened. Provided that happened soon. But my body was an incidental part of me. I was aware of Grychn's body also, and it too was mine. So was the ship. P-grav roaring from thruster nozzles sent a thrill along electronic neurons. Guidance thrusters were my arms and legs. Permaplastic skin felt the cold of space and the warmth of a distant sun. Bits of space dust hit my meteor shield like bugs smashing against a windscreen. I could "hear" gravity. I "saw" with extended frequencies. I "spoke" with spectra other than sound, and louder.

Saturn loomed below. We were deep in his gravity well now. He would always be beneath us. The rings approached, shining with sunlight. We saw them on edge, wavering like a mirage with light reflecting from crystals of frozen ammonia and hydrocarbons. We slipped beside them, skimming close. Stray bits of ammonia ice pattered against our meteor shield like hail on a tin roof. That close, the rings appeared as a translucent band of haze—stars were visible behind them. They were only fifteen km thick. I had the urge to duck into them to hide from the pursuing fighters. But I knew the rings were dense enough to tear us apart at our present velocity. Some of the chunks of ice were hundreds of kilos in mass. How did I know that? Grychn told me. I believed her.

But we got as close as we could to the rings. Ice crystals from them swirled into the vortex of our thrusters, forming clouds behind us. That would interfere with the fighters' aim, as well as slow them down, as they would have to take a path farther away from the rings. They could no longer follow directly behind us. But that would only delay them a little. All they had to do was keep following us. We couldn't hide next to the rings forever.

"Do we have a plan?" I asked us.

"Oh yes indeed," we answered, and I saw the plan. It just might work.

The fighters kept shooting. Quite bothersome of them. Pulsar quanta ricocheted from ice particles in our wake and gleamed like red searchlights within the rings. The hail storm on our roof increased its frenzy, sending a vibration deep into our structural frame. If it continued, eventually we'd shake apart. So we slowed our acceleration. Fingers of Saturnian gravity tugged at us. The fighters closed the gap. Their shots came closer, close enough to raise blisters on our skin.

We had reached the midpoint of our curve past Saturn— in a moment we'd be flying away from the planet.

Now was the time.

We reversed the polarity of our thrusters, and forced them into emergency override. Two hundred gravities pushed from the front, slowing forward velocity. The two fighters flashed past, still accelerating; our relative velocity was too great for them to train their guns on us.

We dropped closer to Saturn. There was a 1,400-kilometer gap between the innermost ring and the fringes of the planet's atmosphere. Of course, "gap" was a relative term. There was still lots of junk there.

We continued to slow.

The fighters had begun decelerating, too. They were still above and ahead of us. Soon they would shed enough velocity to drop down to us. There was only one thing to do.

We entered the gap.

Have you ever been in a bunker that was being shelled by heavy artillery? Well, that's what our meteor field sounded like as fist-sized chunks of ice bounced off it. Frozen ammonia shattered into snow. A cloud of vapor formed around us. But in a second we were through and sailing in clear space. The fighters were now on the other side of Saturn's rings. We were safe from both pursuit and pulsars.

We cut our thrusters. A giant hand stopped crushing our bodies. Our hearts started beating. We gasped air into our lungs.

Our residual velocity was just right, just what we'd calculated it should be—slow enough that we were briefly caught in Saturn's gravity, which caused us to curve in an ellipse around the planet, but more than escape velocity, so instead of being pulled into orbit we climbed away as we came around the planet—like a comet going around the Sun. Our path had been carefully plotted. On the way out we'd intercept Iapetus. On a dead drift. Without any power. Get it? Now we were completely invisible. We'd have to collide with a patrol ship to be detected.

Pretty clever, huh?

You're damn right it was!

And it worked just the way we'd planned. We coasted in an elliptical orbit out to Iapetus. It took seventy-two hours. But the extra time was worth it. I had never made love in zero G before. Apparently Grychn had. She knew all kinds of tricks. Makes you really appreciate Newton's Laws.

Our course had been perfect. Our intercept was precise enough so that we only had to make one orbit around Iapetus before landing. During that orbit we donned spacesuits and spray-painted over the camofilm of the ship and reattached identifying numbers and running lights. Our ship became the *Kestral*, out of Nyssa. We became a Lord and Lady on holiday.

We landed at a small spaceport on the edge of the Ice Mountains. There are only two kinds of mountains on Iapetus—Ice Mountains and Rocky Mountains. One hemisphere is covered with frozen ammonia and hydrocarbons.

The other is barren. A huge crater explains the reason, and also why Iapetus's orbit is inclined—the heat of an ancient collision had vaporized the ice on one side. It was slowly creeping back. Maybe in another billion years the Moon would be evenly sheathed in ice again.

Iapetus had not been colonized. A few mines operated in the Rocky Mountains. Mining was not profitable in the Ice Mountains. There was one city, Atlas, that served both miners and tourists. A few resort domes catered to hydrocarbon snow skiers. Mostly purists.

But Iapetus was rather out of the way. Which suited me fine.

War, elves, combrids, and spooks were all far away.

The timestone waited.

We were safe.

5

We crawled out of our acceleration chambers and showered together to remove residual shock gel. Grychn had a couple of pair of space coveralls stashed aboard. We each pulled on one of the body stockings. Combat armor and battle packs were left stowed in a locker—battle dress would have attracted attention had we worn it. Iapetus was at peace. There was a small combrid garrison in the Rocky Mountains, but their only duties were to settle squabbles among miners and to discourage rebel pirates from using Iapetus as a base. Neither Grychn nor I could pose as combrids on R&R. So it was better to stow away that gear until we needed it.

Grychn had also left some jewelry aboard. She put on a necklace of singing pearls and sapphire earrings. Sonic diamonds, emeralds, and rubies glittered from her fingers and toes. I restricted myself to a single gold earring and my turquoise chargering. No sense being ostentatious.

Besides, I preferred that people look at Grychn. That way, they'd be less likely to notice me.

The spaceport was located in a valley at the edge of the Ice Mountains. A dusty plain stretched for twenty or thirty kilometers to the east, gradually rising to butt against the first range of the Rocky Mountains. Spatters of nickel/iron glinted from their peaks.

The domes of Atlas and two floating towers lay to the west of the spaceport, sitting on the floor of a box canyon, surrounded by snow-covered peaks. Their summits rose steeply to over three thousand meters. The highest was El Diente, marked by a fountain of plasma squirting into space—a gimmick used to attract people to a nightclub on its summit. Glaciers of hydrocarbon/ammonia ice started high in the mountains and ground out of valleys to end in crumbling cliffs less than a hundred meters from the first dome. Skiers made graceful S-turns down the glaciers. Roostertails of hydrocarbon powder rose behind them.

We left the ship and walked across fused obsidian, past rows of parked space yachts, and entered an airtube. We were whisked a couple of klicks away to Atlas, coming out in a commons dome. There was no customs agent— Atlas was a freeport village.

Shops ringed the periphery of the commons, with an open mall in the middle of the dome. A park with grass and flowers and real trees from Earth lay in the center of the mall, with its own stream and waterfall. Songbirds sang from the trees. The mall was crowded with people. Skiers who had finished for the day strolled about, dressed in shining body stockings. Nonskiers loitered, waiting for après-ski to begin. Call-bodies lounged on park benches, displaying their wares to miners rotating back to Atlas for R&R.

Atlas was originally a mining town, and still was for the most part—that was typical of settlements on the outer moons. Prospectors came first, lured to inhospitable climes by the chance of instant wealth. When a lode was struck, a town sprang up overnight, as more miners poured into the area. If the ore was high-grade, a mining town could be quite lavish, as its miners could afford to import the best of everything. But when the mines played out, miners moved to other strikes. With nothing to support the local economy, stores and shops and saloons closed as their proprietors followed the miners to the next lode. The mining town was abandoned. There were hundreds of such ghost towns scattered about the outer moons.

Although the active mines on Iapetus were now deeper in the Rocky Mountains, Atlas still serviced them, as it had the only deep-space port on the Moon. Even if it hadn't, Atlas was in no danger of becoming a ghost town. It had been turned into a resort. The Ice Mountains of Iapetus boasted the best hydrocarbon snow in the System and the most vertical drop to ski. Skiing fanatics came billions of kilometers to try the deep, light powder snow. A skiing vacation on Iapetus had become *de rigueur* for the nobility of Old Earth, as well as for wealthy commoners.

Some of the best skiing was found in the Horseshoe Mountains that surrounded Atlas. The domes of ski chalets grew like giant mushrooms at the foot of the mountains. A hundred-floor hotel tower had been built next to the Anaconda Tower, to accommodate the less affluent. More shops and restaurants and nightclubs were required to cater to skiers.

Liftubes snaked up sheer cliffs to the heads of glaciers at the mountaintops. Skiers could then glide for kilometers down those glaciers. The more adventurous could go on hoverbus ski tours into the interior, getting off on the top of mountains to ski virgin powder that might not have ever been tracked before. For those wanting solitude, the Ice Mountains were the place to go—they were still largely unexplored as well as unsettled.

Atlas was a mixture of the old and new: a raw mining town blended with the pseudoelegance of a resort, whose shops catered to any perversion imaginable.

Grychn and I strolled across the mall hand in hand—a Lord and Lady on their ski vacation. Our faces were still a little haggard from peptide addiction, but the hollows around our eyes had filled in. Bony prominences still showed under our body stockings, where muscle had not filled out yet. But not enough to attract attention. Lords and Ladies sometimes played rough games themselves. Maybe we'd come to Atlas for a rest from those. No one would think to ask. Nor care.

Water babbled in a brook. A warm breeze rustled the leaves of trees. Birds flitted from branch to branch, singing the songs of spring. We passed beautiful call-bodies, but did not look with lust. Pathics touched our minds fleetingly, then withdrew. Peppers smiled behind the windows of their parlors, teeth shining blue, but those also we could resist. Mnemone fumes wafted from other doors. Chips skittered across green felt gaming tables. I could even resist their lure. There would be time for those games later, after I'd found the timestone.

We left the mall and walked through a short tunnel that led to the Hotel Atlas lobby. I registered us as a Lord and Lady, using a name I hadn't used for a long time. But the name matched the chargering I wore on my finger and there was still considerable money in that account. Neither the name nor the account had ever been compromised. I left the hotel bill open. A Lord would be expected to run up other charges. Our lack of baggage did not draw comment.

We rode up the liftube to the ninety-ninth floor.

Our room commanded a good view of the Ice Mountains —I'd wanted that. A bottle of champagne stood in an ice bucket. I poured two glasses. We lay together on womb-skin, sipping wine. A real fire burned in a glass fireplace, radiating warmth into our bodies, blending its heat with that of the wine.

Soon body stockings lay in a heap on the floor.

Wine-wet lips kissed mine, then moved to kiss other places. I let myself relax. We were safe.

My lips sought places that pleased. My tongue touched softly. Smooth skin rubbed against mine, then melted into my flesh. Tactile sensations blended. We were one again, like when we played the mindgame—no, more like when we piloted the gravship. I knew how she liked to be touched, because I was touching myself. Her fingers and lips and tongue were mine, touching me. We made love to ourself, going slowly, savoring each sensation, cherishing each thrill.

A long time later, we coupled, and that also lasted forever. My flesh entered; my flesh yielded to the penetration, as though it had folded back on itself. My mouth kissed itself. Delicious friction stretched tactile fibers; waves of peristalsis squeezed tight. I knew when to thrust deeper, when to withdraw. I knew when to open my legs and when to wrap them tight around my waist. My fingers knew what places to touch, what orifices to enter.

My nipples tightened. A flush burned across my chest, rising into my neck. I played reflex arcs like an orchestra, gradually building nervous tension, until neurons sang with energy. Secretory epithelium exuded. Ducts and vesicles became tumid. Glands stretched tight against their capsules. Then they could hold no more. Parasympathetic ganglions discharged like chain lightning. Smooth muscle contracted. Sphincters opened. Spasms rippled down and around my penis, synchronized with the contractions of my vagina— semen was pumped from within and without. Male and female orgasms were linked in reflex arcs, one triggering another, like a sexual seizure. The frenzy gradually ebbed. Warmth flowed between my legs. I lay quietly, arms wrapped around myself.

Slowly, we became separate again.

Grychn lay beside me with one leg draped over mine, resting her head on my shoulder. Her breath tickled in my ear.

"That was nice," she said. "Much better than in the mindgame—that was real." She licked my ear. "You were good."

"Was it me?"

"Oh, yes. You *entered* me." She laughed at her double entendre. "I mean, I'm sure it was your mind that came into mine, bringing with it your perceptions." Her fingers made circles on my chest. "How long have you been a pathic?"

I thought for a moment. Nels had been right, then. Some of it began to make sense. "Just now," I answered. I felt a tug in my mind—a faint call. Something waited in the cold for me.

"Latent, then."

"That's what Jain Maure said my psyche tests showed."

"I wonder what made it surface now?"

"The timestone. Nels told me it could bring out latent abilities."

She paused. "I'd almost forgotten about it. Everything is so peaceful now." She looked at me seriously. "Why don't you forget about it, too? We don't need it. There's lots of places we could go. Let's just have a little holiday and be on our way."

"I've come too far to give up now. Too much has happened. I've got to find the stone."

"But don't you see? It's become an obsession with you. Why?"

"I don't know. At first it was because I'd seen my own death and was afraid of it. Then it was as a means to obtain power. But I'm not sure now. Except that I've got to find it. I'm sure about that."

She kissed me. "I'll stay with you. I won't leave you now. I'm not going to lose you again." She settled in closer to me. "Have you ever thought that the timestone is looking for you? That it is drawing you near? That it wants you to find it?"

The fire cast flickering light about the room.

I closed my eyes. Dim urgings nagged my mind. Yes, the thought had occurred to me. But I wasn't sure there was anything I could do about it.

That night, the dreams started.

Faces rose to torment my sleep: my own, with eyes of shattered ice, teeth like icicle shards, covered with frost like blue fur; my brother Robrt, eyes bulging, tongue bitten off, blood oozing from his nose; Henri, laughing while we hung, his aquiline features contorted with glee, fire burning from steel eyes; Vichsn, with delight sparkling from retinal reflections; Jain Maure, with copper eyes and full, red lips; my parents, white as marble statues, but at peace; and Grychn—though I couldn't remember what she looked like, I knew she was there also.

The faces superimposed on each other, becoming confused. I couldn't sort out one from another. I knew meaning had to be hidden in the puzzle—if only I could put the pieces together. But a key part was missing. Without it, the rest remained jumbled fragments.

Gradually they dimmed, leaving me uneasy with their memory.

The next day nightdreams were almost forgotten. We went shopping. Grychn bought several new ski outfits. She even talked me into buying one—a body stocking of shiny blue polymer. She said it made me look dashing. We also bought us each a pair of gravskis, poles, and boots.

Then the shopping became serious. I bought a set of topographic maps of the Ice Mountains and two sets of war surplus cross-country skis, and rented a skimmer for a week. The other survival gear we would need we already had stowed in battle packs aboard the ship.

We ate lunch in the café atop the Anaconda Tower. Over coffee, I looked over my maps. Nels had told me where she'd hidden the timestone—in an abandoned mine shaft in the steep canyon between Sunshine Peak and Mount Themis, the two highest mountains on Iapetus. I found the area on my map. It was a remote region, with no camps or habitations within a hundred kilometers. The canyon was inaccessible except on skis—even a hovercraft would have trouble landing on such steep slopes. Which was why Nels had hidden it there.

Grychn had been looking out the window while I looked at my maps. As I folded the mylar sheets, she said: "Let's go skiing for a half-day. There's still lots of powder left."

I looked down to the slopes. Why not? We needed the diversion. "OK," I said. "Let's."

Fifteen minutes later we were atop Peak Nine.

A glacier ground its way down a canyon, to end in ice cliffs. Vertical drop was around three thousand meters. The grade was between forty-five and ninety degrees. A hundred-percent grade was a sheer cliff, so ninety percent was pretty steep. In the low gravity of Iapetus, the slopes had to be fairly steep to get any decent velocity. P-grav generators in our skis also helped augment downward acceleration.

All day the slight heat of the distant sun caused hydrocarbons to sublimate, forming a thin atmosphere. At night, the cold caused them to recondense into snow. Thus, each morning, a new layer of powder snow lay ready for skiing.

Smooth sinusoidal tracks already wound down the glacier, but there was still untracked snow between them. We launched ourselves over a cornice and began making our own S-turns. The snow was about a meter deep and was still light and fluffy. Tall roostertails rose behind us. On the forward half of a turn, the snow would puff into a cloud around my body, blinding me momentarily, before I burst through. It was quite exhilarating: skis swishing, snow rustling against my body, seeing the domes of Atlas far below. Clouds hung like fat snakes behind us, marking our passage.

I pulled up on a small rise about a thousand meters down the glacier. Grychn halted beside me.

"This is great," she said. "It's been a long time since I've had fun." She smiled behind her O_2 bubble.

I returned her smile.

Then I heard the swish of skis uphill. I looked up. A skier burst out of a cloud of snow right above me, swooped by, and brushed me with her hip as she passed. I watched a fine figure bobbing up and down as she cut tight S-turns. I'd just glimpsed her face, but something about it disturbed me—jade-green eyes, hair as black as space, lips gleaming blood red. Then I remembered where I'd seen that face before—at Telluride. And I remembered her name— Michele Kramr. The same Kramr? She must have been. But Kramr couldn't have followed us to Iapetus. The skier must be someone else. Just a close resemblance. But I had to be sure.

I took off after her. She was a good skier, but then Kramr had been an expert also. I pressed hard with my toes, turning my skis to max grav to increase my rate of descent. I sat back on them, so they floated on top of the snow, reducing drag. I slowly gained on the woman.

She looked back. Faint laughter came to me. She increased her speed.

I cut back and forth through her wake, not gaining much ground on her now. I was skiing out of control—I would crash eventually if I didn't slow down.

She saved me the trouble. I saw her lose her balance. She was sitting too far back on her skis—the tails slipped out sideways beneath her, sending her sprawling on her backside in a cloud of snow. I leaned forward to slow my descent and then cut a couple of turns before finally coming to a stop below the woman. She was buried under snow.

I wondered what I'd do if it was Kramr. I had no weapon with me. Maybe she wasn't armed. I still remembered the twenty-three ways. Skis would make it twenty-four.

A form moved beneath the snow. One arm came out, then another. She sat up. Snow fell away from her face. Blue eyes regarded mine. Strands of yellow hair peeked out from a stocking hood. I had never seen her before.

"Do I know you?" she asked.

"I think not. I mistook you for someone else. Sorry."

She smiled. "That's OK." She stood up. Her skis had not released from their bindings. "I think I would like to get to know you." She looked up the hill. Grychn approached. "I party at the Critical Mass. Maybe I'll see you there some time." She smiled. "Don't bring your friend, though." Then she was off again, skiing down the glacier, her fine ass bobbing up and down as she made her turns.

Grychn stopped above me, showering me with snow.

"Who's she?" Her voice was strained.

"Nobody. I thought she was someone else. She was nobody at all."

"Good." Her voice laughed. "I'm glad she was someone else."

We finished that run and made several more that afternoon.

Then we ate dinner in our room, and made love in front of the fire afterward.

With sleep, the dreams came to me again.

I woke with Grychn holding me close.

"You shouted in your sleep," she said. "Quite blood-curdling. What were you dreaming?"

I tried to make fleeting images hold still in my mind. I couldn't. They melted away like cool water seeping into hot sand. Memory of them was fragmented. But still disturbing.

"I'm not sure," I answered. "Something about my parents. And my brothers. I kept seeing Henri hanging Robrt and me. Only sometimes I switched places with Henri. When I was the hangman, I had two other victims." I closed my eyes, trying to push away the faces of Trinks and Vichsn with bulging eyes, protruding tongues. And sometimes Grychn took Vichsn's place. I didn't tell her that.

"I wonder why you should have that dream?"

"I don't know." I kept my suspicions to myself.

"Whatever happened to Henri?"

"I don't know that, either. When they took him away, they gave him a new identity to go with his new memories. Although I can't be sure, I suspect he went to the Combrid Corps instead of the cyborg factories—otherwise they wouldn't have bothered to give him a new psyche. And the Corps likes young recruits—they're more malleable. A lot of combrids have synthetic pasts. No one can be entirely sure of his memories. I suspect Henri died on one of the garrison worlds—maybe he was a hero. Who knows?"

"The timestone is making you dream, isn't it?"

"I suppose."

"We can still leave."

"I can't. Not yet."

"Then go back to sleep. I'll hold you."

I closed my eyes. I felt the timestone calling to me in strange songs, eerie music. And when at last I slept, it again inserted images into my mind to disturb my dream-time.

I saw my own death mask again.

I should have guessed the truth then; I'd been given **all** the hints.

But I didn't.

Truth was harder than that to find.

6

The next morning, we got up late. I couldn't get my body out of bed early—I kept falling back to sleep. I'd wanted to leave Atlas that day, but decided against it because we'd be making such a late start.

I spent what was left of the morning packing the skimmer I'd rented with the gear from Grychn's gravship—combat armor, battle packs, assault rifles, extra ammo, even a spare minimissile I'd found. You'd think we were going into battle. Maybe we were. Anyway, everything got packed and was ready.

I planned to leave first thing the next morning.

That afternoon we went skiing again. I didn't see the woman I'd mistaken for Kramr. We had fun skiing. I was glad we'd delayed our departure. The fun would soon be over. Running an empire would be work.

Grychn wanted to go out for dinner that night. She suggested the Critical Mass, the nightclub on top of El Diente. I could see no reason not to go.

Our liftube rode past sheer cliffs of ice to the three-thousand-meter summit of El Diente. Jets of plasma squirted into space like a giant fountain, or the prelude to an eruption if the mountain was volcanic, which it was not. The plasma came from the thruster nozzles of a fuship ore freighter that had crashed on the summit a century earlier, when Atlas was a mining town and spaceships still flew with the raw energies of fusion. No one had bothered to remove the wreckage after the cargo of radioactive isotopes had been salvaged. When Atlas had become a resort, an enterprising businessman converted the wreck into a nightclub and recharged the fusion engine, using stripped nuclei spewing out of nozzles as a beacon to attract business. So I'd read in a brochure in our hotel room. Sounded interesting enough. Everyone had a sense of nostalgia for the wild energies of the days before gravships.

I felt a little thrill of excitement as we stepped out of the foyer of the liftube into the Critical Mass. I'd seen lots of holos about the days of fusion rockets. Sailors had been fragile men then, not hybrids. The energies had been untamed at that time.

I wasn't disappointed. A clear dome had been constructed around the wreck, which had plowed into the mountain nosefirst. At the center of everything was the fusion thruster: coils of superconductor surrounded a ceramic core, creating a magnetic bottle to hold the extreme pressures and temperatures necessary to fuse hydrogen nuclei into helium. A low throbbing came from the thruster and permeated the rest of the Critical Mass—a whisper of the song sung by dying stars. The fuship's jets protruded from the vertex of the dome. Streams of plasma roared from the nozzles, cutting deep into night. Thermonuclear fire glowed throughout the crystal dome, like angry corposant. Transparent decks divided the dome into three levels.

A hostess handed us each a radiation badge to pin on our chests. This touch of verisimilitude charmed us. Another hostess showed us to a table. Cargo pods had been converted into dining rooms. At the center of each table was a radium candle, which cast flickering blue light on lead-foil tablecloths.

The menus were printed on mylar sheets clipped between aluminum covers stenciled with "Decontamination Manual." The fare consisted of Strontium[90] Steaks, Radon Relishes, Cesium[20] Crêpes. You get the picture.

Grychn smiled, appearing like a specter in radioactive blue light. "Isn't this adorable?"

"A little camp."

"Quaint. Rustic. And adorable. I love it. Makes you realize how crazy those early sailors and miners were. They all died of radiation poisoning eventually." Her eyes gleamed blue in radium light.

Our waiter wore an antique decon suit complete with

helmet and heavy lead gauntlets. I was surprised he could serve us at all in such an outfit. His dexterity in doing so amazed me.

The food was quite ordinary, but they did serve a passable claret. We had two bottles with dinner. Then there was absinthe after dinner. Then brandy after coffee. I overindulged. Especially the absinthe. I felt all warm inside.

War seemed very far away indeed. I had almost forgotten about the timestone.

So when Grychn wanted to try the casino, I agreed.

It was just like old times there. No matter what game we played, we won: craps, roulette, faro, blackjack. We could have won all night. Fortunately, I noticed a croupier staring at us, and had enough sense to quit before she became suspicious.

We went down one deck to the dance floor and took a table on the periphery.

Grychn heaped a pile of chips on the table between us. "The timestone?" She moved them around with her finger.

"I'm afraid so. Its power must be awesome if my mind can make it work from this far away." For the first time, I began to feel a little bit afraid.

Grychn laughed. "At least it has some practical advantages." She paused. "Come on, let's dance."

I let her pull me out on the dance floor, even though I detested dancing.

A huge singing diamond hung directly above. Optical music swirled from its facets and floated over the dance floor, before slowly sinking to become tangled among dancers. The dance floor was crowded. Sweat glistened from naked skin. Jewelry glittered. Silver and gold shone. Tendrils of music tangled among us like singing spiderwebs.

Then I saw a face I remembered and thought I would never see again. Copper eyes laughed above haughty cheekbones. Hair like carbon wool cascaded over naked shoulders. Jain Maure danced across the room from me! What was Dr. Pepper doing on Iapetus? That was too much of a coincidence to accept.

I crossed the dance floor, forcing my way through naked bodies bound up in strands of music. Faces laughed at me. Fingers touched, clinging to my hands, wanting me to touch them. I flung them away. Discordant harmonies hurt my ears as I broke the wires of song. I tried to keep my eyes on Jain Maure so I wouldn't lose her in the crowd.

She had turned her back to me. But I kept sight of her hair.

As I approached she turned. But it was not Jain Maure. A vague similarity, no more. And the eyes were green.

Then I understood.

Chameleons could wear any face, but familiar patterns were easier.

I knew who had followed me to Iapetus.

I turned around and went back the way I'd come. Grychn waited for me.

"Marc, what's wrong? You look like you've seen a ghost."

I had. But there wasn't time to explain. I grabbed her hand and pulled her along behind me. We left the dance floor, also leaving behind a fortune in casino chips. We ran to the foyer and jumped into the down liftube, floating three thousand meters to the valley floor. There, we took another tube to the lot where our rented skimmer was parked. I couldn't take a chance and go back to our room. It might be watched. The skimmer might also be under surveillance. That was a chance I had to take.

We climbed in.

I was glad everything was packed. But then, I'd suspected we might need to make a quick getaway.

As soon as we strapped in and the doors closed, I gunned the skimmer into flight. I headed east, into the Rocky Mountains, hoping to confuse any pursuit. I kept the skimmer a few meters off the ground, hugging the sides of mountains. We'd gone a hundred klicks into the Rockies before I let myself believe there wasn't any pursuit. But there wasn't any. I slowed the skimmer down to a sane speed.

"What's the big hurry?" Grychn asked. But she knew.

I told her anyway. "Kramr was at the Critical Mass tonight. He followed us here. If we don't hurry, he'll find the timestone before we do." I watched her closely for her reaction. I was beginning to suspect something.

She turned her eyes away. "Let him find it. Let him carry its curse."

"You know what would happen then. He'd use it as a weapon. How long do you think your elf friends would stay in business if the spooks had the timestone? Not very long, I'll bet."

"Let's not argue. Go find your timestone if that's what you want."

"That's what I want."

I turned the skimmer and headed in a circular course back toward the Ice Mountains. I wanted to make a wide berth of Atlas. No sense tempting fate. The skimmer was equipped with excellent navigation instruments. The rental agency didn't want their customers getting lost. Transmitters were located on strategic peaks. A computer-triangulated fix was a snap.

Before morning, Mt. Themis stood before us, all ten thousand meters of him. Sunshine Peak stood next to him like a younger sister. A steep canyon separated them. Somewhere up that canyon a mine shaft had been drilled into the side of Mt. Themis.

The timestone waited for me there. I felt its call growing stronger in my mind.

I parked the skimmer as far up the canyon as I could land it, on the last flat spot. It settled into a meter of snow. Stars shone steady in a black sky, but orange fire glowed on the eastern horizon. It would be light soon.

"Here we are," I said. "Are you coming with me, or do you want to wait?"

"I'm going with you," she said, simply.

We pulled on combat armor and ski boots, then climbed out of the skimmer before shouldering battle packs and putting on our skis. I hung an assault rifle from a chest sling, and felt silly doing so. We had not been followed. There wasn't anyone else within a hundred klicks. I had acquired nasty habits. My helmet thermometer read a hundred below. A brisk morning on Iapetus.

Sunlight shone from the summit of Mt. Themis, glaring brightly from hydrocarbon ice. A line of light crept down sheer ice cliffs. Snow that had recondensed that night still drifted gently to ground.

The canyon ran directly west for about thirty klicks, ending in a high pass between the two summits. Several side canyons opened into it. Actually, they were snow chutes—snow that gradually accumulated on the steep mountainsides eventually became unstable from thawing and freezing and crashed down to the canyon's bottom in an avalanche. Over millions of years, troughs had been carved into the canyon walls along natural slide paths. Somewhere up that canyon was my timestone. I wasn't going to get it by standing around enjoying the scenery.

"Ready?" I asked Grychn.

"I guess so." Her voice spoke in my mind. There was no reason not to use e-wave transmissions here.

We began skiing up the canyon. Small thrusters were mounted on our skis just behind the boot heels, and were plugged into the cybernetic systems of our suits. Like any other servo, they were under conscious control. Thrust was varied by willing it so. The skis were surplus from the Tenth Mountain Division, who were garrisoned in the mountains of Mars. But they worked just as well on hydrocarbon snow as powdered carbon dioxide.

Our skis floated on the surface of the snow as we coasted along at thirty kilometers an hour. Roostertails rose behind us. Falling snow rattled against my visor. We were as quiet as ice wraiths and almost invisible in the falling snow. Two pairs of ski tracks were the only evidence of our passage.

"Do you know where it is?" Grychn asked.

"Not exactly. I'll know when we get there. I can feel the stone calling to me." And its urgings grew ever stronger.

The canyon rose steeply in two dimensions, along the bottom and from both sides. Rock and ice towered over us. Snowfields lay in high basins, separated from each other by ridges of jagged rock. Sunlight sparkled from snowdrifts in the high pass. As morning deepened, the snow stopped falling. Gradually the sky became deep orange as hydrocarbons once more sublimed into a thin atmosphere. Stars dimmed overhead in a glowing sky.

Trickles of pentane and hexane dripped from cliff walls warmed by the sun.

I felt wonderful. The goal I'd set for myself was almost within reach. We were tracking virgin powder a meter deep, in a region as desolate and undisturbed as one was likely to find. We looked splendid in battle dress—like images formed in swirling mist. Soon the Terran Empire would fall into anarchy, as the Lords of Earth lost their control to entropic forces. Someone would be needed to put the pieces back together. May as well be me. I was ready to start an empire. Emperor Detrs, the First. I liked the sound of it. Images came to my mind. I became lost in pleasant reverie. It never occurred to me the daydream originated anywhere but in my own head.

I should have been paying more attention to business. I should have noticed a flash and a puff of smoke on the mountainside. My sensors should have tracked a silver trajectory.

Grychn's yell intruded into my fantasy.

"Marc! Look up there!"

I got a glimpse of a frozen face, then pushed it away and let my mind perceive what my eyes were seeing. Grychn was pointing to the right. The mouth of a snow chute opened into the canyon beside us. That didn't concern me. What bothered me was what was going on at the head of the chute. A hundred-meter wall of ice and snow was churning down from the basin there. An old-fashioned avalanche. The only thing missing was the roar of a thousand oceans all at once. But sound didn't carry well on Iapetus.

Not that there was time to be impressed by natural phenomena. In a few seconds, tons of frozen hydrocarbon and ammonia would tumble into the bottom of the canyon, burying Grychn and me. The death mask flashed in my mind again. Was this how it was going to be? Had the timestone let me get this close, only to let me freeze to death at its doorstep?

Not if I could help it.

"Go to max thrust!" I yelled at Grychn, and kicked my own skis to the maximum. I leaned forward over my ski tips to keep them down as the gravthrusters kicked. I forgot to tell Grychn to do the same. It wasn't something you thought about—you did it instinctively because of Corps training. But Grychn had never used powered skis before, nor had she had any hypnotraining. She wasn't ready. Her skis shot out from under her, sending her sprawling on her bottom in a meter of powder snow.

"Frogs!" she cursed in my mind. "Save yourself, Marc, I'm lost for sure."

Luckily, I didn't take the time to think. I had already cut my thrusters back. Then I did a telemark turn, dropping one ski back, unweighting it, and planing the leading ski by canting it into the snow. A conventional parallel turn wouldn't have worked in such deep snow at the speed I was going. A telemark turn was my only chance.

The maneuver caused me to make a tight circle, cutting around and behind Grychn. It was tricky—if I caught the edge of my ski I'd go sprawling myself. You had to plane the bottom of the ski on the snow like it was a slalom water ski. I'd never made that kind of turn before, but hypnotraining didn't fail me. The right reflex arcs had been conditioned.

All the time, a river of snow rushed down its chute toward us. I only saw it out of the corner of my eye. I didn't want to be distracted—or terrified.

When I completed the turn I was behind Grychn, skiing in her tracks. She had managed to get back on her feet, but both ski bindings had released when she fell and her skis were only attached to her boots by safety thongs. She wallowed waist-deep in snow. She'd never get them on in time.

I held my skis as far apart as I could and nudged a little velocity out of my thrusters.

"Turn around! Quickly! Face me. And hold out your arms."

Grychn complied.

As she turned, I reached her. I let my poles dangle by their straps from my wrists, then scooped my hands under her outstretched arms, pulling her against my chest. Her legs hung between mine and her skis trailed behind on their straps.

Then I hit my thrusters to maximum. We shot forward. I damned near fell myself, trying to ski and hold on to Grychn both. But I didn't. A cloud of blue snow swirled around us. Chunks of ammonia ice clattered against my helmet. Others struck my body but felt as gentle as real snowflakes through combat armor. We rose on a wave of snow like a catamaran on an ocean swell. Lateral drag nearly pushed me over. I had to lean toward the wave.

Then we burst out of tumbling snow. Behind us, tons of snow and ice flattened out on the canyon floor, obliterating our tracks. I coasted to a stop, safely out of range of the slide.

Only then did I wonder about the avalanche coming just when we were underneath it. We weren't making enough noise to trigger it—not on combrid skis, wearing combat armor. But it must have been just a coincidence. Some co-incidence.

Grychn pulled herself up so she could peer into my visor. She didn't say anything. I held her until she stopped trembling, then helped her get back into her skis.

We stood side by side. Grychn looked back at the snow-slide.

"Why did you come back for me?" she asked.

"It seemed like the right thing to do."

"Be serious for a minute. I already know you can be as quick on the comeback as anyone. Why did you risk your life to save mine?"

"Do I really need to say it?"

"I think you do. It would be nice to hear, anyway."

"OK." I glanced away, then back. "I guess I love you. Is that enough?" It didn't sound quite so trite at the time. You had to be there.

"I suppose," she answered, but her voice was happy in my mind. "You never told me that before."

"I didn't think I had to."

"Sometimes it helps. Once, anyway."

"Besides, I don't think that slide was meant for you. I was the one it was supposed to get."

"You mean . . ."

"Maybe. I don't know for sure. But let's be more care-ful from now on."

We started out again, gliding up the canyon on silent skis, slowly climbing toward the pass. I stopped a kilometer from the summit, at the mouth of a steep chute coming down from Mt. Themis. The head of the chute was blocked by an ice cliff a hundred meters high—the leading edge of a glacier clinging to the side of the mountain like a giant amoeba. The body of the glacier was about a kilometer wide before the basin in which it lay funneled into the chute. Fingers of blue ice reached up to the very summit of Mt. Themis, three kilometers distant, clawing deep rents in the face of the mountain. Huge chunks of frozen am-monia and hydrocarbon formed a rubble at our feet. Below them lay rock tailings.

Grychn followed my gaze. "Do you think we should be standing here?" she asked nervously. "There's lots of ice up there. It doesn't look particularly stable to me."

"This is it." I could see a dark round hole in the side of the mountain.

"The mine?"

"Yes. About halfway up that chute." Permaplastic bolts protruded in two rows from one wall of the chute. At one time, scaffolding must have been attached to the bolts, but there was no evidence of it now. Chunks of ice falling from the cliff above had knocked it down. It was buried under meters of ice now.

I took off my pack and pulled out a climbing rope and a sack of snap hooks.

"Why don't we just blast up there with thrusters?" Grychn asked.

"The p-grav might set up a resonance in the ice cliff and jar it loose. It looks unstable to me, too. I think climbing will be a little safer." I unslung my rifle and set it beside my pack. I coiled the rope around my waist.

I began climbing. It was an easy climb because of the bolts already drilled into the rock wall. They were spaced at a proper interval and provided adequate hand- and footholds. I inched my way up. A piece of cake. Grychn waited at the bottom.

When I was about halfway up, she spoke in my mind: "Look out, Marc!"

I knew what had happened. Her thoughts had told me. I ducked my head and flattened out against the wall, clinging to a pair of bolts. Fist-sized chunks of rock rattled against my helmet. No big deal. Combat armor protected me from the impact. They would have to be big enough to knock me loose to cause any harm. But I had no doubt chunks that big sometimes did break loose. There were ice boulders as big as houses in the canyon below. They had come from somewhere.

After about a minute the shower ended. I hoped most of the loose stuff had come down. I started climbing again. I could see the tunnel mouth a hundred meters above me. Permaplastic planks timbered its entrance. I continued to climb, slowly and carefully.

Like I said, a piece of cake.

After another fifteen minutes, I hauled myself into the tunnel.

I set a self-tapping eyebolt on one of the timbers. It screwed itself secure. I snapped a hook to it, then looped my rope through the hook before tossing the free ends to Grychn.

In a few minutes she stood beside me in the tunnel.

"Is the stone here?" she asked.

"Oh, yes. It's here. It's been waiting a long time." I heard an eerie song in my mind. I pushed it away. I didn't need any distractions now. My quest was almost over.

We advanced down the tunnel. It was well timbered at first. After a few meters, the tunnel was dark except for dim phosphorescence emanating from the walls. But there was plenty of other radiation for us to see. Helmet sensors perceived more than the visual spectrum. Gamma rays made their own black light. Alpha particles danced like fireflies. Beta particles swirled like shining dust motes.

At the first branching, the tunnels were no longer timbered. Bare rock ribs were scarred from the claws of a mining machine. Rock rubble littered an uneven floor. I knew which branches to take. We crept ever deeper into Mt. Themis, until our way was barred by a wall of jumbled rock.

"A cave-in," I whispered, afraid to speak out loud.

"The stone?"

"Behind the cave-in."

"What now?"

"We dig."

"With no tools."

"We have our hands."

I began clawing at the loose rock near the roof of the tunnel. Battle gauntlets could punch a hole through a concrete wall. They easily served as pick and shovel.

I gradually opened a passage large enough for me to crawl through. I scooped handfuls of loose rock between my legs like a rodent digging a burrow. Grychn cleared them out behind. We talked no further. I concentrated on digging, trying to keep songs, and the images they brought, out of my mind. Mind and body worked smoothly. Chip away loose rock. Push it behind. Pull free more rock.

Finally I broke through to the other side. The blockage was only a few meters thick. I rolled into a clear tunnel beyond. Grychn waited on the other side. The tunnel ended twenty meters away.

"Is it there?" she asked.

I didn't answer.

I saw the timestone, lying atop a pile of rock at the base of the tunnel's raw face. Blue fire sparked from a thousand facets. I picked it up carefully, as though afraid of being burned. I held it in my hands in front of me. Light flickered from the walls of the mine shaft.

I looked into the timestone.

I knew I should not have, but the urge to do so was overwhelming.

A stream of images darted into my mind, like an infinite kaleidoscope. Past and future blurred into one interminable present. I saw all wars, all plagues, all famine, all cataclysms since the beginning of time. And all future ones. History, past and future, was an endless orgasm of death.

My mind was paralyzed with sensory overload. I stood motionless. I could not move. I had looked into the eye of God.

For an instant, I was totally insane.

I didn't have time to sort out all the images. No organic brain could function that rapidly. But a billion images were imprinted in memory. Some of them come unbidden yet.

I could not move. I had to allow an infinity of images to stream into my mind. I had no will of my own. I would do the timestone's bidding. I would be its slave forever. I knew that, but there was nothing I could do to prevent it. I was trapped.

Then stroboscopic flashes of light dazzled my eyes, blinding me momentarily. The terrible images stopped. I could look away.

Grychn stood behind me, holding the assault rifle I had dropped. Its pulsar tube still glowed. She had shot into the stone, where the pulsar quantum had ricocheted from mirrored internal facets. The stone was undamaged. But she had succeeded in freeing my mind from it. I briefly wondered if that was what she had intended. No matter.

There wasn't time to make a rational decision. But my unconscious mind was not constrained by the slowness of synaptic deliberation. Once freed from the grip of the timestone, it grasped the significance of the confusion of images. It knew how to react. Instinct and intuition took over. Blind panic overwhelmed me. Later I would know why. Then, that knowledge didn't matter.

Terror was enough.

I dropped the timestone and ran to Grychn.

I grabbed her hand. "Come on," I yelled. "We've got to get out of here!" We crawled back through the burrow I'd dug. I pulled her along behind me as I ran down the tunnel to daylight. We hardly paused at the mine's entrance. Grychn picked up the rope and rappelled down the chute. I followed. My mind began to clear. Panic ebbed. But I still knew we had to run. I knew what game the timestone played. It was one of death. For me. For Grychn. For everyone.

I had enough sense to retrieve the rope and pack it away. We shouldered our packs. Grychn slung my rifle. We put on our skis and skied back down the canyon. Out in the open, gliding on powder snow sparkling with sunlight, with tall roostertails rising behind us, panic seemed silly. Until an image surfaced in my mind. Then terror seemed quite reasonable indeed. Nels had told me the truth about the timestone. It could conserve entropy. I wished I'd believed her. Not that it would have made any difference.

"What happened?" Grychn asked.

"I'll tell you later." I tried to keep my mind clear. Something else had to be done. The circle must be completed.

We continued skiing down the canyon. I stopped when we came to the snowslide. Something was wrong there. We stood for a moment staring at the wash of jumbled snow and ice. A single set of ski tracks crossed it.

"Someone followed us," Grychn said. "But where is he? There was no place in the canyon to hide."

"Look," I said, and pointed back in the direction we had come.

A figure rose from the snow where he had buried himself, appearing like a ghost rising from a grave. He stood in the canyon just a little above the upper chute. He had probably decided to wait for us to come out of the tunnel, then kill us both and take the timestone for himself. When we came out without the stone, he changed his plans and decided to fetch it himself. Why risk a fight unnecessarily?

He began climbing the chute. Distance made him appear like a bug crawling up a wall. There was no way we could reach him in time to keep him from making it up the tunnel.

"Who?" Grychn asked.

"You should know." *You brought him here.*

"Kramr."

"Who else?"

"Then he's won."

"Maybe."

Images began to reveal themselves. Truth unraveled from a kaleidoscopic weave. I knew what had to be done. There was no other choice. There never had been.

Grychn gussed the same truth. But then she'd known it all along. She emptied a clip at the climbing bug. Bright pulsar quanta flashed up the canyon and into the ice chute. Ice puffed into vapor, enclosing the climber in a cloud of steam that coalesced into a filigree of hoarfrost. He shook off the tendrils of ice and began climbing again. Grychn sprayed another clip in his direction. Again he was not hit. The distance was too great for the accuracy of an assault rifle. I might have been able to hit him if I'd taken a careful rest. But there wasn't time for that. And there was an easier way to take care of both Kramr and the timestone.

I took the rifle from Grychn and pulled my one minimissile from my ammo pouch. I loaded the rifle, then took careful aim. I had all the time in the world, while a bug clambered up to its burrow, slow and lazy.

I pressed the firing stud.

A silver trajectory arced across the sky, just as it had earlier. Light flashed from the middle of a glacier. A puff of vapor rose into a mushroom-shaped cloud. Huge cracks rent the glacier. Ice gave up its grip on rock. The glacier broke into pieces that began slipping down the mountain, until they were funneled into a chute where a bug crawled. Millions of tons of ice poured down the mountain, filling in the canyon below. Huge clouds of snow billowed high, then began slowly settling back to ground. When the snow swirls cleared, a glacier no longer rested in a basin high on the slopes of Mt. Themis. Instead, a jigsaw puzzle of ice dammed the canyon. The upper chute and tunnel mouth were buried beneath several hundred meters of ice. The bug was gone.

"Did you have to do that?" Grychn asked softly.

I said nothing.

"I suppose you did," she answered herself.

*   *   *

Grychn followed me back to Atlas in Kramr's skimmer. We abandoned it in the mountains near town, where it would be found eventually, but nowhere near the place Kramr lay entombed in ice. His body would never be discovered, I was sure of that. Nor would the timestone now. Its tunnel was safely buried.

In our room, I lay in bed. I was tired.

Before sleep came, I let a few images rise so I could begin to be done with them.

7

When I woke, the sun was setting behind the Ice Mountains.

Grychn had her lips on my penis, stirring it to life with her tongue. She looked up and smiled as I opened my eyes, then rose to kiss my lips.

"I thought you might sleep around the clock," she said. "I think we should leave this place soon." She straddled me, letting me enter her. "But not *right* now," she laughed. "In a little while."

She moved her ass up and down. I slid in and out. She placed a nipple close to my lips. I took it in my mouth and stroked it with my tongue, feeling the skin pull taut. Delicious friction tingled.

A long time later we separated. She lay beside me, with her hand close to my face. A ruby glittered in the dying light of day.

"You better leave that ring here," I said.

She snatched her hand away and peered at the gem. "Why?" Her voice told me she really didn't know why.

"It contains a microbeacon. Kramr used it to follow us."

"The cyrines? The patrol craft?"

"Paper tigers, to let us think we'd escaped."

"You know the rest of my story?"

"I think so."

"From the timestone?"

"Partly. But there were other inconsistencies. You

285

couldn't have known I was the combrid who had captured you unless Kramr had told you, because I had not. And he wouldn't have told you for no reason."

"I didn't want to help them, but Kramr turned me into a peptide addict. If I didn't cooperate, he withheld my medicine. I was just supposed to help him find Nels. But when I did, I couldn't get her to tell me where the time-stone was located. Kramr needed you for that. I was sup-posed to find out from you. But when we escaped, I thought we really were free."

"Until the elf city was raided."

"Until then," she agreed.

"You could have told me then."

"I was afraid you'd leave me."

"I would have, then."

Her voice faltered. "How about now?" Amber eyes looked away.

"I'm a different person now."

"A better person?"

"Maybe."

"Do you still love me?"

"Yes." I kissed her to prove it. "Is that important?"

"I think so." She paused. "Just what was the timestone? Why did you leave it behind?"

"Nels was right. It's an entropic crystal. Time manipula-tions use up lots of entropy—that's how the stone works. Death also conserves entropy."

"What else did the timestone show you?"

"A little bit of everything." I had learned how to keep the images away. I'd had lots of practice doing that. Some I didn't want to see. Clairvoyance had a way of hurting inside.

"I'm not sure I understand."

"This timestone is infinitely more powerful than the little one I had. There's no controlling it. As soon as I picked it up, it flooded my mind with knowledge I didn't want. But there was no way I could stop it. When you tried to destroy it, the pulsar flash temporarily blinded me, allowing me to look away. To save itself from perma-nent psychosis, my mind made me run away from it." I laughed hollowly. "If I'd stayed another minute, I'd have been driven insane. But I would have become an emperor. And a vile despot. And a slave to the timestone. Kramr would have become the same, had he reached the stone. So would anyone else. That's what Nels was so afraid of. But there is some good out of it all." I laughed more cheerfully. "Ironically, the vision of death I've had so long was not mine at all."

"Then whose? I thought you'd seen your face."

"A face that resembled mine. A family resemblance. When a chameleon dies, his face finally reverts to its true form. Under all that ice, Kramr finally became himself: his face became his own face."

"A family resemblance?"

"Henri. My long-lost brother."

"Did he know that he was your brother?"

"I doubt it."

She was quiet for a bit. She figured out the truth, guessing the burden I was to bear. "Then you also know when you'll really die."

"Yes." I could push the image away and hold it there.

"How soon?" Her voice sounded funny.

"Not for quite a long time. It seems to be tied up with something very important. Quite glorious, in fact. A soldier couldn't ask for a better death. But the details aren't too clear yet." I wanted to keep it that way. I had learned how to keep away the hurting.

The next question took even longer. She had figured out the truth. "Did you see me dead?"

"Do you really want to know?"

"I suppose not." She kissed me. "But what does it all mean? The timestone. Kramr being your brother. Your quest. My finding you again. There must be some meaning to it all."

"Yes, I guess there is. All moves in a game. An entropic game; a death game. There are moves yet to be made."

"A grim sentiment."

"I'm in an introspective mood."

"What do we do now?"

"We play the game. We get dressed. We go someplace else. We're going to have a few adventures, you and me. And lots of fun. We're going to live in interesting times. No boredom for us. How would you like to be a robber baroness? Or maybe a pirate queen? And later a high priestess?"

"Sounds like fun."

"Then let's get dressed and go."

We stepped out of a liftube exit. The spaceport was before us. Harsh sodium lights blazed overhead, casting yellow glare over fused glass pods. Grychn's gravship stood at its berth.

Snow had begun falling, forming a thick mist. Ghost-faces rose—my parents, pale as alabaster statues; Henri/Kramr; Vichsn, eyes wired with lust; Trinks; Sergeant Pepper, mourning her dead baby; Jain Maure, seeking hurt; Nels; her sailor lover, Mikal Gy. All players in the death game. Grychn would join them too soon, I knew. But I would cherish her while I had her, before she disappeared into the cold empty. We could have a few good times together before her move came. My turn would come still later. I'd join her then. Mist particles connected us all, like fragile webbing. The time matrix, though convoluted, possessed a terrible symmetry.

Sometime I would let the images surface so I could take a better look. Not now. They hurt too much now.

I put my arm around Grychn. I would love her for a long time.

"Ready?"

She nodded.

Mist-faces rose, smiling. We stepped through them and were gone.